RAPUNZI

Sally Ash is the author of two well-received books,
the first of which was runner-up in Romcon's 1994
'Best New Writer' category. She divides her time
with her family between the UK and New Zealand

BY THE SAME AUTHOR

Hedge of Thorns

Matutu

(both Goodfellow Press, Redmond, WA, USA)

SALLY ASH

Rapunzel, Rapunzel

t₂

*It has never been my intention to knock the Roman Catholic Church,
nor do I mean to give offence; indeed, it is always foremost in my mind to respect
my characters. The convent school of St Ursula's exists only in my imagination.
That which happens within its bounds has largely been drawn from my own school
experiences, and those which my friends chose to share with me.*

*I have tried to write a tale which entertains and offers my readers a few
hours' diversion. I believe that I have succeeded.*

Published by
Troubador Publishing
12 Manor Walk, Coventry Road
Market Harborough, Leics LE16 9BP, UK
Tel: (+44) 1858 468828 / 469898
Email: books@troubador.co.uk
Web: www.troubador.co.uk

ISBN 1 899293 44 2

Cover illustration: Laura Donaldson

Typesetting: Troubador Publishing Ltd, Market Harborough, UK
Printed and bound by The Cambrian Printers Ltd, Aberystwyth, UK

*t*₂

t2 is an imprint of Troubador Publishing Ltd

For Pamela R. Goodfellow, who gave me my start,
and with thanks to Sylvia,
who allowed me to plunder her early memories

Prologue

In days long gone there lived a peasant and his wife. In the course of time the wife found herself with child and, as is often the case, she was overtaken by cravings for strange and exotic foods. Sometimes her husband could satisfy these cravings, but on occasion her desires were beyond his ability to assuage, for this was in the era before Welfare cared for the poor of society.

So it was that, one day, the wife looked out of their casement window, and she espied lettuces growing in the neighbouring garden. Now, it was the dead of winter when lettuces are not frequently to be found, but the neighbouring garden was sheltered from harsh winds and frost, and thus plants could flourish within its walls which would otherwise have frozen.

'Husband,' quoth the wife. 'I have eaten nothing but dry bread and turnips for days. Look at those sweet, tender lettuces. How I long to sample their freshness.'

'Nay, wife,' replied the husband fearfully. 'Do not ask this of me. Those lettuces belong to a fearsome old woman. Local gossip has it that she is a witch. Please do not ask me to trespass upon her property.'

But, having espied the luscious plants, the wife would give him no peace. Her nagging filled his ears, morning, noon and night. Finally, the spirit of the lowly husband was cowed; he felt that he must satisfy his wife's desires. He waited until midnight before he plucked up courage, stealthily climbed the wall and snatched a single plant. However, having tasted the crisp leaves, the wife demanded more, so on subsequent nights the husband was forced to scale the wall and steal further lettuces. Clearly

1

this could not continue forever. The old woman noticed the gradually dwindling numbers of her vegetables, and she lay in wait. When, late one night, the husband stealthily descended into her garden, she accosted him and challenged him with his crime.

'Have pity,'' wailed the peasant. 'My wife is with child, and is subject to all manner of strange urges and appetites. It is for her that I stole your lettuce.'

'I have the right to demand payment,' replied the old crone.

'I am a poor man,' the peasant explained, and he turned out his pockets to demonstrate that he had not even one penny.

'Then you must pay in kind,' was the response.

'What do I have that you could desire? Our modest furniture is fit only for your fire. We have not even a mat upon the floor.'

'Then,' replied the witch, 'I shall take that one thing which you will have, and I may not.'

'What might that be, madam?' enquired the peasant, mystified that this person should seek the property of so humble a couple.

'Your child,' quoth the old crone. 'You shall give me your infant child. I am barren, and with time you will have more children.'

The peasant and his wife were shocked to hear these words, but they were powerless to protest. If they did not hand over their infant the father might well be thrown into prison as a common thief, and then his wife and the child would certainly starve to death. So, after the birth of their daughter, they sadly kissed her and handed her over to the keeping of the old woman.

The witch loved the child greatly and cared for her tenderly. She named her Rapunzel. Fearing that she might be corrupted by the world, she placed her in a tower that had no door and one solitary window. There, the child matured to be a young woman, comely of feature and innocent of vice. Her hair, never cut, grew to be luxurious and extraordinary in its beauty. When her adoptive mother came to visit her, bringing food and amusements with her, she would call,

> 'Rapunzel, Rapunzel, let down your hair,
> That I may climb the golden stair.'

This was the signal for Rapunzel to unbraid her hair and allow it to cascade down from the window. Then the old woman, who was mercifully small of stature, would ascend to the tower room in which her adoptive daughter dwelled.

Thus they continued for some years. Then, one day, a young prince came riding through the forest which surrounded the tower. He heard the witch as she commanded Rapunzel to release her locks. Intrigued, he concealed himself behind a tree and watched as the golden tresses tumbled down and the old woman ascended, climbing up the maiden's hair. Some time later he watched as she descended in similar mode and departed back toward the township. He stationed himself under the tower and, imitating the witch's voice to the best of his ability, he called,

> 'Rapunzel, Rapunzel, let down your hair,
> That I may climb the golden stair.'

He waited but minutes before the cloud of golden tresses fell to within reach. Grasping them, he ascended slowly to the window above. You can imagine Rapunzel's surprise when, instead of her adoptive mother, the face and figure of a handsome young man came into view. However, such is the nature of these things it did not take her long to fall in love, and the prince was equally enchanted to discover so beautiful a maiden in so strange a prison. So it was that he visited her daily, always taking care that he was departed well before the witch's visits.

He and Rapunzel discussed how she might escape from the tower and elope with him to his father's kingdom.

'Bring me silk,' said she, 'and I shall fashion a ladder. Then we may escape together.'

The prince did as requested and Rapunzel worked hard, weaving and knotting the silk ropes. One day, however, she forgot to guard her tongue.

3

As the witch, who was gaining in weight as she aged, appeared one day, Rapunzel remarked thoughtfully, 'I wonder that you hurt my hair so when you climb. The prince is taller by far than you, but he hurts my head not at all.'

'Prince?' screamed the old woman. 'What prince might this be?'

But she gave Rapunzel no time to reply. Instead she seized a pair of shears and cut off the maiden's beautiful hair. Then she bade the frightened maid to say not one word, for fear of terrible reprisals to her lover, and she sat down to await the prince's arrival. Shortly thereafter she heard,

> 'Rapunzel Rapunzel, let down your hair
> That I may climb the golden stair.'

The witch tossed the severed locks over the windowsill and secured the other end to the bedstead. Great was the shock and surprise of the young man when he ascended the ladder of hair to find, not his beloved, but an angry old crone lying in wait. Before he could recover his wits sufficiently to grasp the sill, the witch released the severed hair, and it and the prince tumbled down, down, to the ground below. They fell into a thorn bush, which scratched the prince's eyes so badly that he was virtually blind.

Rapunzel bewailed his loss, but without her silk ladder, which the witch seized for her own use, she was once again a prisoner in the tower.

So the time passed, during which Rapunzel's hair gradually grew once more. Finally it was sufficiently long. She took the shears and bravely severed her own locks. Then she secured them, and climbed down the ladder of her own hair . . . to freedom.

It took some years of searching, and many adventures for which we have no time to relate here, before she located her prince. And what a sorry sight he was, his eyes still clouded by the thorns into which he had fallen. Seeing him, Rapunzel was moved to pity.

'My poor love,' she cried and, as she wept, her tears fell into his eyes. Then – wonder of wonders – they were restored to sight again.

The witch learned the hard way that you cannot keep someone you love captive, however high and isolated the tower in which you conceal him or her. She was deeply embittered by her loss, and lived out her days with only forty-four cats for company. She did, however, grow marvellous vegetables, which won prizes at the local horticultural show.

The prince took his bride back to his father's kingdom, where they lived happily ever after, as is the way of all good fairy tales.

The Witch

1

Sydney, Australia.
November, 2002

I am not a witch. I've decided to make that point immediately, although you'll certainly say it's unnecessary. Yes, I know all about the story – and how unkind girls teased Clare that I was, indeed, in some way unusual – but they were wrong. Witches, or witches in fairy tales, act from the very worst motives. I, in contrast, am a very average person; and there has never been a time when I didn't think first and foremost of Clare. I may have been misguided, but that doesn't make me into a wicked person. If you intend to go about castigating honest folks for making genuine mistakes, well, there aren't going to be too many of us left smelling of roses.

As I write this, sitting at the kitchen table and looking out at the back garden, I can feel the spring sunshine on my face. November in Sydney has always been my favourite month, the jacarandas create such vivid splashes of sweet mauve everywhere, the silky oaks are a startling orange-gold. I'm sorry I'm writing this in long-hand but I never learnt to type. Father Flaherty didn't mind if I wrote out his letters by hand as long as the spelling passed muster, and I remembered to send them out. Word processors and the like are the tools of the next generation.

But perhaps I'm going too fast. I'll backtrack, and try to get things into the correct order.

As I intend this to be a record of what transpired, an explanation if you like even if not an excuse, I'll start in 1977, when I first met Shaun and Perdita. In 1977 we were experiencing the first stirrings of the drug culture, you'll remember. Only a hop, step and jump away from hippies, in my view. We in Australia were 'blessed' with the overspill from places like California, some time after common sense in those places had started to make a come-back. 'Alternative Living', they called it, but gobbledy-gook was more like it to me. Any excuse to avoid personal responsibility, while sneering at honest men and women who knew the meaning of the words. Sydney was awash with fey folk who looked as though they'd no more than a nodding acquaintance with soap and water, and who wore beads and clothes that might have come from the St. Vincent de Paul charity shop after they'd distributed the quality items.

I don't need to remind you that my next door neighbour was a gentleman called Mr. Douglas Hamilton. I mention the fact only because I want my record to be complete. The Hamiltons became my neighbours just before my mother died, which was also the year I met Shaun and Perdita. Did you know that Perdita means, 'the lost one?' I'd never call a child of mine 'Lost', so why would any mother name her child Perdita? Lost in what way, I'd like to know? It was as if her mother laid a curse on her from birth, which wasn't so far from the truth I suppose.

I met Shaun and Perdita because they became my lodgers. You'll recall that I leased the basement in those days, because it's one thing to inherit a house and quite another to have the where-withal to pay the bills associated with that house. Working part-time as Father Flaherty's secretary never did bring in a salary you could live on, and as they say, beggars can't be choosers.

Before I let the basement flat to Shaun and Perdita I had a spin-ster lady in there who worked at Grace Brothers as a milliner, but she went home to Ballarat when her mother became ill; and after her departure, the curate at the Anglican Church. He was a very pleasant and quiet young man, even if he was a Protestant. I'm not prejudiced against people just because they're not Catholics. But they found a place for him closer to St Martin's, which is the Anglican church.

So I was in the dairy at the corner of the road buying a loaf, and there was this advertisement board which Mr. Simms runs as a sort of community service, and I picked up a card which said, 'Rooms or Bedsit wanted by quiet couple.' It had a telephone number at the bottom, so I rang up and made an appointment for them to come and look at the basement flat. I know it was quite a daring thing to do because they could have been murderers like Bonnie and Clyde, but the word 'quiet' sounded reassuring.

They were thirty-two minutes late, which put my back up from the start, because I do appreciate punctuality. Being late is extremely rude, in my opinion.

I knew right away that I wasn't going to like Shaun. It wasn't anything to do with his American accent because I have nothing against Americans, I'm not that sort of prejudiced person, but he had 'alternative lifestyle' written all over him. And 'lazy layabout.' And if they're determined to be scroungers, why don't they scrounge in their own country instead of other people's? It was on the tip of my tongue to say, 'I'm sorry, you're too late. I let the rooms to another couple when you didn't turn up,' but then I saw Perdita, who had been standing behind Shaun. My front door's in shadow, and narrow so you can't always see. And when I saw Perdita I was just bowled over. Well, she was absolutely the loveliest person I've ever laid eyes on.

How can I describe her so that my words do her justice? When I endeavour to seek the right phrases they sound trite and inadequate. Words like ethereal and spirit-like; or perhaps I should try dryad. That's a wood nymph. Perdita looked like a creature from the forest or from another world, perhaps peopled with fairies and sprites. Her skin was so clear that it was almost translucent, her hair was flaxen fair. I'd never before understood what was meant by that term but when I saw Perdita I knew at once. Her hair was parted in the middle which was the style you'll remember, and it hung like parted curtains, framing her lovely face. Oh, what serenity. Like the Virgin Mother in Leonardo's famous painting; like the saints whose plaster likenesses were scattered about the parochial school where I was educated. As soon as I saw Perdita I fell in love with her a little, if a woman can say that about another woman.

9

Because I'm not at all like that, you know. The love I felt for Perdita was like the emotion you experience for something too beautiful to be true. A sort of aching love.

So that was that. They moved into the basement rooms, bringing with them such a motley collection of shabby furniture and cardboard boxes that I hoped Mr. Douglas Hamilton and Mrs. Hamilton weren't watching their arrival from an upstairs window.

I never really knew Mrs. Hamilton, she was ill even then, but from the day they became my neighbours I thought that Mr Hamilton was a very nice gentleman. Not at all coarse or ill mannered, like . . . well, like other men I could mention. He doesn't wear a hat, men never seem to wear hats these days, but if he did I'm sure he would raise it politely whenever he spoke to a lady. Even then you got the feeling that when he said, 'How do you do, Miss Galway? Isn't it beautiful morning?' he was raising an imaginary hat. My father would always have raised his hat to a lady, I was sure of that.

At first Shaun and Perdita were just as quiet as they'd claimed to be. You'd hardly have known they were living in the rooms beneath mine, had it not been for the gurgling of water running through the pipes and occasional flushing sounds. Sometimes I saw them leave together, sometimes I saw them return. They rarely seemed to do anything apart. I'd have found that quite touching – we all have a soft spot for true romance, don't we – had I liked Shaun more. But there was always something strange about the man. He never quite met my eyes when he was talking to me, and that was rarely I can tell you; and I resented the way he monopolised Perdita. I very much wanted to become her friend because you could say I was a little bit under the spell of her beauty. I wanted to discover whether her personality matched the loveliness of her physical features. But she and Shaun could have been Siamese twins, the way they did everything together.

And then there was the smell. You could say I was naive and I can only agree with you, but how many single women living my life in Sydney would have been like me and failed to recognise the smell of pot? If it doesn't come your way you do not know. I was

10

simply aware of a sickly sweetness that seemed to pervade the front room of my place, which was above the living room of the basement flat. Often it was accompanied by the smoky aroma of sandalwood and cinnamon, joss sticks being burnt no doubt to mask the pot.

These days I'd know that Shaun appeared spaced out most of the time, his eyes vacant of any emotion not marijuana-inspired. Words like 'spaced out' weren't in my vocabulary in 1977. I thought he was away with the fairies and the resentment built in my breast, I can tell you, because he had a rare and wonderful jewel in Perdita and he didn't appear to appreciate her. However, over the next few weeks certain things, very small events, transpired and the status began to change.

Perdita appeared one morning at my back door, which opens into the garden. Perdita was American too, but her voice was everything you could hope for in a woman. My mother used to quote, "her voice was ever soft, gentle and low; an excellent thing in woman." Perdita's voice was definitely an excellent thing.

'Miss Galway, I wonder if you could lend me half a cup of sugar? I'm making a pie for Shaun, and I'm out of sugar.'

Now, the dairy on the corner is about a two minute walk from my house, so when she asked to borrow sugar I thought immediately that she couldn't afford to buy any, but I didn't care about that because here was the very first occasion when I could extend the hand of friendship. So I asked her to come in and I put on the kettle and I made us a pot of tea, just to have her stay a little longer. We Australians pride ourselves on our appreciation of good tea.

You couldn't say our exchange was very inspiring that day, more small talk than anything significant, but it was conversation and I think I made her welcome. After she'd taken about two tiny sips of her tea she stood and thanked me very graciously, and picked up the sugar that I'd measured out into a bowl, and went back into the garden and down the flight of steps that led to the basement. Our row is on a hill, so the garden slopes away at the back.

But after that day Perdita started to drop in on occasion, just to say the odd word, and the pair no longer appeared to be bonded at the hip, as the saying goes. I saw that as an encouraging sign. We'd talk about this and that, and I always made a point of making her something hot to drink and offering her something wholesome to eat, because she was so thin you could almost see daylight through the girl. Not that she was actually a girl you understand, but neither could you describe her as a woman. Women have curves and are . . . womanly.

Let me tell you a bit about my home. I inherited it from my mother after her death and she'd inherited it from her parents. For the record, and this is a record, it's one of those early Paddington-style houses which you find in central Sydney and certain inner suburbs like ours. As is usual, it's part of a row, with three narrow storeys and the heavy, cast iron work on each of the balconies that cross the width of the house and is called Paddington lace. Originally, I've been told, the wrought iron came as ballast in the sailing ships from England which would transport back the Australian wool.

I really love my house. I was born in it, I'll be happy to die in it. Some of the row houses are a bit dark and gloomy, not to say damp, because what did the Victorians know about sunshine deprivation? They built for the road, and the road was built for convenience, to get from A to B. But not our row. These houses face east/west. The early sun streams into my kitchen and the back garden in the morning, and avoids the worst of the summer heat at noon. Then, in the evening, the front rooms are bathed with light. Just as I like it.

I'm not sure when I first began to notice things going missing; not immediately that's for sure, because I'm no fool and I'd have spotted right enough if anything obvious had disappeared. No, I'd better correct myself there, because I showed myself to be very much of a fool. I told myself many times over in the next few weeks that it could never have been Perdita who filched my small silver pieces; one of the set of brushes which sat on my dressing table, the beautifully wrought sterling sugar dredger from my grandmother. Perdita was too perfect to contemplate such a travesty. Ergo: it had to be Shaun who'd found a way into my house. My love for Perdita, *you understand, was carefully counterbalanced by my dislike for her husband. I tried to set little traps but he/they never fell into them and, to be fair, there were moments when I told myself that I was making the whole thing up. It was my own carelessness and in blaming my detested lodger I was exonerating myself. Thus, alas, do we delude ourselves.*

And then not so long after that Perdita was ill, right in my toilet, right in the middle of drinking a cup of coffee – because I'd discovered that she didn't share our Australian love of a well-brewed cup of tea – and eating one of my delicious lamingtons. For you who've never met a lamington, you take a cube of good sponge cake, and you roll it in melted chocolate to coat the sides and then in desiccated coconut. My mother made wonderful lamingtons and she taught me.

And there was poor Perdita, one minute enjoying her lamington, the next minute clutching her stomach and making for the downstairs cloakroom, only to lose it all into the water closet. Such a waste of good chocolate.

To be quite honest, I didn't really know what to do. Being Father Flaherty's part-time secretary doesn't prepare you for small domestic crises like this. It seemed to me that the best thing to be done was to pretend, once the poor child had finished vomiting and retching, that nothing unusual had happened. But one glance at her, as she emerged from the downstairs cloakroom looking wan and miserable, and leaned against the doorjamb as though her legs couldn't take her weight and I discarded that notion.

'My poor darling,' I cried, running across to her and supporting her against my shoulder, 'Come and sit down. What on earth is wrong with you?'

You'll appreciate that words like 'darling' were, at that time, foreign to me. My mother was definitely fond of me in her way but she never called me, 'darling.' Just Thea, or Dorothea if she was cross. But the word slipped out, as natural as could be.

Perdita sank into the kitchen chair and put her crossed arms on the kitchen table, and sank her head onto her arms. When she spoke it was so low I had almost to guess at the words.

13

'I think I'm pregnant.'

'Pregnant?'

Why should I have been so surprised? Married women were known to become pregnant and a very good thing it was. Procreation is part of the greater plan and in most circumstances to be encouraged. Especially if the parents are Catholic. But the thought that Shaun, that man, was the perpetrator of this act of violation was enough to make me feel quite ill myself. However, I mastered my distaste and said in a calm, reasonable voice, 'Perdita, dear, are you sure?'

'Almost certain.'

'And how far along do you estimate yourself to be?'

'Maybe two months. I missed my period three weeks ago.'

'And have you told Shaun?'

Her voice fell even more. 'No. He'll be mad. He doesn't like kids.'

Now, I'm a good Catholic and I've been a good Catholic all my life, but even I found myself thinking that there were ways of not conceiving babies, if you felt like that. However, to voice such a notion would definitely have been a case of bolting the stable door after the horse has fled. No, on second thoughts that's about as inappropriate a metaphor as I could have chosen; and anyway, moralising wasn't going to help poor Perdita at this moment.

'Would you like to lie down, darling?' I asked.

But Perdita stood, and some of the colour had returned to her cheeks, and she said, 'No thank you, Miss Galway. These episodes don't last long. I'm just grateful that Shaun wasn't about to see me make a fool of myself.'

I thought she looked a bit wobbly as she made her way down the steps that led to their flat but I did admire her courage. We Australians have always placed a premium on pluckiness. We call it the Gallipoli spirit, after the brave Anzac soldiers who fought on that Turkish peninsula in the Great War.

Then I set to work. I've already admitted that I was about as naive as it was possible to be when it came to drugs and the like, but I wasn't so green that I couldn't and didn't put two and two *together at this point. I scrambled into my tweed jacket and I almost flew to Father Flaherty's. He was the only person at that time within my very narrow sphere who might be considered sufficiently worldly to offer sensible advice. I mean, I couldn't exactly ask Mr. Simms at the dairy about the possible effects on an unborn child of whatever nasty concoction Perdita was poisoning herself with; nor could I seek advice of Mrs. O'Riley, who has always looked down her nose at me ever since I first let the basement flat. According to her, taking in lodgers is not a ladylike thing to do. Once I nearly snorted at her, 'Neither is not paying your bills,' but I held my tongue because it would have distressed my mother to have her daughter return vulgarity with vulgarity.*

But, after I had considered and rejected Mr. Simms and Mrs. O'Riley, I could conjure up no other possible source of elucidation to help me solve this dilemma.

Now, I was very fond of Father Flaherty and he certainly had a way with his sermons, but I must confess that in the matter of pregnant young women and unsuitable substances he was absolutely no help at all. He sat there in his favourite leather chair, the one from which he dictated letters to me on Tuesdays and Fridays, and pressed the tips of his fingers together and pursed his lips as though he was about to blow a kiss at someone, and said, 'Dear dear, Miss Galway. Are you absolutely sure?'

'Sure that she's pregnant, Father, or sure about the drugs?'

'Perhaps both, Miss Galway? I mean to say, a spinster lady in her forties . . . perhaps not the first person to appreciate the . . . er . . . to misinterpret . . .'

I know it's not the done thing to wish you could slap the face of the person who hears your confession each week, but I felt very close to slapping Father Flaherty at that moment. What a display of insufferable arrogance. As though one has to experience everything at first hand before one can even offer an opinion. That attitude must sit uneasy on the shoulders of a celibate person given to dispensing sage words to married couples; but initiating a robust debate on that subject would have done nothing to help Perdita and her child. I merely let him prose on for a few more minutes, feeling that he had certainly failed me in my moment of need, then I stood up and thanked him briskly and with just the right amount of tartness, I pride myself, to deflate that worldly-wise bubble a fraction. Then I walked smartly out of the study and down the three stone steps and along the road towards my own house. And as I was passing the house next door to mine, there was Mr. Douglas Hamilton, trimming his roses.

2

As I said before, Mr. and Mrs. Hamilton's becoming my neighbours more or less coincided with my mother's death. This was from old age I should point out, and had absolutely nothing to do with the arrival of the Hamiltons. Indeed, we had expected her to pass away for some time. At the time of their moving into Number 6, I had made a nice plate of lamingtons for the Hamiltons, using my mother's method which is so superior, and I'd taken them around as a 'welcome' gift. When Mr. Hamilton subsequently returned the plate he mentioned how much he and his wife had enjoyed them. He was always extremely well-mannered.

I never did see much of Mrs. Hamilton, although it was some years before I discovered the reason for this. The poor, dear lady suffered from senile dementia. Alzheimer's they call it now. At that time, in the '70s, Mr. Hamilton looked after his wife at home but when her behaviour became more unreliable he found a very nice nursing home for her. And I can testify to his fine sense of duty because when he was about there wasn't a day he didn't visit her there, even long after she could recognise him as her husband. Poor lady, such a tragedy. However, on the day that I saw him trimming his roses and sought his advice, all that was several years in the future.

It took me some courage to approach him, I must say. It was only my fear of what Perdita might be doing to her unborn child that gave me the strength of purpose.

'Mr. Hamilton, I wonder if I might ask your advice?'

Mr. Hamilton paused with his pair of secateurs in one hand and a stem of "Peace" in the other. 'If I can be of help, Miss Galway?'

Did I mention that the Hamiltons were Scottish? Although I subsequently learnt that they had been in Australia for almost twenty years, Mr. Hamilton still spoke with that attractive burr so that even my name, Miss Galway, sounded a little exotic and different.

'I . . . I wonder if you'd be able to spare me five minutes of your time?' I didn't feel quite comfortable discussing somebody's private matters in the street.

Mr. Hamilton put his secateurs down on the front porch and followed me into my own hallway. It's always quite dark in the hallway, except when the evening sun streams in through the pane of glass over the door, so I switched on the light. Then I explained to him as simply as I could about Perdita and her probable pregnancy, and my fear that the drugs in which I was sure she and Shaun indulged might be affecting the baby.

Mr. Hamilton immediately proved himself to be my knight errant, in direct contrast to Father Flaherty. Perhaps he understood because the smell of unusual substances filtered through the common wall to his house.

'I'm sure you're right, Miss Galway, and I admire your spirit. I can't imagine that drugs of any sort, soft or hard, will enhance an infant's development.'

'What do you suggest I do?'

'I'm assuming you'd prefer not to inform the police?'

I didn't know him personally, but at that time Detective Inspector Burley-Brown was a member of the congregation of St. Kevin's. He'd never seemed a particularly approachable person to me. I tried to imagine him taking Perdita down to the police station and grilling her about the use of illegal materials, and I knew that I could never do that. Shaun, maybe; Perdita never.

'I'd prefer not to inform the police, Mr. Hamilton.'

'Then you must talk to this young person and appeal to her as a potential mother. Maternity is the most powerful tool at your disposal. No woman in my experience would willingly set about harming her child.'

I profoundly hoped he was right.

He gave me quite a lot more useful and practical advice before he said goodbye very politely and went back to make sure that Mrs. Hamilton, whose name I subsequently discovered to be Jeannie, was not attempting to burn the house down in his absence. I did hope that I had the strength of purpose to follow up his suggestions. I've never been too good at relationships and I was even worse back then than I am today. I think I come across as gruff when I'm really trying to be direct. Australians, it has always seemed to me, are a direct sort of people.

Anyway, the path was cleared by Perdita's being really unwell. So unwell that the perfidious Shaun actually came looking for me. When I hastened down the back stairs into their flat, there was the poor young woman lying on that wreck of a couch they had the nerve to call furniture, looking so pasty and sickly that you'd think she was suffering from consumption rather than morning sickness. I'd have laughed out loud at the way Shaun hovered in the doorway to the basement, looking completely out of his depth, had I not more important things on my mind.

'You're a better door than a window!' I snapped at him, which felt good because it gave me a bit of authority right away. He stepped quite smartly out of the light so I followed this up by saying, 'and you can make yourself useful by getting this girl a bowl of something nourishing. She looks as though a square meal hasn't crossed her lips in days.'

'What sort of nourishing?'

'Chicken soup? A boiled egg and toast?'

'I . . . uh . . . guess we don't have no chicken soup. Or eggs.'

'You don't have any chicken soup.' It was probably not the right time to correct his grammar, but I was enjoying being in charge.

'Yeah. Right.'

I looked down at Perdita. 'Have you told him?' I asked crisply.

She shook her head slightly, without even opening her eyes.

'Then I think you ought to tell him now.'

'Uh . . . tell me what?'

Perdita opened her eyes then and turned them towards him.

19

Her eyes were a wonderful green. She took a long breath to steady herself. 'I'm . . . we're having a baby.'

'Huh?'

Now most husbands, I'm sure, would react to this wonderful news by hurrying across to their dearly beloveds, dropping down on their knees and expressing their delight. Not so Shaun. He did no more than stand there like the spaced-out nincompoop that he was, goggling at Perdita as though she'd just admitted to being impregnated by an alien being.

'A baby, you dolt.' I confess I didn't hold back on the scorn. 'You're going to be a daddy.'

'I don't wanna be a daddy . . . father.'

'Maybe not. But it's too late for that consideration. Now, do you have any food in this house at all?'

'But . . .'

I could see we would get nowhere with that simpleton. Drugs are like this, I gather. They scramble your brains. Shaun proved at that moment that his brains were more like an omelette than anything else.

'Help me with your wife.'

'Huh?'

I stood and assisted Perdita to her feet. She offered no resistance. 'I'm taking this girl up to my place. You're in no fit state to look after her and what she needs is a sizeable dose of TLC.'

He even stood aside to let us past. He had that slightly dazed look on his unwashed, stubble-strewn face, as though it was all too complicated to comprehend. In retrospect, he must have been completely stoned.

I would like to be able to report that Perdita remained with me for the whole of her uncomplicated pregnancy. To do so would be a lie; but to itemise the ramifications of the next few months would be very tedious indeed. So I'll summarise.

Shaun came down from his drug-inspired high some two days later. These days I know all the vocabulary associated with the drug scene; well, don't we all? Which is why I have no problem, in retrospect, in describing his behaviour; but I can tell you it was

20

extremely strange to me and to my generation at the time.

When he reassembled what was left of his addled wits he came in search of his soul mate – and learned that I had to all intents and purposes kidnapped her. I suppose I should have looked out for signs of withdrawal in Perdita. I thought I knew a little about that because it couldn't be all that different from withdrawal from alcohol, but if Perdita did suffer, she kept her pain from me. In fact, now that she was separated from Shaun I persuaded myself that I was seeing the beautiful interior I'd always expected to find inside the perfect exterior. And if a few small items occasionally went missing? Well, I could afford them, just as I could overlook the small amounts of cash which I might well have picked up myself, accidentally. Oh dear, how we do deceive ourselves.

And how the girl thrived on three nourishing meals a day. She looked less wan, and gained some colour in her face, and finally was blessed with that bloom of motherhood about which poets wax enthusiastic.

Shaun, it would appear, missed her less per se than he missed having a fellow pothead for company. Of course, he compensated quite speedily for her absence. A very strange assortment of odd creatures came and went through the doors of that basement flat during the next few months. You might well ask me why, having separated him from Perdita, I didn't take steps to have him and his spaced-out chums removed by the police. Well, I'm ashamed to say that it did occur to me but I was so absorbed in Perdita's wellbeing, and in the pleasure of fussing over her, that I temporarily put my powers of discernment onto the back burner. And two or three times he'd mount a feeble foray to approach her, and on a couple of occasions I'd go to do the shopping and find that she'd drifted back downstairs to catch up with whatever illegal function was taking place in my basement flat.

But she always appeared to return upstairs with docility and of her own free will. I fooled myself then by believing that she enjoyed my TLC, perhaps even came to love me a little. With hindsight, she was probably just working out what next she could steal without my noticing. Were I a betting sort of person, I'd lay good money she was very nearly the only source of income for that disreputable bunch of lay-abouts. Well, most of them didn't sound Australian, so they could scarcely have been on the dole.

And we did have some nice little conversations, Perdita and I. About family things. Following Mr. Hamilton's advice, I introduced topics like nutrition and infant care and planning for the future. We even discussed possible names for the child. Perdita's choice of name was extremely strange, not to say bizarre. She fancied Ra for a boy, I recall, after the Egyptian sun god or Che, after that revolutionary who helped Fidel Castro. And for a girl she thought Zenobia would be unusual. Or Amphitrite, who, according to Perdita, was some triple-headed pagan deity or the like. Unusual indeed. You can say that again.

It was at this time that I discovered she and Shaun weren't, actually, married.

'How will Zenobia go with your surname, dear?' I asked, innocently enough. Zenobia seemed to be the lesser of the two evil. 'Zenobia Leberman?'

'No, that's Shaun's name,' Perdita replied coolly. 'The baby will have my name I suppose. Zenobia Potts.'

You can see that I was gaining in tact. I held my tongue and did no more than swallow at the thought of any baby going through life as Zenobia Potts. And anyway, I told myself, there was a better than even chance that it might be a boy. Che Potts or Ra Potts was marginally less terrible to contemplate. It did cross my mind to introduce a few of the better saints' names into the conversation. St. Patrick was a fine man after all, as was St. Peter. And I'd always had a soft spot for Saint Cecilia.

As you will imagine, I have very mixed emotions about the whole matter of maternity. Clearly, I have never given birth to a child. Although essentially I raised Clare from her earliest days, I have never experienced that awareness of the infant moving inside me; nor have I felt a small mouth suckle at my breast. These, I believe, are powerful sensations and I regret that Our Lady has not seen fit not to enrich me in this way. But she did bless Perdita, and what a waste of her benediction that proved to be. I seriously doubt

22

that she saw her pregnancy in any way as a period of sanctification. I think her memory of those six and a half months will be of a dragon of a woman who almost forcibly separated her from her soul mate and fellow druggy, who bullied her into eating nourishing meals and forced inconsequential chit-chat upon her, willy-nilly. Perdita, in retrospect, probably hit upon the names which were most likely to irritate me. And she succeeded. How she succeeded.

Mr. Hamilton, that source of all good sense, had gone to the trouble of ascertaining the necessary information relating to an Impending Event. He'd even explained to me how one booked a woman into the maternity wing of the local hospital. So when Perdita went into labour I knew precisely what to do. And, having delivered her at the hospital, and having been informed that the birth was some time away, I returned to my house, and gathered together my resources, and marched firmly out the back door and down the stairs that led to the basement flat, and knocked with an authoritative rap on the door. After all, the least I could do was let that idiot know that he was about to become a parent. The least I could do for Perdita, at any rate.

Now, I should record that during the period of Perdita's pregnancy, whatever modicum of respect I might have held for Shaun had completely evaporated. I tried to put myself in his position, in having his woman semi-kidnapped, and I knew that, were I he, I would have fought like a hyena to have her return to me. Shaun's passive acceptance of my abducting his girlfriend simply caused me to despise him more than ever.

There was quite a pause before the door was opened, and then not by Shaun but by one of his potheaded mates. That sweet, sickly smell rose to meet me like over-ripe fruit. When I peered inside, I could see through the haze that there were maybe five of them, all lolling about on tatty old cushions. They reminded me of marionettes when the puppeteer loosens the strings and the limbs of the dolls sag to the floor in impossible angles.

'Shaun,' I said, 'Perdita's in the hospital. She's gone into labour.'

'Peace, man,' Shaun replied.

That was scarcely a sensible response, in the circumstance. 'I think she might like you to be there.' Even though I felt quite nervous, I tried to make my voice forceful.

'Yeah, man,' said one of the bearded wonders. 'She needs you there.' His words were sensible enough but he ruined the effect by sniggering in a way that made the hairs on the back of my neck rise.

Shaun got unsteadily to his feet.

'Sure. 'T's a big thing, havin' a baby. I guess I oughta go to her.'

But he managed to stumble over the first small obstacle in his way. What a miserable example of paternity. I visualised myself propelling that pothead into the hospital, probably with my elbow in the small of his back. Would the staff there immediately call the police? And how would that benefit Perdita in her moment of need, knowing that the father of her child was being detained at the pleasure of Her Majesty's Australian Government?

'Oh, sit down, you useless idiot,' I said crossly. 'I'll let you know what sex the child is, once it's born.'

I turned around and began to mount the stairs, the abiding vision being of Shaun swaying on his feet, looking at me with the vacant eyes of an addled owl.

The child was born twelve hours later. I can't tell whether Perdita had an easy confinement, or a hard one. I can report that it was very long, for me as well as for her. I found it very difficult indeed to concentrate on the magazines in the waiting room. The baby was, of course, a girl.

3

I want to describe for you the feelings I experienced when first I saw that baby. I assume that most mothers share my sentiments; I'm not so sure about fathers. I did ask Mr. Hamilton how he felt when Joel was born. His reply was quite discouraging.

'I bred ferrets, as a boy in Aberdeen. As far as I can remember Joel looked like a newly born ferret. Red, wrinkled, hairless.'

A ferret, indeed! And his only child, at that. However, I refused to be disheartened by this sadly masculine display of indifference.

'But still yours. Wasn't there the pride of paternity?'

Mr. Hamilton thought for a minute before he said, 'I suppose so.'

That wasn't particularly satisfactory. However, I'm sure that many other people have shared my reaction.

I was ushered in to see Perdita and the baby maybe an hour after the delivery. Certainly, by that time the baby had been washed, clothed and laid in a crib beside Perdita, who looked pale and tired of course, but still absolutely beautiful.

I almost tiptoed to peep into the cradle, as if I was sharing in a moment of homage. And in retrospect I think I was right. Introducing oneself to a very new person, a sentient being recently arrived among us, is a moment worthy of special reverence. And I was not disappointed. She lay in that hospital crib, Perdita's baby, an absolutely perfect, miniature creature. She was the antithesis of Mr. Hamilton's description of Joel; neither red nor wrinkled but smooth-skinned and with the neatest features, a little button of a nose, a rosebud of a mouth. Each miniature fingernail was a miracle, so was the shell of each tiny ear. I couldn't see her eyes because she was sleeping, but her head was already covered with a down of flaxen hair. And even the shape of a beautifully formed baby's head is a miracle in itself.

I don't know why I whispered, although I found myself doing so. 'She's lovely, Perdita. Simply lovely.'

Perdita didn't bother to lower her voice. 'Really? No baby's worth going through what I've been through.'

Didn't new mothers experience a particular euphoria, a sort of bonus or compensation for the effort of giving birth? The books that I'd read suggested as much. But clearly it had by-passed Perdita.

I made my voice as sympathetic as possible. 'I can understand. It must have been very uncomfortable.' What a lie – how could I understand? Although the pain I'd felt when I twisted my knee badly had given me a few sleepless nights. Then I deliberately introduced a more cheerful topic. 'What are you planning to call her, dear?'

Perdita turned her head away and closed her eyes. I did appreciate that she'd be feeling tired; after all, the process is not called 'labour' for nothing.

'I don't give a fuck.'

I couldn't believe my ears. Perdita had always been very lady-like; never given to foul language in my presence, at least.

'What did you say?'

'I said, I don't give a fuck.'

Such words seemed to poison the very air above her cherished daughter's head.

'But . . . your baby . . . and you must register her birth. She can't just be called Baby Potts. So humiliating for her, in later years.'

'Then you name her. If you care so much.' And to emphasise how she felt, Perdita turned her whole body to face the wall, and hauled the hospital blanket over her shoulder in a display that was deliberately dismissive.

I felt quite awkward. I went across to look again at the infant in the crib. Enchanting little thing that she was, she was actually seeking her thumb, in an attempt to suck it. This little action and the way she pursed her tiny mouth made my heart turn over. At that moment, I confess, I was simply overwhelmed with my love for her.

'I'll tell Shaun,' I said as the silence lengthened. I think Perdita grunted. 'I'm sure he'll be along to see you . . .' as soon as his head clears, I added to myself.

Perdita may have grunted again, I've forgotten – because I was, in a way, experiencing the very euphoria that appeared to have passed Perdita by. It was an amazingly heady mixture of total, perhaps you could say obsessive, devotion to that tiny new being, and wonder that the Good Lord could create something so miraculous.

And so that was my introduction to Clare, aged fifty minutes. In my mind I had already decided her name. As there was nothing left to do I said 'Good-bye,' with quiet dignity and then I left. I walked along those interminable corridors, and out the ugly brick doorway of the hospital, and I waited in the rain until I caught the bus; and I can remember the details of how she looked as though it was yesterday, along with the incredible awe that I felt.

In the '70's it wasn't like these days. You weren't sent home from the hospital before you've had occasion to draw breath. Back then they allowed you time to recover your strength, and the nurses helped you to establish breast feeding and made sure that the baby's navel was clean and healing nicely, and that the baby was regaining her birth weight. I realise that you'll be saying, 'What does a single woman, a spinster, know about such matters?' but let me assure you; even then I knew quite a lot. As I said before, you don't need to play the piano like Eileen Joyce to appreciate a quality performance, any more than you must have experienced a car crash to have sympathy for a victim of this misfortune.

I have no idea whether Shaun got his idle hide along to the hospital to greet his new daughter. We never collided if he did, and I made a point of never asking. For myself of course, I visited Perdita on a daily basis and it really hurt me to discover that she wasn't exactly the nurses' idea of a perfect mother. I'd dismissed her nasty little spat of temper about the baby's name as the result of her post-labour fatigue, combined with the unhappy accident that the release of the necessary hormones had clearly not been triggered in her case. So she never, to use the current vernacular, bonded with her baby.

Well, I'd not been infused with endorphins either, or not physically, but it didn't stop me from adoring that precious child.

The nurses assumed that we must be related; perhaps they saw me as an aunt or a very young grandparent. It gave me a certain satisfaction to allow them to think this. So it was that each day when I appeared at the ward they'd leap upon me with tales of Perdita's unnatural behaviour. Evidently she'd refused from the start to breast-feed. The nurses had assumed originally that she'd change her mind. Rather than have them blunt the appetite of little Clare, or Baby Potts as she was still called, so that she wouldn't take to the breast, they'd allowed some hours to elapse and awaited a maternal spark to ignite in Perdita's bosom. No such spark ignited. The baby lay in her cotton crib beside her mother and cried her little heart out. It was as though Perdita were deaf to her pleas for succour. In the end other young mothers, deeply upset on the baby's behalf, begged the nursing staff to come to her rescue.

I wasn't there to see what happened, but I can imagine the annoyance with which they gathered the squalling infant up and carried her off to the nursery to be fed. Then they cornered me when I appeared, clutching grapes and other little treats for Perdita to augment the dreary hospital fare, and poured the whole tale into my ears as though I could work miracles and transform this particular parent.

And yet, Perdita can't have been the first woman to reject her own child, can she?

As far as I can gather, she did not hold her daughter once during those days in the hospital. The nurses moved from annoyance with her to irritation, then to extreme hostility. They did not hold back in voicing their opinion that she was a very unnatural mother. I could have told them that she was unnatural in other ways because the scales were at last falling from my eyes. I no longer saw Perdita as all things wondrous or even as a hapless

28

victim of Shaun's' perfidy. External beauty, I was finding out quite painfully, does not always equate with internal purity. The inside of Perdita appeared to be flinty in the extreme. It stands to reason that a mother should love her child, the wonderful burden she has carried within her for nine long months.

She came home on the Tuesday, arriving in a taxi. I saw the vehicle draw up out of my upstairs bedroom window. There was a narrow gap, so I didn't even have to move the curtain aside. They had no reason to think I was spying on them. Shaun was with her, carrying the white bundle that was his daughter. The baby was squawking with that high-pitched, indignant clamour which is particularly trying to the listener. For a minute I felt quite sorry for Shaun and his obvious confusion and his ineptitude. I'm not sure there are many fathers who would know what to do, when handed a child of a week old. And it was clear that Perdita was not being a lot of help.

However I had made up my mind, in the last few days, that the only course available to me was to be cruel to be kind. Perdita and her daughter had to work their relationship out for themselves. I'd intervened during the pregnancy because not to do so might have had most unfortunate consequences. But surely, surely nature would take a hand and turn this abnormally unsympathetic woman into a maternal being?

How wrong I was. And how, I confess in retrospect, I had misjudged Shaun; because it was he who appeared at my doorstep just two days later, looking as befuddled as ever and as abject, with a bottle in one hand and a screaming, red-faced child in the crook of his other arm.

'Er . . . Miss Galway . . . um . . . .'

Now, I can't pretend I hadn't heard the baby crying. There weren't walls sufficiently thick to filter that sound of painful help-lessness. I'd been forced to bury my head under the pillows to block out the wailing, although even then it appeared to fill the hours of the night until I wasn't sure whether the cries were in my ears or a figment of my imagination. But I'd stuck to my original determination, to allow time for Perdita and her baby to bond.

It was evening when Shaun put in his appearance, the shadows purple and long across the back garden. I pretended that I did not know why he was there, standing on my doorstep. He had several days' stubble on his chin and he looked as baffled as ever, but at least that smell wasn't clinging to him like a spectre.

'Well, Shaun?' I had to speak quite loudly over the din. She had a healthy pair of lungs all right.

'Ah . . . the baby, Miss Galway.'

I allowed myself to peer into the blanket. Below that downy, fair hair the little girl's face was screwed up and as flushed as the wattles on a fighting cock. Her open mouth was a scarlet cavern of gums and quivering tongue.

'Yes?'

'I . . . I guess I need some help. She doesn't seem to like the bottle.'

'And Perdita? Her mother?'

He shrugged rather helplessly. 'I don't think she cares. I think she's still in shock. Whadda you call it? Post-natal something.'

At last I took pity on him. 'Perhaps you'd better come in, Shaun.' I stood aside to allow him into my kitchen, which at that time had red and white cupboards and a matching checked table-cloth.

Now, I hope the irony of the situation is not lost on you. Here was that druggie seeking help from me, me, who'd forcibly separated him from his dearly beloved; me, the seedless raisin who had as much experience of infants as . . . as Father Flaherty, as His Holiness, the Pope. Maybe less. Even so, I held out my arms and took the bundle from Shaun and looked down at his unhappy daughter. And, as if sensing that passage from one person to another, she actually stopped her squalling and opened her milky-blue eyes . . . and looked right back at me.

It was a powerful moment. I can guarantee that no mother in the world could be impervious to such magic. I'm persuaded that had she looked like that at Perdita, this story would be very different. Yes, you could say that we bonded at that minute, Clare and I.

'Give me the bottle.'

I'm an only child, born late in my mother's life. I have no cousins. I'd never fed a baby in my life, and yet it seemed so very natural. Her tiny body fitted so comfortably into the curve of my arm, and I rested my elbow lightly against the kitchen table and Clare, still appearing to focus on my face, sucked at the teat of the bottle as though she knew exactly what she was doing. Perhaps it was the light reflecting on my glasses that held her attention. I'm not sure whether I mentioned before that I wore glasses, even then. I'd been prescribed them while I was still in school, actually.

Shaun stood by, shuffling slightly as though what he was witnessing was a miracle. As, perhaps, it was.

'She seems to like you, Miss Galway.'

'You must handle her with confidence,' I said, amazed at myself because until this minute I had no idea that I possessed such confidence. 'Babies sense these things.'

'Er . . .yeah. I guess so.'

'And what about bathing her? And changing her nappy . . . diaper?'

'Not too good at that, either. '

I had absolutely no idea how good I'd be at such infant-orientated activities; but I do like that sensation, when I have the whip hand. I find that even a little bit of authority induces quite a heady feeling.

Maybe it was that which inspired me to say, ' Bring up the baby's crib, Shaun, and I'll look after her tonight. And fetch me more of her formula. Then you and Perdita can have a good night's rest.'

He looked pathetically grateful, as though I'd bestowed something quite special upon him. I continued to revise my opinion of him.

'That's really kind of you, Miss Galway. We'd be really grateful.'

I pressed home my advantage. 'And have you decided upon a name for her?'

Shaun scratched his chin. 'Not exactly.'

'Then it should be a priority. You must register her birth before she's six weeks old.'

'Uh huh.'

While I continued to nurse his daughter, Shaun departed and returned some minutes later with what seemed to be enough to satisfy the child's requirements for a fortnight, not merely an overnight stay. Of course, a lot of it was familiar to me because it was I who had insisted Perdita buy it, in preparation for the birth. With hindsight I'd probably paid for a fair portion, as well. I recognised the carry-cot which we'd decided was more suitable than a wicker cradle, which we called a Moses basket after Moses in the bulrushes – well, you know that story – and loaded in it were the little stretch suits and the matinee jackets and other items of the layette, as well as a couple of boxes of formula and a sterilisation kit and a changing mat, and two packets of disposable nappies. It's amazing how much paraphernalia a baby requires.

I did see fit to comment upon this major exercise in transposition. 'I said, 'for tonight', Shaun. Not for a month.'

He looked a bit sheepish. 'I guess I thought you might like to choose what you wanted to change her into.'

'I see.'

He made for the door, as though to escape from any more insinuations on my part. 'And thanks again, Miss Galway.'

I looked up from watching the pulse that throbbed in the soft fontanel of the baby's skull. I used one of the very few American expressions that I happened to know. 'You're welcome, Shaun,' I said. And I meant it.

No. I know what you're thinking, that Clare became my responsibility right there and then. Not so. But it is true to say that, over the next few days, I found myself with increasing frequency in the role of baby-sitter.

The baby settled down. Shaun became a little more adept, I assume, because the wailing certainly diminished. Of Perdita there was next to no sight and when we did happen to meet, once, the look she cast my way was painful in its coldness. I felt quite shocked by her overt hostility, as though those cosy little chats we'd shared had never taken place, as though she really resented my charity towards her.

Then, one morning, when Shaun deposited Clare into my keeping, I said, very casually, 'I think I'll take her for a walk, this morning.'

I hoped that the voice I used was as nonchalant as possible, because I confess I had a very important intention in mind. She was such a beautiful child, that infant, and she was to all intents and purposes still Baby Potts. And worse, far worse, she had not been baptised. This failure quite haunted me. I know that the dogma of original sin has been watered down a lot in modern times, in order to make our faith more palatable to the wishy-washy thinking of the modern person, but I was raised in the old school. I could see that enchanting little creature condemned to the dreadful state of Limbo into eternity if I, Dorothea Galway, did not do something about it. So I had quietly consulted Father Flaherty and he had agreed, in the circumstances, to baptise this lost soul for her own sake. In that he did, indeed, show a truly Christian attitude.

I dressed the baby with care, into her prettiest little romper suit. She owned no dresses at all, let alone anything which resembled a baptismal robe, but I doubted that the Blessed Virgin would care what she wore. It was her soul she sought to save. The romper had a pattern of pink and white rosebuds on it and was very sweet, in my opinion. Actually, I had chosen it myself. Then I wrapped her in a soft, woollen shawl which happened to have belonged in our family since before my own birth, and placed her in the carrycot.

This was scarcely an adequate child transporter, because the frame which supported the canvas body was quite flimsy and pushing it was really awkward, but it was the best thing available. And then we walked along the road towards St. Kevin's where I knew that Father Flaherty would be awaiting us. It was quite dramatic, that ten minutes. I had to refrain from looking over my shoulder, in case I should see either of those inadequate parents sprinting along the road in hot pursuit; but, as it happened, our progress was uneventful.

I'd given quite a bit of thought about what to name the child. I did appreciate that her baptismal names might not, in fact, appear on her birth certificate because only Father Flaherty, and I, and

Mrs. Beddowes who stood as her other sponsor with me, would be privy to what was to transpire, but that seemed no reason per se to be less than scrupulous. I selected Catherine Clare Mary, and those were the names Father Flaherty gave her, that cool June morning. Catherine was a very brave woman who died horribly for her Christian faith and it was also my mother's name; Clare means 'clear' and 'bright' and Mary, of course, was the Holy Mother of Our Lord. And oh, the relief I felt when the ceremony was over and I knew for certain that, whatever happened, this was one precious soul we had saved.

I know that Father Flaherty was as aware of the significance of the moment as was I. We had a cup of tea afterwards he, and Mrs. Beddowes who was his housekeeper, and I. Mrs. Beddowes even produced some lamingtons she had made. Poor woman, she doesn't understand the importance of using top quality chocolate.

Clare had behaved with perfect decorum, not even crying when Father Flaherty poured the holy water onto her brow. She slept sweetly in her carrycot as we sipped our tea and wondered together what awful things this innocent child's life might contain in the future. Then I thanked Father Flaherty, and gave him $15 for his trouble, and walked back along the footpath because it would soon be time for Clare's next bottle.

I'm not sure what it was which gave me a strange feeling of foreboding even before I put the key in the lock and opened the front door. It was like a little frisson of sensation that shivered down my spine. At first sight nothing was amiss, apart from a couple of drawers that lay open looking terribly untidy. I'm a neat sort of person, I like order in my life and I don't leave drawers open. But very quickly I realised that these were only the tip of the iceberg.

Yes, I know that you've already guessed. In our absence, and at the very time that the soul of their baby was being saved, my lodgers had moved out and with them had gone most of the valuables that I cherished.

This is the list of items that they'd taken with them:

- The very beautiful, 22 carat gold chain which my father

gave me at the time of my baptism;

- *Two Royal Doulton figurines, belonging to my mother and very valuable;*
- *All of my silver collection, including the candlesticks that were a wedding gift to my maternal grandmother, the silver salver and my tea set;*
- *My Royal Crown Derby jugs, in the Imari style;*
- *The $470 that I kept hidden in a vase in the larder for emergencies;*
- *The $500, rolled into a very small bundle, that lived in the back of the drawer where I kept rubber bands and sticky tape and little skeins of string that might come in handy;*
- *My paternal grandmother's assorted pieces of Waterford crystal which she brought with her as a bride from County Cork in 1894;*
- *One mohair rug of superior quality; and one merino wool rug of equal quality and almost new;*
- *My best two suitcases, which doubtless they used to carry the things they stole.*

In exchange they left me that trashy, jerry built motley of furniture, fit only for the bonfire. And their baby.

4

Now, I don't want to belabour the point, but I hope that the infer-ence has not been lost on you. That stupid and damaging story about the girl in the tower – well, once they'd stolen the lettuce the old woman demanded the peasants' child by way of payment. And that's where the analogy falls flat on its face. I know that in slang talk money is called lettuce, or greenbacks, or something similar, and that I did give them help before they stole my . . . lettuces . . . but I never, never made any demands on them regarding their baby. In fact, I think I took a very moral stand in deliberately stepping back to give Perdita an opportunity to bond with her daughter.

And there was no need for me to do that, apart from moral justi-fication. Given my own inclinations, I'd have gathered that tiny scrap to my bosom and cherished her from the moment of my first seeing her.

But once they had departed, what then? At that moment I was indeed faced with a terrible dilemma. Did I race to the police, explain about my losses and have Clare's parents branded as thieves? Did I shrug and wash my hands of them? After all, in the great order of things I had lost a sum of money, and other material possessions; but to counter-balance that I had gained something I'd given up praying for many years ago, when it became obvious that no man intended to seek me out. I had gained a living, breath-ing baby, a daughter to be loved and to love me.

The conundrum took maybe two minutes to resolve itself in my mind. I hope that my grandmother doesn't think I held her collec-tion of Waterford crystal cheap, but there really was no dilemma. Not when I looked into that flimsy, unreliable carrycot, at its precious contents. As I watched, Clare opened her eyes and stretched out her tiny arms over her head and yawned. I had no idea that so small a person could manage such complex reflexes. There was a pause as though she was assessing things, and had discovered upon consideration that there was a large, empty space in her middle. So she conveyed this fact in the only manner available to babies. She screwed up her little face and gave a half-wail, as though trying out the effect and then, deciding that this was the right course of action, bellowed again with renewed strength. I adored it. I adored watching the steps which led her to that conclusion. I was indeed her devoted slave.

As you'll already appreciate, I did not approach the police.

Strangely enough something which, at the time, I had discarded as foolishness came to my aid. Shaun had, on one occasion, arrived to hand his daughter over to me, and he'd been clutching a legal document in his hand. Have you ever paused to notice how easy it is identify an official imprint? There's the quality of the paper, thick and impressive, to begin with. And he'd muttered something about making me the baby's legal guardian. I can remember that I'd practically laughed out loud. I mean, the idiot had not even got around to registering the child's birth; there was never a hint of a name chosen for her. In fact Shaun had called the tiny scrap 'It', until I'd remonstrated with him. And here he was with a carefully worded, legally sound document, plus a couple of his disreputable chums to witness my signature.

I mean . . . I ask you!

But now I came to wondering whether Shaun had known even at that time that they'd be scarpering; and in his own, inept way had managed to do something decent for his baby daughter. We shall never know. But with that witnessed document in hand I felt that I had a legal claim which would very likely be a great asset, should I ever need to go to court.

And it was I, Dorothea Galway, who registered her birth exactly six weeks after she had first drawn breath. Catherine Clare Mary Galway, it says on her birth certificate. Mother, myself. Father, unknown. And I do apologise to Shaun for that, because I had come to appreciate that he wasn't all bad. Just weak and foolish, the drugs having created a Scotch broth of his head.

I have no intention of describing in detail all the minor events of Clare's early life. To do so would fill several books, and probably bore you to death. Like most 'kiddie' tales, such little anecdotes are very interesting to those involved and decidedly tedious for everyone else. So I plan to summarise and concentrate only on those moments which might be considered to have influenced my future decisions, or which might be thought to be true milestones.

Clare was always a delightful, easy child. I'd assumed that the whole business of mothering must be triggered by a powerful, hormonal charge; nature's way of kick-starting maternal responses, as it were. Maybe so. In my case I'd had none of the physical triggers to kick-start me, and no more did I need any. I found motherhood easier than I could ever have imagined, especially remembering that I was forty-three at the time when Clare and I became a family.

I know I'm above average intelligence after all, and I did win quite a few prizes when I was at the parochial school, and especially for English. I pride myself, modestly, that I always had a way with words. And if you're only half way literate there are any number of books out there, eager to tell you how to handle potty training and two year old temper tantrums. Not that I needed all that much advice about the latter, because Clare was a malleable child. I needed only to say, 'Clare,' in that sort of voice for her to moderate her behaviour.

And, of course, the love I felt for her from our first meeting simply blossomed and blossomed. I had to be quite stern with myself and allow my darling sufficient room to grow. I do understand about the "smother-mothering" syndrome. It would have been easy enough for me to have wrapped her in cotton wool and held her close for ever. But I didn't. When she was four I enrolled her in the infants' playgroup at St. Kevin's, which was run by Mrs. O'Malley, whose mother had known my mother, and they'd been *quite friendly during the war years.*

I didn't see much of Mr. Hamilton during this period. Chiefly this was because he, poor man, was very busy caring for Mrs. Jeannie Hamilton who was becoming increasingly gaga, but it's also fair to say that I was quite busy as well. Small children are very demanding of your time. I did exchange greetings with him whenever we met outside the house and he was quite surprised when he realised that Perdita and Shaun were no longer there and that they had left their precious daughter in my care. That's what I hinted at back then, as though there was always a probability they might return.

I knew differently. Had they contemplated returning, they would never have filched all my valuables. That action seemed very conclusive indeed to me, but I kept the tale of the theft to myself. Their conduct, it seemed to me, was rather like the good Catholic King James dropping the Great Seal of England into the Thames as he fled from the army of the usurping Prince William of Orange. Extremely final.

Clare loved her mornings at the St. Kevin's playgroup. I should record that before I allowed her to take part I had a good look at the other children, to ascertain that there were no nasty little boys who were likely to give her grief. For myself, I've never forgotten my own experience at a similar age.

My mother had saved money out of her meagre housekeeping in order to send me to kindy. Funds were tight even before my father died in the war.

And at the kindy there was a boy called Donal. I can remember him to this day. He was retarded and a lot bigger than the rest of us. Perhaps this was because Nature had compensated for his lack of brain by awarding him extra brawn. Of course, I didn't understand "retarded" at that tender age; I just thought he was very, very stupid. He could scarcely accomplish the simplest task and he was given to barging his clumsy, overweight body into you, if you were in his way. He always seemed to smell of stale urine and as a little girl I hated that, too. In fact, from my very first morning there I went out of my way to avoid Donal.

39

Kindy was run in the PE hall and there were climbing bars up one wall, which were strictly forbidden to the more intrepid small boys except at properly supervised times, and ropes that could be scaled when you were older and stronger, and vaulting horses and other gymnastic paraphernalia. I'd been attending maybe a fort-night when something unpleasant happened. I can't remember the details of how Donal managed to isolate me from the rest of the chil-dren, because even at that tender age I knew there was safety in numbers, and it so happened that at the time the teacher and her helper were both otherwise engaged. I'm sure they were basically good women, but you can't always have eyes in the back of your head. I don't really blame them for what followed. Anyway, Donal got me jammed in a gap between the biggest vaulting horse and the wall and he pressed his large, flat face into mine, which I found frightening enough in itself. I was a timid, retiring child. I remember that his nose was running; his nose appeared to be constantly moist.

'Show me your pee-pee,' he demanded in his thick, hoarse voice.

My mother was a very genteel person. She would never use words like "pee-pee", but even so I had no problem understanding exactly what Donal meant. I closed my mouth tightly and looked fixedly at the floor, although I felt very scared.

'Go on. Take down your pants.'

I was always small for my age. At the time I was wearing a woollen skirt and a hand-knitted cardigan that buttoned down the front and had a line of daisies embroidered about the welts. I remember twisting my fingers together and continuing to stare at the floor. In retrospect, I can't imagine why I didn't scream for help, but at the time I know it didn't occur to me. My mother encouraged quietness about the house and screaming was alien to me.

Donal fiddled with the front of his shorts. 'I'll show you my pee-pee,' he volunteered. 'Here, you can hold it.'

And he tried to take my reluctant hand and place it onto his private parts. Wedged as I was against the vaulting horse, however, my hands locked behind my back, he was thwarted in his attempt. Even so, I confess that some inner compulsion forced me to raise *my eyes from the floor and glance briefly at his exposed member. And oh dear, what an ugly, disgusting sight it was. So wretched.*

It was at this minute that help arrived in the form of Mrs. Williams. Blessed salvation.

'Dear me, what can you two be doing?' she asked in a cheerful tone that said, "enough of this silly play."

Donal didn't have any discretion at all. He didn't even appreciate that exchanging views of each other's genitalia was not considered desirable conduct. 'I'm showing Dorrie my pee-pee,' he explained loudly, so that all about could hear him. Such imbecility.

Mrs. Williams kept her voice very matter-of-fact. 'Now Donal, you pop your pee-pee away and do up your trousers. I think Dorothea would much prefer to play with our lovely building blocks.'

And she took me by the hand and led me off. The relief I felt was overwhelming. Then she guided me into the small, side room and she sat herself down on a chair so that she was at my level and she explained to me that Donal was backward and sometimes didn't quite know how to play. Being bright, I understood immediately. Backward people, I realised, were most unfortunately malformed and were cursed with ugly, wrinkled worms where my lower belly was smooth and pretty. Backward people were to be pitied.

Nevertheless, I didn't return to the kindy. I told my mother that I didn't enjoy it, that I was far happier at home with her. And, because it was probably quite expensive, my mother didn't argue with me. She merely said, 'If you're certain, Thea. If you don't think you'll be lonely.'

I thought that I'd much prefer to be lonely that to face Donal O'Brien ever again.

So it was with that episode in mind that I vetted the children at St. Kevin's very carefully before Clare started there.

At the time when Clare was nearly two, Mr. Hamilton found it necessary to have his wife taken into care. Poor woman, her mental faculties were deteriorating fast, and her behaviour had become increasingly unreliable. Added to that, her sweet disposition also

41

seemed to degenerate and she became given to outbursts of terrible rage. The final straw came when she left the matrimonial bed in the small hours of the morning, evidently intent upon preparing breakfast for her husband and son, although their son had actually died some years earlier. Now, she'd not been safe in the kitchen for many years and Mr. Hamilton had done a good job in securing everything away. But Mrs. Hamilton, like the unfortunate first Mrs. Rochester, showed a strange cunning and countered each of his security devices, even down to sneaking the key her husband used to lock up the stove controls so it could not be switched on accidentally. Then she set a saucepan on the hob, with some substance in it that conflagrated very easily. It gave Mr. Hamilton a terrible fright when the smell of burning awoke him, and he hurried downstairs to discover the kitchen enveloped in thick, black smoke and a real bonfire about the stove. Fortunately, he had a fire extinguisher close at hand and the damage was more to the decoration and surfaces than truly dangerous, but it did clarify matters and help him come to his painful decision.

I know all this because, of course, I volunteered to help him clear the mess up, as soon as I realised what had happened. Because our houses shared a common wall, the horrible smell of burning infiltrated my home as well. And what a mess it was. There seemed scarcely a surface not covered with a greasy, black slick. While we were wiping down counters and cupboards with a strong detergent Mr. Hamilton told me bits and pieces, little anecdotes about the care of his wife. Clearly, the decision to have her incarcerated was very distressing, but I was still impressed by Mr. Hamilton's sense of humour and the brave way he faced his personal tragedy. He has always seemed to me to be a very special gentleman.

After that, his wife no longer demanded all his attention, although he made it a matter of principle to visit her every possible day until her death some five years later. I occasionally asked him in for a cup of tea and when I had cooked more of a certain stew or batch of biscuits than Clare and I could eat, I'd give them to him. Sometimes, I confess, I deliberately cooked more than we required because I admired Mr. Hamilton and I enjoyed our little conversations.

After Shaun and Perdita had debunked with my more treasured possessions and my money, I went to a lot of trouble to clean the basement flat very thoroughly. Once I had rung the office, the garbos arrived to gather up their atrocious motley of furniture. It was fit only for the incinerator. (In Australian parlance 'garbos' are garbage collectors. It's not a trend I admire, the way we Australians create our own slang by shortening words, but I must confess it's very infective. I would not allow Clare to contract certain words of course, such as referring to the birthday of Our Lord as 'Chrissie', which you often hear, but to call a bathing costume a cossie is much briefer and occasionally I even found myself alluding to presents as pressies or a barbecue as a barbie.)

Once the flat was cleaned and aired to my satisfaction I released it, and this time two Australian women answered my advertisement. One of the women was a pretty young thing; I know she was some sort of musician but time has clouded my memory on that point. The other woman was older and taught gym at the local girls' high school. She had rather a masculine air about her, I thought, and she seemed to accentuate this by cutting her hair very short and wearing rather manly clothes. I did wonder about suggesting she might buy something a bit more feminine, maybe floral prints for example, but really it was none of my business if she chose to give that impression. And the pair kept themselves very much to themselves, and Miss Summers was always polite, in her own gruff way. I saw her very toughness as a useful adjunct in a house where dwelled three women and an infant.

Better still, they paid their rental with great punctuality and no unpleasant odours permeated the floorboards into my house.

Something else happened at about this time, which made my life considerably easier and helped in other ways, as well.

I don't think my father's career as a salesman at Grace Brothers can have been exactly spectacular, although my mother always led me to believe he was the very best in his field. I do know that he was extremely well mannered and also a gentle, kindly father. He *would arrive home with little treats for me which I remember to this day; a tiny lamp for a dolls' house, a bull-roarer which sparked and sizzled most excitingly when you wound it up and allowed it to hum. But successful – no.*

He was given, however, to playing the stock market in a very small way and thus he built up a slim portfolio which, after his death in 1945, did augment my mother's meagre war widow's pension. Among these stocks were some issued by a subsidiary of Broken Hill Mining, that gigantic Australian conglomerate. In 1980 this subsidiary was the subject of a very advantageous take-over. Suddenly my modest holding became a small goldmine, and for the first time in my life I had a little money to spare.

Now, I have to confess that money and the workings of money are a mystery to me. I have always been thrifty because my mother demanded that of me, but following the ramifications of the stock market makes as much sense as trying to sort out trends in the pop music world. They could both be written in another language. I happened to mention this to Mr. Hamilton over one of our occasional cups of shared tea and, wonder of wonders, it transpired that he, good man, actually understood what made the market tick.

'Mr. Hamilton,' I said, feeling extremely bold, 'If you could help me invest this money sensibly, I'd be forever in your debt.'

I remember how he looked while he considered my request. He's not a tall man, but to my mind he has considerable presence. In part this is because of his strongly prominent eyebrows and very fine head of springy, silver hair. Probably the greying process was accelerated by anxiety over his wife. He stands very upright and his brown eyes look most intelligent. At the time I made my request we were seated at my kitchen table because Clare was in her playpen, happily arranging her toys. On the table there was a small vase of frangipani, which always smells so delightful. Mr. Hamilton was wearing a blue and brown checked shirt and he'd obviously lost a button off the cuff at some time, and had sewn on the replacement himself. He'd used emerald-green thread, and the button didn't match, either; but I certainly did not intend to presume upon our slight friendship by volunteering to replace it.

The silence stretched so long that I was afraid he'd refuse my request, then at last he said, 'If you're sure, Miss Galway. I'd be happy to advise you.'

'Thank you,' I replied, feeling humble and delighted at the same time. At last, at last I had a legitimate reason to seek him out, to continue our conversations.

As you'll appreciate, I had not placed my small nest egg in unskilled hands. Mr. Hamilton was as good as his claim. He really does understand how Wall Street and the City of London and the local stock market work. Half my new shares were gilt-edged for safety's sake; with the other 50% he allowed a little more speculation. I confess, the money was almost incidental. What became increasingly important in my life were the times when he came around to explain to me what action he'd taken, in the light of this rise or that fall in market value. I really tried to follow what he told me and to look intelligent as he explained. I wanted him to think well of me. And, because our friendship developed through these simple contacts, I was able to ask his advice about raising Clare. His only child, Joel, had died most sadly when in his teens, but Mr. Hamilton must have been influential in his formative years, and I suppose child rearing can be compared with learning to ride a bicycle. The art stays with you. Mr. Hamilton certainly did bring a great deal of common sense into our discussions. So in a second way I was to be in his debt.

5

The tale I'm about to set down next is one of those that I prefer not to think about. It has always been my philosophy that if something unpleasant happens, something which one has no power to resolve, it gains one nothing to dwell on it. Better to put it out of mind and get on with the business of living.

However, because I'm trying to honest, I shall do my best to tell you about what happened to me on one particular evening when I was fourteen.

My mother was not of the nature to discuss with me things like the facts of life. She told me to expect my first period by saying in a matter-of-fact tone, 'It happens, from about when you're thirteen. You'll find that you're bleeding. You're not dying, Thea, and there's nothing to be frightened about. It's a nuisance and it goes on being a nuisance until you're about fifty. Then it stops. If you have cramps you can take a couple of aspirins.'

Then she gave me the most uncomfortable contraption which was supposed to hold a sanitary napkin; but in truth it was very unreliable and the fabric became so brittle after a few washes that it chafed the inside of my legs and made walking an agony. I did point this out to my mother and her response was, 'You're lucky. When I was a girl we had only towelling napkins. My mother made me sew them for myself, when I was about ten. And I had to wash them out each morning. Be thankful, Thea, that you can afford disposable pads.'

I don't think my mother intended to be unsympathetic. It was just her style. She was similarly brusque about human reproduction. Her attitude could be summed up in one word. 'Don't.'

Like every young person, I was curious. It wasn't easy for me because I was three when my father departed for the war and seven at the time of his death; and even in the years before he left, doors in our house were firmly closed. I never saw him as much as in his underwear. So you might say that my only understanding of the male body came from looking surreptitiously at photographs of statues like Michelangelo's David and from that single, fleeting glance at Donal O'Brien's pee-pee.

One summer I asked my mother if I could go to Luna Park with a friend. It would cost her nothing because I had saved up my pocket money for some weeks to pay for the ferry and for the cost of the rides. Because I had carefully removed her usual objection, the unnecessary expense, my mother agreed reluctantly. 'But stay together,' she added as a rider. 'Don't lose each other in the crowds.'

So, on a fine, late afternoon Lorraine Brown and I took the train as far as Wynyard Station and walked down to Circular Quay and boarded the little ferry that transported people across the harbour to Luna Park. I can remember so many small details about that short ride; the ferry was painted crimson red and as it crossed the harbour we had to go under the bridge, because Luna Park is on the North Shore. Looking up at the bridge, I could see the great steel arch and the shadowy forms of the cars crossing. I've read somewhere that there is a gang of painters who do nothing but paint that huge structure. The day they finish at one end, they start again at the other. That's an amazing thought. For the whole of your working life all that you do is scale those girders with your paintbrush and your pot.

At that time, not so very long after the war, the Opera House on Bennelong Point had not been constructed.

You entered Luna Park as though going through an enormous, painted mouth. I was very eager because my daily life was quite monotonous, really; parochial school from Monday to Friday, Saturday school and Mass each weekend. Going to Luna Park was thrillingly out of the ordinary. And it was such an exciting place. As the dusk gathered the twinkling lights and flashing signs glowed brighter and everything was a swirling mass of rides and stalls and happy people intent on enjoying themselves. There was that wonderful smell of spun candy-floss, I remember, and I'd made up my mind to save enough money to buy a cone of the sugary delicacy. Because of my solitary existence, I even found it pleasurable being able to identify with all those other revellers.

I was not a particularly brave girl. Even looking at the more adventurous of the rides made me quail. Lorraine was more intrepid. That's how we came to become separated. She went on a particularly ferocious ride called "The Octopus." There were small cars on the ends of the "tentacles" and as well as the whole structure circling, the individual cars spun round at their own speed. I can recall waving to Lorraine, as she gyrated with her red hair flying out behind her, but I think it was only my imagination that she looked a touch green in the face.

Now, I appreciate that had I waited for her to complete that ride what happened next could never have transpired. However, as I said earlier, we can't undo that which is done. So be it – I wandered away, I think intent upon enjoying that happily antici-pated candy-floss. Yes, that's right, because the queue to buy was quite long. It snaked out of the brightly-lit area into a patch of deep gloom alongside a hoop-la stall, which for some reason was not operating that particular evening. And in the dark shadow a hand quite literally seized my collar and plucked me out from the rear of that line of waiting people. I would have cried out, had I been capable. After the episode with Dugal, I'd reflected in depth and decided that should such a thing ever happen again, I would scream my head off. However, the act of "plucking" caught the collar of my cotton frock hard up against my larynx, thus rendering me absolutely voiceless and then, before I could recover, a large, filthy hand was over my mouth and I was carted, deeply shocked, into the darkness between the unlit booth and the stone wall that formed the boundary of the park.

You can imagine my terror. You read about perverts who pray on children at such places, and I suppose I must have filled that particular pervert's fantasy to a T. I was small, I looked younger than my fourteen years, and was at that minute alone, not likely to be missed. Maybe he had been watching me for the last ninety minutes, maybe he was an opportunist who seized the moment.

I do not plan to describe in detail what happened to me behind that hoop-la booth. Suffice to say that he defiled me, most painfully and disgustingly. I learnt more about a man's physique than I wanted to learn and at the same time I feared for my life. My terror was such that I could scarcely catch my breath. I think at one time I fainted, probably from lack of oxygen, because his foul-tasting hand remained jammed into my mouth so hard that I could not even find the reflex to bite. And it seemed to go on forever. My memory, such as it is, is of tearing, both of my clothes and my person, and searing pain. Then, just as suddenly as my attack had begun, it ended. He cast me down like a rag doll against the rock-face, fumbled with his trousers, and left.

As he departed he spoke for the first time. His voice was coarse and heavily accented. 'I knows where ya lives, little girl. Don't ya go tellin' nobody or I'll come 'n ring you's bleedin' neck as ya lays in you's bed.'

I felt so bad that I could not move. My legs refused to obey me. There was blood on my skirt, my pants had been ripped down and off my legs and I could not even locate them, and my head still felt as though it belonged to someone else. And, worst still, I was consumed by terrible, abject guilt. I knew that I had brought this fearsome assault upon myself, because I had not obeyed my mother. She had instructed us to stay together and I had not followed her edict. What would I say when I saw her? How could I ever explain this terrible thing in confession to Father Rarity?

Hindsight is a wonderful thing. Now, in my sixties, I can share your astonishment that any child would automatically take the blame for a terrible assault such as the one I experienced; but I am trying to record this tale truthfully. And I sincerely felt that the fault was mine.

By the time I crept out from behind the booth Lorraine had sensibly reported my disappearance to the authorities, and a sympathetic policeman was at hand to rescue me, to take me to the

*station and eventually to return me to my mother. Even their nice-
ness and their promises to 'get the bugger' and their repeated
assurances that it was not my fault, could not console me. Once I
had come out of the near-catatonic state into which the attack had
cast me, I found it impossible even to cry. Tears would have been
cleansing and cathartic. They were not available to me; my eyes
remained obdurately dry.*

*My mother was quite nice. She did not blame me, or not in so
many words, but I lived with the knowledge of her disapprobation,
like a wedge that separated us.*

*And that was not the worst. Of course, Lorraine could not be
expected to keep the tale private. That would be asking the impossible of any person with such a story to share. Our fellow students
were still agog when I returned to school a week later. Wide-eyed,
Lorraine narrated to the parochial school children her part of the
events, dwelling on how she initiated my "rescue" by her prompt
action. Not prompt enough, I was tempted to say, but I held my
tongue. But for her valour, according to Lorraine's version, I would
have been murdered, my body flung behind the booths. No point in
my refuting this, or to rebut that my assailant had all the time in the
world to kill me, had he chosen to do so. But no, this was
Lorraine's chance to be a heroine, her fifteen minutes of fame. In
essence I was unimportant, except as a vehicle to reflect her glow
of righteousness.*

*How desperately I wanted it all to die away, but even when the
Reverend Mother spoke in assembly, pointing out that I was the
victim of this crime, not the perpetrator, I was still the object of
interest. Curious eyes followed me about the playground and my
blessed anonymity, behind which I had sheltered all my school
days, was shattered forever. I would always be the girl to whom
"something nasty" had happened. It influenced my thinking to such
an extent that I left school as soon as I legally could, shortly before
my fifteenth birthday. Essentially, it ended my education.*

The police let me down, too. They never did catch my attacker.

At this time it might be sensible to tell you a little about Clare, per se.

As you will appreciate, in those early years I was quite anxious that she might have inherited some of the character flaws of her natural parents. The first item to report is that at no time did she exhibit any of the symptoms of drug dependence. Such knowledge was in its infancy back then; indeed, as I have already recorded, I did not even know the vocabulary. But it stands to reason that I should follow the research findings as they appear in our daily papers.

However, in the matter of foetal drug distress, Clare appeared to have been blessed; and in other ways as well. I don't think I am biased when I say that in the child I saw the nicer qualities I had hoped to find in the beautiful Perdita. She was an easy infant, a winsome toddler. Even Mr. Hamilton mentioned what a delightful child he found her. She has always been shy, but shyness is certainly not a sin and can, on occasions, be charming. The way Clare colours up in moments of social stress is extremely touching.

I also sought in vain for characteristics of her father. Of course, it is reasonable to say I did not know the young Shaun and, presumably, there was a time before his personality was drowned under the pervading nature of the substances he abused. I've read that dependence such as that is often the recourse of an inadequate personality. Perhaps it was so with Shaun. How can I tell? I have no knowledge of his early history, his family background, his former life. If his was an inadequate personality, he did not hand on this shortcoming to his daughter.

I did know a little more about Perdita, because we'd conversed quite happily and at length during her pregnancy. She was always cautious about giving me too much in the way of hard facts; for example I have no idea which part of America was her hometown, and America is a large country, almost as big as Australia and considerably more populated. I do know from these talks that she was an only child and that her father was a professor at a small, liberal arts university. She called it a college, which is our name for certain high schools, but having read widely I can translate these little anomalies of language. Maybe it is from her grandfather that Clare inherited her brains, because from the start she was a clever, almost a precocious, little girl.

And from Perdita she certainly gained her looks, although perhaps she was even more lovely. She always had a certain fragility about her, those fine-boned features, the fairness of her hair and skin that suggested she might be delicate of constitution. This, I hasten to write, was in direct apposition to the robust good health she enjoyed. Of course there was a year, her first at St. Kevin's, when she seemed to go from one cold to another, one bout of bronchitis to the next, and all of which I managed to catch from her, but I'm told that this is normal in children when first they encounter new strains of germs and the like.

And, most remarkable of all, she had these great, wonderful eyes. You read about people whose eyes are as green as cats' eyes. The colour of Clare's, however, reminded me more of sea green. Most striking, almost unique in my experience. And her fine, dark lashes set them off. Oh yes, she was a child out of the ordinary, my daughter. I became used to people turning to look at her in the street as I trundled her pushchair along to the dairy or across the High Street to the butcher's and the greengrocer's. Sometimes I wondered what people thought, glancing from her to me, and trying to find a likeness, but I wasn't bothered by their implied question, their slightly raised brows.

As Mr. Hamilton said, after he came to know that Clare was now officially mine, 'Miss Galway, the accident of giving birth does not create a mother. A mother is the woman who walks the infant in the night when she's curled up with the pain of colic, and who teaches her to use the potty and who mops up the vomit when she misses the pan. A mother recites with her the alphabet and reads the "Just So" stories to her and introduces her to the ideas of honesty and decency. In all these things you are her mother, Miss Galway. You may rest easy in your bed.'

And, in faith, I knew him to be right. My daughter would have the education denied me by circumstances. I was punctilious in my reading to her. We progressed from all the old nursery rhymes to children's literature, not just those that spring to mind like "Winnie the Pooh," but also Australian classics, like "Snugglepot and Cuddlepie." Should you not be familiar with this tale, it tells of the adventures of two gumnut babies and is quite delightful, as well as *introducing our young people to the flora and fauna of the bush. And when she was older we shed a tear together over the sad death of brave little Judy in "Seven Little Australians."*

No one had to teach Clare to read. She taught herself, just by following the words as we explored together the delights of the printed word. This intrinsic ability must have been another legacy from her birth parents and I could not but be grateful.

Clare, as a little girl, had an imaginary friend. She's not alone in that, I know, but Clare's friend did seem different from those of other fanciful children. The friend's name was Bunny, and she appeared very shortly after I'd read her the tale about the bunyip. A bunyip is a monster which appears in Aboriginal legends and, although I'd been careful not to read her anything particularly scary, I do think this is how she selected that name for her companion.

I was introduced to the mythical Bunny one afternoon when Clare announced, 'Bunny's been very naughty.'

'Who is Bunny?'

'She's naughty?' Clare repeated, but she seemed unable or unwilling to clarify further.

So I changed tack. 'How do we know that she's been naughty?'

Clare looked at me sideways. 'She ate the last Anzac biscuit.'

So I assumed that this last, delicious, morsel had slid down Clare's throat and here was a valuable scapegoat. This made sense to me at once.

'That was very naughty and greedy of Bunny,' I said quite sternly.

'Yes, very naughty,' Clare echoed.

And that might have been all, had it not been that, when I looked in the tin, the sugar-biscuit was still sitting in there, totally intact. And so it went on, in subsequent days and weeks; a litany of Bunny's misdeeds which might have been invented to excuse Clare's own naughtiness, but never were. Clare continued to be the good little three-year old that she'd always been.

I decided to discuss this behaviour with Mr. Hamilton. He listened in silence as I explained Bunny's more recent "appearances."

'And she never, actually, perpetrates the misdemeanour?' he

asked. *'So there's really no need to have invented a scapegoat?'*

'No need at all.'

'I think Clare would like to be naughty herself,' Mr. Hamilton continued after a few minutes' thought, *'But she's not sufficiently brave. So she gives voice to her possible transgression, in order to test your response.'*

'Then am I responding correctly?' I ventured. *'I try to sound firm, but not angry. I don't want Clare to fear me, even when viewed in the light of her companion's supposed crimes. Nor do I laugh at this Bunny.'*

'Dear me, no!' Sometimes Mr. Hamilton's Scottishness made him sound as though he'd arrived from Aberdeen only yesterday. *'To laugh at Bunny would be very heartless. Her little friend is probably very real to Clare.'*

'And you think I'm handling it correctly?'

'Aye. I can't imagine any better way to handle it. And I'd take no further action, unless Bunny's sins become too extreme.'

I changed tack slightly. *'Did Joel have imagined companions as well?'* I liked to introduce topics in which we might have a common bond.

'No. Joel was a very down-to-earth child. More in my mould than his mother's. She had a most poetic side, in her heyday. Joel was more interested in dismantling our telephone to discover how it worked, than allowing his imagination to let rip.'

'His loss must have been deeply painful, both to you and Mrs. Hamilton,' I ventured. Even the thought of my ever losing Clare made my chest tighten and my throat constrict, despite her being such a healthy child.

'The loss of any child is painful. The loss of an only child is probably worse. Jeannie took it very hard.'

Oh, how I would have liked at that minute to reach across the table and lay my hand comfortingly on his, to demonstrate my sympathy. But such a move was alien to me. Instead I came out with one of those platitudes which sounds better in one's head than when voiced.

'I'm sure the Good Lord had a reason to take him.'

54

I could almost feel Mr. Hamilton withdraw and knew that I had made a mistake.

'You may well be right, Thea, but not being Christian I can't share your faith that there's an order in such things. If there is a God, it seems somewhat unjust to me that he should have seen fit to rob me of my only child and, in essence, my wife.'

The oft-touted remark in moments like this deals with our not being given burdens larger than we can bear, or a reminder of all that Job had to suffer. Being intelligent I appreciated that neither comment would be suitable. So I sat in shocked silence until Mr. Hamilton stood and politely took his leave and went back to his own house. The words I used in farewell came out by rote because my head was still reeling.

I'm not sure whether the greater part of the shock came, however, from discovering that Mr. Hamilton was not a Christian, or because he called me Thea.

Clare took her First Communion shortly before her seventh birth-day. I wondered whether this was too young, but Father Flaherty was an advocate of early First Communions. In one way it was a blessing that he influenced me to have Clare's name put on the list to attend Saturday School and be prepared for this important rite of passage. I've always been small, or petite as they say in the larger department stores. PETITE SIZES they put on the sign, as though those of us not blessed with inches will be offended by the word SMALL. Even at nearly eight, when I took my First Communion, I was smaller than the other children. And, because it was so very important to me, I'd kept the very fine dress my mother had made for me for that special day. It must be remembered that we were not at all well-off in those days, even if my father was supposed to be one of the best salesmen at Grace Brothers. My mother had made my dress herself, lovingly and by hand, and I've kept it, because it is one of the very few manifestations of affection that she ever showed me. Outward displays of warmth were foreign to her personality.

The dress was made from tana lawn and as delicate a fabric as you can imagine. If you know the tales of the Brothers Grimm, you'll recall that in one the king promises his daughter to the hand of the suitor able to find cloth so fine it will pass through a wedding ring. When I read that story, it occurred to me that the tana lawn of my first communication dress was sufficiently insubstantial to do just that. And my mother had meticulously created a host of tiny pin tucks, vertical up the bodice, horizontal around the skirt. How I loved that dress, which is why I had folded it away in blue paper in the days when I'd hoped and assumed that some man might ask me to marry him and bear his children. When this did not materialise, I very nearly forgot about the slim parcel, packed in a cabin trunk in the loft, but when Father Flaherty approached me with his suggestion regarding Clare, my mind flew to this hidden treasure.

I hauled the cabin trunk into the centre of the loft and unwrapped the blue paper, fearing somewhat that even at six Clare might be larger than I had been, a full year older. However, I was not to be disappointed. I soaked it in milk, then washed it with care and pressed out the pin tucks. Clare was as delighted as I could have hoped. I explained to her how precious it was to me and she stood very still as I slipped it over her head and did up the tiny, mother-of-pearl buttons down the back. I'd always loved those little buttons. And, wonder of wonders, because she was slightly built she could wear the dress without my even having to let out the side seams. It was a little on the short side, but not too much because my mother had thought showing one's legs was a sign of vulgar breeding, and the hem had very nearly brushed my ankles.

I coached her in her catechism, as my mother had taught me to say it by rote. It did seem to me that this generation of children is nothing like as well versed in the Tenets of Faith as we were. When I was to take my First Communion, I had to recite by heart the Apostles' Creed, the Act of Contrition, the Confiteor, the Litany of the Virgin Mary, not to mention the Seven Sacraments, the Seven Deadly Sins and the Seven Virtues. Some of these I also learnt in Latin; the Magnificat, Ave Maria and so on. And, according to my Irish grandmother who was still alive at that time although with scarcely a tooth in her head, as a girl in Ireland she'd been expected to learn the entire catechism in Gaelic, as well.

So when you think about it, in having to know only the brief version that is considered adequate, Clare got off very lightly. She learnt it in the way a sponge soaks up water . . .

1. Q.   Who made you?
   A.   God made me.
2. Q.   Why did God make you?
   A.   God made me to know Him, love Him and serve Him in this world, and to be happy with Him forever in the next.
3. Q.   In whose image did God make you?
   A.   God made me to His own image and likeness.
4. Q.   Is this likeness to God in your body or in your soul?

. . . . . *And so on.*

Picking things up came so easily to Clare. Even though she did not need to know more than the early tenets of faith, by the time the great day came she was conversant with almost all the doctrinal points of the catechism. I don't mean that she knew it all by heart, but we did have some happy discussions about the meaning of being a true Christian.

So Clare went to her First Communion. I'd have liked to suggest that Douglas Hamilton come with us to mark the importance of the day, but knowing how he felt about Christianity, it didn't seem altogether appropriate. But I should have liked a man sitting beside me on that special day and sharing my pride, especially a man like Douglas.

58

The Maiden

6

Clare was wearing her new red shoes. Each had a strap across the top, and a buckle at the side. Her socks were new too, and very white. Some girls turned the tops of their socks down but Clare liked the smooth lines they created when not folded over. She quietly admired them while Father Flaherty talked to the class. He was telling the children all they had to know, before attending their First Confessions and taking their First Communions.

Father Flaherty was really boring and talked in a funny way. That was because, according to Mummy, Father Flaherty came from Ireland and they talked that way in Ireland. He wasn't very good at making the boys pay attention. The nuns at St Kevin's wouldn't have let them get away with it. Sister Paul was really crabby with naughty boys. She whacked their fingers with her ruler. Perhaps Father Flaherty should get out his ruler; then he'd have the boys' attention all right.

The girls sat demurely on one side of the kindy room, the boys the other side, divided by a space in which Father Flaherty walked up and down. Clare thought all boys were stupid. They were always creating a row and interrupting interesting lessons, like sums and reading. Not that Father Flaherty was interesting, apart from the black bump on the side of his nose that had stubby little whiskers growing out of it. He always seemed to smell of fish, as though he ate it every day instead of only on Fridays, as did Clare and Mummy. Mummy explained that eating fish on Fridays was a mortification of the flesh, but the snapper was cooked with a little

59

butter and a sprinkling of parsley so that it tasted delicious; so Clare had decided that mortification was probably a good thing.

Clare watched the boys from under her lashes or, if she turned her head a little, sideways, in a peepy manner. The boys were swinging their legs quite vigorously and nudging each other. One pinched the boy next to him and the neighbour said, 'Ow,' and retaliated with a punch. Father Flaherty raised his voice a little but behaved as though he hadn't noticed the bad behaviour. That was a pity. Clare had thought they might get into trouble and not be allowed to take their First Communions.

Father Flaherty was the priest and he was talking about sin and it was easy to understand that sin meant being naughty, like the boys right now. Clare, however, found it a lot harder trying to separate mortal sin from venal, when he launched into a description of both. Was swatting a bluebottle a mortal sin? Or stepping by accident on a spider? They both died, after all, and killing was a mortal sin. Father Flaherty had talked earlier about being unkind to animals, which was far easier to comprehend. Actually, Clare would never be unkind like that anyway. She would have liked a little black and white kitten to sleep on her bed and to chase a bit of paper tied at the end of some string. She would have called it Socks. But Mummy was allergic to cat hair, so there was no pet at the Galways' house. If she couldn't have a kitten, Clare wouldn't have minded something small and furry, but anything that reminded Mummy of a rat was out of the question. Even if it didn't have That-Sort-of-Tail-Ugh. Mr Hamilton had pointed out a jerboa to Clare, when they visited the nocturnal house at the Taronga Zoo. A jerboa was an Australian sort of desert rat and really sweet with its huge, bright eyes, although it did have That-Sort-of-Tail-Ugh.

Mulling over happy thoughts about possible pets was far more interesting than grappling with moral uncertainties, especially when being explained as they were in the wrong sort of vocabulary.

Clare had no real idea of what First Communion was all about except that it was very special, that she was expected to wear Mummy's own First Communion dress and a beautiful veil a little like a bride's; and she might receive a present. She wondered whether Mr Hamilton would give her a present as well, but it didn't seem likely, because she knew he thought going to church was "a load of superstitious twaddle."

And, before you were given God to eat, and His Blood to drink, you had to attend your First Confession. Clare was not looking forward to her First Confession. In fact, she was counting down the days to the Big Event with almost as much dread as excitement. Unlike those boys, she had nothing to confess. She could recite the opening sentences with ease . . . 'Forgive me, Father, for I have sinned. This is my First Confession . . .' but had absolutely no idea how to continue. And subsequent thought, and more carefully expressed questions asked of Thea, did very little to enlighten her in the following days.

Come the hour, she approached the compulsory unburdening of her soul with dread. Even drawing aside the crimson curtain of the confessional was hard, and the dark interior, with its grill on one wall and wooden seat, looked more forbidding in nature than comforting; a dark cave smelling of stale-body odours, nothing like the welcoming refuge which Father Flaherty had described. He had also implied that they would sleep better when they had shared their burden of guilt with God. Clare, modestly smug in her six-year-old rectitude, slept very well without it.

She entered and seated herself. An ornately carved crucifix, with Christ's face twisted in His agony, dominated the wall. In the dimness she could make out Father Flaherty's plump silhouette on the other side of the grill. The wart on his nose looked like a minia-ture volcano, spouting larva. The growth fascinated and repelled her at the same time.

'Forgive me Father, for I have sinned . . .' she whispered.

'Speak up, child, speak up.'

Clare tried to obey, but the second time her voice came out even quieter. She could hear Father Flaherty sigh noisily.

'Well? How have you hurt the Lord? What sins have you to confess to Him?'

Silence might be interpreted as a sin. Something was definitely expected. She clutched at straws. 'I said, 'Shut up' to my mother.'

'You did, eh?'

Clare had never said 'shut up' in her life. 'No, Father. That's a lie,' she whispered.

Another gusty sigh crossed the space from confessor to confessee. 'Lying is a sin. You must say ten "Hail Mary's" and think about honesty. Have you other sins to confess?'

This was more frightening than anything else, ever, in her life. Clare felt like leaping from the wooden bench and seeking the familiarity of the church, and light, and sweet fresh air. Then inspiration sprang to her rescue.

'Father, I've got a friend called Bunny and she does all sorts of very naughty things.'

On the other side of the grill Father Flaherty shifted a little testily. 'Then your friend Bunny should come to confession herself.'

Clare, comfortable at last with something worthy of sharing, grew bolder and consequently her voice louder. 'She can't, Father. Her mother won't let her. I said I'd confess for her.'

'And what has this friend done?'

Clare thought fast. What fearful crimes had Bunny dared to commit? 'She emptied all the new packet of tea leaves down the toilet and flushed them away and her mother was cross.'

'That was wasteful and naughty.'

'And she took her First Communion dress and she cut it all up, so that she could have a shop-bought dress like the other girls. With frills.'

'Harming material things is wasteful and a sin. Especially if her parents could not afford a new dress. The church preaches thrift. Does Bunny appreciate that?'

'Bunny doesn't care.'

Father Flaherty paused thoughtfully. 'Perhaps you could persuade this little friend Bunny to come to our classes with you?'

By now Clare was on well-walked territory. 'And then she stuck a pair of scissors into her mother. And she called her an ugly old pig.'

'She did? A pair of scissors? Dear, dear. That's very sinful.'

It was a gloriously heady feeling of power, of familiarity, of personal knowledge of transgression. 'And she cut off the thing on

Father Flaherty's nose when he wasn't looking, and she took a hammer and she hit her mother on the head with it. Lots of times. There was blood all over the kitchen.'

The heavily rotund figure sat up abruptly. 'Clare! I think your sin might be letting your imagination exceed your better judgement. You will say a hundred "Hail Mary's" and apologise to your good mother.' Father Flaherty launched into a hasty absolution, then concluded abruptly. 'That is enough. Good day.'

The use of her name startled Clare out of her enthusiastic flight of fancy. When the priest had talked of the anonymity and confidential nature of confession she had assumed, somehow, that although she could see him, he was not similarly empowered. He did not know who sat on the other side of the wall. In her reckoning he had taken on the guise of a blind, steadfast God, incapable of shock or offence.

Once outside the booth she reverted to form. Downcast eyes, shy smile; never a foot out of step. She was, however, aware that Father Flaherty always looked at her a little differently after that First Confession. His look was appraising, thoughtful. Even Clare knew that Bunny had badly overstepped the mark.

There were, however, two interesting post scripts to this little episode. The first was that Father Flaherty underwent a small surgical procedure to remove the wart that had so long adorned his nose. According to Mrs. Beddowes, his housekeeper, this was prompted by the current concern about skin cancer. The father thought it sensible to take precautionary measures.

The second was that Bunny's excess had shaken Clare almost as much as it had her Father Confessor. As a result Bunny, from that time on, was kept more firmly under the hatches. She emerged seldom and was never again known to do more than contribute the occasional, inappropriate swear word.

If ever – heaven forbid – Douglas Hamilton were asked to record his hobbies and pleasures, maybe for some hypothetical *Who's Who*, he knew that he would list his roses high. There was something so intrinsically perfect about them. So beautiful that, had he to offer some proof of the presence of God, he might to be forced to suggest one, flawless bloom. Perhaps *Peace*, with its sheen of rich cream and hint of rose and the faultlessness of its shape.

However, such a proposition was never likely to manifest itself. And, come to that, by way of refuting his own argument in favour of the presence of a deity, he could well point out his own personal history. What sort of all-powerful being, capable of authority over good and evil, would have prescribed so terrible a sequence of events? Douglas felt that he'd experienced more anguish than any one man deserved.

As he trimmed *Elizabeth of Glamis* (slightly flat-faced, but an abundant bloomer and fine, near-coral shades) of her exuberant growth, Douglas' thoughts slipped, unbidden, back to his early days in Australia. They'd arrived, the three Hamiltons, so brimful of excitement and visions and hopes. Well, he and Jeannie at any rate, because Joel at three was really too young to do more than echo his parents' enthusiasm. Which, indeed, he had done in full. And in those early years there was no reason to presuppose a tragic end to the dreams.

Joel was such a grand wee lad. Intelligent, sturdy, willing to try anything. Perhaps Douglas would have liked to see in his make-up more of Jeannie's poetry and Jeannie's vibrant personality, but that was only because he regretted the lack of such flights of fancy in himself. Douglas used to joke, during their courtship, that his woman lived her life amid a flurry of exclamation marks, in a world where the shapes and colours were more vivid, more brilliant, than for other mere mortals.

Joel, however, took after the scientific, factual Hamiltons. Behind him stretched a long line of Scottish Calvinists who had weathered a thousand Aberdeen winters and grown on a daily intake of oatmeal to be as tough and rugged as the city's granite face. Tough? There was a jest. A bitter, deeply unfunny joke, because fourteen year old Joel, who never suffered from the usual coughs and colds of childhood, had transmogrified in a mere two hours from the light of his parents' lives to the death of their aspirations. Meningitis. The secret, lurking killer whose presence they had never so much as envisioned.

It would have been easy to blame Jeannie's slide into dementia on their son's precipitous death. Easy but untrue, because even before that terrible period she was becoming forgetful and acting in a bizarre, unreasonable manner. Hindsight, that wonderfully precise attribute, told him that the seeds had already germinated by the time they escorted Joel to the crematorium and returned home with what was left of him in a totty-stupid little urn-thing. But perhaps Joel's death did accelerate her decline. Jeannie, fast losing touch with day-to-day reality, had seemed to find comfort in that urn, crooning to it the nursery songs she'd sung to the infant Joel.

'Dance to your Daddy, my little babby,
Dance to your daddy, my little man.
You shall have a fishy, on a little dishy,
You shall have a fishy when the boat comes in.
Dance to your daddy, sing to your mammy
Dance to your daddy, my little man.'

And Douglas could recall how the toddler Joel had rocked from side to side on his sturdy little legs, and clapped his plump small hands and beamed at her with their shared pleasure.

None-the-less, the moment Jeannie was gone into the hospice where she would spend her last years, Douglas deposited the urn in the bin. Remnant ashes in a vase held no connection with his son, no sentimental link. He preferred to cherish his memories.

Douglas, moving from *Elizabeth of Glamis* to *New Dawn*, which in early summer had covered the dividing wall with pink profusion, could hear the very small Clare playing in the Galway's garden. From the snatches of conversation that drifted over she was conducting a tea party for her dollies and teddies. Douglas, growing up as one of four brothers, appreciated that he knew amazingly little about girls; but there was no doubting that Clare Galway was a fetching wee thing.

There'd been an occasion, only recently, when he'd felt it beholden upon him to take Clare off Thea's hands for a brief period. He'd never really known a lot about his neighbour until the day Jeannie had tried, very nearly successfully, to render them all to charred remains as ashy as that horrible urn's contents, and Thea had so willingly come to his aid. And my word, how the wee woman had toiled. She was amazingly strong for one so slightly built. And then they had somehow drifted into an easy, but not exactly intimate, friendship.

But until the other day Douglas had considered Clare only as an accessory to her adoptive mother; certainly charming, but with no personal association. He'd actually dropped by at Thea's with a paper to sign and you didn't need to be a forensic scientist, which Douglas was by training and by vocation, to read the pain etched between his neighbour's brows and in the sightlessness of her eyes.

'Woman, are you all right?' he'd asked.

She had put a hand to shield her face from the sunlight. 'Oh, it's nothing, Douglas. Just my usual migraine. I'm afraid I have them, occasionally. The doctor talks about a cluster.'

'Then get back into the dark. These papers can wait.' And at that moment he'd had an uncharacteristic flash of insight. 'What about Clare?'

'Clare?' Thea had repeated stupidly.

'Yes, Clare. Is she at school?'

'School? Today's Saturday. She's at her Saturday class. With Father Flaherty.'

Ah, Douglas had thought. Catholicism. It didn't even allow you the luxury of a day off. 'Then have her come across to me, as soon as she's home.' He had another thought. 'Perhaps she needs fetching from the church?'

Thea looked a ghastly greeny-white, as though she was about to faint, as though she were developing verdigris. 'No. No. Mrs O'Neil said that she'd collect Clare, along with her Kathleen.'

'Then you get onto your bed, woman, where you belong. I'll keep Clare with me until you're feeling better.'

She'd half closed her eyes. 'If you're sure, Douglas. That would be such a Christian kindness.'

At other times, in other circumstances, talk of Christian kindness would be exactly the tinder to kindle a sharp rebuttal from

Douglas, but he recognised that Thea was scarcely herself, and held his tongue.

And so, half an hour later, Clare skipped around and knocked on his front door; and thus Douglas began a voyage of discovery into the make-up of the embryonic-woman's mind. And a truly delightful voyage of discovery it proved to be, certainly for Douglas, but apparently for Clare, as well.

At this time she was six and a quarter. She and Douglas spent the afternoon playing games, because it was as wet as only Sydney can be in autumn. Just the other day they'd had four inches in a little over twenty-four hours and Douglas had actually thought with a touch of nostalgia of the bone-chilling cold of Aberdeen's winter. They played *Old Maid*, which Clare taught Douglas, and *Go Fish*, which Douglas taught Clare and which had been a favourite of Joel's. Clare confirmed his hitherto only suspected conjecture that she was very quick on the uptake and amazingly bright. Until they were stretched out on his carpet, head to head in their individual determination to beat the other, Douglas had rather feared that this might be a painful exercise. Too close to the territory that was uniquely Joel's. He need not have worried. The blond hair in place of Joel's crisp brown head, the long, curling lashes against fair, fine-textured cheeks in place of Joel's intense, dark gaze, did nothing to rekindle his sense of loss. And, moreover, there was a gap of twelve-plus years separating the two children who presumed to pit their wits against him. Against him, Douglas Hamilton, acknowledged champion in the Hamilton family of *Go Fish*?

It was with reluctance that he suggested to Clare, some time later, that perhaps she should find out how her mother was feeling.

But that was only the start. It seemed so easy to suggest that maybe he could drive her out to see the animals as Koala Park? Of course Thea would be welcome too but Thea, it transpired, was involved in some parish function and was only too happy to allow Clare the chance of so exciting an outing. So Douglas and Clare went alone, driving through the inner suburbs, across the great span of the Harbour Bridge, out through the affluent residential areas of the North Shore.

Douglas had not been to Koala Park in years; it was a first for Clare and through her wondering eyes Douglas experienced the pleasure of re-discovery. Not just of the native fauna, although there was something so comical about the tank-like squatness of the wombat, and quite cuddlesome in the koalas which were presented for curious eyes. There was also the satisfaction of seeking with upturned eyes the round and furry posteriors wedged into gum-tree forks which indicated other, sleeping marsupials Then there was the fun of feeding the emus – although carefully, because those small heads atop sinewy necks and hefty bodies did not speak of any great intelligence, and certain birds could prove quite aggressive. Douglas had no desire to return his charge minus the odd finger and be faced with inevitable explanations.

But . . . best of all . . .Clare, he learnt, also shared an interest in things botanic, albeit embryonic. So he could point out to her the fine, crimson blooms of the native waratah and the spider-like grevillea that grew in the carefully tended borders of the park, and the fine-cut leaves of the wattle family.

Some hours later the pair returned home deeply satisfied and bonded in their mutual pleasure in flora. And even the drive in a car held novelty value because Thea, of course, did not own a vehicle of her own. Douglas had not anticipated it but he felt, increasingly, that Clare depended in part upon him, as much as did Thea in entrusting him to supervise her portfolio.

The Convent of St. Ursula's is more than sixty miles from Sydney, built on a very fine site that looks out towards the Blue Mountains. The sisters who live within its confines come from many parts of the world but in the greater part are of Irish stock. Two thirds of the order of nuns are teachers, the other third dedicated women who have forsaken the world in order to enter a life of prayer. Occasionally, especially on feast days, the two parts of the convent overlap.

These days, when education is so largely community based, a school such as St. Ursula's must be considered something of an anachronism. Its very isolation acts against it. But it was to the good women of St. Ursula's that Clare Galway's education was entrusted. She began there as a pupil the February after her eighth birthday. The resolve to send her was taken most painfully by her mother, who loved her above all things. In fact, the decision was reached because of a small, somewhat charming event.

Until then Clare attended the local parochial school which was run by lay people under the auspices of Father Flaherty's governing eye. Clare was clever, she read early and easily and enjoyed school. She might well have continued there for some years.

Thea walked with her each morning to school and collected her each afternoon. This was not quite as precious as it might seem. The traffic that raced along the road between the Galways' home and the school seemed to increase in size and volume daily.

Between these two points was another educational establishment, a private, Anglican prep school. It was necessary to cross the entrance drive to this school, and parents arriving to collect their sons created a further hazard for the incautious. Although the children were clearly being raised in a faith close to heathen in Thea's book, she could not but admire the general turn-out of the boys, their courtesy and their smart uniforms. They still wore boaters, a custom of which she approved and which has unfortunately been discarded by so many schools. Thea and Clare both thought the boaters looked very chipper, especially when worn with the summer blazers of maroon and white stripes. Frequently the Galways, on their way home, were forced to stop at the kerb by a stream of departing cars. On this particular afternoon a smartly clad mother and her small son stood alongside them and the children got into conversation, as children will.

'What's your name?'

'Clare.'

'My name's William Sinclair Lewis Brandon. How old are you?'

'Seven. But I'll be eight in May.'

Over the children's heads Thea's eyes met the young mother's and they shared the smile of all parents in this situation, a little embarrassed, but delighted by their offsprings' making contact. The admiring glances directed Clare's way always made Thea swell with justifiable pride. In return she allowed her smile to compliment William's mother on the fact that he was a fine, manly little chap.

'What school do you go to?' William asked.

'St. Kevin's.'

The stream of expensive cars seemed to continue forever; Jaguars and Mercedes and Mazdas, all bearing home the scions of the privileged.

'What's your best lesson?' William persisted.

'English,' Clare replied. 'But I like sums, too. I know all my tables, up to the ten times.'

'I know all my tables, too. Up to the twelve times.' He paused, then added out of courtesy, 'but that's because I'm eight. You'll know your twelve times when you're eight, too.'

At this moment the lights changed and the pedestrian traffic was able to continue on its way. But after that, it was surprising how frequently the two couples coincided at the crossing. The children would exchange a few sentences, Thea and the other mother did not actually converse, but they would smile at each other in a mildly conspiratorial way. And this boy, Clare carefully explained to Thea, was as far removed from the naughty boys who had their knuckles rapped at St. Kevin's as chalk from cheese. She hated all those boys, she confided, but she liked William Brandon.

Then, on the 14th of February, they arrived a few minutes late at the entrance to the prep school and young William all but pounced upon them. His unexpected appearance certainly made Thea jump.

'I've been waiting for you. I thought you'd never come.'

Thea, holding Clare's hand, knew by the convulsive small movement of her captive fingers that she had been startled as well.

'My teacher wanted to talk to Mummy.'

William produced a scarlet envelope from behind his back, like a rabbit plucked from out of a hat. 'This is for you. Happy Valentine.' And he grabbed the brim of his boater, leaned over and kissed Clare boldly on her cheek.

It wasn't the kiss, it was the suddenness of it that shocked. Clare's hand twisted nervously in Thea's warm clasp.

'You can be my girlfriend if you like.'

William's mother, now in evidence against the school's wrought iron entrance gates, beamed her approval.

'Say thank you, Clare,' Thea ordered. 'Thank William for the card.'

Clare lowered her head and looked at William from under her lashes. She was enchantingly pink in her confusion. 'Thank you, William,' she whispered.

But it was this small episode that galvanised Thea into action. A Valentine card today, a kiss on the cheek; harmless in themselves. But in the great order of things she saw this to be the very small wedge in the door. And what would happen when the door opened wide? Clare needed to be protected from handsome small boys who would grow into handsome adolescents, and then young men, young men brimful of testosterone . . . and on the prowl.

Clare enjoyed gathering together her uniform. Although it had been streamlined from earlier lists, which included dresses of tussore silk for Sundays, and little was required in the way of formal exterior gear because the girls were mostly confined to within the grounds of the school, it still seemed a vast pile. A lot of the uniform could be bought from Gowings, downtown. They went in the train and got off at Wynyard Station. Then they walked along Pitt Street. It was all very exciting. Once home, Clare tried on the green and white checked dresses which had white collars, and the bottle-green blazer, and the matching winter skirt and pullover. Thea ordered Cash's woven name tapes and spent long hours sewing them, as ordered on the clothes list, to the inside of each collar or the turn-over of each sock. Shoes had to be named with a soldering iron under the instep of each, except black sports' pumps which you marked with difficulty on the inside. Mr Hamilton came to their rescue there, because he actually owned a soldering iron. Each item, carefully labelled and folded, was laid out on the spare bed to await packing.

Because Thea had no car, they faced a formidable journey to the school. When Thea had taken Father Flaherty's advice originally and gone the first time to inspect St. Ursula's, it had involved a train journey with a connection, then a bus and finally a taxi to take her to the entrance door. Clare, however, had skipped around to Mr Hamilton's to show him her smart new clothes, which was how Mr Hamilton came to learn of her impending departure, and in the end he volunteered to drive them to the school.

This was at total variance with his opinion. Douglas was, as might be anticipated, outraged to hear of Thea's plans for Clare's exile.

'Have a heart, woman,' he argued. Clare could hear this, because she was seated at the time on the stairs which led upstairs from the hallway, and the living room door was not quite shut. 'What sort of preparation for life will a convent education give her? Haven't you heard? There are two sexes inhabiting this planet – and, like it or not, Clare will have to learn to live with both.'

It was harder to eavesdrop on Thea because when she was upset or backed into a corner she let her voice drop.

'The sisters are noted for the quality of their education. Clare deserves the best. St. Ursula's will give her the very best.'

Douglas snorted. 'Clare would learn if you locked her up with the Angus and Robertson Encyclopaedia. Learning's not her problem. Relationships are more difficult for her, witness her shyness. And you're exacerbating it. What do you want for her, Thea? That she grows up like the couple downstairs?'

'I don't follow you.'

'I mean lesbian, woman. Do you want that for her?'

Thea's reply was stiff. Clearly she didn't like the drift of this conversation. 'I have to tell you, Douglas, that Clare herself is delighted by the idea.'

'An eight year old child? And what does she know about it?'

'I've described to her how very pretty the place is. And they have a wonderful music department. And art. Clare will be extremely happy.'

Clare had no idea what "lesbian" meant. She crept upstairs to her bedroom, and looked it up in the dictionary which Thea had given her for her birthday. It said *a. of Lesbos, island in the Aegean Sea, home of Sappho. n. a lover of women.*

Clare wondered why this was an undesirable state, which it

72

certainly was if you gave credence to Mr Hamilton's accusatory tone. After all, she certainly loved Thea, who was a woman. But then again, she also loved Mr Hamilton, who was a man. And why should he not want her to grow up like Miss Summers and pretty Miss Browning downstairs, who were always really nice and gave her small gifts for her birthday?

Nonetheless, it was kind of him to drive them all the way to St. Ursula's, especially after he lost the argument about her education.

Thea had not exaggerated when she had talked about the beauty of the setting. Positioned as it was on the top of an escarpment that towered several hundred feet above the valley floor, and surrounded by wide, sweeping lawns, the convent looked like an echo of colonial Australia. They approached the conglomerate of cream-painted wooden buildings up a long, tree-lined drive. The red trunks of the enormous gums were twisted with age and there were banks of rhododendrons and azaleas which must look wonderful in the spring. The air was filled with the pungent aroma of eucalyptus. Magpies contributed their throaty warble, as though they were welcoming the trio.

Douglas unloaded the elderly, battered cabin trunk which had been removed with some difficulty from the loft, divested of its contents and re-packed with all the paraphernalia necessary for a new student. Then he seized a long, metal pull beside the great front door and have it a hefty tug. Clare could hear the responsive clang, some distance away. Several minutes later the door was opened by a nun.

Clare knew all about nuns because several attended Mass at St. Kevin's. She knew, from gleaning bits and pieces of other people's conversation, that the nuns at St. Kevin's concerned themselves with ministry among the fallen women of King's Cross. This had given rise to some rather confusing thoughts. How many women of Sydney spent their time tripping over? And why did people pull grave faces at the mention of these unfortunates? However, she also knew that St. Ursula's was not a haven for injured ladies, but was a select educational establishment which would introduce her to the marvels of mathematics, the grand relation of arithmetic and as far removed from sums as was Earth from Venus, and foreign languages and hockey, among similarly privileged daughters of the select few.

This nun had a kind face and introduced herself as Sister Winefride. She explained in a strongly Irish brogue that she was in charge of the Junior School, which would include Clare among its number, and she was to take Clare there right now while her parents sorted out pocket money, and offertory for the Mass, and other small obligatory contributions such as the fees.

She smiled cheerfully, took Clare by the hand and said, 'Say goodbye to your mam and da. Say, "See you at half term, tra-la!" '

Thea bent down so that her cheek was at kissing level and Clare had the feeling that she was about to cry. Thea never, never cried, so Clare found this amazing in itself. It might have inspired synchronous tears of parting in Clare, but at present she was in the thrall of the Great Adventure which Thea had so successfully sold her. So instead she kissed Thea's soft, gardenia-scented cheek, and allowed Douglas to hug her and say goodbye in his gruffest manner, and was then led briskly away to the Junior House by Sister Winefride. The good sister, clearly intent upon forestalling any unwarranted bid for freedom, tightly clutched Clare's hand in a manner at total variance with the inconsequential stream of chatter that issued from her mouth.

The Junior School stood apart from the Senior School. The upper floor was divided into dormitories which were again subdivided into cubicles. The cubicles were separated from their peers by low wooden walls with much-layered varnish, and each contained two small, slatted beds. Every new girl was put with a seasoned student who could show her the ropes. Clare had the good and bad fortune to be placed with Lyndal Murphy, eight years and eleven months old, sassy, foul-mouthed and experienced beyond anything Clare, or even Bunny, could possibly have envisaged.

7

Clare sat on her small, wooden bed and watched Lyndal from under her lashes. Lyndal stared back. Clare tried to gauge what that stare meant. More confrontational than conspiratorial, she concluded. Definitely a challenge.

They exchanged names, ages, birthdays. Clare thought that Lyndal's plump darkness was very pretty, but she knew that Thea would disapprove of Lyndal's voice, because Thea considered most Australian voices to be uncultured, made Clare articulate clearly and forbade her to use certain colloquial words.

'Where d'you live, eh?' Lyndal asked. She said "d'you" as "joo". Thea would notice that as once; so did Clare.

'In Sydney.'

Lyndal pulled the sort of wry face that suggested living in Sydney was the saddest thing which could happen to a person.

'I live on a station near Nyngan. We've got four thousand sheep and a thousand head of run cattle.' She looked challengingly across at Clare. 'You got any brothers?'

'No.'

'I've got six brothers.' This was stated with perceptible pride. 'You got any sisters, eh?'

'No.'

'I've got one big sister, but she's married. She lives in Wollongong. I'm an auntie.'

Pecking order satisfactorily established in Lyndal's favour, she relaxed a little. 'Why are you at St. Ursula's?' But she didn't wait for a reply. 'I'm here to make a lady out of me. My dad thinks I'm too much of a tomboy.' Clearly being thought a tomboy was also a matter worthy of respect.

Actually, this was only the start. The facts, as pertaining to Clare, reduced her status in the eyes of Lyndal and the other small girls step by step. She had no father, they didn't even own a car. She lived in a terraced house with neighbours that abutted it. They shared their address because her mother actually let the basement flat to lodgers. She had no pets. Worst of all, she was good at lessons and did not have the wit to conceal this fact. The one thing that actually saved her hide was her looks. The girls thought she was pretty, and she was certainly modest about this fact. In fact, she found approval by being thoroughly self-effacing.

The first few days were very strange indeed. Lyndal was a careless sort of guardian, rather in the way that a mother duck will abandon her offspring without a backward glance. If Clare took the trouble to keep up, Lyndal showed her the ropes; but if Clare happened to be in the lavatory at the time that a bell rang, Lyndal did not bother to wait. Clare would be forsaken to find her own way about the confusing maze of buildings that comprised St. Ursula's Convent.

The teachers were kind. She felt most comfortable when in the classroom.

The community's time was punctuated by the calls to pray. They seemed to spend long hours on their knees. When in the simple, sparsely furnished chapel with its less tasteful share of nineteenth century plaster saints, Clare would see the handful of remaining nuns not part of the teaching staff. By the 'eighties most of the sisters had abandoned heavy, impractical wimples and habits in favour of simpler garments. This still did not allow the concession to the summer heat of bare legs, but the stockings they adopted were at least lighter in weight. Only two of the really elderly women stuck to the old-fashioned, all-enveloping attire. One of these was pointed out to Clare as Sister Christopher, who was led to and from services by her fellow sisters in Christ. Local lore pegged her age at no less than a hundred and twenty, she was totally gaga but very much beloved. Sister Christopher was held up to the girls as a paragon of goodness, whose example they should all aspire to emulate.

Life, Clare discovered early, revolved around keeping your guilt quotient nicely balanced. Too many transgressions, like Lyndal's regular portion, led to a litany of sins to be confessed. Too few, and you came to the confessional sounding either pious or a liar. Apart from Good Friday, confession was taken by one of the senior nuns from the non-teaching order. She had a habit of intoning a sorrowful, 'Tch tch,' regardless of your crime, prior to reciting the absolution. It did occur briefly to Clare to release Bunny from her enforced retirement and really liven things up a bit, but the cautious side of her personality took command and put paid to that notion.

Most of the daily offices were led by the Reverend Mother, who was a figure of awe, but on Sundays a man was permitted into the hallowed halls of St. Ursula's. Father Sheedie. His arrival always coincided with a period set aside for letter writing, and as his small VW Beetle put-putted its way along the drive the younger girls would exchange glances and the older girls who supervised the junior letter writing would colour up and look pleasingly confused.

Father Sheedie wasn't at all like Father Flaherty. He was tall and young and handsome. His voice rolled richly as he intoned the Mass. It was noted by people like Lyndal, who was an authority on these matters, that he never allowed his eyes to stray when serving the Host to the seniors girls. Even the green checked uniform dresses could not disguise the fact that the senior girls had breasts. In some cases they had very bulgy breasts. His deliberate attempt to keep his view unfocused gave Father Sheedie an interestingly myopic appearance. Sometimes, if you were really lucky, his face would turn brick red. When this delectable situation materialised the younger girls would exchange nudges and attempt to stem their giggles.

Sundays were very much enlivened by the priest's arrival. Observing the response he inspired in the older girls, and they in him, gave Clare an early, if untranslated, understanding of the power of sex.

Catholic dogma was reinforced in other ways; not just scripture lessons but in the conduct of the women among whom the girls lived. Sometimes their example was inspiring, on other occasions it touched on the bizarre.

Sister Winefride ruled the Junior House with a rod of iron, ameliorated by her generally cheerful and kindly personality, but about a month into Clare's first term Sister Winefride disappeared into retreat, and Sister Mary-Catherine temporarily took her place. Sister Mary-Catherine was of the old school. Vespers prior to bedtime was not enough. Each small girl was ordered onto her knees beside her bed for fifteen minutes of personal mortification. Clare had not before known the meaning of mortification. Now, in the absence of any carpet or mat to cushion the floor of the cubicle, she discovered it to mean very painful knees. And that was not all. When found curled in her habitual foetal position prior to sleep, Sister Mary-Catherine expressed her disapproval most forcefully.

'Jesus, Joseph and Mary! Look at the child. Has Sister Winefride taught you nothing?'

Clearly an answer was needed. 'I don't know, Sister.'

'And are you a wee animal, child, to curl yourself up in a ball?'

'No, Sister.'

'Then lay yourself down like a true Christian, not like a dormouse.'

'I don't know how a true Christian should lie, Sister.'

'Jesus, Joseph and Mary. The child is an ignoramus. You lay on your back, child, with your legs straight and your arms folded in a cross over your chest.' She rearranged Clare to her satisfaction, placing her arms in the correct position essential for ultimate salvation. 'Now you are prepared, if Jesus should choose to enter you in the night.'

This might have been intended to be reassuring. To Clare it proved the opposite. For the first time in her life she did not slip into easy, untroubled sleep, but lay awake, fearful that the Lord might select her for special treatment in the dark hours of the night.

A second episode during that first term stayed with her as well, as another example of mortification.

At the end of every meal the cups, saucers and plates were passed down each long table and stacked by a senior girl. Cutlery was put in a bowl of hot water, scraps were disposed of into another bowl, slops from all the teacups were concentrated into a single jug.

A younger nun had arrived recently from another establishment. Totally unconfirmed gossip among the girls had it that she'd cast a carnal eye upon another sister, and had been removed from her original convent in order to help her regain her sense of mission. She certainly looked an unhappy young woman and, on occasion, close observation might detect moistness about the eyes. On this particular day she approached the Reverend Mother, seated at the head of the High Table, just before the closing grace. The girls could not hear what was said, although there was no mistaking the surprised response of the Reverend Mother.

'If you're certain, Sister. If you feel that is what you must do.'

As the girls sat in stunned silence, Sister Brigid moved from table to table, drinking from each the slops collected in the jugs. Finally she returned to the top table and knelt at the feet of Mother Scholastica.

'Thank you, Reverend Mother.'

'And may you be blessed, Sister.' The older woman rose to her feet. The girls, knowing this to be their cue, followed suit, accompanied by the scraping of bench-legs and shuffling of feet. 'Girls, what you have just seen is an act of extreme mortification. I should be most proud to think that any one of you had the faith of Sister Brigid and the resolve that she has just displayed.' And while the girls exchanged bemused glances, she launched into the benediction.

Clare made the very private vow, at that minute, that nothing, absolutely nothing, would persuade her to enter Holy Orders if it involved partaking of other people's spit.

One of the less pleasant things about school was the business of doing your business. Regularity, according to Sister Winefride, was very close to holiness in the Lord's esteem. Every morning after breakfast, when the junior girls assembled in the common room, she opened a large register and called out their names.

'Marie Abbotts?'

'Yes, Sister Winefride.'

'Pauline Abrams?'

'Yes, Sister Winefride.'

'Stephanie Cornwall?'

'No, Sister Winefride.'

'See me afterwards, Stephanie.'

'Yes, Sister.'

'Clare Galway . . .'

If you said, 'No,' Sister Winefride gave you a spoonful of liquorice. Lyndal loved liquorice. She was prepared to suffer a dose of the squitters, if that was the price you paid for the delicious sampling. Clare, however, loathed the flavour and dreaded the possibility that at some time in the future her digestive tract might betray her. This fear was so real that at half term she shared her anxiety with Thea. Thea was thoroughly sympathetic because she, too, disliked the thought of compulsory liquorice. So she bought Clare two packets of mild laxatives, pleasantly sugar coated, which she could store in her locker as insurance against future constipation.

This small act of kindness had unexpected ramifications.

Lyndal, after the first few weeks as official guardian, had virtually ignored Clare, although occasionally this cold-shouldering spilled over into open hostility. Despite all her obvious shortcomings of background, Clare was liked by the other children, and Lyndal's hostility arose directly from jealousy. In an attempt to restore her position as most popular girl, Little Miss Murphy gathered about her a posse of cronies prepared to follow her lead unquestioningly. When the girls reassembled after the half term break, Lyndal's behaviour became openly confrontational.

'What are you hiding?' she challenged, as Clare secreted her little cache at the back of her locker. The laxatives had been removed from their packet and transferred into a less conspicuous paper bag.

'Nothing.'

'They are too. They are something. I bet you're hiding lollies, eh.'

Clare averted her eyes. 'They're not lollies.'

'Lollies are contraband. You've brought contraband into school. Hasn't she kids?' Lyndal's cronies agreed in harmony, as their dictator ordered.

'They're not contraband. Not sweets or anything, I promise.'

'Oh yeah?' Lyndal jeered. 'We don't believe you, do we.'

Clare could have removed the paper bag and hidden it in her desk, but for some reason she didn't. Perhaps it was Bunny's influence.

Three days later the 'sweets' had disappeared. There had been twenty-four individual doses in that bag. Lyndal and her gang amounted to four so they had, perforce, prescribed for themselves six laxatives apiece.

The quartet missed chapel that evening, which was very nearly a mortal sin. They described the terrible, gut-wrenching gripes they suffered in vivid detail to all who were prepared to listen. Even so, unable or unwilling to explain their theft, they were forced to accept public humiliation. Clare could not have cared less.

That, however, was not the end of the tale because Lyndal, interestingly, did not take offence. Indeed, she assumed that Clare had deliberately set her up for what happened, and she actually admired Clare for doing so. Such spunky behaviour met with whole-hearted approval.

'You can be my friend, if you like,' she announced after lights-out a few days later, as though conferring the ultimate honour. 'We've got a gang, me and Stephanie and Jane and Caitlyn. You can be in our gang.'

Clare was torn. To be included in the Lyndal circle would certainly ease things for her, because Lyndal was a born leader, but there were certain aspects of her new friend's personality that were harder to accept. To begin with, she swore like a shearer and lied her head off if it suited her. And she was an appalling skite, to the extent that her determined showing off was painful to watch at times.

81

But not to accept the extended hand of friendship was to place yourself in an impossible situation. The opposite of being a friend was to be an avowed enemy. There was no room for manoeuvre in between. And in Clare's imagination she could see long weeks and years ahead until they, too, became big girls with breasts, during which period Lyndal cold-shouldered her, and turned out the lights on her when she was in the bath, and generally made her life a misery.

She yielded. Figuratively, she grasped the extended hand. So on Clare was bestowed the title of official Best Friend. This gave her a novel status, something she had never before experienced. Hitherto the external observer, the odd man out, she became accepted. She was one of The Set. She was In.

There was a price to pay. Probably there always is. Clare helped Lyndal with her schoolwork, because Lyndal might have six brothers and be an auntie but she had not been meticulously coached in her nine times table by Thea, nor had she been read the *Just So Stories*, nor could she fathom out the mystery of dissecting and parsing a sentence.

In exchange she told Clare all that she knew about sex.

Directly opposed to Lyndal's instruction was the teaching recorded in the Catechism. With her almost photographic memory, the learning of the Catechism had been no more than a minor assay in Clare's education. And Sisters Mary-Catherine and Winefride were constantly present to reinforce the official tenets of the church. This manifested itself particularly in their interpretation of the sixth Commandment. The sixth commandment dealt with adultery, but in catechismal doctrine this did not confine itself to bad behaviour within marriage. It included such wickedness as immodest plays and dances. Goodness alone knew how the good sisters translated lewd conduct into taking sinful pride in one's own body, but in the minds of the nuns such was a given.

Clare received her first lesson in undue immodesty very early during her time at St. Ursula's. Sister Winefride rounded the corner of the cubicle divide to witness the horrendous sight of a very small Clare standing in her pants and vest . . . *about to divest herself of these . . . in full view of the world and her own eyes.*

She was openly scandalised. 'Holy Mother of God, Clare Galway!' She pressed one hand against her lips to reinforce her dismay. 'And your mother a good Catholic woman. Has she taught you no modesty?'

Clare, unaware of how she might be transgressing, stood very still. From the other side of the cubicle divide came the muffled giggle of another small girl.

Sister Winefride rounded on the offender, affording the atrophied Clare a brief moment to draw breath. 'And that's enough from you, Madeleine Martin. You'll be saying ten Hail Mary's if I hear another sound escape your lips.' She turned back to Clare but her voice had lost some of its heat. 'Now, Clare, let me explain how we do things here in St Ursula's. Perhaps your mother has been remiss, although it's no great offence in a little girl. But we know that our bodies are a constant source of the many sins of the flesh and we must be careful to conceal them from sight to the best of our ability. Remember this: nakedness is an affront to Our Lord. Practice now and it will be easier when you're older. When you wish to put on your nightie, you must first take your dressing gown and put it over your shoulder . . .' and she carefully spread Clare's robe about her slight frame ' . . . and then you undress beneath it. Keep your eyes modestly averted at all time and that way you can avoid breaking God's commandment. Do you understand?'

'Yes, Sister Winefride.'

'Then you're a good girl. And perhaps you can study your catechism, especially from 209, which explains everything that is a sin against holy purity. Then you will never be caught unawares.'

'Yes, Sister Winefride.'

But it was easier said than done. Struggling to extricate your arms through the narrow outlets of an under-garment while keeping a robe strategically balanced around your shoulders took some skill and Clare thought the whole thing grossly stupid. How could looking at her bony little knees and skinny thighs be considered sinful? A check in the catechism did nothing to make the position any clearer. The nearest sentiment to echo Sister Winefride's strictures

83

merely stated that the sixth commandment was broken "by amusements that we may commit."

Clare obeyed the nuns because hers was not an openly confrontational personality and she saw nothing to be gained in not obeying. After a while she became quite agile at dressing and undressing essentially by touch alone. But through her veins ran the blood of Perdita Potts and Shaun Leberman, and obedience did not equate with acceptance. To the end of her school life she considered it totally illogical that an intelligent God might make us in His Own Image and then forbid us to rejoice in this fact.

St Ignatius Loyola is reputed to have said, '*Give me a child until he's seven, and I shall give you the man.*' St. Ignatius Loyola did not meet Clare Galway. Clare might outwardly be a Cradle-Catholic, having been immersed in Catholicism practically from birth, but the longer she was to stay at St. Ursula's the more she came to the conclusion that such total devotion was at variance with what Jesus must have intended for us. Entirely of her own volition she came to hate the obsession with mortification of the flesh.

The hot milk episode was perhaps the catalyst.

Clare had always been subject to headaches, usually bearable, occasionally ferocious, and as she approached adolescence they came with greater frequency. On such occasions, when only darkness and total quiet would allow them to dissipate, she would make her way to the san where Sister Margaret Mary held sway. Sister Margaret Mary was wonderful, in that she would dispense codeine and fiercely guard your right to complete absence of noise; but she also thought that a glass of hot milk worked wonders. Clare detested hot milk even more than she loathed liquorice. The way the revolting skin gummed itself to your upper lip was cause enough.

'Drink it, dear. It will make you a better person.'

Clare, stretched out on a crisply white bed in the san and starting to feel the beneficial effects of the analgesic, carefully propped herself up on one elbow.

'How can forcing me to drink something gross make me a better person?'

Sister Margaret Mary smiled indulgently. 'It's a matter of discipline.'

To Clare it was more a matter of vowing to give up so unreasonable a religion as soon as possible. Perhaps she could become Buddhist, and never again have liquorice or hot milk forced upon her. But there was no point in sharing this distinctly contrary opinion with the good nun who was, after all, an ally when it came to her headaches.

'What's the benefit of discipline, if there's no reason behind it?'

'Och. True faith is not based on reason.'

Clare lay back and closed her eyes. 'Then perhaps I'll never find true faith, either.'

Sister Margaret Mary looked suitably shocked. Clare was quite a pet among the teaching staff, because not only was she very good at her lessons, but she wasn't ashamed of her braininess. To hear a favoured daughter mouth such heresy was painful. She resorted to the convent's classic reproof.

'Blessed Mary, Mother of Jesus! Don't let dear Sister Christopher hear such blasphemy. It would send her to her grave.'

Clare did not bother to open her eyes. 'As dear Sister Christopher's marbles have been rattling for years, I can't imagine my paucity of faith will influence her one way or another.'

'Clare Galway! You will say ten "Hail Mary's" for your lack of respect.'

Clare recognised that the opposition was unworthy. It was only fair to hit at targets of your own weight. So she picked up the cool hand of the good nun and placed carefully it on her brow. 'Darling Sister Margaret Mary. It was the headache talking. Really it was. Not me'

And, mollified at least in part, the sister left her to the dark and the soothing efficacy of the analgesic.

8

Very early Lyndal's little band of cronies found themselves a hangout in the surrounding bush, which was sufficiently private and secreted to give it a feeling of audacity. It was in an area clearly demarked as out of bounds, which added an extra frisson of excitement, and the girls had to approach it cautiously so that their progress was not noticed by either the sisters or the prefects who helped to maintain law and order within the school.

They worked together to improve the camouflage, hauling several broken boughs into position, adding twigs and strips of bark until from the outside it looked like an enormous, shaggy beaver's lodge and inside there was sufficient space for five girls to gather, even if they had to draw their knees close to their chests in order to fit in. It was a fortunate accident of nature that severed gum boughs clung to their leaves as they changed colour from grey-green to dry, brittle brown. In the eyes of Lyndal's gang their little clubhouse was the last thing in concealment.

They called themselves, with a staggering lack of imagination, 'The Secret Five,' and carefully toted down to their den contraband sweets and soda pop which had been smuggled in after half term exeats. For some reason candy tasted far more exciting when not sanctioned, and even lukewarm, fizzy lemonade was polished off with pleasure.

Lyndal was always the leader, and in all their years at the convent her position was never challenged. Eventually the gang lost interest in consuming illicit junk foods, but that early association set the tenor for their friendships, and a loyalty developed among the five that endured over the years. There were some occasions when Clare wondered why she stayed within the group, but rational thought always advocated maintaining the status quo. Not merely for cowardly reasons, because to be within was far easier in the long run than to be without, but also because Lyndal in her own way could add that certain something to the intrinsic monotony of school life. Lyndal dared to do and say the things which Clare would never venture to attempt or voice. Consequently, she spent quite a lot of her spare time in detention.

The other factor which weighed in favour of 'The Secret Five' was Jane Sullivan. It was important that the group, consisting as it did of an uneven number, did not pair off; Lyndal considered that, if quizzed, they would all automatically cite her as official 'Best Friend', and such status held considerable cachet within the convent. In secret, Jane and Clare agreed that actually they were best friends. Nothing too obvious came of this avowal; just the shared look that acknowledged an occasional and tacit questioning of a Lyndal-truth, or the apportioning of the last piece of ginger cake, but that attachment, if nothing else, cemented Clare's membership.

All other factors aside, Lyndal's position was secure because she had exclusive knowledge of boys. In truth, she was a world authority. None of the other girls had as much as a brother – or none that counted. Stephanie was one of three daughters, the eldest of whom was already a senior at the convent. Caitlyn, like Clare, was an only child, although that was where the similarity ended, because Caitlyn's father was Very Important in Parliament and holidays for the Roberts family meant London and Florence. Jane was the solitary fruit of a second marriage. Her two half-brothers were married and had their own families by the time she put in an appearance.

Lyndal ruled supreme because she was able to answer all the questions that her subordinates threw her way.

Boys, Clare learnt in the close confines of their secret den, had a different form of external plumbing. This made weeing much easier if you were out in the bush. Other children might have gleaned this basic fact in the early years of school, but St Kevin's had seen to it that boys and girls were separated at all times apart from lessons, and there had been no Donal O'Brien to initiate and enlighten her. Evidently a boy had a spout, which was called a willie, or a dick, or a winkie. The grown-up word was penis but nobody used that, because it was so ugly. Willies, according to Lyndal, were objects of hilarity, nature's practical joke perpetrated on males, apart from the afore-mentioned advantage when in the bush. It was very important that you didn't butt brothers in the area of the willie because it was very painful and they were likely to retaliate to your distinct disadvantage.

There were jokes aplenty. A favourite, which Lyndal frequently repeated upon request was, 'what is long and stiff and has a hole at one end and whiskers at the other?' The answer was, 'a toothbrush.' This response was calculated to send The Secret Five into fits of giggles, even though they had no idea what it meant.

The stiffness was a problem. Jane had seen her small nephew, when his nappy was being changed. He certainly had a willie but it was neither stiff nor was there a single whisker present on his plump, smooth, baby tummy.

'But men do have hairy bellies,' Lyndal could contribute to this deeply scientific discussion. 'When my dad's wearing his cossie, you can see hairs going all the way down from his tummy-button, into his . . . you know what!' And within the confined space they fell about again in a transport of giggles.

Underneath the willie, the innocents were instructed, a boy had two small balls. These were also exceedingly ugly because they were all wrinkled, like walnuts. Names for these balls were goolies and nuts. Caitlyn was the proud owner of a *Where do babies come from?* book. In it they talked about testicles, but testicles was an even uglier word so the girls agreed that 'balls' was easier on the ear. It did not pay to bash these either, if you valued your hide.

Having satisfactorily demonstrated her knowledge of the male anatomy, Lyndal progressed to congress, as pertaining to the animals on her parents' station. Male animals, she informed them, 'serviced' the females of their ilk. People fucked or shagged if they wanted to make a baby, but you didn't use those words in relation to animals.

She was quite lyrical when describing the mating habits of rams and bulls, but her most vivid description came when the girls were about ten and Lyndal had been privileged to watch a stallion put to a receptive mare. All other things aside, it certainly explained the necessity for stiffness.

'The stallion's willie is *enormous*,' she said, adding emphasis by opening her eyes wide and showing the approximate length with her hands. 'And he waved it about as he mounted before he got it into her cunt. Dad had to help him aim it straight. I thought that it must hurt the mare, going in like that, but you could see that she enjoyed it.'

'How?' Stephanie breathed, leaning forward in her eagerness. 'How could you tell.'

'Well, she sort of rolled her eyes and the skin all along her back shivered up and down.'

'Do you think that happens with people, too? Do women roll their eyes and shiver? Or does it hurt?'

'It hurts at first,' Lyndal told them wisely. 'My mum told me that. She said, 'don't you even think of doing it, Lyn, until you're thirteen. And take precautions. I don't want you getting yourself in the family way at sixteen, like Diane. And expect it to hurt at first.'

There was a profound silence, as the girls thought about this.

'I don't think I want to do it at thirteen,' Caitlyn remarked soberly. 'Not if it hurts.'

'What are precautions?' Jane asked doubtfully 'Aspirin, do you mean?'

Lyndal bestowed on her the look reserved for the brain-dead. 'Don't be stupid. Precautions are what you use to stop babies coming. Frenchies. Condoms.'

'Oh . . . but . . . ' But in the light of such scorn, Jane dried up.

Lyndal had yet to complete her description of the thoroughbred's prowess. She was inclined to respond testily if her narrative was derailed.

'And when the stallion pulled his willie out, after he'd done it, it was all droopy. He got down off the mare and it hung there, sort of shiny and wet. Then it shrivelled up and disappeared into his belly.'

'Do men's willies shrivel up into their bellies, after they've done it?'

Lyndal had to confess that she didn't know. 'But I'll ask Patrick, when I'm home,' she promised.

Diane was Lyndal's older sister, who had been forced into a precipitously early and unwise marriage. The ages of her brothers ranged from twenty-three to sixteen months her senior. Patrick was the brother closest to her. He went to St. Xavier's College and even if half Lyndal's tales were to be believed, he was more than happy during holiday times to share cosy, exploratory sessions at the back of the shearing sheds. And he was also useful as the girls' prime source of grubby jokes and double entendres.

Clare lay awake long nights and wondered about all that she learned. Clearly you were exposed to many more interesting things, if you were fortunate enough to be born into a farming family. Animals on farms seemed to do nothing but fornicate. She could understand why, in Lyndal's eyes, life in Sydney was a poor alternative. She tried to add an ugly little worm-thing to William Brandon and thought that she'd have preferred not to know. She liked William as he was, in his shorts and crimson-striped blazer and smart boater. And the thought of dear, kind Mr Hamilton having something so unfortunate was even sadder. She resolved to ask Thea for further erudition, when the time was suitable.

Half term provided the opportunity, but Thea proved very disappointing.

Guided by Douglas, Thea had always been open about Clare's origins. She was, evidently, "a donated child" given into the safe-keeping of her adoptive mother because her parents, who loved her very dearly, were unable to provide for her. In the official version, Thea and Clare were the joint beneficiaries of their selfless munificence.

Thea had always been rather vague when questioned about the reasons behind their inability to maintain and raise their daughter, which allowed Clare to create an entirely fictitious but very pleasant scenario all for herself. Clare knew that her mother was a very beautiful young woman, that her father cared for her after the birth because her mother was too ill. He tried very hard, according to Thea, but was incapable of sustaining this effort. Men were like that, where babies were concerned. It wasn't unknown for mothers to become ill, after experiencing a birth.

Because of all this, Clare knew that Thea had never been wed, but she had no knowledge of how sketchy Thea's own understanding of things sexual actually was. However, Thea was determined to do her best by her daughter. In order to prepare her better for the ripening of her body than Mrs Galway had done in Thea's own case, she overcame her embarrassment and bought an instructive booklet from the Catholic Bookshop. It was called, *Your Sacred Body*, and, although it did run through the business of reproduction in sketchy outline, it was more into informing the reader about the sins of the flesh. The ultimate sin, evidently, was masturbation or "defilement of the body."

In *Your Sacred Body* a simplified diagram informed you of the basic organs but it certainly skirted around stiffness, as relating to masculine anatomy. You could, however, learn quite a lot about the ribcage and the workings of the heart, were you sufficiently interested.

Clare returned to St Ursula's, and to Lyndal's human biology lessons, little better off.

There were drawbacks to the distance St. Ursula's was from Sydney. I was deprived of seeing my daughter for long periods and I missed her very much. Fortunately, the school owned a minibus and so the girls could be transported to and from the railway station at the start and end of half-term breaks and holiday periods. This did save me a great deal of time in travel. The mainline train came as far as Central Railway Station, and I would catch the suburban train to meet Clare. I always made sure I arrived with plenty of time to spare, although it did mean hanging around on that draughty station. Even when she was old enough to make the trip by herself, I made it a point to meet her. Not only did she have the very sort of looks that must appeal to white-slave traders but, apart from exeat breaks mid-term, there was always the cabin trunk to manhandle on and off carriages.

However, for her twelfth birthday I resolved to make the occa-

sion memorable by taking a picnic tea up to St. Ursula's. I had the permission of the nuns, of course. Visits from parents were confined to two a term and always on Sunday afternoons. This made it especially difficult for me, because the trains run less frequently on Sundays. At this time Douglas seemed to be abroad quite a lot. His work did occasionally take him overseas. Did I mention that he was, and is, an authority on ballistics? He is quite frequently asked to testify as an expert witness in court cases all around the world.

Because I would have to carry everything, I planned my little treat with care. I assembled all Clare's favourite teatime items, which I prepared and stacked neatly into plastic containers with resealable tops. There is nothing more unpleasant than sandwiches that curl at the edges. Then I put the boxes into two portable bags, with a tablecloth folded neatly over the top, and some paper serviettes and also a rug for us to sit on. I had to set off at seven thirty in the morning from my home, because there was only one train going up to the Southern Highlands on a Sunday morning and it really catered for people who wanted to go bush walking.

I took the suburban train to Central Railway Station, then transferred to the mainline train. The trip out of the city was particularly enjoyable because the day was clear and bright. May in Australia comes in late autumn. The deciduous trees planted by the early settlers were still a glory of red and gold; most picturesque. Although we rarely get frosts where we live, they do experience quite harsh drops in temperature inland. Once the train started to leave the coastal plain and climb there was ample evidence that today would be one of those bright, frosty days which give way to warm, brilliant sunshine later. I thought how fortunate that was. It was a lovely day for a picnic. I hoped that Clare would be anticipating our meeting with as much pleasure as I was. I had suggested in a letter that she invite two of her little friends to join us, and I had included them in my catering calculations.

After I disembarked from the train, I boarded the bus that took us to the township nearest the convent. As I had anticipated, I was the only person not clad for hiking in bush-pants, sturdy boots and thick woollen socks. These people really could learn a little about consideration to others. Being hit on the head by a bulging haversack is not a pleasant experience, especially if you're short, like me. My head appeared to be in range quite frequently.

Then, from the township I took a taxi to the school. I think the driver charged me extortionately. He said it was Sunday loading but I have only his word to go on. I wondered whether he would have had the gall to charge Douglas in the same way; but Douglas has no need for taxis on Sundays, having his own car.

Anyway, I was still grateful for the ride, because my arms were getting quite tired from toting those two bags about. And I was right about the day. It was sparklingly sunny at St. Ursula's, and as we drove to the school I felt quite grateful to my father, that he'd had the sense to invest in that BHP subsidiary. It was because of him that I could afford such a fine educational establishment for my daughter.

Clare was waiting for me with two little friends, a dark, plump child called Lyndal, and a nice little girl with brown curls, called Caitlyn. Clare looked a bit embarrassed when I started to kiss her so I patted her on the shoulder instead. As, by the age of twelve, she was about an inch taller than I am, I felt a little awkward myself, caressing her like puppy.

A nun who was unfamiliar to me suggested that we all sit in the library to talk, but I explained that I had brought a rug, so that we could picnic. I did think that the way Lyndal and the other child exchanged looks was a trifle ill mannered and I really can't see why they did. Picnics are always pleasant, and certainly nicer than being cooped up in a stuffy room with all the other girls and the visiting parents.

The sister suggested that we take our tea things and sit on the lawn behind the building, because from there the view of the Blue Mountains was spectacular. This is what we did. I spread out the rug for us and we sat down and had our tea. As we ate several magpies serenaded us with their melodious warbling. I do think that it's unfortunate magpies have such a bad reputation, because the sound of their trilling song is delightful. It reminds me of gargling that my mother made me do with ti-tree extract, when I *was suffering from laryngitis.*

The other girls seemed to enjoy the food although, for myself, I should have been most ashamed if Clare had giggled in that common way. I did wonder, also, how a child with such an unrefined voice could have found her way into a select ladies' seminary like St. Ursula's, but I concluded that maybe the sisters were having trouble making ends meet. Perhaps they had had to lower their standards. However, I would certainly recommend elocution lessons for that particular girl.

Clare was mostly silent although she, like the other children, certainly did seem to appreciate the food I'd brought. Seeing them tuck in made all my effort worthwhile.

Unfortunately, only an hour after I arrived I had to pack away the plastic containers and the tablecloth and the rug and be ready for the taxi I'd already booked to return me to the bus station. But it was a most enjoyable hour, because I could see that Clare looked very well and she was able to tell me that she was preparing for her confirmation with the local priest, whose name was Father Sheedie. She said that he stayed after Mass on Sundays to give them an hour's instruction. Just the mention of his name made the girl called Lyndal start giggling again. Sniggers like that are very unattractive.

And so I took the bus to the railway station, and the train back to Central, and finally the train to our own suburb. I walked in the door eleven hours and ten minutes after I had left that morning, but it was all worthwhile, because Clare had been most appreciative of my birthday gift. I had bought her a very lovely copy of the Missal, with a white leather cover and a really beautiful picture of Our Lady inside. I decided it had been a very nice day indeed.

Here is a list of the food I took for that birthday picnic. I can remember it as though it happened yesterday:

- *Egg and chive sandwiches,*
- *Cucumber and cream cheese sandwiches,*
- *Sausage rolls, made with my own, home-made flaky pastry,*
- *Cream puffs, with whipped cream. (I would not have dared take* that *in high summer!)*

- *Viennese slices, with my own raspberry jam,*
- *Ginger beer,*
- *And, of course, a lamington for each of us. Into one I pressed a candle, as a small birthday cake, so that Clare could blow it out.*

Thea's picnic became the subject of a great deal of ribaldry. Not just her car-lessness, or her carrying a rug and a tablecloth and paper napkins all the way to school, although all received their share of attention. However, even knowing that Clare was adopted, Lyndal refused to believe that anyone could have a mother who was so old. She was more ancient than Anna-in-the-temple, when Jesus was presented. Jane's father was old, but men were different. Lyndal decided that Thea was actually a witch, and must have kidnapped Clare from the maternity wing of the hospital. Warming to her theme, Lyndal expounded upon this tale. There was probably, somewhere in Australia, a bereft mother still mourning for her lost child. Had Clare thought of putting an ad in the *Sydney Morning Herald*?

Clare hated all this equally for herself and for Thea, whom she loved, but she knew Lyndal too well to mount a counter-offensive. Given the right encouragement, Lyndal could run a topic to death. It was much better to allow her minor cruelty to play itself out naturally. Clare had watched Stephanie be persecuted similarly because her father wore a particularly unfortunate toupee. Rather than square up to Lyndal and risk her swapping targets, Clare had quietly shown her support by sharing with Steph her weekly sweets allowance from the tuck shop.

She did think that the others of the Secret Five could have come equally surreptitiously to her aid, especially Jane, whose father was at least as old as Thea and who was her very best friend. She didn't expect anyone to confront Lyndal or to challenge her version of things, but she would have appreciated some subtle token to indicate that they sympathised with her. When none materialised it made her realise that, in their eyes, Thea might well have been a witch who had snatched her from her infant's cradle.

9

Not being privileged, like Lyndal, to observe first hand the wonders of nature in the raw, the rest of their sex education for four of the Secret Five came from books, and very inadequate it proved to be. Quite a few cheap paperbacks were regularly smuggled into school, of the bodice-ripper variety. These would be perused after lights out, under the sheets and with the aid of a torch. You knew quite quickly where the sexy bits were, because the novels would open at that place and the pages would become discoloured with thumbprints.

According to all that the girls read, kissing was of paramount importance in the business of sexual relationships. Sort of the open-ing salvo, frequently undertaken reluctantly, despite the best inten-tions of the participating couple.

'Dash it, woman', the hero would say (darkly handsome, at least thirty and owner of a vineyard in France.) 'Why do you have this effect on me?' And, goaded beyond all bounds by the sweetly innocent sexuality of the heroine, he would seize her, kiss her deeply until her senses reeled, then fling her from him and stride moodily away. At this moment the heroine, who'd been secure in her extreme hatred of his cold powerfulness, would be forced to reconsider things in the light of his masterful magnetism.

All such romances dwelt at some length on that first uniting of lips and its effect on the blushing maiden. There was much talk about heightened sensations, allied with feelings of moistness and weakness of the lower extremities. The Five gave it a great deal of thought.

'We ought to practice,' Caitlyn suggested tentatively. 'Before we have to. Boys will know if we're experienced or not, by the way we kiss.'

And evidently it was important, in the great order of things, to be seen as experienced, because that was perceived as desirability. Once you'd taken the plunge, so to speak, other boys fancied you as well. Even Clare knew that, if only second hand and through her perusal of the vital literature.

'But how? How can we practice?' Jane looked glum, as well she might. 'Kidnap Father Sheedie after mass?'

Scarcely sensible, even if he were the only male to come within their sphere. You could, however, practice on your knee. They discovered that by pursing your lips you could create quite a satisfactory slurping noise, if sufficient vacuum was created. This, however, did absolutely nothing to the vigour of your legs and moistness levels fluctuated not one whit. Moistness of what? Clare wondered. Or where?

Or you could try out your technique on a well-placed arm. And then there was the problem of tongues, the employment of which, according to Lyndal, definitely separated the men from the boys or, in this case, the greenhorn from the slapper. This really did look to be an insurmountable barrier towards the necessary attainment of experience.

'Perhaps we should use each other,' Steph suggested eventually, with a modicum of gloom. She glanced around the scandalised faces of her friends. 'Well, who else is there? And it's better than being utterly useless when we try the real thing,' she continued defiantly, in the face of their overt misgivings.

Caitlyn giggled and shrugged. 'Why not?' She turned to Lyndal, took her shoulders and kissed her vigorously. The other three watched, open-eyed. It seemed to last a long time. Then Lyndal broke away.

'Not bad, for a start. But I don't think your teeth should clash like that.'

It was too much for the girls' senses of humour and satisfactorily broke the sudden tension. They rolled about on the ground with mirth which, as they were on a wide rock-slab, was quite uncomfortable.

Then Steph turned to Caitlyn. 'Try with me, this time. But no teeth.'

The others followed proceedings with interest. Caitlyn actually closed her eyes and looked as though it wasn't too bad.

Lyndal turned to Jane. 'Come on, Saint Jane. You can always confess it afterwards. 'Bless me Mother, for I have sinned. I kissed my friend and it was nice, nice, nice.''

Jane, pinker by the moment, turned quickly aside. 'I'll try it with Clare. Okay, Clare?'

Clare took a deep breath. 'Okay.'

She shut her eyes and thrust out her face, lips slightly parted. Jane, having decided to take the plunge, apparently did not believe in doing anything by halves. This was no chaste meeting of the lips. This was the full treatment. Clare thought it utterly revolting. It was like a slug invading the sanctity of her mouth but a very muscular, intrusive slug, all slime and wetness. The slug tasted of peppermint because they'd recently eaten Polos and that, at least, was a mercy. The taste of liver, or liquorice, would have been the last straw.

And this was to constitute a sea-change in your life, when some grotty boy actually did what Jane was doing? In which case, maybe the convent life did beckon. She broke away. Jane looked at her appraisingly, as though trying to assess her own prowess and subsequent appeal.

'Was that okay?'

'I . . . suppose so. But I don't think I'll bother again, thank you. I think I'll stick with my knee.'

So Clare watched, while the others perfected the art of bussing. She felt awfully goody-goody and hated that, but she hated even more the feeling of that horrible, exploratory muscle inside her mouth.

When they were about thirteen the Secret Five, along with other girls of a similar age, were privileged to the ritual of Reverend Mother's Talk. For this the good woman selected a small group at a time and lectured them about the changes taking place in their bodies, about boys and about the virtues of chastity.

To giggle was to risk death by firing squad.

Lyndal's gang was actually divided for Reverend Mother's Talk, although they compared notes later. Clearly, Mother Scholastica was on safer ground when talking about the onset of menstruation and the general way this was handled within the school. You could, for example, be excused certain physical exercise if you suffered from tummy ache or gripes, but to treat these five days each month as a period of illness was to misconstrue the Lord's purpose. She was also quite straightforward when describing the evils of masturbation; there was definitely an echo of *Your Sacred Body* in her use of words like 'defilement'. In fact, the general tenor of her talk was that bodies, by their very nature, were mildly distasteful; they were also subject to terrible temptation and urges therein, which should be sublimated at all times. This was scarcely new territory, bearing in mind the insistence that one was expected to wield a sponge by touch alone when abluting, and to go through the ludicrous ritual of robing and disrobing twice daily beneath a dressing gown. Now, by way of reinforcement, there were dark hints of Original Sin. God-fearing people should be on guard against rogue manifestations of Original Sin at all times. After that, however, it all became more complicated because this was definitely a case of the Lame leading the Blind and the Halt. Lyndal, for example, knew a great deal more, even if her approach was coarsely basic and her choice of words cruder by far.

'The Lord gave us a sex drive in order for people to procreate,' The Reverend Mother concluded. 'That is the sole reason. It behoves you, as young Catholic women, to respect the sanctity of your bodies until the time comes for you to marry and bear children for Our Lady.' She paused, surveying the gaggle of girls whom she had gathered to sit on the carpeted floor of her personal study. 'Now, are there any questions?'

'Does Jesus think it's important for us to have families?' Stephanie, seated beside Clare, ventured. They had swapped surreptitious nudges and pinches as the talk progressed.

'Of course. It's one way that we can spread Christianity. And His Holiness the Pope loves a large family.'

'Does His Holiness think being a nun's a waste of time, then?'

asked one cheeky girl. 'I mean, nuns don't add to the Catholic family, do they.'

Clare could almost see the firing squad priming weapons at this audacity. Not even Lyndal would have dared to voice such heresy.

Mother Scholastica looked sternly over the top of her glasses at the bland face of the young woman who'd had the temerity to challenge her words.

'There are other missions in the world, Nicola-Rae, as well as enlarging Jesus' kingdom on earth. And, girls, maybe I should emphasise that chastity is not a negative quality. By taking a vow of chastity, sisters and brothers in Christ are also contributing positively. Perhaps you will think about that. Now, you may go. Nicola-Rae, you will write a two-page essay for me on the detrimental effect of bumptiousness.'

Outside Mother Scholastica's study Clare and Stephanie and Jane exchanged glances.

'Pathetic,' Stephanie whispered. The looks of the other girls agreed with this assessment. 'She doesn't know anything, does she.'

'But it's not her fault,' Clare pointed out fairly at they wandered down the corridor towards the common room. 'How can she know, not having ever *done it*? All she can tell us is book learning. And she doesn't even know about Frenchmen with vineyards.'

'But she did try to be helpful. You have to say that she tried.'

They agreed with that, too. Poor Reverend Mother was at a distinct disadvantage, neither having been raised on a farm nor having the advantage of Lyndal's erudition but she had, indeed, done her best. Clare wondered how she'd have got on, being in the same group as Lyndal. She was relieved not to have gone through that personal embarrassment. She could imagine only too well Lyndal's contributions and asides to this particular lecture.

Kissing aside, in most things the Reverend Mother's little homily was too late. All the members of the gang except Clare had been menstruating for some months. They called it "onion time", and were continually overwhelmed by their own brilliance. " *'The curse is come upon me,' cried the Lady of Shalott*." Spelling not regarding, the transition was easy; curse – Shalott (or shallot) – ergo; onion time.

The girls' bodies were poised on the fulcrum of womanhood. In Lyndal's case, this meant that her childish plumpness had rearranged itself in a very pleasing form. She definitely had breasts. She also had hair under her arms and *down there*.

She was more authoritative than ever because she had Done It. She'd actually waited until she was thirteen and Patrick had been happy to oblige. She shared it all with her henchmen, one lazy Sunday afternoon. The five had abandoned their den as babyish some time before. They were sitting in the shade on a ledge of rock that overlooked the valley. They had claimed this particular shelf of rock as their own and were fierce in defence against any unfortunates who attempted accidentally to stake a counter-claim.

Lyndal's rationale was stunning in its simplicity.

'If it was going to hurt, I didn't want to look stupid with a boy I really like and someone I want to be my boyfriend,' she explained to her henchmen. 'You'd look really dumb screaming and yelling, when he wanted you to look pleased and happy. I though it wouldn't matter if I screamed with Patrick.'

'Isn't it a mortal sin, doing it with your brother?' Jane asked doubtfully. 'Are you going to confess?'

Lyndal's look was withering. 'Don't be stupid. Of course it's not a sin. My dad says that it's normal for kids to want to roll in the hay. Nature's way of learning, that's what he says.'

Stephanie was more interested in other aspects of this rite of passage than in the state of Lyndal's soul. 'And did it hurt?'

She who held centre stage looked quite proud. 'It hurt like mad. Patrick really had to push hard. And I bled afterwards, like onion-time.'

'But aren't you frightened you're going to have a baby?'

Again, Lyndal's expression reflected her intrinsic superiority. 'Course not, dummy. Don't you remember anything? I told you about protection, ages ago. And I've got something to show you. Here.' She withdrew a small, foiled packet from her uniform pocket. The printing on the outside read, *Super-Stud de luxe. Your*

101

Pleasure Guaranteed, Your Safety Ensured.

Clare, to whom it was presented, opened it gingerly. 'It's a balloon?'

'Don't be stupid. It's a Frenchie.'

'What's a Frenchie?'

'A *condom*, you idiots.' The girls with long memories might recognise the word but were still somewhat in the dark. 'You use it so that you don't get pregnant.'

'Isn't that a mortal sin? Aren't you meant to have babies for the Lord?'

Lyndal reduced Jane to silence with another withering look. 'Really. You don't know anything. My mum would kill me, if I got in the club. She nearly flayed Diane alive.'

Clare was holding the small, latex object as though it might bite her. 'But what do you do with it?'

'Oh, give it to me!' Lyndal snatched the condom. She stretched it over two fingers. 'Doesn't that suggest *anything* to you?'

'Does it . . . does it . . .?'

'Of course. The boy puts it on his cock. Before he does it.'

"Cock" was a new, exciting word that they'd learnt only recently. "Cock" implied stiffness, and these days nobody was in doubt about the necessity for stiffness. Lyndal was nothing if not thorough in her pursuit of scientific authenticity.

'Where did you do it?'

'At the back of the shearing shed, under the throwing table.' For the sake of the unfortunates who did not know about station living, she added, 'that's the table where they throw the fleeces for rolling and packing, after they're shorn. There's a pile of old sacking there so it's quite comfortable, although it stinks of sheep wee and pellets.'

'How did you do it? Like the stallion?' The story of the thoroughbred's prowess had made a profound impression on Steph.

Lyndal made the sort of noise that signified total scorn. 'Honestly! Animals do it that way. It's called mounting. People never do. You lie on your back, dummy. And the boy lies on top of you.'

'How can you breathe, if he's lying on top of you?'

102

'You do feel a bit squashed,' Lyndal admitted. 'But it only lasts a minute or two.'

Caitlyn was brave enough to pose the ultimate question. 'Was it nice?'

Lyndal screwed up her cute little nose, with its sprinkling of freckles. 'Not really. It was all over so quickly; and Patrick was wearing his great heavy boots, so I got bruises on my ankles where he kicked me.'

'He kicked you on purpose?' That was a shocking thought.

'Oh, no,' she replied airily. 'He said sorry afterwards. He said he couldn't help it, once he got started. Oh, and his face got redder and redder and he puffed and panted as though he was running a race.'

There was a period of silence as her audience absorbed all these new facts.

'Did you do it just the once?'

'Yes. Just the once.' Lyndal paused and looked wisely around. 'I want to save myself, for my real boyfriend.'

'Do you think you'll enjoy it better, when it's your real boyfriend?'

'Of course, because I'll love him. I don't love Patrick. He's just my brother. But he did say that he enjoyed it. He gave me three old copies of *Playboy* to say thank you. And he stacked the dishwasher when it was really my turn. Mum asked him if he was feeling okay and Dad said, 'What have you done to Lyn, that you're being so nice to her?'' Lyndal giggled at this memory.

'Gosh. What did Patrick say?'

'He turned really red and he mumbled that he hadn't done anything. That's when Dad talked about nature's way of learning and he laughed and pinched my bum, and told Patrick he was a great, hairy galah.'

Fortunately, Clare's reading did not stop with the bodice-ripper genre, and through her perusal of everything the school library could offer, she began to appreciate that perhaps Lyndal was not always the most reliable of informants. There was no way she could separate herself from the Five without making life at the convent totally untenable, nor would she want to. How else would she learn about interesting things like wet dreams and circumcision, were Lyndal not at hand to educate her? But in her reading she encountered heroines who thought that virginity was worth preserving, and that copulating with your brother was definitely frowned upon, and that men should respect you.

So, between the extremes of the Reverend Mother and *Your Sacred Body* on one hand and *penny-dreadfuls* and the casual promiscuity of the Murphy family on the other, Clare, in the end, got the balance about right. Unfortunately, however, she was unlikely to put any of her knowledge to good account. She had absolutely no chance of meeting boys of any persuasion because school holidays were exclusively dominated by Thea.

And there was worse for, by the time you were fourteen, it was essential that you received Letters. Not just any letters, but letters from boys. There was a sort of pecking order involved here too, so that an envelope adorned with the crest of Riverview, one of the top Catholic schools, was far more enviable than a *billet doux* from a less prestigious educational establishment. Clare saw herself once more becoming of an outsider as, predictably, first Lyndal but very soon afterwards Jane and Caitlyn, became the happy recipients of fat, juicy epistles.

Jane gained extra respect because she had met a boy when holidaying in Rome and they had struck up a correspondence. Better yet, he was nineteen and was at university.

'Does he know that you're only fourteen?' Clare asked. At least she'd started to menstruate, at last.

'I didn't lie, if that's what you mean.'

'There are sins of omission, as well. If he asks your age and you say, 'well, I've not had my seventeenth birthday yet,' you're not exactly lying but you're certainly letting him think you're sixteen.'

Jane was busy braiding her hair while this exchange took place. When she pulled it up into a French pleat she did look nearer to seventeen than fourteen. And her body had changed shape even more extremely than had Lyndal's. Where before she'd been a skinny sort of beanpole, she was now tall, big breasted and had

104

learned to carry herself well. Clare envied her so much that she wondered whether she should confess it as a sin.

In the matter of letters Clare was becoming desperate, and in her desperation she remembered William Brandon. She'd scarcely given him a thought in years, but unless he'd moved she decided it couldn't be too hard to locate him. She knew that he must live within walking distance of his old prep school, although he would have finished there some years ago. By her estimate he must have celebrated his fifteenth birthday a few months ago.

So it was that she spent some time during half term scanning the telephone directory for Brandons, then eliminating them by district until she was down to three. The Brandon with the initials W.S.L. and with an address about half a mile from the Anglican prep school appeared the most hopeful.

She had to wait until Thea was otherwise occupied, and even then it took most of her courage to dial the number, but she hit the jackpot at first shy. She actually recognised Mrs Brandon's voice, all these years later. Then she had to explain her request to William and that was even harder. She became so confused that William, perhaps taking pity on her, interrupted her disjointed sentences.

'It is Clare, isn't it?'

'Yes. You gave me a Valentine card, once. Do you remember?'

'Of course. You were my first sheila. I was madly in love with you.' Sheila was not a word which indicated respect, but desperation made Clare overlook that. However, before she could speak William continued, 'Clare, I can't understand what you're saying. Can we meet somewhere? Then you can tell me what you want.'

'I don't think I can. My mother . . . '

'Sure. I understand. But don't you ever do the shopping, or something? Walk to the shops on the High Street?'

'Yes, but . . . '

'Then tell your mother you're needing things for school. There's a little park off Captain Cook Avenue. Do you know it?'

'Yes.'

'Well, meet me there in about half an hour. Okay?'

It seemed so simple that Clare was in awe. In all the romantic novels which managed to escape the sisters' eagle eyes and circulate for under the sheets perusal, masculine decisiveness was rated highly as a most desirable attribute in your love. William had just demonstrated to a T why it was so to be admired. And she didn't even have to lie, because there was quite a list of things she really did need.

She approached the small park feeling incredibly shy, even wondering whether they would recognise each other. Six years was quite a long time. She need not have worried, however. William had shot up, gained width in his shoulders and a nice, deep voice, but he still looked very like the small boy who had surprised her with his card.

He was leaning against the back of a wooden bench and, because it was warm for October, he was wearing shorts. Short shorts. He had very hairy legs. He stood up as she approached and Clare had a sudden terror that he might try to kiss her, or something embarrassing like that, but, instead, he came around to the front of the bench and sat down, and indicated that she should sit beside him.

'Clare, g'day,' he said, and smiled. He had very nice teeth.

Clare sat beside him and glanced across. 'Hello.'

'Tell me what you want. I'm sorry I was a real hairy galah on the phone.'

'That's all right. I was a galah, too. As you said, it's easier to talk face to face.'

He put an arm along the back of the seat, but mercifully it did not make contact with her.

'Then fire away.'

Clare twisted her fingers together and kept her eyes lowered as she tried to formulate her request. 'I'm at school at St Ursula's.'

'I know. I met one of your old chums from St Kevin's. She told me that your mother had sent you there. Is it gross?'

'Heavens, no!' She paused. 'I mean, it's a bit churchy. We're very religious because it's a praying order, as well as a school. And the food can be dire. But it isn't gross.'

'I'm at Grammar, now.'

Clare knew all about the Grammar School. It was one of the most scholarly establishments in the city. You had to be really brainy to be accepted for Sydney Grammar.

'The problem is, because we're a long way from anywhere we don't see too many boys.'

'I suppose not.'

'And, because of my mother, I don't get to meet any boys in the holidays either. None of her friends have sons; in fact, not many of them have children at all.'

William cocked his head to one side and looked at her enquiringly. She could feel her face colour.

'So, what do you want me to do?'

Visions of Lyndal and her brother leaped into mind. Great white cockatoos! Surely William didn't think she was asking him to emulate Patrick, on the pile of sacking . . . at the back of the shearing shed . . . which smelled of sheep wee and pellets . . .?

She took a deep breath. 'Write to me.'

'*What*?'

'You go to a day school, so you don't understand. All the girls in my set get letters from boys. It's really important. I don't even have any cousins who could write to me. And I don't have a single friend who's a boy. Apart from you.'

William scratched his neck, which she read as a sign of acute embarrassment.

'Clare, I think you're just as pretty as when you were seven. In fact, you're prettier. But I've got a girlfriend, already.'

'Oh, I don't expect to be your *girlfriend*,' she hastened to reassure him. 'I'm just asking you to write once or twice a term.'

'Write what?'

'Write pretend things.'

'Pretend what?'

Clare thought of some of the extracts Jane read aloud for their approval, and how her face would fill with colour and she'd crush the sheet against her chest and become quite confused. But her boyfriend was nineteen. Boys of fifteen would probably not write stuff that made your cheeks turn pink.

'Just things. Say you can't wait to see me in the holidays, tell me a bit about what you're doing. And I'll write back, although my letters will be really boring because nothing ever happens at school.'

'And that's all?'

'Yes, that's all.'

William grinned at her. 'You could make stuff up, when you reply. Just for the fun of it.'

Clare read from this response that William was receptive to her appeal. 'So you'll do it, for me?'

'Why not? As long as that's all you want.' He looked at her quizzically. 'I wouldn't like to make Frankie jealous.'

'Is she your girlfriend? Frankie?'

'Yep. Francesca Buchan.'

'Oh.' Until this minute Clare had absolutely no desire to have a boyfriend, any more than she wanted to do *that*. Such things were way, way in the future. But looking at William, with his nice smile and his hairy legs, she felt suddenly jealous of Francesca Buchan.

'Lucky her.'

William was as good as his word. His first letter arrived a scant week after she'd returned by way of train and minibus to school.

The arrival of letters at the convent was a matter of considerable excitement. The postie came in his van about dinnertime and after dinner, during which time the senior sister on duty scanned the incoming letters and parcels for undesirable content, the girls would assemble in the common room while a prefect called out their names and distributed the mail. Clare's first epistle did not go unnoticed. Nor did the fact that the envelope bore a very impressive, embossed crest on the back flap.

Clare had practised in her mind what she would say, at this particular moment. A throw-away line would be ideal. Something like, 'Oh, it's just from William,' as though William's missive was almost incidental, among the hoard of men crowding her life. Instead, eyeing that envelope, she felt colour climb up her neck and infuse her face. She had no idea what it signified, but it looked far too expensive and ornate to be a school crest. And her fingers shook as she prised the back open, taking care not to rip the embossed insignia.

Darling Clare, William had begun. Clare rather fancied being Darling Clare. *I hope you got back to school okay. The rest of the term will be very hard for me. I've got a calendar in my bedroom and I'm going to count down the days until you're home again.*

Clare thought that this was extremely satisfactory. William was playing along nicely, even if the rest of the letter described in painful detail what had happened during the test against South Africa . . . *in case you weren't able to follow the match on the tellie. Are you able to get to a tellie for the test series?* Clare knew no more about cricket than that you hit a ball with a bat and ran up and down a strip of mown grass. Cricket was neither Thea's nor Douglas's thing. William ended his first epistle by writing, *I lie awake at night and think about you. Sometimes my eyes are wet, wanting you. All my love, William.*

In her return letter she suggested that he could tone down the endings or she would be embarrassed, and she asked him about the crest. His reply was something of a shock. William's father, it appeared, was the Leader of the Opposition in the New South Wales legislature. The crest was that of the House. His dad had brought a few envelopes home, at William's request. He was entitled to do this, William explained. It was all totally above board.

So his letters continued in the following years. They did not meet again in the holidays because this might make Frankie jealous, but through the letters they exchanged Clare came to know a great deal about William. She thought that Frankie Buchan, to whom he remained loyal for the duration of their correspondence, was a very fortunate person.

10

Clare was still fourteen when she had her very first experience of sexual conquest: memorable for that, but scarcely something about which to raise the nation's flags.

They'd gone to Coal and Candle Creek, Douglas Hamilton driving, Thea providing the picnic food for the little party. Coal and Candle Creek was a long way north, in the Ku-Ring-Gai Chase National Park, and it took them more than an hour to drive there; across the Harbour Bridge, along the Pacific Highway to Gordon, then branching off through St Ives and into the bush-clad hills. But it was worth it because the picnic area was lovely, alongside a tributary of Cowan Creek, and quiet and beautiful. There were great gum trees and kookaburras, and while they were eating the chicken drumsticks that Thea had cooked on the picnic area's barbecue, they watched an enormous goanna explore one of the litter bins in quest of rich pickings. A goanna is a huge, monitor-type lizard and this particular specimen stood as tall at the shoulder as a small terrier. It had small, stupid eyes and skin with the texture of eucalyptus bark and a forked tongue like a snake's that flicked in and out. Clare thought it was wonderful.

Douglas wasn't too good at barbecues. He thought cooking was exclusively woman's work, even if it was out of doors, but fortunately Thea was happy to oblige and take up the tongs. Thea, Clare thought, would be happy to do anything to oblige Douglas. She'd probably jump through fiery hoops, should he ask it of her.

After lunch Clare swam in the salty water of the inlet while Douglas wandered the shore and Thea read her book. Then they changed places; Clare stretched out in the diffused shade of the gum and Thea joined Douglas to explore the shoreline.

There was another family who had taken over the next door picnic table, and they appeared to have reached a similar stage in proceedings. The only person left at the table was a man of about middle age whom Clare noticed idly, as she fiddled about to find her place in her latest reading. She was into Dickens, having discovered the humour of his writing. She could hear the little pleasurable screams of the man's children and wife as the children splashed in the shallow water of the creek. The man's wife was a lot younger than he was, and pretty, and Asian. Probably Filipino. She'd also watched their three children who were gorgeous, black haired and golden-skinned.

It took Clare some time to realise that the man was studying her. He hadn't moved from the other bench, so they were separated by several yards and there was certainly nothing threatening about him, because her mother was only a shout away and several other families were also enjoying the place and the day. But the man was definitely observing her. Very deliberately Clare rearranged herself on the blanket so that she could bend one leg, raising it and point-ing her toes just a little. That was the pose she'd studied exhaus-tively in the *girlie* magazine which Patrick had supplied for Lyndal's gang. It lived under Lyndal's mattress and could only be perused in strictest privacy, because knowledge of its presence would probably lead to instant expulsion for the reader. Actually, the models in that publication were photographed mostly on their backs, had no clothes on and lay with their eyes half-closed and their mouths half-open. It occurred to Clare that she would look very silly, lying like that in her bog-standard Speedo cossie. She wished that she'd developed breasts, but to date that part of her had done no more than swell a little about the nipples. Not exactly inspiring.

The man didn't even make a pretence of doing something else. He had the newspaper in front of him on the table, but he certainly wasn't reading it. Without looking in his direction, Clare raised herself and reached for her comb. Kneeling, she very slowly began to groom her wet hair, drawing the comb with deliberate strokes the length of the strands. As she completed each motion drops of water splattered heavily onto her thighs. She didn't once look at the man but she could sense, somehow, that he was enjoying watching her. Then he took the newspaper and placed it over his thighs and his groin.

There was no more to it than that, because Clare could see Douglas crossing the grassy verge by the road and Thea following him a few paces behind: but for those few, short moments, she understood the motivation behind the bodice-ripper. She had felt amazingly powerful.

Her fourteenth year was also memorable for her confirmation. Douglas who, despite his severe reservations, did appreciate its significance to Thea, drove her from Sydney for this special occasion. The Bishop came out from Sydney, and the service was so lovely that Thea wept. Lyndal had been confirmed last year, so was only a member of the congregation this year. She shared with the gang that she thought Thea might melt away from exposure to her own tears, like the Wicked Witch of the West in *The Wizard of Oz*, after Dorothy drenched her in water. Clare gritted her teeth and retorted that Thea was not a witch, but a much-loved parent. Jane quietly squeezed her fingers in sympathy. Clare was sorely tempted to ask Lyndal how she could square up having sex with her brother, and with some kid called Gary, and another kid called Greg, with what they were taught in the catechism? Once again, however, she held her tongue.

This turned out to be quite a lot easier once Jane, Caitlyn, Steph and Clare made the discovery that they shared serious doubts about the Gospel According to Lyndal Murphy. It became accepted, after they'd realised this, that you never actually did the things which you claimed to do and this was not really lying, because you kept your fingers crossed. Jane led the way, by explaining that she and the nineteen-year-old were no more than platonic friends. He lived in Toulouse and attended the university there. She would probably never return to Europe, or not in the foreseeable future. But, although she was still a virgin, he *had* kissed her.

'What was it like?' Clare asked.

'Nice. Really nice. It wasn't like our practice session and he didn't do that stuff Lyndal told us about, all wet and swapping saliva. He just ran the tip of his tongue along my teeth so that it tickled. And he had lovely, smooth, olive skin.'

'Do you wish he really was your boyfriend.'

Jane looked around, as though fearing that the walls might have ears. 'Promise not to tell?'

Caitlyn's, Steph's and Clare's heads converged in a tight cluster of flaxen, mouse-brown, strawberry blond and dark hair. The only reason they were able to have this conversation was that Lyndal, yet again, was serving out her time in detention.

'We promise. On the cross.'

'He has a friend called Jean-Claud.'

'NO . . .!'

'Yes. He's gay. But promise not to tell Lyndal, won't you?'

Sister Brigid left the convent that year. She found that she did not have the vocation. Mother Scholastica led prayers for her, as she went back into the secular world. Mother Christopher died the following month. She was three weeks short of her century. Everyone cried at her funeral and two girls became so hysterical in their grief they had to sleep in the san overnight.

When Clare was fifteen the next opportunity to test out her sex-worthiness made itself manifest, if that is not to overstate the situation.

Whenever she and Thea turned up for Saturday evening Mass at St Kevin's, the same altar boy was in attendance. He was about sixteen and would not seriously have attracted Clare's attention, had there been any competition. But beggars cannot be choosers. Clare elected to dismiss his mild acne and concentrate on his profile, which in certain lights did remind you of Leslie Howard in *Gone With the Wind*. Of course, the chance of their becoming acquainted was as remote as her visiting Mars, but she could try out a mild sort of flirtation, through eye contact. The altar boy, whose

113

name she knew to be Damien, would slip a sly glance her way as the official party processed along the aisle; and, because Thea always insisted on their sitting in one of the front pews, he would look across the altar rail at her when he should have been concentrating on holier matters, like the chime of bells that announced the presentation of The Host. Clare found it impossible to return his glances directly, but she was adept at peeking from beneath her lashes, and on the occasions when their eyes did meet she could feel the colour rise pleasantly in her cheeks.

This inoffensive amusement continued right through January, without Thea's being aware of it, but – even so – not promising to lead anywhere. Then, shortly before she was due to return to St Ursula's, Damien managed to manoeuvre himself, in his kneeling position behind the altar rail, so that she could see more of him than usual. He should have been mumbling the *Agnus Dei* with the rest of the congregation. Instead he made a very explicit gesture with his hands, the thumb and forefinger of one hand creating a circle, the forefinger of the other hand repeatedly thrusting through the ring so created.

Clare was thoroughly shocked; shocked firstly because anyone who was Lyndal's friend knew exactly what *that* meant, but even more disgusted because the gesture was so inappropriate in the middle of the Mass, in a place of sanctification. William, she thought hotly, would not have done anything so inappropriate. Although one had to remind oneself that William was Frankie's property.

But it was shocking in another way, because it made Clare question the precise message she was putting out. Had she encouraged Damien to do something as rude as that? Had her eye-flirtation been seriously misinterpreted? Or was he merely wanting to impress someone whom he saw as taboo, with his street-cred?

She made certain that she no longer met his eyes . . . and spent the rest of the service envying Frankie Buchan.

During that Lenten term a bunch of the senior girls became struck by a bout of extreme devotion. This manifested itself in an epidemic of kneeling during dinnertime. The girls vied with each other to outdo this display of homage, coupled with self-denial of food. It added a certain thrill to lunchtime, although privately Clare thought the girls looked very silly, kneeling and reciting their rosaries as their peers and juniors munched their way through shepherd's pie. The episode lasted five days, and seemed to be gaining new recruits, before Mother Scholastica put an end to it.

'You remind me of the Pharisees, girls,' she said as she rose to recite the grace. 'You may remember that they thought public prayer was superior to private penance. This behaviour will cease, as from today.'

Nonetheless, each Lent was devoted to some form of fasting, and there was a certain rivalry about how self-denying you chose to be. Giving up lollies for Lent was seen as far too easy, and could be construed as good for you, so scarcely a sacrifice. And during Lent they spent even more time on their knees. Older girls, if they were sufficiently dedicated, were encouraged to join the non-teaching nuns in all of the daily offices, instead of the customary three. On occasion this meant leaving lessons halfway through, as the bell calling you to worship began to toll. None of the Five, now renamed "our bunch" in acknowledgement of their senior status, ever saw fit to join these committed girls, although Jane was definitely closer to sanctification than her friends.

All five, however, did keep vigil in the chapel during Holy Week. This meant setting your alarm on your watch and praying that it would waken you at some unearthly hour. The year she turned sixteen, Lyndal was privileged to draw the period from 2:00 am to 3:00. Terrified that at so early an hour she would be at her deepest slumber, she also secreted a primed alarm clock under her pillow. Both watch and alarm proved their reliability, but even so Lyndal dozed an extra ten minutes. Still foggy with sleep, her uniform awry, her hair a mess, she tottered to the chapel to be greeted by an irate Sister Margaret Mary.

'Have you no sense of dedication, Lyndal Murphy?'

Lyndal didn't even try to conceal her yawn. 'I'm here, aren't I, Sister? I think I did very well.'

Sister Margaret Mary all but snorted. 'I'm happy to think that there is at least one person who approves of you, Lyndal, even it is only yourself.'

In the business of turning Lyndal into a young lady, as required by her father, the convent had to all intents and purposes failed. Nor, until her last year with the good sisters, did they ever really comprehend just how subversive was her influence. In part this was because her disciples were robustly grounded in their mores and their morals. In Caitlyn, Clare, Jane and Steph, St. Ignatius Loyola was proven at least partly correct.

Lyndal's voice had certainly been modified, as had the crudity of her vocabulary – at least in the nuns' presence. Her scholastic education had also come on by leaps and bounds, in no small part because of the long hours Clare spent coaching and testing her. Rather than depart St. Ursula's as soon as was legally possible, she now hoped to train as a nurse, and so stayed on to sit her HSC. Such a possibility would never have crossed the minds of her first year teachers.

In the matter of chastity, however, she was at a total loss. By fifteen she had entered the list of the select few who met their current boyfriends on a regular basis and engaged in enthusiastic sessions of sex. Despite the remoteness of the convent, it was all too easy.

Everyone in the top two years knew about it; how to escape the convent, and the location of the trysting place. Few girls were so driven by their hormones that they needed to avail themselves of the knowledge.

However, by the time they returned in the February for their final year at the convent, Clare found herself once again isolated. She was the only girl not to have Done It. William had left Sydney Grammar at the end of the previous year, having completed his HSC in the top 5% of the nation. He was now taking a year out, before he went to Sydney Uni to study law. He was still "with" Frankie who, like Clare, would not sit her HSC until the end of the scholastic year. He still wrote letters to Clare, although this now meant no more than postcards with exotic stamps from wonderful

116

places like Bali and Kuala Lumpur. All of "our bunch" except Lyndal knew that there had never been any real connection between Clare and William, apart from their correspondence. This had not mattered until now. Now things were different. Caitlyn had been seeing and sleeping with John for nearly a year. *It* had hurt a lot, they used condoms, and she was having trouble equating the employment of contraception with Papal doctrine. She had discussed this with her priest at home but could not bring herself to renounce all sex, as suggested. Sex, she could tell them, was fantastic. Jane had finished with her French guy in favour of Simon, who was local and whose parents knew her parents. She planned to become engaged as soon as she left school. Simon, evidently, had a brilliant future as a merchant banker and was already earning indecent sums. Once she'd met Simon she decided not to take Holy Orders. *It* had hurt like mad.

It was like Ten Little Indians, a countdown that ticked along with the inexorability of a primed bomb. They were down to two. But then, during the long summer holidays, Steph had met Dane, and lost her virginity at her parents' holiday place at Terrigal. *It* had not hurt, she told them.

So that left Clare, who never met boys during the holidays except to exchange glances with them across the altar rail at St. Kevin's.

Holiday treats with Thea had graduated from trips to Taronga Zoo and on the ferry to picnic at Manly, to visiting the current exhibition at the New South Wales Art Galley or excursions to The Rocks to wander through the Saturday stalls and then to buy themselves a nice little lunch. They might attend an outdoor concert at the Domain. On none of these occasions was Clare likely to connect with someone of the opposite sex. She did, however, form a very strong idea of what she sought in her ultimate boyfriend. Foremost among her ideals was respect. He would certainly not be coarse, like Damien. Words like 'sheila' would be banned, although she had to admit that William had never again put a foot wrong. But, sadly, William was still the property of Frankie, and Clare honoured that prior claim.

Australian men were notoriously macho, as though the feminist movement was for other nations but not for the Real Men of a Sunburnt Country. Clare, however, would know that her boyfriend respected her from the first time they made eye contact. The novels she read fostered this strong determination. In them, heroes such as Mr Rochester won through, despite the obstacles fate threw in their way. Clare wasn't particularly impressed by the thought of an earlier, mad wife, but she did admire the romance of it all.

There were moments when she was close to despair. Only the knowledge that she was one year away from uni kept her afloat. Surely, surely, at the uni there would be some boy who liked her enough to seek her out. She knew that she was pretty, but she also knew that prettiness and sex appeal weren't the same thing. Giving a middle-aged man a cock-stand was a two minute wonder and could scarcely count for much. Caitlyn, on the other hand, was quite plain and wore glasses, but the boys evidently thought she was terrific. Jane, clearly, was wonderful in every way and she had the advantage of breasts that were really attractive. Clare's own chest had only recently started to develop, which was why she supposed herself to be sadly lacking in boy-appeal. Stephanie had her own sort of glamour; and Lyndal was . . . Lyndal. Small, dark, vivacious, oozing potency; bossy, opinionated, the show-off of all time. Part of the fabric of school life, and constantly entertaining. Just Lyndal.

The Prince

11

As requested, Tom had pulled down the blind across the window to darken the cabin. When he awoke however, after a fitful few hours of sleep, he returned it to the halfway position. According to his calculations their flight was approximately three hours out of Sydney. At any minute the artificially short night would summarily end, as lights were switched on again and the attendants brought around breakfast and coffee. He glanced out the window. The red-hot line on the horizon was the vanguard of the sun's reappearance; dawn, about to break. Way below stretched the expanse of the Pacific, the serene blue broken by not so much as an atoll. Until you flew over it, you really didn't appreciate its vastness. A full third of the world's surface.

Coffee, he thought, would be more than welcome. A civilising agent. He rubbed a hand across the stubble on his chin, weighing up the advantages of getting to a cramped lavatory now, or waiting until he'd weathered the tedium of entry to a foreign country and could relish the leisurely privacy of a hotel room. The hotel room won.

He fished into a pocket and located the immigration form. Then he found his passport and started to fill in the relevant details. Name: *Goulding, Orford Thomson*. Date of birth: 6. 9. 68. No, that was the wrong way around for Australia. He scratched out the first two numbers and wrote 9. 6.

Orford Thomson. What could his parents have been thinking about, landing him with an epithet as ugly as that? There weren't

119

many things about his brother that Tom envied, but as a kid he did envy him his name. Anthony Wilbur, his brother was; known as Will. Wilbur, Tom had decided early, was a real man's name. But who the hell had heard of anyone called Orford? Apart, that was, from a distant relative who might be persuaded to leave his infant namesake some sort of legacy? A total waste of time that exercise had proved to be. When the old man died he left his considerable wealth to a televangelist.

And the Thomson? His mother's maiden name. He could recall as a kid resenting that, too. He'd have been happy enough being a Thomas; there were some mighty fine Thomases, starting with the great Edison, himself. But he, young Tom, was saddled with Thomson. Back in those days he'd called himself O.T. Goulding so the kids at school had given him the nickname of Otee.

When he thought about it, a lot of his childhood seemed to have been filled with resentment. And it had started with the family name. Goulding. He could remember, as a twelve-year-old, inspecting his developing schnozz in the hope that therein he might find just the trace of an Ashkenazi profile. Couldn't Goulding have been Gold at one time perhaps, or Goldman? Wasn't there, in the more recent history of the family, one Abraham Goldstein who had pushed his way through the turnstiles to face the immigration board on Ellis Island? Such a notion held huge, romantic appeal to young Tom. From there, this mythical great grandfather might well have spent his apprenticeship in the sweatshops of New York and emerged, some time later, with a fortune entirely of his own making.

That was Real America; a nation formed by a rich tapestry of antecedents who gave rise to the exquisite mongrel, blessed with the sterling characteristics of many older civilisations. *There* was a legend you could get your teeth into. But, according to the authorised version of the family history, their roots were essentially Anglo-Saxon and boringly British at that. There wasn't a lot of romance to be milked from such humdrum stock. Another disappointment.

In a way, Tom thought, accepting from the attendant a heated washcloth and allowing it to rest, folded, across his brow, in a way he'd been forced to despise his family by the very ordinariness of them and their way of life. The warmth of the cloth felt good, although he knew it would cool quickly.

He closed his eyes and thought about his parents. Dale and Thelma. He'd not spoken to them in seven years, although he had sent them a card, the last few Christmases. No fear of *that* letter being returned, stamped that the addressee had departed to foreign parts, address unknown. Not Tom's father and mother. No siree! They still lived in the same home in which he'd grown up, a very standard house of two and a half bathrooms on a very standard subdivision, the sort reproduced ten thousand times throughout Middle America. Interior decoration pegged in the 'seventies.

That, of course, was not the reason for which he despised them. If you did that, you'd be despising a goodly half of the populace. No, his grievance came from their lack of ambition, their being prepared to settle, unquestioningly, for this and no more. It was their acceptance of this essentially humdrum existence against which he'd rebelled. That, and their assumed mantle of superiority. A snobbishness of the very worst sort, Tom reasoned, because they had so little about which to be snooty.

The cloth had chilled rapidly. He swiped it across the nape of his neck then handed it to the waiting cabin attendant.

Dale. His father. Lying back against the cushioned seat with his eyes closed, his nose being teased by the aroma of impending breakfast, he could picture the guy down to the last detail. Cleft chin like his own, but therein any physical similarity ended. He could imagine Dale's hair, greying at the temples, picture that characteristic half-grin which was at the same time apologetic and a tad confrontation. Lower the chin a fraction and he was placatory. Raise it a similar distance and his dad could demonstrate that he was a man to match any other man.

Dale had worked most of his adult life as a salesman, for the one company of any size in the town. Marketing, in the terminology of today. He and Thelma had grown up there together, in that self-same town. Tom didn't know whether his father's career ground to a halt, halfway up the promotional ladder of middle management, because luck didn't favour him or because he wasn't particularly capable. Tom thought the latter was more probable. But you didn't despise people because they weren't all that successful. You despised them because they acted like they were, when every indication was to the contrary. Especially, in the credo of Thelma and Dale, it was vital that you put on a brave display around the neighbourhood.

And that was the essence of the matter, the root cause for Tom's scorn. That determination to act superior. It was imperative, in his parents' book, that you be seen as one step ahead of the pack. In their case this translated into such paltry, trivial victories. The Christmas lights needed to be out of storage, strung and lit the Saturday after Thanksgiving. The Sunday – and you had failed. And it stood to reason that the Goulding display must be the very best. If the Fords, two doors along, bought illuminated reindeer why, the Gouldings must of necessity have Santa and his sleigh installed before next weekend. If the Wilsons added a gigantic nutcracker, then the Gouldings must display two such monstrosities. Indeed, only financial limitations prevented them from sporting an entire row of the grotesque, glowing figures.

Will went along with all this nonsense. Will was two years older than Tom, and mean as a female skunk in season. Tom felt no more than scorn for his parents' pathetic worship of mammon, but he really loathed Will.

He flipped a page in the passport and glanced at the photograph that endorsed his identity in visual form. Had he not looked so like Grandpa Thomson, he'd have thought Thelma had brought the wrong baby home from the hospital. You heard of such incidences; infants swapped accidentally at birth and raised in homes where they stood out like the proverbial sore thumb. It would have made sense, because he had found from so early an age that the things his parents and brother held dear were of absolutely no importance at all.

And his mother? Thelma, with her pert features and peach-coloured hair, still set in the cotton-candy bubble of the seventies? Her role in life was to endorse everything her husband and firstborn son did or said or thought. Thelma might give lip service to the advances engendered in women's lib, but that was as far as it went. Had anyone suggested that she, Thelma Goulding, should stand up and be counted, or even give birth to a single original notion, she'd probably have suffered palpitations on the spot. Tom, imagining her now, did allow a momentary softening. Thelma had been a good mother and a kind one. He owed her that. She might be as limited in her ambitions as her husband, but she had one characteristic for which Tom did admire her. Loyalty, even if, in his opinion, misplaced loyalty.

He must have been a real stinker during his teenage years, Tom mused, because he'd been so determined not to toe the party line. He'd been resentful and hypercritical and downright ornery. He'd gone around with a perpetual scowl on his face, waiting to take offence, refusing to be placated. He'd allowed his disappointment in his family to colour his views about everything else. And he never gave Will the time of day, so the atmosphere between the two boys was tense as Mt St Helen's before the eruption.

The cart was, finally, being pushed along the aisle. Coffee, at last. He swung the small table up and out of the armrest, in anticipation. Amazing, the way just the smell of fresh-brewed coffee could awaken your taste buds.

It was probable that he, Tom, would have rebelled against the sobriety and intrinsic boredom of his upbringing anyway, despite his parents' best efforts. In retrospect, and allowing a more charitable frame of mind, they probably felt they had shown great forbearance in letting him attend school a couple of thousand miles away, in California. Everyone knew that only weirdos chose to live in California. When he dropped out of school before completing his second year, he knew they would blame the subversive influence of those wacko San Francisco types. And why not? he reflected. They'd seen none of that sort of nonsense in Will. Will, the darling blue-eyed boy, had emulated his parents step by tedious step. He'd followed their dad into the same company; he'd married a local girl. Tom had no doubt that he appreciated all the correct virtues. *His* Christmas lights would embarrass nobody.

Pancakes for breakfast, with two microscopic sausages.

Scarcely an orgy. Probably just as well, though, because by this time into the flight you were starting to feel like the sacrificial lamb being fattened for the slaughter.

When Tom had seen fit to drop out, he recalled, it was the easiest thing in the world. San Francisco in 1988 had been rich with opportunities for those turning their backs on corporate America and rejecting the values for which it stood. That's what he'd told himself he was doing; that had been his rationale at the time.

He could remember so clearly the feeling of overwhelming relief as he walked down the broad, impressive steps of Berkeley, dumped his last assignment (for which, incidentally, he'd been awarded a perfect score) and its accompanying text book into the nearest bin and headed for the city and its run-down, less salubrious, areas. Mistress Luck appeared to grant him her blessing. He'd not been forced, even, to spend the first few nights of apprenticeship in the shelter of some doorway among the drunks, the kooks and other derelicts of society. Six hours after his abdication he'd been satisfactorily screwing a broad not so much younger than his mother. Which, for some reason, made it all the sweeter. The ultimate snub, so to speak. Remembering now, seven years later, he could allow himself a wry smile. Actually, she'd been quite a lay.

Tom's 'drop-out' period had lasted two and a tad years, and thinking about it now made him cringe. He was not proud of that interval. He'd have been happy enough to remember it as a time of creativity, had he been creative. But writing the definitive American novel was not for him, he'd never understood poetry, thought philosophy was for the birds and knew himself to be totally without talent, where art was concerned.

Instead, trying to find something worth something within himself, especially something that separated him from his bourgeois family and their pretensions, he'd snorted or shoved up his nose every substance available. You couldn't get away from it – drugs cost serious money. He'd found the wherewithal by servicing an assortment of equally spaced-out women of uncertain age until he'd settled with one particular woman, in one squat as, in essence, a kept man. Another reason to cringe. This retrospective stuff, he concluded, did not make a comfortable travel companion. And all brought about because he'd had to fill in an immigration form. Once aboard this train of reminiscence, however, it was quite difficult to switch off the mind and disembark.

And there were things on the plus side, on which he could dwell. In retrospect, when he was able to step back and try to find some small aspects of which he need not be too ashamed, he could thank his lucky stars he'd never gotten as far as main-lining, and had emerged from his Beat period free of any hideous disease. More good luck than good judgement, Tom could admit soberly; just as he could probably thank Thelma's and Dale's sturdy, non-dependent genes that these days he was drug-free and not a hopeless addict, well down the morbid spiral to sorry extinction. He'd seen enough kids go that way.

He'd never before found anything for which to thank his parents. It was this year, when he'd finally come to his senses, that he'd sent them a Christmas card. It had been the first contact since he left home, so at least they knew that he was still alive. He remembered that he'd not gone so far as to add an address. Was that because he was ashamed, or because he still didn't wish to share? Did he harbour some residual fear that Thelma and Dale would hot-foot it to the West Coast and attempt a sort of emotional kidnapping?

Waking up each morning with a clear head, neither throbbing nor half a second short of being split by a gigantic cleaver, had been a new experience. It stood to reason that, after two years of being stewed out of his brains, it wasn't going to prove easy to come clean. Which brought his thoughts neatly around to Bob. Tom would be eternally grateful that his friend, himself an ex-pothead, had been prepared to offer a sofa and support during that early, critical period. They'd been touch and go, those weeks. But it had allowed Tom the opportunity of a new beginning. The chance to re-create himself.

Bob had been the catalyst then, and subsequently the guru. He'd introduced Tom to the computer – and it was like a door opening, a light switching on. The technology made total sense to him. He'd discovered that he did, indeed, have a talent that was all his own, and the discovery was wonderfully empowering. He could understand the language of Visual Basic, and programming, and analysing systems. That was when he'd enrolled at the local college and emerged, after a decent interval, literate and employable. And clean.

So he'd become employed. Until then he had shared the apartment with Bob, and you knew there were some things that could never be repaid. Bob had that generosity of spirit which Tom feared was sadly lacking in himself, or at least where his family was concerned. It was his new employment, he recalled, which had taken him to a new part of the country. The great Northwest; Seattle, where CompuSoft was based. And it was from there that he'd sent a second card to his parents, informing them of his good luck and his job. That he didn't, this time, send an address was not from ill will, but because he still didn't have one.

In the next couple of years he'd actually changed addresses quite frequently, but this was more to do with his promotion within CompuSoft than with any basic restlessness. In fact, he was beginning to like the idea of putting down some sort of roots.

It was still a marvel to Tom that his employers had recognised his problem-solving talent so rapidly, and were prepared to reward him accordingly. When your self-esteem has taken a hiding over a period, albeit it self-imposed, it's quite a surprise to find yourself valued. CompuSoft sent him out on a consultancy basis, to soothe ruffled corporate feathers and to set up the more complicated programs. For these two tasks, which came so easily to him, they paid him the sort of sums that he'd considered at first to be downright indecent. Funny how, after a period, you found yourself taking such things for granted.

Sometimes he'd pause to wonder which particular god he'd had the good fortune to please. It was as though his star in the firmament was smiling down on him, without his having done anything to deserve it. To have a job that he enjoyed, found sufficiently challenging to keep him interested without being too stressful, must be anyone's idea of heaven. That Seattle suited him like a hand-lasted shoe was the icing on the cake.

He could have chosen to live anywhere this side of Millionaire's Row. Attracted to the water and to the individuality of the setting, he'd bought himself a houseboat on Mortlake. He'd decided at that moment that he must, indeed, have died and gone to heaven. He could remember lying awake, that night when he moved in to the first home he'd ever owned, listening to the night noises of the city, watching the lights of traffic descending the approach to the floating Evergreen Bridge, hearing the slap-slap of wavelets caused by a launch chugging quietly through the cut toward Lake Union, and wondering whether life could be more perfect. He knew that in the morning he'd wake up to drink his coffee looking across toward the eastern line of the Cascades, snow-clad because it was November, their outlines sharp and crisp against a clear, peach sky.

Maybe, he'd thought, he should send Thelma and Dale a post-card with his address. But maybe not. There was the feeling that it was still too specially his, too new to share.

Tucked into his wallet were two photographs. The first was of Elliot's untidy features, bisected by his array of none-too-perfect teeth. Elliot had become part of his life within weeks of buying the houseboat. That meant, Tom calculated, that they'd been a serious item for nearly three years.

They'd met up one moist, fall evening, when he'd been wandering along the waterfront looking with indifferent eyes at the refurbished piers and their assorted merchandise, and thinking idly about Thanksgiving, and Christmas, and gifts.

Elliot was a brown mess of a dog, of no recognisable breed but a miscellany of three hundred assortments; the total, Tom could recall wryly, at that particular moment disgustingly smelly and uninviting. Tom didn't particularly want a dog. Elliot had been pretty dim when it came to getting this message. He'd done a great deal of tongue wagging and pleading, but it was the way his face very nearly smiled which finally won over Tom's heart. He'd needed to establish that there was no bereft owner and no other strings attached, before he forked out $100 in vet's fees alone. The vet had reminded him with some tact that Elliot was in the twilight of his canine years but did concede that, once sanitised, he was in a fit state to share the houseboat. So added to the vet's account had been the $155 for which a doggy beautician, and that in itself was a joke, had robbed Elliot of the more matted and tangled portions of his unkempt overcoat and de-scaled his teeth and rubbed salve into the torn pads on his paws. Elliot, Tom remembered, had appeared to consider this a very fair bargain, in exchange for two square meals a day, plus lodging plus love. They'd settled down on the houseboat as a couple, to happy domesticity.

The second photograph in his wallet was of Sandi. Sharp featured, elegant, poised. Not a hair out of place on her sleekly groomed head. She'd given it to him the other evening, quite casually, making a bit of a joke of it. 'In case you forget what I look like, among all those bronzed Australian beauties,' she'd said. And laughed.

Sex became a habit. Being robbed of regular, satisfying sex when first he arrived in Seattle had not pleased Tom at all. He'd set about correcting this omission pretty damn quick. He'd met Sandi through work and had appreciated almost immediately that he'd, as the saying went, hit the jackpot.

Sandi, he thought, fulfilled his particular requirements as satisfactorily as he fulfilled hers. Basically, that meant with no strings attached.

Tom regarded sex as an appetite, to be nourished in the way that one nourished other, more material hungers. During his Beat years in San Francisco his ability to gratify quite a number of women had kept him, marginally, on the correct side of the law. He thought he was pretty good at it; correction, he prided himself on being something of a pro.

Sandi certainly seemed to agree. She'd never once voiced dissatisfaction, after a vigorous session of fornication.

Sandi, he'd concluded, was the '90's ambitious woman. She reckoned she was in charge of her life, her career, her body. Tom saw no reason to disagree with her. She worked downtown for a major advertising company, she adored progressive jazz and sushi, and sex. She did not adore children, or country music, or other people's emotional baggage. She didn't think a lot of Elliot, either. It was the one small bone of contention between them. Elliot felt he was entitled to part of Tom's bed, once they were through with the sex. It meant that Tom and Sandi more often than not met in Sandi's smart apartment. Sandi seemed to like it that way anyway, because she claimed to enjoy tossing together trendy little salads and other, fat-free concoctions. There were moments when Tom would have liked to sit down to a slab of rib or an order of French fries, instead of her substitute, fat-free cheese, which reformed itself into an indigestible ball in his innards, but he kept these thoughts to himself.

And, of course, it was Tom who had to get up and make his way home in the small hours. That seemed to appeal to her, too.

12

One of the nicer things to happen in 1994 was that Tom was able to pay back in part his debt to Bob Squire. A job came up in CompuSoft that could have been tailor-made for his buddy. Tom called and suggested that Bob apply. So it came about that not only did Bob become a colleague, he also became a neighbour. In the intervening years he had met and married Joey. It seemed only right that while the pair was house hunting in the area they should bed down on Tom's sofas. Joey fell in love with the whole concept of living on the water. She waxed lyrical about the feeling of falling asleep on a gigantic waterbed, she loved the compact nature of everything. Even the obvious drawbacks, such as having no guaranteed parking space, did not deter her. When the vessel immediately adjacent to Tom's became available, Bob and Joey signed the lease and moved in.

Tom had been more than happy. Having close contact with your neighbour removed the one disadvantage to his present life, his need every so often to abandon Elliot. The old guy was too far on in years to appreciate vacations in kennels and, as though aware that here was his chance, he'd applied himself with all his canine logic to charming Joey. He'd succeeded. In fact, he'd succeeded to the degree that Tom had occasionally to remind him where his true loyalty lay.

It did mean, however, that when Tom was asked to go to Sydney in the New Year of 1995, he could leave knowing that Elliot would be happily spoiled and cosseted. Personally, he was more bothered about missing out on his skiing.

His spec was to establish the new CompuSoft software for one of Sydney's leading merchant banks. Estimated time, seven weeks.

His contact, who would initiate him and smooth his way within the bank, would be one Greg Allsop.

And so, in this deceptively simple way, the prince was nudged in the direction of the maiden, as the story dictates.

Tom would have considered himself fit, by any standards. The Cascades, the mountain range that separates the western, coastal strip of Washington from the more arid interior, had an almost magnetic draw for anyone who'd been raised on the wheat-lands of the Midwest. In recent years Tom had scaled Mt Si with enthusiasm, joined an overnight party to conquer Mt Rainier, inspected the crater of Mt St Helen's and trekked his way up other, equally demanding trails.

None of these excursions equipped him in any way for the hike up the escarpment before him. To begin with, this ascent appeared almost vertical, and secondly, the temperature must have been well into the upper 80s. The rock was brick red, and the parts not crumbly were inclined to be frighteningly slippery. Each foothold had to be tested with care, if he was not to find himself descending in a terrible corkscrew of death, toward the valley floor far below. And he'd last seen Greg at least an hour ago, at which time he'd set off enthusiastically, claiming that if you followed the track it was impossible to get yourself lost. Famous last words. Terrible words. The trail, to all intents and purposes, seemed to peter out within a mile. In the total absence of any other clue, Tom opted to follow the only apparent route that might take him toward civilisation. Up.

And a lot of good this sensibly thought-out, rational decision was proving to be. Granted, the path of sorts certainly aimed uphill, and thus held the promise of more hopeful things at the top. Following it was considerably harder. He paused once more to take his bearings, allowing himself a glance down and backwards toward the thick canopy of dusty-green bush from which he'd emerged only recently, followed by an upward sweep of his eyes toward the incredible, burning blue of the Australian sky. His only ally was the sparse scrub that struggled to maintain a hold on the nearly vertical face of rock. The heady, pungent scent of eucalyptus was almost overwhelming.

It sure cleared out the sinuses; which would be more comforting if you weren't contemplating the possibility that your bleached bones might one day be found by a future generation of hikers.

Why the hell hadn't he stuck to Greg like glue, instead of agreeing in his stupidity that they split up and meet again by the car?

And, as if to reinforce the alien nature of the bush, his ears were repeatedly assaulted by the harsh, jarring cries of birds, none of them familiar to him, all of them appearing to mock his progress. But progress he was making, albeit measured by feet rather than yards. More than an hour of excruciatingly slow ascent brought him nearly to the top of the cliff face. A further half hour of scrambling about boulders and shed gum-bark, which had the slickness of plastic sheeting, took him the next stage, in the direction of where he imagined the car-park might be.

And then, as though to reinforce this hope, he heard girlish voices, laughing together and chatting. Civilisation, at last. The thought was almost overwhelming.

Tom straightened his shoulders, brushed back the clump of hair that sweat had gummed irritatingly to his forehead, and headed toward those voices. Grateful out of all proportion for the less challenging nature of this terrain, he rounded the thick, knotted trunk of a gigantic gum tree and almost fell over the speakers.

Clearly the girls were the more surprised, because the shrill screams of a thousand cicadas must have masked Tom's stumbling arrival; ergo, they had not the benefit of knowing that anybody was within earshot. It was a close thing, however. There were two of them, seated on a flat slab of rock, knees drawn up to create a surface against which to rest her arms, in the case of one, and her cheek, in the case of the other. The loose braid of ash-blond hair on one head, already unravelling, suggested that they had been idly grooming each other.

They were wearing identical dresses of green and white checked gingham with white collars, clearly some sort of school uniform. One of the girls, Tom noticed, was small and dark, with short hair, bangs and a fully developed figure that the school dress did very little to conceal. The other girl, she of the long ash-blond hair, happened to have the most wonderful green eyes. And her loveliness was such that it very nearly took Tom's breath away, and made the words he was about to utter stick in his throat.

The little brunette recovered her wits first.

'Where did you come from?'

Tom indicated with a shrug of one shoulder. 'Down there.'

'From the *valley*?' Her tone suggested that this was totally impossible. Tom was inclined to agree with her.

'Yup. From the valley.' He slipped his arms out of the backpack's straps, deposited it on the ground and sat down beside the pair. 'Mind if I join you?'

The gorgeous blond scooted herself across the smooth slab of rock as though she'd just encountered Quasimodo on a bad-hair day.

'Don't worry. I haven't the strength necessary for rape. Not after that climb.'

The dark girl tittered, the blond smiled a little nervously, but stayed as far away from him as the rock permitted.

The smaller girl's gaze was bold and curious. 'Nobody ever comes up that way. It's too dangerous.'

'You're telling me.'

At this moment Tom had an almost overwhelming urge to do nothing but stare at the fair young face before him. Because he'd noticed, however – who couldn't – her hasty shuffle, he deliberately turned away, reached inside the backpack to locate his water bottle and then concentrated on drinking deeply. The original ice had long ago melted, but the water tasted sweeter than anything he'd ever drunk in his life. It slipped like smooth syrup down his throat, making him feel human again. Farewell Quasimodo; welcome back Tom Goulding. Out of the corner of his eye, he observed the two young women. Obviously still at school, so they couldn't be more than seventeen or eighteen, although those goddamn awful dresses made guessing their ages a bit of a lottery. The brunette appeared the older and her look was downright calculating, as though she were sizing him up as shrewdly as he was them. The fair one certainly had less breast development and her expression was almost childlike.

Incredibly ingenuous. Almost . . . almost, he thought to himself, naive to the point of absurdity. Could she be one of those unfortunate people about whom you occasionally read? An idiot savant?

The dark girl had watched his every movement with overt interest. Now she stood, brushing her hands against the back of her skirt to remove any vestige of debris that might be clinging there, and incidentally giving him a very good idea of how well formed were her nether regions. She picked up a cotton hat and jammed it carelessly onto her head.

'Come on Clare. We'll be in for it if we don't get back soon. Vespers at five-thirty.'

Tom tucked the empty bottle into his pack. 'Can you direct me to the road? How far away am I?'

'How long's a piece of string?'

Sassy baggage. He stood and hid his mild irritation. It probably was a pretty dumb question.

'We left the car in the parking area at the head of the trail. There's an engraved map-plate that shows the possible tracks. Do you know where I mean?'

'I might.' But her shrug gave little ground for hope.

He turned to glance at the blond girl. She had also climbed to her feet, so that he could see she was at least of average height and very slender. She had bowed her head but was watching him surreptitiously from under the rim of a similar cotton hat. The dark sweep of her lashes juxtaposed against the fairness of her skin. Apart from the jumble of voices that had led him to them, Tom had yet to hear her speak.

He addressed her directly. 'Do you know the place?'

The girl lowered her gaze and shook her head slightly.

'Perhaps I could come back with you? To your school, I assume.' He swung his backpack over one shoulder. 'There must be someone there who can direct me. Or I could call Greg, my companion, on his phone.'

The pair exchanged glances. Then the dark girl shrugged. 'Okay. But we'll have to get going. It'll be worth it, just to watch Sister Fachtua's face when she catches sight of a really, truly, breathing man.'

Sister Fachtua. He'd caught the ramification. 'So your school's a convent?'

'Yeah. And the sisters think all men are in league with the devil, lurking behind the gum trees and waiting to rape their precious charges.' She met his eyes challengingly. 'That's us.'

'You're safe with me,' Tom replied. 'I told you before that not even the most determined rapist could undertake that climb and have the strength left to attack anyone.'

He followed the pair along the trail. That way he could watch the graceful way the blond child moved, and how she glanced at him every now and then from under her floppy cotton hat. She was worth watching.

They reached flat terrain and the path became smooth and well worn, no longer a challenge. The brunette spoke over her shoulder.

'I suppose that's what the founding order must have reckoned on, when they sited the convent here. An impregnable citadel of maidenly virtue.' The giggle that followed suggested that the original nuns had sure gotten it wrong.

She walked in a calculatedly provocative way, Tom noticed, watching her progress before him. Each movement of the hips was accentuated and she wriggled her butt like a hooker seeking to attract customers. She was also extremely aware of his presence; you'd have to be a moron not to read the message she was conveying.

A few hundred yards along the trail it widened out into a sunlit opening, then the bush-line fell away and there, before them, were the sturdy, cream-painted buildings that indicated a school. There were also several dozen similarly clad girls in assorted attitudes of inactivity, and the veiled figures of at least two nuns. The only concession to modern living in evidence was that their calves were visible although clad, even in the heat of an Australian summer, in black hose. The arrival of Tom and his escorts created quite a stir, as though the presence of any man was particularly bizarre, to be compared with the invasion of a multi-headed creature from Mars.

The person approaching him certainly thought that his intentions toward her protégés were of the most dishonourable sort. She charged at him like a tigress intent on defending her cubs, a truly formidable opponent. She stopped a scant three feet from Tom and he had to restrain himself from stepping hastily backward. Was this the intrepid Sister Fachtua?

Somewhat phased by the force of her offensive, he found his voice with difficulty.

'Ahem, excuse me, mam . . . Sister. I was wanting your help . . .'

Where was the wretched Miss Provocative when he needed her help? The whiskers on this old girl's chin alone were weapons that could do mortal damage. But a sideways glance showed his potential seductress of only a few minutes ago had been reduced to the status of meek schoolgirl.

'My help, young man? My HELP?'

The lioness's eyebrows were wicked black lines that met above her nose and she had an aggressively hirsute mole beneath one eye.

'Well, yes. I . . . er . . . became separated from my companion. We were trekking in the valley . . . and er . . . '

'He climbed up the escarpment, Sister Fachtua.'

It was the first time he'd heard the blond girl, whose name he knew to be Clare, speak.

'Yes, and you said nobody except a fool would attempt such a thing, Sister Fachtua.' So Brunette had found her voice again. Not before time.

'Hold your tongue, Lyndal Murphy. And you too, Clare Galway.' The nun drew herself up until she could very nearly look Tom in the eye. 'And as for you, young man, intruding into a place where you're less than welcome . . .'

But clearly the enormity of his crime was beyond anything imaginable, and words at this minute failed her.

Tom decided that confrontation might very well give these silly children something to discuss subsequently, but would not help him locate Greg and the car. A touch of the blarney must surely be more acceptable.

'Sister, I do beg your pardon. I had no idea when I dragged myself up that terrifying cliff that I'd be breaking into a convent school. But now that I'm here, I'd be more than grateful if you'd let me use your phone. Then I'll be on my way.' He'd very nearly said,

136

"m'way." From where on earth had that Irish accent arisen? From watching *The Quiet Man* as a kid? But it did seem to do the trick. The old girl with the beard appeared decidedly mollified.

'Of course, Mr . . . ?'

'Goulding, Tom Goulding.'

'And you're from America.'

Was that good news or bad? Good, it would appear. Maybe her Irish relations were on the mailing list of Noraid. Recipients of arms for The Cause.

'That I am.' That darned Irish accent again; hell, it was catching. He cleared his throat, only too aware of the circle of green and white clad girls who by now encircled them.

'Holidaying in Australia, maybe?'

'Actually, I'm working here for a couple of months. In Sydney. Computers.'

'Ah, yes. Computers.'

The way she said it suggested that PC's had some mystic appeal, maybe a private line to God's throne. No, that was the wrong connotation; more likely they were seen as the e-mail link with the Blessed Virgin.

Again Tom cleared his throat. Time was ticking by and from the girls' lack of recognition it seemed likely that he still had quite a hike to locate Greg and the car.

'Ahem . . .'

Clearly mollified, Sister Fachtua's voice dropped a couple of decibels and she very nearly smiled. 'You'll be wanting some refreshments, Mr Golden. After your terrifying climb.'

'Goulding, Sister. And although I'd sure like something to clear the dust out of my throat, I think the phone is more pressing.'

The good nun inclined her head graciously. When she smiled a dimple appeared in each cheek. 'Indeed. The telephone. Follow me, Mr Gosling.'

The car, Tom, and his erstwhile hiking companion were reunited two hours later, by which time Tom's temper had simmered down in direct apposition to his state of footsoreness. They turned back

137

toward the vast sprawl of the city. Greg drove his somewhat decrepit vehicle as though it were a high-powered sports car, despite the narrow, winding nature of the road. They began the descent from the plateau, toward Sydney and the flat, coastal plain. Greg needed much of his concentration to keep them from dropping over the edge. Nevertheless, he thought it hilarious that Tom had managed to get himself lost with such facility on a track that 'any moron could follow' and felt obliged to share his opinion. Tom came very close to a serious sense of humour failure, but his good temper was salvaged by his own, racy account of what had followed his invasion of the convent school. Greg redeemed himself by proving to be a pretty acceptable audience.

'After I'd managed to contact you, I was fed and watered, and then sort'a displayed for this bunch of nubile wenches like a prize biology specimen,' he continued. 'All in these green and white uniforms and with white bobbie socks like the kids in that Olivia Newton John movie, 'Fifties style.'

Greg was laughing so hard that he had difficulty seeing the road. He wiped his eyes. 'What can you expect, a regular guy dumped down among a herd of sex-starved sheilas?'

Tom sobered up unexpectedly. 'Actually, it was quite ghoulish. The girls didn't actually slaver, and the nuns were kindness themselves, once they understood I was there by mistake, and not in the business of ravishing their ewe lambs, but you could almost hear the hormones racing in those kids. Well it's not natural, is it, jamming a couple of hundred adolescent girls together in that isolated place?'

'You frightened that they might've attacked your virtue? Held you there as a sex slave?'

'I damn near was ravished by the first kid I met. Given half a chance she'd have jumped me.' Lyndal Murphy, potential seductress. She'd practically undressed him with her eyes. Then the image of the other girl, the beautiful Clare, invaded his thoughts. 'And there was this fair girl, who must be the loveliest kid I've ever seen.'

'The one you'd have chosen to do the ravishing, given a choice?'

'Yes . . . no.' Thinking about Clare, she simply didn't enter into that category. 'Actually, she wasn't like that at all. She was sort of . . . pure. Not sexy, really. Just . . . beautiful, in the way that artists used to paint women. Like Botticelli's *Venus*; you just can't imagine her jumping into the sack. Do you understand?'

Greg caught his change of mood and temporarily sobered. 'Frigid.'

Tom hated the thought that the enchanting Clare might be considered anything less than perfect. 'No. Chaste. There's a difference.' He shrugged. 'Anyway, confined in that place, guarded by a pack of old crones with whiskers, there's not much of a chance I'll ever lay eyes on her again.'

Greg, still needing to keep his eyes on the road, risked a quick glance. 'Do I detect a note of regret in your voice?'

'Nope. I like my women sophisticated. And I'm not in the business of cradle snatching.'

Then, to indicate that the subject had run its course, Tom opted for silence, and turned his head to look at the passing scenery. Because there was more to the afternoon's events, the concluding part, which he had no intention of sharing with Greg Allsop.

The convent, it transpired, did own a minibus but it was out of commission. Tom, having accepted gratefully the refreshments that had arrived for his enjoyment, had faced a five kilometre hike back to where the car was parked.

'I'll have one of the girls walk with you to the road,' Sister Fachtua said authoritatively. 'Lyndal Murphy, you always appear to have an excess of energy; witness your determination to talk for hours after lights out. You will be excused vespers and will escort Mr Goldsmith to the gate. You have precisely twenty-three minutes to do so, and I'm timing you.'

'Yes, Sister.'

The voice was meek enough, but Tom was privy to the grimace that accompanied Lyndal's reply. And to the gleam in her eye.

Tom would have chosen Clare Galway to accompany him, but felt that he couldn't exactly voice this preference. So he shouldered his backpack, thanked the sisters for their hospitality and followed the suspiciously mild Lyndal as she led the way through the host of gingham-clad girls and their sizzling hormones. He could almost feel the regret of their gazes on the nape of his neck. What the heck? So he'd added a frisson of excitement to a dull Sunday afternoon, and would possibly figure in the masturbatory session that followed bedtime for half a hundred young women. Scarcely skin off his nose.

The convent's drive wound through enormous, ancient gum trees and great banks of rhododendrons, then down a dip that clearly led toward the road and ultimate civilisation. At some distance away to the left he could see the gleam of sunlight off water.

'Is that a lake?'

Lyndal had been surprisingly quiet during the last few minutes, contenting herself with walking beside him. Now she turned in the direction he was indicating.

'Not really a lake. It's more of a large pond, where the stream has been dammed.'

'Do you swim there, then?'

'Never! It's totally out of bounds.'

Aha, thought Tom, it seemed the lady was mighty quick with her denial.

'Would you like me to show you?'

'You've just told me it's totally out of bounds.'

Lyndal turned on a hundred megawatts of power. 'We could accidentally get lost.'

'Get lost? Off this drive?'

Her smile was dazzling. 'Why not? It's only a couple of minutes and I'll bet you're a fast worker. And I'm not a virgin, you know.'

Tom made his voice as chilly as he could. 'I have no doubt at all. You don't need to convince me.'

She added coquetry to her arsenal. 'Then why not? Just a quickie. I won't snitch on you.'

'And risk having the gorgons who guard you hack my balls off with their teeth?' Tom replied soberly. 'No thank you, Lyndal. I value my manhood too much for a minute's casual gratification.

140

Even to please you.'

Lyndal appeared to give up the chase without too much rancour. She waved casually in the direction of that gleam of water.

'We do go swimming there, actually. When the nuns are asleep. We creep out and skinny dip. It's fantastic, on hot nights.'

'All of you? Regularly?'

'No, just a few of us. The rest are cowardy-custards.'

'Does Clare swim with you? Or is she a yellow-belly as well?'

He was aware of Lyndal's shrewd glance. Was he as transparent as all that?

'The blessed St Clare Galway has never broken a rule in her life. When she leaves this school she's going to be beatified, as the first step towards sanctification.'

'Really? As holy as that?' His tone was mild, uninterested.

Lyndal met his eyes boldly and defiantly. 'As holy as that. She never, never swims with us.' She stopped walking and pointed ahead. 'And there's the road. Turn left when you reach the gate. Even a yellow-livered girlie like you can't get lost from here to there.'

For some reason Tom chose not to repeat that conversation to Greg.

13

On the following evening, at about eight o'clock, Tom found himself behind the wheel of a rental car, driving along the Hume Highway, the arterial road that leads toward the Southern Highlands and then the Blue Mountains. In the time that he'd been in Sydney he'd had no need for a car, so the business of negotiating this vehicle on the wrong side of the road, combined with the often-expressed impatience of metropolitan drivers, took a fair bit of his concentration. The fact that he was actually in such a situation, however, came as no surprise at all.

He'd realised very quickly that a certain educational establishment had all the fascination of the lorelei, the attraction of some monstrous electrical magnet. Or, to be more precise, a certain person within those walls.

Just to leave the city and achieve the first half of the ascent into the hills took about two hours. Tom spent part of that time coming to terms with the traffic, more minutes were used gainfully in making sure he knew where he was going, but once he'd left the suburban sprawl behind there was plenty of opportunity to contemplate the obvious truth – that he was either a depraved voyeur or a brainless idiot. Either option weighed heavily toward the fact that he might very well find himself behind bars before the night was out. How would it look on his résumé? *February 1995: arrested in the grounds of St.Ursula's Convent School for Girls, as a Peeping Tom*. Not exactly a positive career move.

There was no question in his mind that he was definitely several sandwiches short of a picnic, and becoming more degenerate by the minute. And yet . . . and yet . . .

Clare Galway. Clare Galway. What had she done to him, in one brief hour and with two shy glances? Cast a spell on him. Totally bewitched him.

As the scenery became more rural, cultivated fields yielding to gum trees and more gum trees, undulating pasture being regularly bisected by deep, bush-clad valleys, Tom turned over in his mind reasons why he was actually going along with this mindless stupidity. To get his kicks from watching a bunch of hot adolescents skinny-dip? Crap. He'd not been fooling when he told Greg Allsop that he liked his women sophisticated, more in the mould of Sandi Schmidt. Polished. No one in his right mind would mistake Clare Galway for a woman with knowledge of the world. From what he'd seen she could scarcely put one foot in front of the other and breathe at the same time. Then . . .why the hell?

In the bright moonlight that followed the brief period of twilight, it was easy to retrace the previous day's drive until he could recognise the fork in the road that led to the convent's entrance. Only yesterday afternoon he'd hiked along this very stretch. Tom parked the car several hundred yards short of the gates and well in from the verge, partly concealing it by reversing into the surrounding scrub. Even that simple act endorsed what he had already concluded. He was a certifiable nutcase, about to gain a police record as a sex-criminal.

He avoided walking along the drive. It didn't seem likely that the good sisters had installed CCtv, by his reckoning they probably considered their very isolation to be sufficient security, but there was no need to take unnecessary risks in this dumb business. He estimated that the pond Lyndal had so carefully pointed out could be no more than half a mile from the road. By the time he was within range, his eyes had fully adjusted to the dimness of the hour.

It might have been sign posted, so clearly did the gleam of moonlight off the surface indicate the location of the dammed-up stream. Tom crept on stealthy feet from eucalyptus to shrub to eucalyptus, pausing as he approached to ensure that he was still alone. There was nobody about. But then, when did the nuns see fit to retire to their bedrooms? Or maybe they slept in cells. Any sensible guy would have checked on Catholic rites of worship as well, discovering precisely when the last service of the day took place.

Behind the pond the undergrowth was thick, and the rock less craggily uninviting. He found a smooth surface, largely screened from view by a useful cluster of slender ghost-gums, seated himself and prepared to wait.

The silence was almost scary. In the daytime the high-pitched screams of cicadas had blocked out the more mundane noises of the bush. Stilled, the only sounds were the trickle of water as the stream escaped over the dam wall, soft rustlings of small nocturnal animals going about their nightly affairs, and the occasional calls of unidentifiable birds.

He didn't have long to wait. He'd timed it well. A few minutes after ten his watchful eyes made out the shape of three young women wending their way carefully through the fringe of trees that separated the pond from open ground. They were briefly silhouetted against the silver-white of moonlit grass, then they were enveloped by the gloom of the surrounding shadow. As he'd expected, one of the girls was Lyndal, the second was Clare. The blessed St Clare who never broke school rules. The third girl was unknown to him, but easy to identify because she was reed-slender and by far the tallest.

They approached the pond carefully, although obviously familiar with the terrain. At the edge Lyndal paused to peel back her robe, lifted her arms high in a movement marvellous in its theatricality, then slid into the still, dark waters. The tall girl followed with a minimum of fuss. Clare, Tom noticed, was more circumspect. There was a brief moment as her robe fell to the ground and a fine shaft of light spotlit her still childish breasts and softly rounded belly, then she joined her friends in the welcoming coolness of the pond. Had he been there in the role of voyeur, he would have considered himself cheated. But he was no sex-absorbed spectator, he was . . . what? A guy fascinated by a kid he had met only briefly? Captivated by her, obsessed by her. And even thinking about the smoothness of her skin and the silkiness of the sweet water brushing against it, and knowing that she was no more than twenty yards

144

from where he sat concealed, was satisfaction enough.

They swam, the trio, in slow easy circles. They stopped to tread water, talking quietly together, never raising their voices above a whisper, never splashing or indulging in the least hint of horseplay. Their young bodies slipped effortlessly through the water and he could almost feel its refreshing nature in the heat of the night, as though he was in the pool with them, sharing the sensation.

They stayed there about fifteen minutes, all told. Then Lyndal, again the ringleader, led the way out of the pool. Budding dramatist that she clearly was, she emerged to best effect, lingering on the smooth stones adjacent to the pool, allowing the filtered moonlight to play on her nakedness, the fullness of her breasts and roundness of her behind, before donning her robe. Clare, again, showed greater modesty.

'Give me my robe, please.' Although her voice was no more than a whisper, he could hear the words clearly enough.

Lyndal picked up the discarded garment, appeared about to hand it to her companion who was still kneeling in the shallowness of the pool's edge, then seemed to change her mind.

'Come and get it, Goody-Twoshoes!' She hoisted the robe into the air behind her.

Clare held up a beseeching arm. Tom found that he was holding his breath.

'Please, Lyn. Don't be mean.'

The teasing lasted probably less than a minute. To Tom it might have been an hour. Then the third girl intervened.

'Oh, give it to her, Lyndal. You're being a bitch.'

'Spoilsport.' Lyndal tossed the garment toward Clare's outstretched arms. 'Here you are, cowardy-cat.'

Was it his imagination that she turned to look directly at the clump of ghost-gums behind which he was sheltering? Goddamn, it had to be a trick of the light or his eyes deceiving him. By not by so much as an indrawn breath had he betrayed his presence.

He gave the girls a full ten minutes to return to their dormitory before he crept away from the pool and headed on silent feet toward the car.

He was back the next evening and the night after that, and the ritual was repeated. The swimmers were not always the same, although Lyndal and Clare were each time of their number. On the third evening the party had swollen to five, which Tom thought risky, if for no other reason than the success of five young women creeping covertly back to their beds in the middle of the night must rely on nuns who slept very deeply indeed if they intended to avoid detection.

The nightly excursion did nothing to enhance his work potential. Although the return drive into Sydney was clearly shorter, because most sensible people had long ago sought their beds, it still meant that he spent almost four hours on the road. Then long workdays, as he customised the bank's program, demanded almost more than he was capable of producing, after a row of seriously contracted nights.

And all because he was under the spell of a certain child/woman, one he was privileged to see, at best, for fifteen minutes, in exchange for that four hours of travel. And that quarter-hour did not even include the opportunity to speak to her.

The situation was so farcical that by Thursday he began to long for the arrival of the New South Wales police, maybe complete with baying tracker dogs and large flashlights, to escort him to a convenient cell and eight straight hours of uninterrupted slumber. So when, on Friday evening, and once more secreted in his customary hide to the rear of the ghost-gums, he noticed a small scrap of paper lodged behind a loose strip of bark, it appeared almost in the light of a prophetic manifestation.

There were four girls, that sweltering night. The appeal of the cool water must be almost irresistible. The difference was that Clare Galway was not of their number. As soon as he appreciated that she wasn't present, Tom would have preferred to creep away. His only interest in being there, on that now-familiar slab of rock, was to lay eyes on his goddess, his beloved. In her absence the whole thing took on a different flavour, a flavour for which he had no taste and in which he had no interest. Inside his head he could almost hear himself, defending his actions to the interrogating cop.

146

'I didn't bother to watch them,' he would say. 'Once I saw Clare wasn't there.'

He could imagine the cop's look of incredulity. 'There were four pretty kids skinny-dipping in a pool in front of you – and you chose not to watch 'em?'

'That's right. I wasn't there for the kicks. I was there because she's cast a spell on me.'

'Yeah, sure. And the moon's made out of green cheese. Pull the other one.'

How did you excuse your actions in such a situation? There was only one possible defence. Plead insanity – and with justification.

It was as he turned his head away, totally unresponsive to the healthy young bodies quietly treading water and perfecting their side-stroke technique not twenty yards from him, that his eye fell on the strip of paper. And he knew, because the spot was by now so familiar to him, that it had not been there yesterday.

The lure of the water must have been stronger that evening, or the girls were becoming more confident. They swam for fully half an hour before Lyndal began the familiar ritual of leaving the pond and executing a series of theatrical poses, which gave ample time for her moonlit charms to be appreciated, had he chosen to appreciate them. Was it his imagination or were the actions of the other girls equally bold? There was no doubting that at least two were giggling, quite openly. Then Lyndal did something that caused Tom to freeze. She looked directly at the ghost gums behind which he was concealed and said succinctly, 'Enjoy the show, Mr Tom Goulding. It's your last.'

Then, linking her arms with her friends, all four turned back toward the school buildings, keeping to the deep shadows that the gums threw across the mown grass as they went.

Tom sat there completely still, in total shock, for some time. He would hear their sniggers in his nightmares.

He waited more long minutes before he slunk away, and he was nearly back to the road before he dared switch on the miniature light that he carried on his key-chain. The words on the scrap of paper said, "Meet me by the gate. Clare."

She wasn't at the gate, when he made his stumbling way past the last of the great, red-barked trees which seemed to stand sentinel at the convent's entrance. Despite the heat of the night, the disappointment was like the sudden impact of icy water. It was almost a physical reaction, which seemed to course down his spine like rippling goose-bumps; the same sensation of chagrin as all those early Christmases, when the longed-for gift turned out to be a sad facsimile, the Hong-Kong alternative, because Dale had spent the allotted sum on yet another set of illuminated peppermint candy-canes.

Almost weeping in his frustration, Tom started along the road toward his car.

'Mr Goulding? Tom?'

He froze.

'Mr Goulding, It's me. Clare.'

And then he saw her, a deeper shadow against the assorted shades of night, the darkness making it impossible to identify individual features. She was leaning against his carefully concealed car.

He drew in a sharp breath. 'Won't your friends know you're missing?'

'No. I said I had a migraine, so Sister Margaret Mary let me sleep in the san. I do have migraines and my head did hurt a little, so it nearly wasn't a lie.'

Tom hesitated. 'Thank you for the note. Why do you want to see me?'

'To warn you.'

'Warn me?'

'Yes. Lyndal's my friend, but she's going to snitch on you. Tell Reverend Mother that she's seen a man lurking in the grounds. Because you're not interested in her. Because you wouldn't do . . . you know . . .'

A short distance behind the scrub, which he'd fondly hoped camouflaged the car, there was a bank covered with long, dry grass. Tom seated himself and indicated for Clare to join him. Up close he

148

could see that the pale garment she was wearing was no more that a skimpy nightie. Her feet were bare, her ash-blond hair fell in a fat, loose braid down her back and her face in the reflected moonlight was a perfect oval. Just the sight of her made his heart leap into his throat and his chest tighten agonisingly.

It was an effort to keep his voice normal. 'Then what will happen?'

'Oh, last time Reverend Mother called in the police and they caught the man.'

'So I'm not the first.'

'No, but the other man was different.'

Tom had no desire to know about some previous sucker; nor did he want to hear gory details of the guy's fate.

He cleared his throat, which felt uncomfortably constricted. 'Do you know why I came, Clare?'

She bent her head slightly. The perfect line of her neck set his heart thumping wildly again. 'Yes.'

'Why?'

Her voice was no more than a whisper. 'To see me.'

'And did that bother you?'

She glanced up, meeting his eyes. 'No.'

'So you expected me to come?'

'Lyndal said you'd come. She said she'd baited the trap.'

Lyndal would, Tom thought. Man-eater that she was.

'Did she bait the trap for the other sucker? Then tell the Reverend Mother?'

Clare began to fold the edge of her nightie. 'Oh no. He wasn't like you at all. He was a Peeping Tom. He even had a record, the police said.'

'So you don't think I'm a Peeping Tom?'

'No.'

They sat in silence for some minutes, Clare apparently concentrating on the pleating of her hem, Tom content merely to study the gentle curve of her cheek, her silhouette, the length of each slim calf.

Then he said, 'Clare, how did you know I was there? I thought I

149

was pretty well concealed. Dark shirt, dark pants and shoes. Nothing visible.'

She turned toward him and smiled. 'You don't read many detective books, do you? Even an amateur knows that you have to rotate your watch inwards.' She leant over and swivelled the face of his watch around until it was against the inside of his wrist. Tom wanted to grab her hand, capture it in his own, but dared not break the perfection of the moment.

'So I'm a real idiot? Failed at the first hurdle?'

She smiled again. 'I'm sure you're very good at other things. Computers, for instance.'

'Yeah. But that doesn't make up for not having street-smarts.'

'You're more street-smart than me. Actually, I'm the most un-street-smart person in all of Australia.'

He recalled that his first impression had been something like that. He'd even wondered whether she was the full dollar.

'What makes you say that?'

Again she turned her face to him. 'Not being street-smart isn't the same as being stupid. I'm clever at other things, and that includes self-knowledge. I do know me.'

And she wasn't frightened of him either, Tom thought. Didn't see him as a potential threat, which was gratifyingly true and pretty complimentary.

'And that little show of Lyndal's . . . Deliberate?'

'Of course. She adores an audience; she's a born actor.'

'And the other girls . . . they knew I was there all the time, as well?'

'Yes.'

The whole concept was hard to swallow. These sweet young things had actually been putting on a demonstration exclusively for his benefit. So much for the innocence of youth. He thought of Lyndal Murphy prancing and parading in the moonlight, and he winced.

'Then . . . what did she say? Why did you . . . they . . . all come?'

'She dared them. She dared me, too. You can't turn down a dare. It makes you look chicken.'

The tone of her voice was so calm, so easy, that clearly she was not struggling with the same doubts and objections that were flooding Tom's thoughts. It was all so smutty, somehow. Not at all the image which he cherished; not enchantingly chaste, in the way he wanted her to be. He changed the subject.

'How long have you been here?'

'Ages. I knew Lyndal would stay forever. As I said, she's a real show-off. So if tonight was to be her last performance, she was bound to make it good.'

Too true, Tom thought. The baggage had given him a great run for his money tonight; sadly wasted, should she but know it.

'No, I meant how long have you been at the convent?'

'Since I was eight.'

'And how old are you now?'

'Seventeen, nearly eighteen.'

Confirmation of what he already suspected; and he was a jaded, over the hill guy of twenty-six. He'd lived a lifetime in those eight additional years. Suddenly he felt very tired.

'Clare, it's nearly midnight. You ought to be in bed.'

He stood and held out a hand. She took it obediently and Tom pulled her gently to her feet. Through the flimsy material of her nightie he could make out the triangle of darker hair between her thighs.

'Will you come back again?'

Tom rubbed the back of his neck. 'How can I, with every cop this side of Sydney lying in ambush?'

'You mustn't go to the pool again, but I won't either. In fact, if there are going to be police patrolling the grounds, swimming will be off for a week or two. But there are other ways. Other girls meet their boyfriends, all the time.'

So help me, Tom thought. You paid a fortune to secure your adolescent daughters in a hilltop fortress away from predatory males, and then discovered that they behaved like prostitutes in a French whorehouse, with the morals to match. Down to putting on strip shows for the passing trade. And here was he, fast becoming one of the predatory males.

'Clare, I'd like to see you again, but can't we meet legitimately? Out in the open?'

He could almost hear her amazement. 'Of course not. The sisters would have hysterics. I'd be isolated for weeks, or perhaps expelled. They think men are after only one thing.'

'Most guys probably are,' he replied soberly.

She met his eyes squarely. 'But not you.'

He answered softly and with total honesty. 'No, not me.' But even to utter the words astounded him.

'Then you'll have to believe me. There's only one way we can meet.'

Tom groaned inwardly. So the covert life was still to be his. Tom, the outlaw, with a price upon his head.

'Okay. I believe you. Tell me what I have to do.'

14

The sense of unreality stayed with Tom throughout the long drive back into the city. It was in some ways like an out of body experience, something that was happening to him, but not of his own volition. He was the bystander, the observer.

How else could he explain, even to his own good sense, the peculiarity of his behaviour, crowned as it was by his acknowledgement that the overwhelming feeling he had for Clare Galway owed absolutely nothing to lust? He knew the feminist jokes about the male brain being lodged somewhere south of the navel – who didn't – and in the past he'd probably have agreed with this perception, at least when certain decision-making was concerned.

But he'd sat on a grassy bank at eleven-thirty one Friday night with an enchanting nymph of a girl, and longed . . . to hold her hand.

Hell, he was definitely cracked; not just two clowns short of a circus but also, goddamn it, missing the three rings, the elephants and the big top itself. He was wacko. Off the wall. A first-class nutcase. The only rational excuse had to be sleep-deprivation.

But at least it was the weekend and he had no need to emerge from his hotel room until two, when Greg Allsop, still determined to gain brownie points with the Big Cheese by the quality of his escort work, was scheduled to pick him up. Today he'd organised sailing for them, at some place called Middle Harbour.

Of course they met all the time at work, Tom and Greg, but within the huge corporate building another pecking order already existed. Tom was expensive; he was costing the company mega-bickies, as the Australians expressed it. When Tom said 'Jump,'

Greg replied 'How far, sir?' and might well have pulled his fore-lock, were he not the proud owner of the currently trendy, close-shaven head.

It certainly never arose during the week for Greg to drop more than the odd hint about people who couldn't follow their noses along well-worn tracks, and actually invaded the hallowed domain of a convent school.

Tom needed that long, deep Saturday morning slumber, just to regain the strength to counter Greg's version of cheesy cracks.

Given his own way, he'd have arranged to see Clare within the limits laid down by the good sisters, her guardians, even if that meant tamely chaperoned tea parties. He held deep misgivings about the furtive nature of all these shenanigans. It wasn't even as though he harboured dastardly thoughts of ravishment.

And, most of all, it smacked of underhand and underhand was kissing-cousin to lying. Tom had a deep-seated abhorrence of anything that strayed from the clear, unvarnished truth. It stemmed from Thelma and Dale's attitude, and the necessity in those early years of maintaining face. When money was short you put on a charade, a farce. It wasn't as though they'd been reduced to maca-roni and cheese, because Thelma was pretty good at making potato chowder taste good, but it was the secretiveness that went along with it which he found so distasteful.

Will couldn't understand why Tom objected. In his eyes, Thelma's, 'It'll be our little secret,' about this or that created a sense of family. Us versus the world. Mostly, this had applied to vaca-tions. On Dale's salary they couldn't take grand trips to Disneyland like others in the neighbourhood, but it was important to pretend. Tom would have been happy had they gone camping somewhere upstate; Thelma had other plans. She even resorted to clipping out extracts from vacation literature, so they could feign that the Gouldings, too, had tasted the delights of the Magic Kingdom, were familiar with the thrill of Back to the Future. Thelma even went so far as to test her sons, so that they came up with compatible tales. Will considered this stuff neat; an exercise in imagination designed to hoodwink their fellows, and to allow a certain posturing. Will was great at swaggering. Even as a nine-year-old it bothered Tom, to the extent that threats of parental retribution had to be invoked. As a nineteen-year-old it had irritated him far more.

He thought about all this as he drove along the highway toward the Southern Highlands, on the way to his first date with Clare. Date? That was a joke. On his way to another clandestine meeting, the only difference being that this time Clare had set the trysting place.

He passed the turn-off where on previous occasions he'd secreted the car, passed the convent drive, continued south a couple of kilometres until he saw, as directed, a clearly signed trail head. According to Clare, who had it on the good authority of her peers, you could hide your car behind the scrub, just in case a prowling cop happened by. Tom, following instructions to the letter, did wonder whether this ploy would work after rain, when the red clay must surely show every tyre-mark, as incriminating in its way as a set of fingerprints. However, during his time in Sydney they'd experienced not one drop of rain, so the ground was bone-dry. Car adequately concealed, he set off along the trail. Clare had said that after about twenty minutes he'd come to a fork; he must take the right hand branch, which would eventually lead to an overhang of rock. To the girls at the convent this was a well-known and oft-used rendezvous. She would be there to meet him.

'What about other kids?' Tom had asked, wondering haplessly how many couples were already in residence and busy making out.

'Just us,' Clare had replied. 'You have it on a sort of first-claim basis. As soon as I say I claim the Rock, it's ours for the evening.'

'Have you met other guys there, before?' Tom was forced to ask.

'Oh no. You're the first.'

'But you know all about it?'

'Of course.'

Tom wasn't sure whether or not he should be reassured.

In the bright moonlight the trek along the path was a breeze. He knew that he must be approaching the convent grounds, but from the west, and several hundred feet further down the escarpment.

The hard-packed soil presented no hazard under his sneakered feet, apart from occasional stretches of exposed rock that might well make the trail hazardous in wet conditions. The night was so still he felt he could hear his heart beat; and his feet were given wings by the knowledge that he would be seeing Clare again. The enchanter; his goddess.

The path forked; he began the climb to the right. This was much less frequented terrain, scarcely a trail at all. He had to scale slippery outcrops, using the tough shrubs alongside to haul himself up, hoping that they were firmly rooted and wondering as he did so how many other young swain had performed just such a feat in the pursuit of love. Half an hour after he'd left the car, he reached his destination. The area beneath the overhanging shelf of rock was in deep shadow.

'Clare?'

From somewhere in the gloom a disembodied voice replied softly, 'I'm here.'

'Are we alone?' Until his eyes adjusted, he hadn't a clue.

'Don't you trust me?'

Tom groped his way toward the voice. 'I don't trust anything about this business. It's too devious for me.'

'More devious than watching us skinny-dip?'

He winced. 'Yup. This time you're implicated, as well. I don't like that.'

'And you don't think I was implicated in all the other evenings when you came.'

'I guess.'

He sank down beside her, despite his misgivings grateful to be there, even more grateful that so was she; fully aware that he'd burnt his bridges, anyway.

Clare put out a hand and laid it on his wrist. 'Thank you for coming, Tom.'

The feel of her fingers, cool on his skin, created a ripple of sensation. 'You couldn't keep me away. I told you, you've bewitched me.'

She pulled her arm back. He was aware that she'd turned her

head away. 'Don't say that.'

'Why the hell not? It's true enough.' He took her hand in his, resisting her attempt to draw away. 'It's some sort of magic, I think. Maybe the gum trees do it, maybe they exude a substance that enables spells to work.'

His eyes were becoming accustomed to the blackness. He could see that Clare was wearing a dark-coloured towelling robe over her night attire, and that her feet were bare.

'Who do you think cast the spell? Me?'

Tom shrugged. 'I can't tell. Perhaps it was you; perhaps it was your buddy.'

Clare turned to him. 'Lyndal? Gosh no. If she could do that, it would be her sitting here right now, not me.'

Mention of Lyndal prompted Tom to ask, 'What about the cops? Have they been patrolling the poolside? Roaming the tennis courts every evening?'

Clare shook her head. 'Lyndal changed her mind. It's too hot to forfeit swimming, just out of spite.'

'I see.' He reached over and traced the outline of her brow with one gentle finger. 'Why don't you like the idea that you've bewitched me?''

'I just don't.' Beneath his fingertip she shivered slightly.

Sensing something, he asked quietly, 'Because . . .?'

Clare took his other hand again. She was so close he could smell the sweetness of her hair, her skin.

'Because I'm adopted. My adoptive mother, Thea . . . well, the other girls tease me that she's a witch. They say she must have kidnapped me as a baby. That's why.'

Tom could hear the residue of pain in her voice, and more than anything he wanted to comfort her. He drew her close so that her towelling robe tickled against his bare forearms.

'I'm sorry. No more bewitching. I won't say it again. It's just old-fashioned sexual attraction brought me here.' He stroked her hair in silence for a minute or two, then changed the subject. 'She's kind to you, your adoptive mother?'

'Yes. Very kind.'

157

'Then you know it's not true anyway, what the other girls say. And does it matter? Really?'

'It still hurts, even if the hurt isn't for me. And Thea's so much older than their parents, which makes her appear different again. And she's really old-fashioned.'

'None of that's important, if she's a good parent. And you love her.'

'I suppose not.'

He put one finger under her chin, making her look at him. 'You don't sound particularly convinced.'

'It doesn't matter.' Clare dismissed the subject with a small shrug. 'Tom, we don't have long. Let's talk about other things.'

'For instance?'

'Tell me about you.'

'What do you want to know?'

'Everything. Are you married?'

'Of course not.'

'Do you have a girlfriend?'

She was looking directly into his eyes. Did Sandi constitute a girlfriend? Not in his understanding of the word.

'There is one woman; I suppose you'd call her that. But not really. Girlfriends imply strings attached, and she and I have no strings attached. No commitment to each other.'

He could feel Clare's withdrawal and wondered whether he could begin to explain a relationship that wasn't a relationship at all.

'Then what am I?'

He drew her close again. This was easier territory. 'You're the beautiful young woman I met one afternoon, after I barged into her school. You're the person whose image has invaded my dreams and made working damned near impossible, because thoughts of her keep on cropping up between me and the console. That's who you are.'

Her shoulders relaxed again. 'And . . .?'

'And what do you want me to say?'

She paused, then replied quietly. 'I don't know.'

158

'Let me explain, Clare. I'm a programme consultant. I live in America, in Seattle. I expect to be over here for about another two weeks, then I'm scheduled to go home. I can say, "I think I'm in love with you," and it would be true. But I can't hope to forecast what's going to happen to us.'

'I understand that.' They lapsed into silence, then Clare asked, 'How old are you, Tom?'

He nuzzled his face into the hollow between her head and shoulder, rubbing his cheek against the rough fabric, imagining the smoothness of her skin beneath. 'Old enough to be your father.'

'I don't believe that. How old are you really?'

'Twenty-six.'

'Then you're being stupid. I'm nearly eighteen. Boys of eight don't father babies.'

'I feel old enough to be your father.'

'That's not the same thing.'

Tom countered by repeating her question. 'And what am I, to you?'

She looked down, twisting his watch inward on his wrist as she had the other evening. 'You're the first man who's ever looked at me . . . in the way you looked at me.'

'Then, young woman, let me give you a bit of sound advice. When a guy looks at you the way I looked at you, don't invite him in. Take to your heels and run.'

Clare, close to him, turned her head so that she could see into his eyes.

'No, that wasn't necessary. That's what was so different. I knew straight away that you didn't have anything ugly on your mind. No dangerous intent, not even the trivial stuff that would make the nuns have a fit. That's why I wanted to see you again.'

'And you're not disappointed?'

'No.' She paused, while thinking about this. 'No, not at all. I feel totally safe with you. And . . . I don't want this to sound melo-dramatic and silly, but I feel as though we were pre-destined. As though there was something out there, maybe someone, with a greater plan; and we're part of it.'

Tom smiled. 'Shades of *Some Enchanted Evening*?' But wasn't

159

she describing in different words the very sensation he'd experienced, of being bewitched?

'Perhaps.'

Again they lapse into silence. Tom was happy to hold her close in the quiet, and to let his fingers toy with her long, unbraided hair.

It was Clare who broke the silence. 'What's the time?'

He glanced down at his wrist. 'Ten past eleven.'

'I'll have to go. Another girl has booked here for eleven-thirty.'

The familiar feeling of revulsion swept over Tom. There was something so tacky about meeting in this way, in this place. 'How do you get out so easily?'

'The fire escape, off the senior dorm. With the convent being out here in the bush, and all the buildings being wooden, most of the dorms need to have fire escapes. Everyone uses that one because it's furthest from where the nuns sleep.'

'But don't they ever check, after lights-out?'

'Practically hourly.'

'And how come you're not caught?'

Clare sighed. 'Poor Tom, how pitiful. No street-cred. We put a dummy in the bed, you idiot.'

'It must be a pretty good dummy.'

'Of course. It's one of those blow-up figures, the sort that sad blokes use. Lyndal got it, naturally enough. And we have different wigs, fair and dark, long hair and short. You'd have to get really close to realise it wasn't the actual person it's supposed to be. And Sister St Francis, who's the senior matron, is dreadfully short sighted. That helps.'

Once more Tom was threatened with the sense of unreality. Whatever had happened to the age of innocence?

'Tom . . .'

'Yes?'

'I'll have to be going.' Another pause, while he waited.' Will you kiss me?'

'You really want me to?'

'Of course. Otherwise I wouldn't have asked.'

She turned within the circle of his arms and Tom kissed her very

160

gently on the lips. 'Okay?'

'All right, I suppose. Now will you kiss me the other way?'

He was still. 'What other way?'

'Properly.'

'Clare, are you sure?'

In reply she wrapped her arms about his neck and raised herself slightly so that their mouths were level. So Tom kissed her properly, swimming in the sensations the action roused within him, wondering whether she was feeling even a fraction of something similar.

She broke away and in the dim light smiled. 'That was better. Not at all like a slug. Thank you.'

'Like a *slug*?'

'I'll explain some time.' She stood, drawing her robe more tightly about her, re-tying the cord. 'Will you come again?'

'If you want me to.'

'You know I want you to. But not tomorrow, because the Rock is fully booked.'

'Is there nowhere else?' Tom asked fretfully. This place had all the appeal of a whore shop. He dared not even extend an exploratory hand because he fully expected to find the discarded etceteras of others' lovemaking.

'Not that I know about.'

'Could you come further along the track? If I do a recce?'

'I suppose so.'

'Then meet me . . . oh, on Monday, down by the fork. And be sure to wear sneakers. Those rocks are lethal.'

Tom made excuses not to share Sunday with Greg and his fiancée, Dawn. It was no sacrifice; Greg's relentless jokiness began to grind after a while. Instead he bought cold chicken from the deli near his hotel, along with bread and fruit and an outsize bottle of water, and returned to the Southern Highlands. He thought, as he wove his way through the hotchpotch of Sydney's suburbia, that this car had covered the ground so frequently in the last few days it could probably find its own way there, if put on auto-pilot.

161

There was no need to go through the complication of hiding the wretched vehicle. His reason for being in the area this afternoon was sufficiently legitimate. He hiked down last night's trail, surprised at how different it looked in the brilliant sunshine. Australian flora was novel as well, distinct from anything he'd encountered at home. Without knowing a thing about botany, he could appreciate the great black spikes that towered dramatically twenty feet from the centre of clumpy, spiked leaves and the general resilience which allowed tenacious shrubs to find foothold on the most hostile of surfaces. The strange cry of a bird cut through the high-pitched screams of cicadas. 'WHOO- wee-eep!' It sounded like a whip being cracked. And occasionally parrots of startling scarlet or vivid crimson broke from cover and flapped leisurely into the bush.

When he reached the fork, he could appreciate more fully the ascent he'd undertaken in the dark hours. And, knowing approximately where to look, he could make out the overhanging shelf of rock. He wondered whether any intrepid wench was entertaining her boyfriend under that projecting canopy at this moment but discarded the idea. Even a very myopic nun might miss an errant student in broad daylight, and to be seen breaking cover from that general direction would be to court disaster. For a similar reason he'd not even considered risking a sight of Clare Galway, this afternoon.

Instead he continued along the lower track, keeping a weather eye out for any likely meeting place. A few minutes later he found what he sought. He had to abandon the track and push his way through the leathery-leafed shrubs that abutted it, but his first thought proved correct. This site was much smaller than the Rock, and the canopy overhead would offer less than half the shelter in inclement weather, but the surface was smooth and relatively less cluttered with the habitual debris of gum leaves and bark. At the far end of the narrow ledge a blackened circle of stones suggested that, at some time in the past, other hikers had discovered and made use of the spot.

He seated himself, legs dangling over the edge of the shelf, and enjoyed his lunch, conjecturing as he bit into a chicken drumstick and washed it down with water what Clare might be doing at this minute. Ten past two; a very sophisticated hour for lunch. Would she and Lyndal Murphy be wandering down to the place where first he'd encountered them, last Sunday? Might they be discussing him? He hoped not, he thought not. Clare had intimated as much. But then, he really knew so very little about her. Gut feeling might not be the best arbiter.

The view before him was spectacular. The near-vertical side of the escarpment, up which he'd scrambled so painfully last week-end, stretched dramatically away to the right; the floor of the deep valley was thickly wooded. Beyond, against a dazzlingly cerulean sky, the far cliffs shimmered in the haze of summer. It was easy to understand why they were called the Blue Mountains.

Last Sunday. Only a week ago. How come his very thinking, his whole way of life had been rendered topsy-turvy in so short a time? Clare might not like the suggestion that magic was involved, but she'd certainly voiced the same thought in other words. And Tom, himself, was not in doubt. There was no other explanation of what had happened that suited his rationale.

15

In the next days Tom made two important discoveries. The first was that, once acclimatised, the average human body could adapt perfectly well to sleep deprivation. Only sad guys needed more than six hours a night. The second, and equally important, was that there was no need to compromise on standards at work, merely because fifty percent of your brain was actually some distance away and involved in totally irrelevant matters. He set about his tasks with a surprising clarity of thought, quite unclouded by the images of a certain young woman, which constantly came between his eyes and the PC monitor.

The nights took on a pattern of their own. Secreted in their own, private place, he and Clare would meet and talk and go their separate ways. Thus, he knew more about convent life than he'd ever imagined possible, and quite a lot about her adoptive mother, and the sheltered nature of her upbringing, and a certain neighbour called Mr Hamilton who appeared to feature quite frequently. And Clare, in turn, learned at least in part about the workings of a multi-national conglomerate and corporate life. Tom described for her his houseboat home; how morning sun could transform the Cascades and, of course, told her about Elliot. He left any mention of Sandi out of these conversations and Clare saw fit not to ask again, perhaps fearing what she might hear.

Their meetings always ended with a kiss, but that was as far as it went. Body contact was confined to hand-holding and close, but restrained, proximity.

What might happen in the future was, of course, a topic of

considerable interest. Tom tried to imagine a life that did not include Clare, and failed.

'If we hadn't met,' he asked one night, 'what did you plan to do with your life?'

'Sit my HSC at the end of the year. That's our Higher School Certificate. Then go on to uni.'

He'd talked enough to Greg and other Sydneysiders to be conversant with the Australian penchant for abbreviating any word that could be shortened.

'And what would you study?'

'Modern languages. Japanese, probably. I'm doing that and French for my HSC.' In the semi-darkness she pulled the sort of face that stripped her of half a dozen years.

'Say no more. You've impressed me already. So you're the studious sort.'

Clare didn't play at being mock modest. 'I find learning easy. Especially languages.'

'And does your mother approve?'

'Oh, she considers education the most important thing in the world. She just wishes she'd had the chance.'

The long drive back to the hotel afforded Tom ample opportunity to reflect on all of this. Knowledge that Clare was fast becoming an integral part of his life could not fully counter his reluctance to be seen as a cradle-snatcher. It seemed to Tom that the obvious course of action was for her to continue with her education. They could marry after that. He wondered whether there was any long-term CompuSoft assignment likely to crop up this side of the Pacific. Such a solution would address both problems but, if not, he'd have to make sure he returned on a regular basis to be with her. They might become engaged. That would allow official acknowledgement of their relationship. A ring was not ideal, but better than nothing. He could even imagine himself approaching the elderly mother, figurative cap in hand, to seek permission to court her only child. The idea brought the ghost of a smile to his face. He could hear himself trying to explain that theirs had been a whirlwind, but totally chaste, relationship.

So things continued for the better part of ten days. It was on the Wednesday prior to his departure that the status quo altered.

The weather had been threatening to break for several days; today the atmosphere was menacingly charged, the sky yellow and oppressive. Tom, driving yet again toward the Highlands and the convent, thought that they might well become soaked before the night was out. Had it been possible, he'd have considered getting a message to Clare, cancelling their date. But that was impossible and, anyway, this ultimate meeting was too precious to squander for the cowardly fear of a soaking.

As he made his way along the familiar trail, the sky was parted by a sheet of brilliance, followed some seconds later by the anticipated rumble of thunder. The intervening gap suggested that the storm was still some distance away. With luck it might veer to the north and spare them. Before he reached their private haven, two more flashes illuminated the canopy of the valley far below. Was it his imagination, or was the storm retreating?

'Tom?'

Nature's display of pyrotechnics enabled him to notice, briefly, that as well as the usual robe Clare had brought along a functional, wet weather garment. The thunder crashed with increasing vigour as he seated himself beside her.

He leaned across to kiss her gently. 'I was afraid you mightn't come. Not with this weather.'

'You think I'm chicken?'

'Nope. I was being practical. I simply imagined sopping wet footsteps leading from the fire escape to a certain bed. Even a myopic old fart would need to be blind to miss a trail like that.'

'No problem. I'll just take off my shoes, once I'm back. Assuming that it does start to rain.'

'And you're not frightened by the thunder?'

The look she bestowed on him was at once scornful and endearingly youthful. Tom's heart turned over.

'Well, thank you for coming, anyway. You realise this is our last chance to meet until I can wangle another flight?'

Clare was seated with her knees drawn up, very much as she'd been seated that first time he'd seen her. Her nightie was too short

166

to cover much; the lightning briefly illuminated the long, smooth line of her thighs. There was no denying that solid rock did not make for comfortable lounging, nor did the debris of dry gum leaves equate even marginally with the luxury of pile carpet, let alone inner springs. But then, Tom thought wryly, this had been an unusual courtship from the outset.

He had arrived determined to suggest that they become engaged before he left for Seattle. It had appeared an easy enough suggestion when tried out in his head. Now it seemed far more complex in implication, as though in absentia he was becoming too possessive, laying claim to her.

Clare, he noticed tenderly, was keeping her eyes averted, as though she too was struggling with a private agenda.

He had an uncomfortable sense of foreboding. 'Is anything up? You're not in trouble, are you?'

'No. Nothing like that. It's just that . . . well . . .'

'Well, what?'

She glanced across at him. 'Tom, will you do something for me?'

'Sure. If I can.'

She knotted her fingers together beneath her knees. 'Will you have sex with me?'

He was stunned into silence. 'I . . . can't.'

'You mean, you're impotent?'

Even that slur upon his manhood did no more than pinprick. 'Hell, no. It's just that I can't. It's not right.'

But he knew, even as he said the words, that his concept of Clare might not necessarily be her own. Purity was in the eye of the beholder.

'Because I'm a Catholic?'

'That, and other reasons.'

'But they don't count. And I'm over-age, so it's not illegal. Nor would it be rape or anything. Not if I've actually asked you.'

Tom, still in shock, redirected the conversation. 'Why do you want me to?'

Clare looked out over the darkened valley. 'I'm the only one of us who's still a virgin. For some reason, it's thought to be really important, the difference between being a kid and being a woman. I've been seen as different all my life and I absolutely loathe it. That's why.'

'It's a pretty dumb reason for . . . having sex. In order to emulate your buddies.'

She glanced at him again. 'So you won't? Not even when I ask you.'

He paused to select his words with care. 'Listen, Clare. You'll be at university within a year. Are you imagining that all the guys there will regard you as a freak? Forget it. You're far too lovely. They'll be falling all over themselves to get you between the sheets.'

Hell, why had he said that? The very thought of other guys casting carnal glances her way gave him a fit of the screaming heebie-jeebies. That was the focal reason why he wanted them to be engaged.

'But I don't want other guys. I'm asking you.'

He took a deep breath. 'Clare, we can't. All other things aside, we haven't any protection. Even if you're Catholic, it would be wrong to risk getting you pregnant.'

By way of answer she reached into the pocket of her robe and pulled out a small package. 'That's not a problem.'

He winced. 'Lyndal?'

'Of course. Actually, they've been in my pocket ever since the first time we met at the Rock. Lyndal . . . the other girls . . . can't imagine a bloke who wants to do anything except shag. They think we've been doing it all the time.'

Again, he cringed. Why was it that any mention of that wretched bimbo removed some of the lustre? Not to mention Clare's use of words like "shag." He summoned his strength and tried another ploy.

'And why me?'

Clare took his hand and counted out her reasons with his fingers. 'Because you're kind. Because I know you haven't been meeting me just for sex. Because I trust you.'

'Trust me? In what way?'

She looked up to meet his eyes. 'From what the other girls say, it hurts sometimes. I can trust you to be gentle.'

He paused. 'And you've thought about this? Really thought about what we'd be doing?'

'Yes.'

He found he was holding his breath until his chest felt unnaturally tight. He exhaled slowly. 'My darling, I'm not prepared to have sex with you; but I will make love to you. There is a difference, you know.'

'You will? Really? Thank you.'

She had discarded the all-weather coverall; now she knelt up and peeled back the robe, then crossed her arms and pulled her short nightie over her head in one fluid movement. Tom, almost overwhelmed by the powerful response this action kindled in him, fumbled for his belt. He was all fingers and thumbs, as though the magnitude of his emotion rendered him clumsy. Finally bare, he leaned across to kiss her, playing as he did so with her cascade of blond hair, then ran a tender finger along the smooth skin of each inner thigh.

'You see, this is the difference between sex and making love. Sex is all over in a few minutes. Love-making comes from the heart, and it takes time.'

And so, in the most unreal of surroundings, and as the forces of nature gathered strength and played out their histrionics, the prince introduced the maiden to the masculine physiology, and then deflowered her to the mutual satisfaction of each.

Then the rain came.

It was no more than Act Two of the drama; as though the gods themselves wanted to demonstrate their power. The overhanging rock provided next to nothing in the way of shelter. Even huddled together as far back as the ledge allowed, with their feet in the blackened circle of embers, slanting shafts of water ricocheted off the edge and stung against the parts of their bodies and faces that the waterproof could not cover. Clinging together wasn't only from choice; the mutual warmth was welcome, too. Even speaking became difficult, amid the incessant cracking and rumbling.

Clare's hair hung in dripping strands, her face was covered with

169

beads of rain. Tom put his mouth against the moist semicircle of her ear so that she could hear. 'How long is this likely to last?'

'It can go on for ages. Hours, if there's no wind about to move it on.'

Tom wondered how the storm had crept up on them, appearing, it seemed, out of nowhere. 'There must be some wind up there.'

Clare shivered. 'Let's hope so.'

The possibility of pneumonia raised its ugly head. Tom attempted to think practically.

'Would it be better if we tried to get you back? We could at least get as far as the Rock. It must be drier there. Or we could make for the car and I could drive you back to school.'

Clare giggled. 'That would be fun. What would you tell Sister St Francis? "Here's your star pupil. I've just fucked her."'

'Don't say that. Don't use words like that.'

She turned to kiss him on the cheek, damp lips against damper skin. 'You're awfully romantic, aren't you.'

'I guess. Where you're concerned,' Tom replied miserably.

They lapsed into silence as the rain beat relentlessly down, splashing against them as though teasing their inability to escape it. Then, as suddenly as it had started, the storm ceased. Just evaporated away. One minute the sky was ink-laden and oppressive, the next it was a wide, star-strewn expanse, the storm no more than a diminishing bank of cloud.

Tom stood with difficulty. There wasn't a part of him that didn't ache, including his dick. Evidently Lyndal's current beau must be a midget, if the size of that condom was any indication. That part which he held most dear had not taken kindly to being half-strangled. Was it possible to get gangrene of the penis? And two hours of sitting on rock, not to mention being soaked to the skin, had done its own peculiar damage. He pulled Clare to her feet. Her sneakers and legs were splotched with mud from the driving rain, her hair was a mess, but she still managed to look lovely.

Together they inched their way back onto the path. It wasn't easy, because what was a straightforward trail when dry now became treacherous. Once more Tom had to be grateful for the tenacity of the Australian flora and its ability to provide sturdy handholds. They stopped at the fork in the path.

Tom took Clare in his arms and kissed her. Properly. 'Does it feel any different, being a real woman?' he whispered.

She smiled up at him. 'It feels . . . full.'

'Is 'full' the Australian word for satisfied?'

'I suppose so. Thank you, Tom, for being so nice.'

'Most guys would like you to say, "for being such a tremendous lover. For being so good at it." '

Clare fiddled with the top button of his shirt. 'How would I know? I've had no other experience to compare it with.'

'But you enjoyed it?'

She reached up to kiss him gently. 'I enjoyed it a lot. I think you must be a real stud.'

Words like stud should not be in her vocabulary, either. Not in an ideal world.

'You know that this is goodbye, for the present?'

The monumental events of the night had wiped from his mind his determination to suggest they become engaged. Should he suggest it now? But the thought of dropping on one knee in mud was too farcical to contemplate, and Clare deserved better. Moonlight alone was not enough. She deserved a romantic setting and violins and flowers. He knew already that he'd be back, perhaps to coincide with her school-break in April. That way he could approach her mother. He'd had enough of this hole-in-the-wall sort of dating.

'Yes. When are you likely to be in Sydney again?'

'Soon. I promise.'

'And you'll write?'

'I've promised that, too.'

Their clothes were beginning to steam, as the summer heat reasserted itself. Perhaps he could discard the possibility of pneumonia.

'We look as though we've just showered with our clothes on.' He kissed her again. 'Clare, you have to go. But be careful. That incline's going to be hideously slippery.'

171

She looked reluctant to leave. 'I will.'

Tom watched her set off up the track which led toward the Rock, and subsequently the convent. He tried to imagine her creeping across the waterlogged lawn, up the iron steps of the fire escape, discarding her soaking clothes – where? – and padding on damp feet back to her bed. Was there a handy towel to wipe away the telltale sequence of moist footprints? And what might be the punishment for girls discovered to be keeping midnight trysts? A thousand Hail Mary's? A diet of bread and water? Instant expulsion?

He turned his back and started along the path to the car. He'd gone less than a hundred yards when he heard her scream. You read of sounds that curdle the blood. This sound did just that to Tom. On feet urgent with terror, he retraced his steps and pushed his way up the face of the escarpment toward the Rock. Adrenaline gave him a turn of speed he didn't know he possessed. He did not have all that far to go. Clare lay in a crumpled heap, still clutching the perfidious shrub which had abandoned its perch and betrayed her. Her foot seemed to lie at an appallingly unnatural angle.

'Clare?' No reason to whisper now. That scream could well summon the entire sisterhood, were they on the prowl. He thought she had fainted, but as he knelt beside her she opened her eyes.

'I'm sorry.' Her voice was fuzzy with pain.

'No need to apologise, darling. Not your fault.'

'It's my ankle.'

'I can see.'

He leaned over to stroke the hair back from her brow as he thought. Damn it. This was not the moment for panic. This was the time to be totally practical. He glanced up. The climb to the Rock was hazardously steep at the best of times, almost impossible when carrying an injured young woman. Had he been dumb to imagine that she could undertake it after all that rain? But that implied hindsight. He could save the self-flagellation until later. Now, his immediate task was to get Clare to shelter and treatment. He looked again at the contorted joint. No doubting that it was broken; normal feet couldn't turn themselves like that.

'It's going to need setting, probably under anaesthetic. Is there a hospital anywhere near?'

Her face was distorted with the agony. 'Not for miles. The local hospital was closed down last year.'

'Then what about a doctor?'

She tried to rise, then quickly gave up the attempt and sank back onto the ground. 'There's Doctor Moses. He comes to the school.'

'And you know where we can locate him?'

'No.' She closed her eyes. 'He just appears.'

Should he make the ascent himself, and summon help from the nuns? That way risked his falling, as well. The thought of them both lying injured, perhaps until morning when Lyndal and her cronies made the interesting discovery that Clare was not in her bed, concentrated the mind wonderfully. And, anyway, what could even the most intrepid of women do in such a case? Summon a helicopter? Maybe hours away.

'I'm going to take you back to Sydney. I know where there's a casualty department. I've seen the signs.' Many times, he could have added, but was grateful at least that the information had sunk in.

The two kilometres back to the car were a nightmare for them both. Tom did his best, with what was available. He made a rudimentary splint out of brushwood, lifting the injured joint as tenderly as he could, first cushioning it, then strapping the whole with strips of his own shirt, reinforced by the cord of Clare's robe. Then, as carefully as he could, he lifted her in his arms. Clare knotted her fingers behind his head and thus they proceeded by careful, painful inches along the track. The surface had developed the consistency of melting ice, slick and slippery. The possibility of their both ending up several hundred feet lower down the escarpment was never far from Tom's mind, and added extra caution to every step.

He knew that Clare was doing her best to be brave, that each tiny jolt must be excruciating, and he admired her determination. Even so, every now and then a moan escaped her. And the journey in the car was another agony because, sick and shivering with shock, she could not even lie, but was forced to lean up against the door, so that her leg could be extended along the seat.

Tom simply drove, as fast as the law and common sense dictated. He did not attempt conversation because Clare had enough to contend with. Nor did he allow himself the luxury of blame. That, too, could come later.

They arrived at the casualty wing of the hospital he'd passed so many times three hours after Clare had first slipped in the mud.

16

It was only when Clare had been admitted and subsequently carried off to some inner sanctum for treatment that the enormity of what had happened fully hit Tom.

'Here. You'll need this. You'll find the public toilet along the corridor.' The young nurse tossed him a functional towel and indicated with her head.

Still stunned, Tom wandered along the dimly lit passage and switched on the light of the men's restroom. The brightness of the neon strip made him blink owlishly, but more appalling still was his own reflection, confronting him in the mirror. He'd not really appreciated just what a mess he was, sodden, splattered with mud from head to foot, his sneakers encrusted with an extra inch or two of clay. His hair stood out in grimy clumps, looking like a dead animal slapped on his head.

As he washed the worst of the storm's legacy off his face and arms he thought for the first time how they must have appeared, bursting as they had into the hospital lobby at three in the morning. Clare was still clad in skimpy nightie and robe, she was wet, muddy and in shock. The efficient reception nurse had shown little curiosity, so perhaps the staff saw them as a couple caught in the bush, maybe camping, when the accident occurred.

Stickler for the truth that he was, Tom could at least draw slight satisfaction that they'd not asked hard-to-answer questions. But that was only the first hurdle.

As clean as was possible in the circumstances, he abandoned the soiled towel and made his way back to the deserted visitors' waiting room. It was functional and unlovely, although someone had tried to cheer it up with a set of boldly coloured prints. A pile of dog-eared magazines had been carelessly gathered into an over-flowing heap. The artificial-leather chair emitted a fart like a whoopee cushion as Tom sat down and gave himself up to his misery.

How had they managed to turn an occasion that was essentially pure and lovely into something so tawdry and ugly? And what the hell was he to do now?

He tried to think rationally. It was just after four in the morning. If Clare's scream had been heard, there might well be nuns out scouring the bush at this minute for their lost ewe lamb. He had no idea what distance separated the convent buildings from the Rock, so he couldn't even conjecture. Had she not been heard, the convent would still be asleep and Clare's absence would not be discovered for another couple of hours. Clearly, he would have to inform the sisters that she was safe. The poor old bats deserved that reassurance. But still a dozen questions would need explaining, most of which made him cringe to contemplate.

He wondered whether Lyndal, whom he knew to share the cubicle with Clare, would waken in time to deflate the decoy doll. If not, that ruse was over for good. Clearly, fire escapes by their very nature could not be barred, but the nuns would find some other way to protect their nubile charges. Probably, he conjectured, it would lead to a gorgon sleeping in every dormitory. A pity they couldn't employ eunuchs like those in a harem. Either way, it would certainly mean the final days of the St Ursula's Whorehouse, at least for the foreseeable future.

But that didn't free him from blame or solve anything. He'd have to confess his part in what had led up to the accident . . .which led to another moment of panic. You couldn't expect to experience a deflowering without some blood. Hell, in medieval times they'd triumphantly paraded the nuptial sheets. He all but groaned. The Reverend Mother would probably demand his balls on a plate . . . not to mention Clare's adoptive parent. And, added to that, he was scheduled to fly back to Seattle in . . . he glanced again at his watch, still turned inward on his wrist . . . in nine hours.

176

He shifted uncomfortably on the chair, dropping his head onto his hands. What a goddamn mess it all was.

'Here, I've brought you a cup of coffee.'

Tom looked up. He'd not heard anyone approach. It was the nurse who had so opportunely presented him with the towel.

'Thank you. That's good of you.'

'That's okay.' She sat down beside him; chirpy, wide-awake and eager for something to break the monotony of a quiet night. 'Your girlfriend will be all right. She's in the operating theatre right now.'

'Yes, I'm sure she will be.' Tom wrapped his hands around the mug, not appreciating until now how welcome it was. 'Thank you.'

'You were pretty stupid, weren't you. Camping in the bush when there was a storm warning. Or didn't you hear the forecast?'

'I guess I'm pretty stupid.'

She stood, nodding sagely. 'Well, we all learn by our mistakes. You'll know better next time, I s'pose.' She turned at the door. 'I'll let you know when you can see your girlfriend, once she's in the recovery ward.'

Tom came to life. 'Er . . . nurse . . . I guess there's a public call box somewhere? I need to make a few calls.'

'The payphone's down the hall. Feel free.'

Even so, he waited for two long, unhappy hours before he braced himself to do so. During that period of enforced reflection he had decided upon a certain course of action. His first call would be to the convent; his second to the airline, his third to Dorothea Galway. Airline aside, he wasn't sure which call he dreaded more. The telephone system of every country has its own peculiarities, guaranteed to mystify foreigners. Sydney's system proved no exception. Its hostility put the crowning touch on Tom's frustrations.

The young nurse appeared at his side just as he returned the hand piece to the wall-mounted receiver.

'You can come now. She's awake.'

Tom followed obediently, feeling rather like a reprimanded puppy as he trailed his escort along miles of sterile corridor.

Clare's hair was still tangled and limp but the rest of her had been washed. She lay against the crisply white pillow looking wan and drained. Seeing her, Tom was almost overwhelmed with his love for her. The power of his emotion made his legs feel quite shaky.

'Here, have a seat.'

Tom thanked the nurse and sank gratefully onto the proffered chair. He took Clare's hand in his own.

'Hi.'

'Hello. Are you okay?'

He smiled tenderly. 'That's my line; I should be saying it to you.'

She returned his smile faintly. 'You know what I mean.'

'Yup.' He glanced at the nurse, who was still hovering.

She took the hint. 'I'll leave you alone, then. But don't be too long. Clare should get some sleep.'

Once the door had shut behind her he said, 'I called your school.'

She closed her eyes as though to block out all the implications of that simple sentence. 'Help. What did they say?'

'Well, I gather they'd yet to discover you weren't tucked up in your bed. I'm not sure which emotion took precedence, after that. Relief that you weren't lying at the bottom of the cliff, or rage. Probably rage. They sure were mad.'

'They?' Clare queried.

'Uh huh. I was handed from the old girl who answered the phone to the Queen Bee. And she has the ability to freeze your blood with a well-chosen word.'

'Mother Scholastica. She's actually quite nice. On a good day.'

Tom spoke with feeling. 'Not when she's accusing you of kidnapping her star pupil. And that doesn't include mention of words like seduction and sin.'

Clare squeezed his hand. 'Poor Tom. But that was really brave of you, taking the punishment for me.'

'No more than any guy would do.'

'Not true.' She opened her eyes again. They looked incredibly green against the pallor of her skin. 'It's today that you're flying home, isn't it?'

'Was. Past tense. I've managed to reschedule my flight.'

'You see, that's why you're brave. You could just have leaped onto your plane and fled the country.'

'Leaving you to face the music? Forgive me!'

She intertwined her fingers through his. 'Anyway, thank you. I feel much braver knowing that you're here with me.'

He leaned over and kissed her brow. 'And now, my darling, I need to let your mother know about what happened. Even if the Queen Bee has already informed her, I should make contact.'

'Oh, poor Tom. Worse and worse.'

He couldn't but agree. The very thought of the impending discourse turned his stomach into knots. But it had to be done.

'I was looking in the directory. There are dozens of Galways listed and I didn't know which was yours.'

Clare gave him the number and he wrote it down on the back of a very crumpled receipt that he found in a pocket.

He spoke soberly. 'Strangely enough, I'd had this idea of getting in touch with her, anyway.'

'My mother? Really?'

'Sure. I was going to suggest that we got engaged, maybe when I was next back in Sydney.'

Clare looked at him with widened eyes. 'What? You were going to ask *her* permission? Even before you asked me to marry you?'

He smiled at the vigour of her response. 'Not necessarily in that order. But I did have it in mind. And from what you'd told me she sounds the old fashioned sort, who might appreciate a bit of formality.'

'You were hoping to wheedle your way into her affections. Get in under the door, so to speak.' Her voice was stern. 'Cajole her.'

'Something like that.' He sobered up again. 'But your accident has kind of put a new complexion on things.'

Clare closed her eyes once more and he could see that she was reacting to the medication. 'That's the understatement of the year. She's going to flay us alive.'

'Perhaps we deserve to be flayed alive.'

'Maybe. But Tom . . . don't explain how I came to fall. Leave that to me.'

'You don't think I should tell her?'

'No. I know how to handle her. Just tell her that I'm here, and all right. Okay?'

'Okay, if you're sure.' He kissed her brow again, in tender farewell. 'Wish me luck.'

Fleetingly she squinted up at him. 'Good luck, Tom.

The conversation started well enough. Evidently the convent had not yet made contact.

'Mrs . . . Galway?'

'Miss Galway. Speaking.'

'Right. Miss Galway . . . my name's Tom Goulding, and I'm calling to tell you that Clare has had an accident.' This elicited no response so he hurried on. 'Not too serious. She broke her ankle.'

'Her ankle. I see. But not too serious.'

'No, ma'am.' His mother would be delighted, could she but hear this display of good manners. Validation for all that early ear-bashing.

'Did she fall, then?'

'Yes, she slipped in the mud.'

'This morning?'

It would have been so easy to say 'yes.' Let her find out later, when he was a few thousand miles away. But the truth was the truth was the truth.

'No, ma'am. Last night.'

'There was another pause as though she were assimilating this. 'Mr Goulding, last night's storm didn't break until near midnight. How could Clare have slipped in the mud then?'

He swallowed. 'Perhaps it would be better if you asked her that.'

The tenor of the woman's voice changed, became sharper and more insistent. 'And are you speaking from St Ursula's, may I ask?'

'No, ma'am. I'm calling from the hospital . . .' and he named it, ' . . . where I brought her. After the accident.'

180

The silence stretched along the line, laden with all the implications that had yet to be voiced. Speechlessness in itself was incriminating, Tom thought wretchedly. Perhaps he should plead the Fifth Amendment.

'Then clearly I should thank you, Mr Goulding, for coming to her rescue. And for informing me.'

Worse and worse. 'I don't deserve your thanks, Miss Galway. It was the least I could do.'

'And how is my daughter now?'

'Sleeping. Her ankle's been set but she's very tired. And suffering from shock.'

'I suppose she is.' Another pause. 'But she's able to receive visitors?'

'Yes, ma'am.'

Her voice was crisply decisive. 'Then I shall ask my neighbour to drive me to the hospital.'

'I could drive you myself, Miss Galway, if that would be easier.'

'No thank you, young man. I believe you've played your part.' And the phone went dead.

Tom stood, his back against the wall, and tried to assimilate the different strata of that brief conversation. Miss Galway appeared to be one step ahead of him, at all times. He had the feeling that she had read the situation, decided to put her own interpretation onto things, and to play it that way.

Was he being fanciful, his imagination influenced by his overwhelming assumption of guilt? Surely, at some time, she was going to ask about his role in all this fiasco. Then why not immediately? Why had she delayed asking that vital question? Well, he decided, returning the phone to the cradle, if he were about to meet his future mother-in-law, it behoved him to clean up a bit; change his clothes. He was pretty sure that to Miss Galway cleanliness would be seen as next to godliness.

They met ninety minutes later. By that time Tom was showered and wearing fresh chinos and shirt. He'd tossed his sneakers into the bin, unwilling to set about the task of cleaning them, finding that even to look at them was distasteful. That encrustation of mud spoke volumes, seeming to accuse him of so much by its very presence.

He was standing awkwardly in the visitors' waiting room when the pair walked in and he had an odd sense of deja vu, which was completely false and really stupid, because there was no earthly way that he and Clare's mother could have met before. And yet, as the upright figure came through the archway, he recognised her immediately. She was, perhaps, smaller than he'd anticipated and neat as a pin, from her straight, iron-grey hair brushed severely back from the brow, to her trim feet. She was wearing a lightweight skirt with a muted pattern, a crisply ironed white blouse and frameless glasses. Her features were nondescript, neither plain nor pretty, but somewhere in between. Tom knew her to be around sixty but, greying hair aside, thought that she might have been taken for twenty years younger.

Her escort was similarly lacking in height, but he carried himself with considerable dignity, which gave him stature to compensate for his lack of inches. Sharp, bright eyes surveyed Tom from either side of a ferocious nose, as prominent as an eagle's beak. His brows were like a bramble thicket, wild and disorderly.

'Miss Galway? I'm Tom Goulding.'

He held out a hand; the neighbour shook it. Clare's mother contented herself with a slight inclination of her head.

'Someone will be along to take you to Clare,' he pressed on gamely. 'She's expecting you. And I gather she'll be discharged this afternoon.'

'Indeed.' Hell, she could get a world of meaning into two syllables. But then she seemed to come to his aid. 'That sounds hopeful.'

'So it was quite a straightforward break?'

Tom turned gratefully toward the neighbour. 'Yes. Thank heavens, Mr . . . '

'Hamilton. Douglas Hamilton. I'm Miss Galway's neighbour.'

Hamilton; that was it. He should have recalled the name, because it cropped up frequently in Clare's conversation.

'I believe Miss Galway has one or two questions she'd like to

182

ask you, before she goes to see Clare. Perhaps it would be better if we all sat down.'

Tom braced himself for the worst. He glanced around the waiting room. It was still too early in the morning for the casualty wing to be getting into its stride. Three minutes after eight. At this moment the only other occupant was a young mother who was breastfeeding her baby, while her toddler was having a bead removed from up his nose. Tom knew all about the in's and out's of this trauma, because the young mother seemed to think her child's medical history was of universal interest. This, Tom had been informed, was the fourth time little Mitchell had seen fit to shove a foreign object up his nostril. Evidently the hospital looked upon their arrival as continuing episodes of an ongoing soap opera. Greeted them by name, and all. He hoped that she was more absorbed in nourishing her small daughter than listening to the inquisition about to ensue. Not that he could do anything about it, anyway.

'Sure.' The damn chair farted of course, but he could find no cause for amusement.

Miss Galway looked at him intently. 'I'm having difficulty placing you in this story,' she began. 'Do you work at St Ursula's? A gardener perhaps, or the driver of the school bus?'

'No, ma'am, to both of your questions.'

'So how was it that they asked you to drive Clare to hospital?'

She knew, Tom thought. She'd already talked to the Queen Bee. What she was wanting was for him to say something incriminating.

'I happened to be there.'

'*There*? At St Ursula's? And what time might that have been?'

He winced. 'As you reminded me yourself. Around midnight.'

There followed a long silence. Tom glanced at their fellow occupant. She was watching with undisguised interest, her mouth hanging open with overt curiosity. Even the baby rolled a round blue eye his way, apparently more engrossed in this potential lynching than in her sustenance.

'Mr Goulding, do you know my daughter?'

He blinked. It seemed the stupidest question.

'Yes. Of course.'

Mr Hamilton cleared his throat. 'I believe, Mr Goulding, that Miss Galway means "know" in the biblical sense.'

He'd agreed, at her suggestion, that Clare should break this news, but in agreeing he'd not really anticipated so direct a charge.

He swallowed. 'Yes, Miss Galway. Ma'am. I do.'

In his imagination this would be the time of retribution. He'd already figuratively removed his shirt for the lashing to follow. Maybe it would prove to be cathartic. He expected to see Clare's mother swell with righteous indignation, let fly at him in her rage. Instead, she seemed to crumple as though all her stuffing had been removed, like the Scarecrow's straw in *The Wizard of Oz*.

Tom was unprepared for this reaction and it made him feel a hundred times worse. But what the hell could he say that would not exacerbate the situation? To apologise would be as crass and insincere as blustering. There was a lot about Clare's accident for which he held himself responsible, not the least of which was allowing her to attempt that precipitous ascent in such conditions, but he refused to degrade what had happened between them by abject expressions of regret.

'I did not force myself upon your daughter, Miss Galway.'

The small woman appeared to draw herself up. She spoke with steely dignity, as though each word was being dropped into a bucket of iced water. 'I did not assume you to do so.'

Tom's torture was brought to an end by the arrival of an orderly. 'Mrs Galway? I'll take you to see Clare.'

She stood. 'Will you come with me, Douglas?'

'No, Thea. You go yourself. I'll meet you here in half an hour. Give Clare my love.'

Left alone, Douglas Hamilton seemed to relax.

'Come on, young man. Let's go outside and you can tell me exactly what happened. I'm in need of a smoke.' He patted Tom's back, as though their heights were reversed and it was he who towered some seven inches the taller. 'Filthy habit, but there it is. Too old to teach an old dog new tricks.'

17

Outside the day was still pleasantly mild, the summer heat not yet building. Douglas and Tom wandered around the side of the low complex of brick buildings that comprised the hospital, until they happened upon a secluded courtyard. The presence of several benches suggested that convalescing patients probably sought fresh air in this small oasis, but this was the hour of the post-breakfast snooze and the courtyard was deserted.

Douglas sat down. 'Does it bother you if I smoke?' His voice, Tom had noticed earlier, had an attractive Scottish burr.

'Of course not.'

He took his place further along the bench as the older man flicked a lighter and inhaled sharply. The morning sun was warm and soothing, the air sweetened by the fragrance of a pink frangipani growing in the adjacent garden.

'And I think you could do with a dram of this. You're looking drained.' Douglas reached inside a pocket, produced a hip flask and handed it to Tom. 'You do drink?'

It was so unexpected a gesture that Tom was taken by surprise. 'Sure; although generally not quite so early in the morning.'

'From what I can gather, it's also very late into your night. Have you managed any sleep at all?'

Tom accepted the hip flask gratefully. 'No. But then you could say I don't deserve any.'

'Now, why should I say a thing like that? I can remember being young myself, amazing as it might seem to you.'

Tom took a sip. Neat malt whisky. As the mellow liquor slipped down his throat, he could almost feel the metamorphosis within him. A re-awakening of the nerves and fibres and muscles.

'I still think I should explain.'

'I'm hoping you'll do so; expecting it of you.' Douglas drew deeply on his cigarette, exhaled with equal satisfaction and turned to look at him. 'But first I'd like to do a little explaining myself.'

This was even more unexpected. From all that he had heard, Tom had assumed the small man to be Miss Galway's champion. He'd even braced himself for a man-to-man sort of dressing-down, include phrases like, "conduct unbecoming," and "most ungentle-manly behaviour."

'What, exactly?'

'A bit of background. I have a great deal of admiration for Thea Galway and a vast reservoir of love for Clare. I've known her from infancy, from when her parents skipped off abandoning her with Thea. An enchanting child. But not exactly an advantageous start in life, one might say.'

'You mean, her parents just disappeared?'

'I mean just that. And in many ways Thea has done a fine job, and Clare has not disappointed. However, that said . . .'

Tom was feeling better by the minute, thanks to the contents of the hip flask. He turned to face his companion, intrigued.

'However . . ?' he repeated.

Douglas frowned slightly, so that his untidy brows were united across the high, beaky nose. 'Thea, like most of us perhaps, is the product of her upbringing. In her case, that means being the old-fashioned sort of Catholic, brimful with oppressive culpability, assuming that sin is lurking in wait between the paving stones. For myself, I see such religion as intolerable, trading on guilt as it does. However, I am neither Clare's natural nor adoptive parent.'

Tom was wondering how all this pertained to last night's events, but it seemed easier to stay quiet. No doubt Douglas would get to his point, given time.

'I have never been in the position to do more than advise. I hope my advice has been wise; occasionally it has been acted upon.' He paused, as though selecting his words with care. 'Now, add to the

186

religious angle Thea's own, celibate adolescence, and I think you'll see where I'm heading. Her own mother sounds, from what she has told me, to have been a repressed old harridan with vinegar coursing through her veins in place of warmth. So, well-intentioned woman that she might be, Thea never had the opportunity to meet a lad at the street corner; she has not, to my knowledge, experienced that rush of hormones which occasionally knocks us off balance. Do you get my drift?'

'Yes.'

'Worse than that, to my way of thinking, she refused to accept my suggestion that Clare would be better prepared for life by attending the local co-educational high school. To her, St Ursula's was quite literally the answer to a maiden's prayer. In this case the prayers of two maidens, Misses Dorothea and Clare Galway. Her much loved darling, and Clare is a truly beloved child, would be able to grow up safe from the disturbing influence of the opposite sex. She would be highly educated, chaste and pure.'

Tom was starting to experience a happy sense of well being. 'She was right in two out of the three. I think Clare is pure and she's certainly well-educated.'

Douglas turned to him again. 'And here's where you come in, I assume. So please pick up and continue the story.'

Tom sketched through the early part of the tale, from how he had met Clare when he'd stumbled upon her and Lyndal, down to bravely confessing to his part as reluctant voyeur, although hastening to explain to this unusual man his true purpose for being in the grounds of St Ursula's.

'I'm sure you're right about that sort of existence. It's totally unnatural. I had the creepiest feeling, when I was surrounded by all those kids that first afternoon. You could almost hear the hormones screaming for release.'

'Carry on.'

'Clare wrote me a note; then met me, out where I'd left my car. She appeared to know even where I'd park.'

Douglas inhaled again and watched the pattern of smoke as he released it. 'Not hard. You'd have driven out of Sydney. She's bright. She'd merely have walked along the roadside until she located your vehicle.'

'Do you appreciate that the after-dark comings and goings at that establishment make Grand Central look like nothing? They have their own trysting place, they have a booking system. Clare even arrived with a condom in her pocket.'

The eyebrows arched. 'A condom! Really? I give them top marks for that. The sisters can't have succeeded in totally cowering their spirits.'

Thinking about Lyndal and the other bathers, Tom thought that quelling their spirits was the last thing the nuns had managed to do.

'I found it grossly tacky,' he confessed. 'But Clare poured scorn on my suggestion that we should meet legitimately. In fact, it seems to me those kids get a kick from the clandestine nature of it all.'

'Think yourself back. Wouldn't you?'

Tom agreed reluctantly. 'Perhaps. Being on the other side, as it were, I hated it. And most of all I loathed the Rock. It has all the appeal of a brothel. I had to scour about for another place, more private.'

'And might I ask how long these assignations have been going on?'

'Just short of three weeks.'

'Really? I think the phrase these days is, "you're a fast worker."'

Tom grinned. 'More appropriate would be to say, "desperate." I've finished my assigned period here. They're all set up and running smoothly. I forgot to mention that I'm a computer consultant. I should have been flying home today.'

'And where is home?'

'Seattle, Washington.'

'I see.'

They sat in silence a minute, Douglas puffing contentedly away, Tom happily allowing the sunshine to recharge his batteries. Then Douglas changed the subject, sparing Tom the necessity to complete his narrative. Perhaps, he thought, the final act could be assumed without being spelled out in detail.

'Might I ask your intentions? I know that sounds old-fashioned, but I'm an old-fashioned sort of fellow.'

188

'Totally honourable, I promise. In fact, I was going to suggest we announced our engagement, next time I'm in Sydney.'

'You don't think Clare is rather inexperienced to commit herself to one lad? Especially the first lad she's ever had any dealings with?'

A small cloud formed on the horizon of Tom's euphoria. 'Uh huh. I have thought of that. Plus the fact that she should complete her education.'

'So . . .'

'So that was why I'd just suggested an engagement. Not marrying immediately, or anything too drastic.'

Douglas had finished his cigarette. He stooped to stub it out, then carefully dropped the butt into a small, metal box which he took from the inside pocket of his jacket. 'I assume you're hoping that a ring will deter other young hopefuls?'

Tom shrugged. 'I can't lock her away again. Nor would I want to. A ring's about the best I can manage.'

'Let me put it to you this way, Tom . . . I may call you Tom? . . . Might it not be better to keep your relationship informal? For Clare's sake more than for yours, I'll admit. But you have the experience, perhaps the sophistication, that she at present lacks. I gather that you love her very deeply. Maybe she feels the same about you. But you have no way of knowing whether she'll outgrow that love, when she meets other young men. Fellow students, if and when she does go to the university. At present you have, one might say, a captive, untested heart.'

The thought of losing his goddess was so painful that Tom all but cried out. He knew that Douglas had reason on his side, was, in fact, giving voice to the very fears that created his worst nightmares, but accepting them was no easier for all that.

'You're asking an awful lot of me.'

'An act of faith. I know. But perhaps you'll consider what I'm saying. For Clare's sake.'

Tom shrugged. When he was with her he felt so sure that she shared his growing passion. When apart, the doubts clustered as forebodingly as the clouds heralding last night's storm.

'I guess I have no choice. Although I can promise you I'll do my damnest to woo her.'

'That is different. A happy wooing could well be a very uplifting experience. For both of you.'

Because the subject appeared to have run its course, and because to belabour it was to lay himself open to flagellation, Tom returned to an earlier topic. 'You say that Clare's parents actually abandoned her. That does sound desperate. Can you tell me more?'

Douglas had the courtesy to allow the redirection of the conversation. Perhaps, having made his point, he saw no reason to continue.

'A strange couple. High on drugs most of the time. Thea stepped in there too, as it happened.'

'Stepped in? How?'

'I scarcely knew her at that time, but with hindsight she showed considerable courage. In the 'seventies we weren't as conversant with the effect of drugs on the foetus, but I'd witnessed the problems of alcoholism, and it occurred to me that drugs must be similarly harmful. When Thea sought my advice we discussed this, and as a result she more or less kidnapped Perdita. She kept her from her druggy chums and forced healthful fare upon her through the pregnancy. Clare, as a result, suffered absolutely no ill effects.'

Tom sat up abruptly. 'Did you say Perdita?'

'Yes. Perdita and Shaun were her natural parents. Why do you ask?'

'It's just that I happened to know a Perdita, as well. In San Francisco. It's an unusual name.'

'As I remember, Clare's mother was Perdita Potts. The father was something like Leberman. They weren't married, of course.'

Tom relaxed again. 'The Perdita I knew was Perdita Svenson. Clearly another person.'

'And living in San Francisco, you say?' Douglas glanced at his watch. 'I think our time is up. Thea will be wanting me to take her home.'

They both stood. Douglas turned to Tom and held out his hand.

'I've enjoyed our conversation, and I think we understand each other. Don't be too hard on yourself, young man. Clare is an exceptionally beautiful child. I'd fall in love with her myself, in another incarnation. Or were I to believe in such things.'

Tom took the outstretched hand. 'I'll never forgive myself for letting her try to climb that hideous trail. I should have insisted on taking her back by the road. Even driving her to the school, if necessary.'

Douglas raised one brow into a perfect question mark. Tom found himself fascinated by the mobility of those two shaggy features. It was as though they had lives of their own.

'That would indeed have been interesting. In fact, I'd have been prepared to pay a goodly sum for the privilege of witnessing your arrival at the door of that establishment of incorruption. Your reception would have been truly an education. And I'd add an extra $100 to hear the beauty of your explanation.'

Tom grinned, warming to Douglas Hamilton by the minute. What a guy. He could understand why Clare thought so highly of him.

'You're right. It might have taxed my powers of oration. And I've enjoyed meeting you too, sir. I hope I have your approval . . . for my wooing.'

The brows met together, parted, were raised. 'Maybe. Maybe. If I consider you're good enough for Clare.'

Clare was released later that day, into the waiting arms of her mother. They departed in a taxi. Tom was not even allowed the luxury of driving them home. Nor was Douglas Hamilton present to offer support. It was good to have an ally, but in the business of future courtship it took only a glance at the frosty exterior of Thea Galway for Tom to know that in her he had at least one formidable foe.

Clare looked subdued and pale. It was evident that she had been crying. Snails' trails of silver down her cheeks were proof, if proof were needed. Her ankle and foot were encased in plaster and a candy-striped nurse pushed her in a wheelchair to the waiting vehicle. Tom longed to take her in his arms and wipe away her tears, but when he approached them Thea Galway said tartly, 'I think you've done enough damage, Mr Goulding. Kindly step aside.'

Tom did know where they lived now, but it did not seem sensible to press his claim at this minute. Better to let them talk things over, parent and child, settle down, come to an agreement as to how they would approach the reverend sisters at St Ursula's. Would Clare be expelled under a cloud of disapprobation, and forbidden to sit her entrance exams to the university? Did a full confession to the priest, followed by an act of extreme contrition, equate with forgiveness? Tom had no idea. He was privileged only to watch the taxi speed away, taking with it his goddess and her mentor. Her personal gorgon. Perhaps the girls of St Ursula's were right. Perhaps Thea Galway was a witch.

Back in the impersonal comfort of his hotel room, released for the couple of days he could spare before the pressure of work claimed him back, he began to reconsider the discussion with Douglas Hamilton. At the time he had been warmed by the guy's consideration in producing that Scottish liquid magic, and by the good sense he exhibited. But, upon reflection, Tom wondered if he'd not actually been taken for a patsy. Played like a fish on the hook.

Did the Galways' supportive neighbour actually have another agenda? Could it be that the whisky and the man-appealing-to-man talk was simply a way to soften Tom up, prior to issuing the death-blow to his and Clare's relationship?

You could read it that way, but on reflection Tom decided not to do so. There was too much about Douglas Hamilton that he liked, and it would need a very devious mind to be so open at one minute, so deceitful the next. And, the crunch, he needed an ally. Even if their aims at this minute did not totally correspond, it might be that in the future he could persuade Douglas to side with him. In the meanwhile, he'd make one final attempt to contact Clare tomorrow, before he boarded the plane to Seattle and home. All other things aside, it would be good to see Elliot.

It seemed curiously strange to be lounging in an overstuffed armchair and not contemplating a lengthy drive to St. Ursula's. He wondered whether the adolescent nymphomaniacs were on bread-and-water rations. Remembering that painfully tight condom, he might have said, 'serves them right'; but instead he felt sorry for the girls.

He fell asleep in front of the television at four-forty seven and slept through until morning. Then discovered that his back ached like an over-stretched shoetree.

18

You can criticise me as much as you like, but I'll defend myself to the end.

When that young man telephoned to tell me about Clare's accident, it was as though I'd been anticipating such an event all of her life. And, of course, dreading it. Just the sound of his voice made me go cold.

I'm not going into the "nature" versus "nurture" argument again, it receives too much airing as it is in my opinion. But you must accept that Clare's birth parents weren't a pair well versed in ethics, or not in the way I understand the concept, and it seemed to me Clare needed all the help she could get to combat the influence of her particular genetic inheritance. And, as reinforcement to my belief, there was always the influence of Bunny, lurking in the wings as it were. Not that Bunny did, actually, surface – but I lived with that possibility. There was no doubt in my mind that Bunny was the naughty little girl Clare would have liked to be, given the opportunity. And what a catastrophe we might have faced, had she and Bunny actually decided to swap places.

That was the prime influence in my selecting St. Ursula's for her.

Now, I don't want this to be taken out of context. I am not overly influenced by those unfortunate events in my early life, the small affair of Donal and his wee-wee, and the very disgusting thing that happened at Luna Park; but you can forgive me for thinking that there are, in this world, certain men and boys with only one thing on their minds. And am I to be castigated because I wanted to spare my darling from truly unpleasant experiences like that?

St. Ursula's seemed so very right. Even the name, for it was the blessed St. Ursula who was reputed to have led her eleven thousand virgins on pilgrimage from Britain to Rome. I've often wondered a bit about that number – eleven thousand is a vast horde for one stalwart figure to lead – but even if history has distorted the number a bit, the idea of a brave troupe of chaste women certainly appeals to something in me. And then there was the convent's position, more than twenty kilometres from the nearest township, and that in itself no more than a small, shopping centre, supplying the farming community. And the Reverend Mother, an admirable woman, assured me that they did nothing to foster visits from the town's young men.

In a lovely, rural place, she explained to me, with handsome old buildings set in a very fine park, the girls could grow into a community of happy, well-educated young women. They could be sheltered from the seedier aspects of modern city life and spared the influence of less refined people.

But despite all this, my darling, my darling, *was ravished by an interloper, an intruder into that happy community. And an American, to boot. It appears that every time a person with a Yankee accent enters my life he or she's up to no good; apart from the blessing of leaving me Clare, of course.*

And then you expect me to be polite to him. To welcome him as a guest? The very creature who has defiled the person nearest and dearest to me?

All very well to tell me that she was not unwilling. I know all about the temptations of the flesh; not at first hand, exactly although I can remember feeling quite . . . wobbly . . . on occasions when I was a girl, although my mother soon shook it out of me. But I'm a reader, and I've read enough to accept that handsome young men can be quite persuasive, if they set about getting under your defences. And then Father Flaherty in his day, and the new young priest after him, have frequently taken the sin of copulation outside of blessed matrimony as text for their sermons. And very powerful speakers they have been as well, although it did strike me as more than a touch hypocritical that, after years of exhortations against the sin of unnatural practices, Father Flaherty should confess to being overly fond of the altar boys, to the extent that he retired most suddenly three summers ago. Extended sick leave, they called it. Thank goodness the young priest has such an exemplary character.

But I'm straying from the subject of Mr. Tom Goulding.

I knew, the minute I clapped eyes on him, that we were in trouble. It would have been easier had he not been more than average good looking. Had I been able to point out to Clare that he shared his features with a male orang-utang, it would have eased my path; but even I, ready to hate Mr. Tom Goulding, had to admit that he was very film-star in his appearance. He has that sort of glossy, dark hair which will probably go silver early but in a most distinguished way, and fine hazel-brown eyes, a cleft chin which is often a very attractive feature, and creases down his cheeks when he smiles that would turn many a head more susceptible than mine. And, like all Americans, his teeth are very even and white. I've often wondered why that is. You see it from the Osmond family to their presidents, so I've concluded it must be a national characteristic.

You see, I've been totally honest in my description, because I'm trying to set the record straight and prove that I'm not a biased person. Simply, at this minute, a deeply upset and anxious parent.

Also in his favour, I suppose, I should record that he seemed to have quite a manly physique. I won't attempt to describe it, because words like pec's don't come easily to me, but I can record that he is maybe an inch or so over six feet and neither hollow chested nor beer-bellied.

So, what was to be done? There was Clare, at home when she should have been at school, her foot encased in heavy white plaster, looking terrible and admitting to me that she was no longer the pure young girl who had returned to St. Ursula's only a few weeks earlier. I dismissed her avowals that Tom was "different" and "respected her" as silly, adolescent babble. How could she know that he was different? Come to that, how did his supposed reluctance to do what he had done signify respect?

'That's the ploy every man uses,' I all but snorted. 'And has done so, since time immemorial. They're adept at it, especially

196

worldly, practised men like that Mr. Tom Goulding. And you can stop your snivelling . . .' I added, ' . . . because you won't be seeing him again, except over my dead body.'

Clare's snivelling turned into a veritable Niagara; but I was being cruel to be kind.

'But he'll be leaving tomorrow,' she wept. 'I'll die if I can't see him before he goes home.'

'Nobody ever died of a broken heart,' I retorted. 'And I'm proof of that.'

She actually stopped crying long enough to ask, 'You? How come?'

Then I wished I hadn't raised that matter. 'There was a young man, once,' I muttered.

'And you were in love with him?'

'I won't go as far as to say that. But I liked him, yes. I thought about him.'

Clare mopped her eyes with a tissue. 'And what happened?'

'Nothing happened. Any more than will happen to you. My mother put her foot down, very firmly. Pointed out that he was grossly unsuitable. Not even of good stock, let alone a Catholic.'

'Oh, poor Thea. I never knew that you suffered from unrequited love.'

I'd made her a cup of tea and buttered a scone, and as I spoke I put them carefully within reach, because she was scarcely mobile with that great, heavy impediment of plaster.

'And no more I did. I knew that my mother was right; he was not a suitable person at all. Although he did have very regular features. Rather like Gregory Peck, I thought at the time.'

But even with these diversionary tactics I couldn't prevent her thoughts from returning to that irritating male who had intruded into our happy, peaceful lives. I could see she was going to be thoroughly tiresome. So, in the end, I returned to my respected counsellor. I left Clare watching television, with her leg up on the sofa and a pile of cushions behind her back, and the box of tissues close at hand in case she was overcome by another fit of weeping. Then I went out my front door and up the neighbouring path and rang the bell.

'Ah, Thea. I've been expecting you. How's the invalid?'

Over the years I have come to respect Douglas' wisdom and to rely upon it. We don't always see eye to eye, which stands to reason, his not being a Christian; but on the whole his advice has always been of the soundest.

He stood aside so that I could enter, and led the way along the narrow passageway to the room that opened out at the rear of the house. When Jeannie was alive, the Hamiltons had decided to have the wall between the kitchen and sitting room removed, making a larger living area. For myself, I would never paint a room that particular shade of green – but tastes differ, as we all know, and men are notoriously lacking when it comes to such matters. Then he poured me a small tipple of his best malt whisky. In our years of friendship I've developed quite a taste for a quality whisky, just as I think I have educated Douglas' palate in the matter of fine tea.

'Sit down, woman. You're making me nervous.'

Perhaps I should digress here briefly, to explain his use of that word. Douglas calls me "woman" in two ways. When he's being friendly, I tell myself "woman" is nearly a term of endearment. When he's annoyed, there's an implied exclamation mark after the word, "woman!" which signifies his displeasure. Today's woman was definitely of the former variety. It was clear he appreciated my anxiety. So I sat down.

We sipped in silence. Then Douglas said, 'I trust you allowed that pleasant young man to drive you home from the hospital.'

I understood from the way he couched the sentence that he knew this not to be the case.

'We got a taxi. Unlike you, I can't sweep things under the carpet and pretend nothing has happened. This has been a truly terrible day. I was very upset.'

'Of course you were. And with justification. No accident is pleasant. But be sure that you don't shoot the wrong target.'

Sometimes he speaks like this, and at such times I have difficulty following his drift. Perhaps it's because of his police training.

'As far as I am concerned there is only one culprit, only one true sinner.'

'Woman, don't start pedalling your Christian gobble-de-gook at me!' There was very nearly an exclamation mark after that "woman." 'Stand back a minute, do, and get what has happened into perspective.'

I can't recall all that followed, not in detail, but he then proceeded to read me a lecture about how lucky Clare really was and, by implication, me. In Douglas' opinion, Clare was most fortunate that her first love affair was with so considerate and thoughtful a lad. I confess that neither word would have sprung to my mind, were I asked to provide a description of that particular person.

'You would not listen to me when I was pointing out the advantage, to a child such as Clare, to be gained from a co-educational school. Instead you assumed that by shutting her away in that nunnery you were going to inhibit her sexuality. Well, m'dear, you were always destined to fail.'

Even expressions such as 'm'dear' could not sway me.

'But . . .' Then I closed my mouth firmly. We'd had this argument so many times before. I stood my decision, but accepted that at this time I certainly needed Douglas, and his good counsel, more than he needed me. In my head I counted to ten, so that I would not say something I later regretted. Then I asked quietly, 'what, then, should I do?'

Douglas poured himself another dram but I shook my head when he offered to refill my glass. I know my limit.

'If you really want Clare to throw herself at this young man, fall headlong in love if she's not there already, and make a precipitous, unfortunate marriage, then you should forbid her ever to see him again. There's nothing like a bit of healthy opposition to strengthen the resolve; and if you doubt my words, just consider how helpful the harsh regimen of persecution was to the start of your own early church.'

Anticipating what he was about to say, I began to wish I'd accepted a second tot of whisky. I knew I should not enjoy his next words.

'You want this affair to die a natural death? Then guard your

tongue and hold back on your feelings of outrage and anger. You should welcome the young man into your house, you should even encourage the friendship. Clare has only this year before her examinations. Then she'll be at the university. And once there, did you really imagine that, with her looks, she was going to escape the attentions of her fellow students?'

'I thought . . . I suppose I thought . . .'

'Well, woman? What did you think?'

'I thought, perhaps, that her studies would keep her occupied.'

He drained his glass. 'Then brace yourself for some long and lonely nights. You're in for a period of major heartache.'

'But if I welcome . . . this . . . young man . . . can I expect her to lose interest in him?'

Douglas shrugged. 'Who can tell? He's as aware as you are of her youth. I tell you, Thea, he's a decent young fellow. You should be thanking him for not just walking away and breaking your darling's heart. Many lads have taken the coward's way out, in the past. Many will in the future. And if time proves that his and Clare's affection is enduring, well, you will have all the pleasure of preparing for a wedding.'

I had to swallow very hard at the mention of marriage. Why, Clare was still only a child! And I can't pretend that I was converted to Douglas' way of thinking. I knew I should always be distrustful of the person who robbed my darling of her innocence, but for the greater good I appreciated the importance of concealing my dismay.

I realised, at that minute, how fortunate it was that I'd introduced mention of Reggie Fosgill. Although he was, in fact, no more than a shadow I my mind – the memory of a memory, so to speak – it did give me a hook onto which I could pin my apparent change of mind, without looking foolish.

Tom Goulding came to say goodbye on his way to the airport. I believe it was only the knowledge that his departure would at least give me breathing space which allowed me to get through that terrible hour.

200

Of course, anybody else observing the pair out there in my back garden would have perceived a very touching little scene of farewell. I, in contrast, was only too aware of the intrusive nature of Tom Goulding's presence. At the back of the house my garden slopes away in a series of terraces. I pride myself that it is very attractive. There's a huge magnolia tree which dominates one level, magnolia grandifolia. *I have a delightful photograph of a very small Clare under that tree, face upturned, arms outstretched in a childish attempt to capture one opaque, descending petal. That photo, framed, was a little Christmas present from Douglas one year.*

At the time that Mr. Goulding knocked on the door, Clare was sitting in the shade provided by the cover of huge, glossy leaves. I hid my feelings of intense dislike and did my best to welcome him, although even to my ears the words sounded insincere.

'Good afternoon, Miss Galway. Ma'am.' Sycophantic. I think extreme politeness is as repellent in its way as gross rudeness.

'Good afternoon, Mr. Goulding.'

He had a large bunch of lilies in one hand. 'These are for you, ma'am. A sort of apology for Clare's accident.'

Lilies. An emblem of Our Lady, a symbol of purity. How dare he! Had he no sense of propriety?

I swallowed and said as graciously as possible, 'Lilies. How nice. Thank you, Mr. Goulding. I shall put them in water right away.'

'Tom.'

I stiffened. 'I beg your pardon?'

'My name is Tom, ma'am.'

I inclined my head. 'I think, at present, I prefer to say Mr. Goulding.'

I knew that I had offended him; nor could I undo that. A leopard cannot change its spots overnight. He followed me in silence along the hall and down the back steps into the garden. Only a blind man or true Philistine cannot have been impressed by the picture Clare presented, as she sat under the magnolia. She was wearing a very simple little sundress, deep green with a trim of broderie anglais,

201

her hair was in a long braid, although I noticed that she had taken trouble to plait it down the back of her head in a complicated pattern. The great, accusatory cast was the only discordant feature. As he followed me, I thought I heard Tom Goulding draw a sharp intake of breath and for once I was in sympathy with him. She appeared to have grown up suddenly; nor had she ever looked more lovely.

'Please go on down. I shall be in the kitchen, preparing us refreshments.'

There was method in my saying that. From the kitchen window I had a very clear view down the garden and I didn't want him to think he could start billing and cooing in a distasteful manner. After all, you can't always tell whether Americans share our sense of decorum.

I was too far away to hear their conversation, nor did I wish to, but in the privacy of the kitchen I did not have to compose my face to conceal my hatred. My hatred. Yes, it's a harsh word, and I choose it deliberately. I hated Tom Goulding, and all that he represented.

If you were in sympathy you might have described the little scene taking place outside as touching and romantic. If you shared my feelings you'd use words like maudlin and sentimental; stomach churning, like an overabundance of sugary foods. His dark head, her fair, so close together, the way they looked into each other's eyes. Even observed from a distance that look was more intimate than any kiss. I simply had to turn away, or I would have gagged.

I'd gone to the trouble of making a jug of lemonade. I use my mother's recipe which calls for a teaspoonful of tartaric acid, rather than the more customary citric. I do think it's superior. I had also made elegant little cucumber sandwiches, cut into triangles and with the crusts removed, and cream puffs with freshly whipped cream and, of course, my lamingtons. I thought that Mr. Tom Goulding might as well understand that we knew how to do things properly. He rose as soon as he saw me coming down the steps and came to take the tray from me. I thanked him as graciously as I could, thinking at the same time what a veritable Uriah Heep he was.

I saw as soon as I seated myself on the rug that I'd spread out on the lawn that Clare was wearing a new ornament, a teardrop pendant. She kept fingering it and I noticed that there was an unnatural spot of colour highlighting each cheekbone. The pendant looked disgustingly expensive. You can tell that by the quality of the chain. Low carat gold has a brassy look to it. I wished he would keep his exorbitant gifts to himself.

'And when do you intend to return to Australia?' I asked innocently enough.

'I'm not sure, ma'am, until I get back to work.'

'Ah yes. Tell me about your work.'

'Tom's a computer consultant,' Clare informed me, and I hated it that she was so knowledgeable, because it spoke of intimate little tête-à-têtes when such information was exchanged. 'He's sent on loan to any company that wants to install a new CompuSoft program. Tom customises it for them.'

'Indeed. Very interesting.'

For myself, I have no understanding of computers, and absolutely no interest. I do appreciate that they make matters like banking and finance easier, and Douglas certainly sings their praises with regard to his police work, but as far as I am concerned they might well be written in Swahili.

'But I shall be back as soon as my work allows me.'

Words like that, spoken with such vigour, made my stomach tighten into a knot again. I put down my glass of lemonade because I didn't want him to see that my hand was shaking. Why could he not just disappear back to America and leave us in happy, ignorant peace? But, as well I know, there is no turning back of the clock. As Omar Khayyam says,

The Moving Finger writes; and having writ,
Moves on; nor all your Piety nor Wit
Shall lure it back to cancel half a line.

Much as I would like it, I could never erase the events of the last twenty-four hours, nor cancel as much as one syllable.

203

He didn't stay long. After all, he had a plane to catch. I let them have exactly five minutes alone to say goodbye, and I deliberately went into the toilet so that I didn't have to watch them embrace. I can't tell you the relief I experienced when he finally climbed into his car and drove away. It was like the sun coming out after a spell of wintry weather; like reaching home when you've undergone a long, tiresome journey. Even Clare's obvious dejectedness did nothing to abate my sense of elation.

After I had tidied away the tea things Douglas appeared, as we had arranged. He had volunteered, good neighbour that he is, to drive Clare and me up to the convent. I had quite a few things to say to the Reverend Mother and I was most grateful that Douglas had offered to come with me. There are occasions when the support of a man is useful, such as when moving heavy furniture around, and informing nuns that they have been negligent in their guardianship. And, to quote Douglas, attack is by far the best form of defence.

19

In a way it was a relief to be home, even though the weather in the great Northwest was dark, forbidding and drear. Typical of late February. Iron-grey cloud masked the familiar peaks of Mount Hood and Mount Rainier as the plane circled the airport before descending. Seattle had an ominous blanket in place of a sky. It was quite an eye-opener to Tom to realise how his life had changed in the weeks he'd been in Sydney. He felt like a dishcloth that has been put through an old fashioned mangle. His namesake, Grandmother Thompson, had one such, and as a small boy he'd occasionally been asked to supply the manpower, finding satisfaction in stretching his muscles and watching the great iron wheel turn. His emotions felt squeezed similarly dry.

Elliot greeted him like one reprieved from Death Row, as though Bob and Joey next door had put him on seriously reduced rations and deprived him of all form of affection. Knowing this to be the opposite of the truth, Tom was able to crack a few jokes about cruelty to dumb animals.

During the long hours crossing the Pacific, around the constant supply of food and entertainment, Tom had tried to think rationally. The first item on the agenda, once clothes were laundered and CompuSoft informed of his return, would be to break it gently to Sandi that whatever there was between them was no more. Tom had no great misgivings about this. He liked Sandi well enough, and was happy to exchange their strictly sexual relationship for friendship. There was no way he could remain loyal to Clare while screwing another woman, and he had every intention of being loyal to Clare unto death. He was comfortably aware that Sandi knew the rules. She'd talked far too often about her dedication to her career, her horror at the thought of matrimony. To reinforce this aversion, she'd even regaled his ears with little anecdotes about other rocky relationships, in which too much was asked.

How could he explain Clare to her? A sprite of a girl ten years her junior, who had turned his thinking and his life upside down; had literally bewitched him, to the extent that he'd found himself prepared to break the law in order to make contact with her. Somehow, whichever way he tried to put it in words, the whole story of the skinny-dipping nymphomaniacs of St Ursula's, and his own craven role, sounded far-fetched in the extreme. Probably, he concluded, Douglas Hamilton aside it was a tale to be shared only with Clare, and then in their old age. Rocking side by side on the front porch, their blond-headed grandchildren playing happily at their feet, they'd be able to laugh together at that memory.

He'd had the good sense to stop at the airport Duty Free and buy Sandi an opal. It seemed compulsory to return from Australia bearing opals. He hoped that she did not misinterpret the fact that he'd been forced to settle for a ring. The only other gems available, without his going into serious debt, were triplets, wafer-thin slices of stone glued together to enhance their colour. He'd thought them tawdry compared with the milkier stones, and he did not want his and Sandi's easy association to end cheaply or acrimoniously. For a similar reason he called and suggested that they meet over a meal.

He might not have bothered. The evening was doomed from the start. The difference between a classy farewell and an expensively celebrated happy homecoming is far too narrow to be gauged with ease. Easily misinterpreted. He should never have selected that ring. Even an intelligent, sophisticated woman like Sandi was liable to misunderstand a gift like that. Tom realised very quickly just how stupid he'd been.

The restaurant he'd suggested overlooked Lake Union. Tom had selected it because of the excellence of its gastronomic repute. Lights rippled across the stretch of water and as they finished their meal a small float plane put down quite close to the restaurant and chugged across to the jetty. The atmosphere was comfortable and friendly. Now would seem a suitable time to offer his parting gift.

Sandi opened the small package and literally cooed at its contents. Then, to his considerable embarrassment, she slipped it onto her ring finger.

Hell, what did you say on such an occasion? He took a deep breath and mentally launched himself off at the deep end.

'I didn't mean it for that finger, Sandi. It's not an engagement ring. In fact, it's a sort of farewell ring . . . a goodbye gift.'

'F . . . farewell? Goodbye?'

He winced. 'Not absolutely goodbye. Not if you're happy to remain friends. I really would like us to be friends. But no more sex.'

'No more sex?' She all but shouted it. Tom, becoming more scarlet by the minute, glanced uneasily about at their fellow diners.

'No. Not really.' And keeping his voice low, he launched into his rehearsed little description of meeting Clare and falling in love.

Sandi looked as though she was going to cry. Like most men, he loathed the very thought of a scene. And here he was, about to be embroiled in the father and mother of all scenes in the centre of a very crowded restaurant.

'Sandi, let's go.'

He tossed on the table a pile of twenty-dollar bills, aware that the waiter was about to receive the tip of a lifetime, and helped Sandi into her coat. Her face was tight, her lips clamped together as though at any moment she would lose it.

Outside the night air was still, but bitterly cold. Certainly not the temperature for idle loitering.

'Let's walk.' Tom put a hand under Sandi's elbow and guided her along the path. There was a crispness to the last, wintry leaves underfoot, and an Arctic sharpness about the air. 'Sandi, I'm really sorry. I thought you'd understand.'

She spoke with difficulty. 'Understand what?'

They picked up the path which circled the lake. 'Are you warm enough, if we carry on?'

Sandi shrugged, then repeated her question. 'What was I to

understand? Being dumped?'

'Not exactly. Not so crude. But understand that a relationship like ours would always come to an end. It was intrinsic from the beginning.'

'Why should I understand that?'

Tom felt increasingly helpless. You thought you shared a mutual language with someone, that you were playing the game by an identical rulebook, and then discovered that the language had no common root, that the rules of the game had been rewritten.

'You told me often enough how you felt about marriage and commitment. Surely that meant that if, or when, I discovered someone I wanted to marry, we'd part. I thought that was obvious. I'd assumed it would be perfectly painless, for both of us.'

There was a sturdy railing along the walkway. Sandi stopped and leaned against it, looking out across the lake toward the dramatic silhouette of the old gasworks. She wiped a tear angrily away.

'You're a fool, Tom Goulding. You know absolutely nothing about women.'

Tom, joining her against the railing, kept his mouth shut. It seemed safer.

She made an effort to regain control of her voice. 'Think about it, for a minute. Imagine a couple, not so different from us. There she is, this successful woman, getting on well in her job, enjoying her life. Someone like me, say. Then she meets a guy who gives her the hots. Maybe someone like you. And this guy says, very clearly, "I'm not interested in getting tied up. What I want is sex, exciting sex with no strings attached."' Sandi turned her head to look at Tom. 'What does that woman like me say? "Oh dear, no. I'm only interested in a relationship that has a future." Then the guy like you replies, "Tough luck. Bye bye," and wanders off to search for someone else. Or instead the woman like me says, "Isn't that amazing! I feel exactly the same way. All I want out of life is lots of exciting sex. Certainly no kids, no commitments." She mouths all that garbage because this is what the guy like you wants to hear. And to make him feel comfortable she reinforces it. She says, "Do I look like Susie

208

Homemaker? Forgive me!"' She paused, ostensibly to blow against her hands, but Tom heard the catch in her voice. 'But all the time she's hoping and hoping that he'll change his mind. That one day he'll say, "This casual stuff is for the birds. Why don't we make it permanent?" That's what she's hoping, Tom. And instead he gives her a rock and tells her he's met someone else.'

'I'm so sorry, Sandi,' Tom said miserably, as this easiest of all his tasks grew in enormity before his very eyes. Then he made matters worse by adding, 'It was pretty expensive, the opal. Not a triplet or anything.'

'Damn the bloody opal!' She dashed one hand across her eyes. 'Oh fuck!'

And she grabbed Tom's jacket lapels, buried her face against his chest and burst into noisy, inconsolable tears. Tom held her close, upset for her, mad at his own obtuseness, and totally unable to rectify things.

It was late April before he could return to Sydney. By then Seattle was enjoying a spring with all the implied hope of a rainbow, and in Sydney autumn was flexing its muscles. Tom tried explaining at length to Elliot that he was not being abandoned because of a transgression, and Elliot put his head to one side and looked at his master with wise brown eyes, as though he totally understood.

During the period of separation Tom and Clare had corresponded regularly, so that Tom knew all about the nuns' mortified reaction to Douglas Hamilton's choice phrases of censure.

'I was told to leave the room, of course,' she wrote, 'but even waiting outside Reverend Mother's study I could hear it all. I really felt sorry for them. Of course, the minute Thea and Douglas had driven off they reverted to form and ladled on the icy treatment, which I suppose I deserved. There was a lot of talk about honour and the breaking of trust. Each time one sister dried up the next one picked up the theme to voice her outrage. By the time they'd finished, I felt as small as one of the junior girls. AND, you won't be surprised to know, Jane and I are no longer a prefects, which is tough on Jane who's only met her boyfriend a couple of *times, but who was brave enough to own up in the face of the Holy Inquisition. Lyndal held out longest, of course, although she's always been the ultimate sinner, so to speak. As well as that, they've instituted a system of special monitors, girls whose beds are plonk against the fire escapes, and whose duty it is to patrol each dormitory. Ghastly toads, the lot. The problem is, the fire escapes must be easily available at all times, for obvious safety reasons.*

'The good news is that they've not kicked us all out, because I'd have found it hard to transfer to another school and pick up my HSC studies.'

In return Tom sent her long, detailed letters, occasional small gifts, and descriptions of the places to which CompuSoft sent him. In March that was Tokyo, in early April, New York. Not too sure whether her letters might be censored, he refrained from avowals of eternal adoration, confining himself to a simple, 'all my love, Tom.' But all the time thoughts of her were just behind his eyes, at the forefront of his consciousness.

Sandi, a couple of weeks after the appalling moment beside Lake Union, called and asked if they could still be friends. Dreading a repeat performance, Tom replied cautiously, but it appeared that Sandi had come to a few painful decisions.

'Just friends, Tom. I've got another boyfriend. Honest.'

So they met for occasional lunches, and one Sunday afternoon walked with Elliot along the Burke-Gilman trail, which led from the university around the shoreline of Lake Washington, and was not too taxing for elderly pooches. Sandi even made an effort to be friends with Elliot, as though her aversion to him might have tipped the scales in Clare's favour. Tom was careful not to look too closely, in case the new-boyfriend disclosure was no more than a face-saver and he might see in her eyes a desperate longing he knew himself unable to fulfil.

But, once seated in the plane, knowing that Clare was a mere eleven hours away, Tom could let rip his feelings of exultation, that he was on the way to see his goddess. He thought that the grin plastered across his face probably made the rest of the passengers assume him to be an idiot, a few sandwiches short of a picnic; but he could no more wipe it off than he could stop breathing. Just the thought of Clare had that effect on him.

She had taken the train and then the bus to meet him at the airport, and she seemed to his starved gaze even lovelier than his memory had suggested. And in jeans and a shirt that matched her eyes instead of the checked school uniform dress, she looked as though she'd gained a handful of years. There was no sign of the all-embracing plaster cast, nor any evidence of the injured ankle in her walk. Tom knew from her letters that the hospital had given her the all clear a week or so back, after a period of intensive physiotherapy.

'How were you able to escape from home?' he asked, after they had embraced. Clare smelled of apples and Tom permitted them a proper kiss, even in the midst of all the people gathered to meet the incoming flights.

'Thea has decided you're not so bad, after all. Or Douglas has persuaded her.'

'Honest Injun?' Awesome thought. Would an obligatory halo follow?

'Honest Injun. But I'd not rest on my laurels, if I were you. I think her resolve is only skin deep. Basically, she sees all men as the implacable foe. With the exception of Douglas, of course.'

'That's me. The foe.'

He grinned down at her, unable to mask his delight at being with her again. He picked up his two duffel bags and Clare led the way toward the taxi rank. Of course, being classified as not so bad did not include being admitted to the house as a guest. Tom was booked into a small hotel on Captain Cook Avenue which, he was reliably informed by their brochure, overlooked an attractive and scenic park. It did seem to Tom that the witch had miscalculated there. It was far more difficult to transgress under the eagle eye of a parent, than when you had access to a hotel room. While waiting for an available taxi, and with Clare by his side with her hand affirmatively in his, even the thought of inner springs induced an erection that was painful in its urgency.

In retrospect, that happy ten days was a halcyon period, somewhat like the eye of the storm before hurricane forces return with renewed vigour. Clare and Tom did the usual tourist things, they wandered along Circular Quay, they kissed in the ink-blue shadows of Cadman's Cottage. They viewed all of Sydney from the heights of Centre Point, which made Seattle's Space Needle look like a presumptuous midget. That particular day was diamond-bright, the autumnal sunshine glinting off the facets of the buildings. The air was so clear Tom fancied they could see as far as the Southern Highlands and the venues of their earlier meetings.

Sydney continued to turn on its best weather, as though approving of Tom's determined wooing. On two evenings he was invited as a guest to share the evening meal with Thea and Clare. Despite Douglas' presence, and his easy conversation, they were stiff, awkward occasions because Thea might give nodding approval to Tom's presence in principle, but nothing could hide her inner hostility. She went to a great deal of trouble with the meals, which Tom appreciated. Determined to seize any opportunity, he was fulsome in his praise, but even then managed to draw from the older woman no more than a tight, reluctant smile. Noticing the steel-girder set of her shoulders, he wondered if she was capable of relaxing.

He and Clare made love, frequently and with great pleasure.

One evening, shortly before his precious ten days were up, Tom braced himself, and told her about how he had parted with Sandi. He even tried to explain how badly he had misjudged their relationship. At the time they were sitting in a seafood restaurant overlooking the harbour.

'Oh dear,' Clare commented, as he finished his confession. 'Poor Sandi.'

'Was I as dumb as I sound, even in my own ears?'

'I'm not sure, because I've never been in that situation. I've never had to pretend, unless you count William Brandon's letters.' Tom had been told about William a long time back, during clandestine midnight meetings.

'I though I was being totally honest with her, from the start.'

Clare selected a fat, green-lipped mussel and scooped the contents out of the shell. 'Honesty is relevant. You have to establish

212

the ground rules.'

'So I realised, too late.'

She placed the empty shell on her side plate and reached into the bowl for another. 'Anyway, what is truth? Your perception may be quite different from mine.'

Suddenly the conversation seemed to have moved into far deeper waters than his uncomfortable, but not too damning, confession. Quite philosophical. Tom knew, however, that in this matter he was on sound territory.

'Truth is total. Like black and white. I don't believe there are shades of grey.'

'You're wrong. Truth has hundreds of manifestations, all manner of faces. For example, Caitlyn and Jane and I quite often don't tell Lyndal the truth. It makes life so much easier.'

'I'm not sure that counts. But in my book the truth is the truth is the truth.' He spoke soberly, because this was so important to his way of thinking. 'Believe me, Clare, I learned that the hard way.'

She pushed the bowl of mussels his way. 'Aren't you having any more? They're delicious, don't you think?' Then she returned to his statement. 'How did you learn the hard way? By example?'

'The antithesis. When your folks live a lie, reality becomes your teacher.'

Clare discarded another empty shell. The small lamp that lit their table cast a soft glow on her face. Her lips were shiny with the sauce from the mussels.

'You make your parents sound like FBI informants; given new identities and names, plonked down in some anonymous small place to live out the rest of their lives.'

Tom smiled slightly. 'Maybe that's what happened and they could never bring themselves to tell me. Us. My brother and me.' He sobered again. 'However, I think it's more likely they created the new identities all for themselves, without the assistance of any agency.'

'Tell me.'

Tom helped himself to the final shellfish.

'Imagine your one goal in life is to be successful; the junior

213

VP. Maybe, even, the senior VP. And you fail, utterly. You reach the point when you know that, try as you might, success is always going to elude you. And I guess it hurts. So you kid yourself; you pretend. You don the external trappings of success, as far as the inadequate salary will allow you. And your family's drawn into the farce, forced to adopt the same set of wonky values. Will and I were raised on an entire tissue of lies. We had to learn to read between the lines.' He paused. 'Maybe that happens in other families. It sure was the case at the Goulding residence.'

Clare took her time thinking this over. Clearly the concept was new to her. 'You mean, create a show for the neighbours?'

'That, plus . . . plus . . .'

'Thea's always direct. She never does anything just for show.'

'There are other forms of lie. I'll bet she traded in maybe's.'

Clare frowned slightly. 'I don't understand.'

He shrugged. 'Come on, they're in all parents' vocabulary. "Mom, can we go to Disneyland?" "Maybe," meaning no. "Mom, can we trade in the old wreck for a new Chrysler?" "Sometime," meaning no. "Dad, I need new sneakers. Can I buy Reeboks with air soles?" "Perhaps," meaning no. All lies, all designed to save face.'

Again Clare took her time sorting this out. Then she weighed in on behalf of Tom's yet-to-be-met parents.

'You're being grossly unfair. Even if they knew they couldn't afford whatever it was you asked for, at least they held hope alive for you.'

'Is that right, though? Holding the possibility just beyond reach. Why not tell me the truth? Why not say, "I'd love to have a new car as well, Tom. But the company pays me peanuts, because I'm not too good at what I do there, and so we can't afford one."'

The waiter appeared and cleared away their plates. Clare waited for him to depart before she commented, 'That's really cruel. You'd be asking your parents to flay themselves, just to appease your idea of what's valuable.'

'Absolute truth's about the most valuable thing we have avail-

214

able to us.'

'Do you really think that?' She took a soft bread roll and toyed with it, crumbling the white interior onto her plate as she considered the strength of his conviction. 'Do you think that even a half-truth's wrong, in any circumstance?'

Tom looked directly at her, intent upon holding her gaze because this was unconditional and of such importance to him that it dwarfed all else. 'I believe it totally.'

'So you'd never lie to me? Not ever?'

'Not ever.'

The bread roll was reduced to a mess of crumbs. Clare discarded what was left.

'It's never been much of an issue with me, Tom. I just told the truth because I was expected to, and lying meant having to explain it in the confessional. But I've often told white lies to save someone's feelings. And to keep clear of Lyndal's nasty side.' Her voice dropped to a whisper. 'I hope I can live up to your ideal. It sounds frighteningly absolute.'

He took the opportunity to lean across and kiss her gently. 'I have no doubts whatsoever. In my eyes, you're perfect. But you know that already, don't you.'

Two days later he was back on the plane. As he crossed the Pacific, Clare was on her way up to St Ursula's for her second-to-last term at that establishment, life in which, after her accident would never be the same again.

The Thorn Bush

20

Douglas Hamilton had originally visited Australia from his native Aberdeen to testify in a particularly nasty trial, in which his ballistic knowledge swayed the case in favour of acquittal. To his and the police's considerable relief, the true culprit was later apprehended and imprisoned.

After the trial Douglas had stayed on a couple of days, and he liked what he saw of Australia. There was something about the quality of air which in a way reminded him of Aberdeen, but Australia had the advantage of masses of sunshine and an aura of youthful vigour which appealed, and was in stark contrast to the rather tired presence he imagined he saw in his home town. So he went back to Scotland and sold the idea of moving half way around the globe to Jeannie and to the very young Joel. Despite all that had happened since then, Joel's tragic death, Jeannie's gradual decline into the bleak world of Alzheimer's, he had not regretted their move. Scotland, after all, was not immune to meningitis. It was one of those distressing, unforeseeable things which could strike anywhere.

When Jeannie's illness became more debilitating, Douglas more or less retired. He filled what free time he could manage by writing a manual for future forensic experts, but he still kept a metaphorical toe in the door. Plus, he followed any information which became available, so he could keep abreast with new developments. After Jeannie's enforced incarceration, following the episode of the fire in the kitchen, he began again to accept commissions on a consultancy basis. His expertise made him quite valuable and he was called upon regularly, and not only in Australia.

So it transpired that he was asked to testify in California. They wanted someone from outside of the state. Total impartiality was essential. Douglas was happy to oblige. He didn't know San Francisco, but it was a city about which everyone had heard, and of which very little adverse was said. He though he might fit in a visit to Alcatraz.

The case dragged on for longer than he had expected, but San Francisco lived up to his expectations. He rated it a beautiful city. It was not until shortly before he was due to return home that another reason for being in that fair city surfaced in his mind.

It was a long shot, but he had nothing to lose by firing a few arrows into the air. There was just the possibility that one might find a target, as it fell to earth. And he was not to be disappointed.

He told Thea about the successful launch of his arrow and its rami-fications, shortly after he was home again. Spring was in full flower in Sydney. That meant the jacarandas were wonderful blotches of mauve and the silky oaks were a startling gold, and the Illawarra flame trees looked as though they were on fire. Thea had asked him to share a cup of tea with her and he was happy to accept, because he was in harmony with her at present, and had been so for several months. The good woman had taken his advice and not behaved badly to that decent lad who was so besotted with Clare. They had shared a couple of meals, all four together, back in April and again when Tom had managed a week in Sydney to coincide with Clare's August school holidays.

Douglas still supported Tom. He knew that Thea found the whole concept of anyone courting her precious child painful, but if Douglas could do anything it was to smooth the path to adulthood for Clare, and ease the accompanying pain for Thea.

Thea had set up a small, portable table on her top terrace. This she had carefully laid for tea. Thea approved of doing things prop-erly, and Douglas approved of her for that nicety of habit. There was an embroidered cloth and napkins apiece, and bone-handled

218

sterling silver knives which Clare's parents had managed to over-look eighteen years before.

Eighteen years. It seemed like only a few weeks ago that Thea had shown him that truly bonnie baby, and now she was grown into a truly bonnie lass.

'Something happened, while I was in San Francisco,' Douglas began, accepting a smoked-ham sandwich, the crusts of which Thea had carefully removed. 'But I want your promise that what I share with you is for your ears and mine alone, at this minute. Perhaps things will change, later.'

'I hear it's a lovely city,' Thea replied noncommittally.

'It is that. Rather European in its character, I felt. But, like all large cities, it has its seamy underbelly.'

'I'm sure you're right.'

'Aye. Well, it has often occurred to me that one day Clare might like to know something about her birth parents.' He saw Thea's back stiffen, so continued quickly, 'With no intention of displacing you in her affections, I'm certain. But occasionally one is asked about inherited tendencies of a medical nature, and I have no doubt whatever that Clare, being an intelligent wee girl, will have created some grand, fictitious rationale behind their precipitous departure. It might be necessary, at some future date, that she knows the truth.'

Thea spoke carefully, which amply illustrated how painful she found this line of conversation. 'I have never deviated from our original explanation. She has always appeared happy enough. Isn't it sufficient to know that they loved her?'

'And that in itself is a lie.'

'I'd be willing to lie a thousand times, to spare her the ugly truth.'

'Aye. I believe you would, and that is admirable, woman. But still the opportunity presented itself, while I was in the States, to pursue this line of thought.'

Thea put her cup back on its saucer with a clatter. 'You found them? Perdita and Shaun?'

Douglas frowned. 'You're leaping ahead too fast, woman. Let

219

me take things in order.' He leaned over and helped himself to another sandwich. 'My interest was kindled by something young Tom dropped into our conversation, after Clare's accident. He mentioned that he knew a Perdita . . .' he glanced across at Thea, who was sitting very still, '. . . and you have to admit it's an unusual name. I ask you, how many Perdita's have you known in your life-time?'

'One was enough, thank you.'

'Just so. And the same for me. That's why I pricked up my ears.'

'And was it? Was it the same woman?'

Douglas frowned at her again. 'Not so hasty, woman. Let me tell you at my own pace.' Having finished the sandwiches, he drew a packet of cigarettes out of his pocket. 'Do you mind if I smoke?' He never did indoors, but when outside Thea was generally accepting of his lifetime vice. He waited for her nod before lighting up.

'Where was I? Ah yes. With Tom. He said that the Perdita he knew had the surname of Svenson. In its own way, that's about as unusual as Perdita. I thought it might not be too hard to use my contacts in the police department, and trace one Perdita Svenson.'

'And did . . .?'

He held up a hand to silence her, then concluded that he was inflicting a form of Chinese water torture on the poor woman. 'Aye. I did.'

'Oh dear.'

Her voice was so bleak that Douglas wondered whether he had misjudged the whole thing. But surely eighteen years was long enough to create a sturdy emotional buffer.

'If you're worried that the mother might hurry back to Sydney to claim her daughter, you may rest easy in your bed. In fact, as far as Perdita is concerned, she has no daughter, and never did have.'

Thea's face seemed to have frozen. 'So you saw her? You actually saw her?'

'I did.'

'How . . . how was she?'

'Dissipated.'

Thea looked as though she was about to crumble. Douglas,

220

already regretting that he had mentioned the whole affair, leaned across the small table to place his hand on hers.

'Thea, pull yourself together, and let me tell you. There is more to this story than you can possibly imagine.'

And he launched into an account of what had transpired, that Friday afternoon of the previous week.

I can't condone what I did next. There is no excuse at all for my actions, and I have spent many unhappy hours on my knees in an attempt to excise my guilt.

I do know that it would not have come about, had Clare not provoked me.

She sat her exams, and then finished her education at St. Ursula's. I never had a doubt that she would feature well in the table of exam results, when they were published in the Sydney Morning Herald. *I was, of course, very annoyed with her that after the despicable events of February she should have been stripped of her prefect's badge, but there is no use in crying over spilled milk as the saying goes, and I'd had my say, back then. Not to mention the culpability of the sisters, into whose care I had entrusted my daughter. In* loco parentis, *is the phrase; but their laxity of supervision was most remiss.*

Douglas Hamilton drove me to the final, end-of-term assembly. We in Australia do not have a ceremony of graduation as they do in America, but the convent made quite a big thing of Speech Day, with the Bishop giving the end of year address and presenting the girls with their prizes and certificates. Then there was a very pleasant tea, laid out on trestle tables under the gum trees on the side lawn. They had let the sandwiches curl at the edges, which was unfortunate and would not have happened had they wrapped them in cling film. I wondered about suggesting this to them, for future years.

Clare and the other girls had almost been forgiven for their sin, after they had fully confessed and received absolution. Clare won three awards and two certificates. I must record that my heart was swollen with pride at that minute, and I confess she did look truly lovely. I know that we should not place too much credence upon

221

external beauty, but it is very hard not to be influenced, on occasion. It was the first time I had laid eyes on that Lyndal Murphy since Clare's birthday picnic and, according to Mother Scholastica, Lyndal Murphy was the ringleader behind the sinful shenanigans that went on. I was not surprised. I still remembered her ill-mannered sniggering. I was more surprised to see her still at the school, and being awarded a certificate for most improved student. I should have removed her and her bad influence from the place, forthwith. However, I was not prepared to allow my disapproval of one young woman with sadly loose morals to colour the day.

So all that was very nice. But, once she was home, Clare seemed to change. You may attribute it to a latent adolescence, and in the absence of any other explanation I could not but agree with you. I had read all about adolescence and quietly prided myself on how easily Clare appeared to have passed through that particular stage, giving me no heartache at all until That Man intruded into our peaceful lives.

But now she became moody and insolent, and very careless indeed. It was like having a stranger in the house. And the only time she appeared happy, with a pleasant look on her face, was when Mr. Tom Goulding telephoned from Seattle. How I detested that man. And he must have spent a fortune on his phone bills, because they would talk for long hours. Of course, that had not been possible at St. Ursula's. The girls did not have access to a telephone, although one could call in, in times of emergency. Now the pair made up for lost time. Daily conversations; and the rest of the day I had to live with an ill-humoured, sullen young woman who was no longer happy to accompany me to the Art Gallery, or to visit the new extension to the Power House Museum. Even my suggestion that we go to Manly on the ferry and buy our lunch on the beach, generally a sure-to-please treat, did no more than evince a monosyllabic response.

Christmas approached. I suggested that we took the train and attended the Carols by Candlelight evening in the Domain.

'Go yourself,' Clare snapped. 'If it's so important.'

'But you love the carols.'

'Well, I can't come. I'm expecting a call from Tom.'

And that is how I came to lose my temper.

I regret it. I really do. I understand now why they talk about "seeing red". When I had an infection in my eyes as a child, my mother put antiseptic drops in them and suddenly the world turned yellow. When Clare told me so rudely to "go myself", rejecting my offer in favour of yet another whispered conversation with you-know-who, it was as though, suddenly, I saw everything through a film of bright scarlet. Somehow the words just spilled out of me.

'And you'd be only too happy to go if it was your precious Tom with you,' I screamed. I never scream, but it was as though something inside me had snapped. Clare looked quite surprised. 'Well, let me tell you some hard facts about your precious Tom, facts that I'll wager he's never seen fit to share with you. To begin with, do you know about his druggy past?'

'He doesn't have a druggy past.'

'Oh, no? That's all you know. Well, I know better. He dropped out of university after less than four terms, your whiter-than-white Romeo; and he joined forces with a bunch of miserable no-hopers, living in no better than a hovel, and sniffing and snorting and smoking drugs, and doing all the disgusting things that dropout layabouts do. So how's your hero now, m'lady?'

Clare had turned quite white. Had I been in control of myself in the usual way, I would have noticed that and ceased my ranting, but I was beyond restraint. It was because inside me there was this huge weight of resentment, which had been growing like a canker of hatred in the long months since February.

'And that's not all. As though being a pot-head and a festering sore on the face of humanity's not enough, ask him what he knows about Perdita Svenson!'

Clare had her back to the wall as if she needed a solid support. Clearly, she had never seen me so inflamed; I have never seen myself in such a mode. It was equally shocking to both of us.

'Who's Perdita Svenson?'

'Only your mother, my girl!'

'My . . . mother? How does Tom know my mother?'

'That's for him to tell, and you to find out. That's all I can say to

that. But you should ask him how it feels to be a kept man, and to offer sexual services in payment for room and board. Ask him how he likes fornicating with older women. Older, druggy whores and prostitutes. Then tell me how much you like your precious Tom Goulding.'

'I don't believe you.'

'Don't believe me then. What's it to me, madam? But perhaps you'll believe Mr. Hamilton, if you don't see fit to believe me.'

I was beginning to run out of steam. The red had quit my eyes and I felt as though I had been through a terrible passage. As, indeed, I had. With my vision becoming restored, I could see that Clare looked truly terrible. For a minute I thought she was going to faint, then she just crumpled down against the wall, her legs giving way under her until she was an abject figure on the floor.

I forgot about myself. I forgot about my rage. For eighteen years I had cared for this child, and loved her and patched up her grazed knees with plasters and kisses. Awkwardly I knelt beside her.

'Clare . . . dear?'

I put out my arm to comfort her as I had done so many times, but Clare pushed my arm away.

'Don't touch me. Leave me alone.'

'Let me get you a cup of tea.'

'I don't want any tea. Go away, Thea. Go away. I want to be alone.'

I stood shakily and went on wobbly legs into the living room. I sank down on the sofa. The slam of the front door told me that Clare had gone out.

What have I done? I asked myself over and over again. What have I done? What have I done? Then, as the frightening realisation dawned, I wept. I wept and I wept, first for the awful thing I had just done to Clare, and then for the awful thing I had done to Tom Goulding, and after that for the awfulness of having broken my promise to Douglas. And soon I was also crying for the little girl who had been molested behind the hoop-la stall and had been unable to weep healing tears at that time, and for Donal O'Brien who was retarded, and for all the slights and rebuffs and curious glances I had experienced throughout my life. I wept for the things I could not undo and for the things over which I had no power.

I cried for the past, and I cried for the future. Most of all, I cried for the loss of my daughter, which I knew to be inevitable because how would she ever forgive me?

21

It took quite a lot of adjustment to consider Christmas and high summer in the same breath. Tom, once more on his way across the vast expanse of the Pacific in the comfortable seat of a QANTAS plane, thought about sun-drenched beaches and the dusty heat of the bush, and contrasted them with the skiing at Steven's Pass he'd been enjoying only last weekend. Definitely bizarre.

Elliot was becoming accustomed to being abandoned, although Tom had explained to him that this time it would be for the briefest of breaks. He would be back, he made clear, for work on the 29th of December. Bob and Joey had a particularly tasty treat secreted away until the day after tomorrow, which would be Christmas Day. It was a specially softened morsel, manufactured with elderly canines in mind, because Elliot was showing his years. Walks were more laboured and had to be shorter in duration. Only on rare occasions did he gather together his resources and gambol like a youngster. He was, however, all the more precious to Tom because he offered such unconditional approval whenever the key turned in the lock and Tom arrived home again.

Tom had hoped that Thea would soften her stance sufficiently to allow him room and lodging, but he accepted with as much grace as he could muster his relegation to the hotel abutting the park. Being excluded from the family circle was frustrating but, on the plus side, the hotel did afford more privacy than they would have managed, were they in residence all together. He was coming to know the geography of that small park quite well, and liked it. Each morning a flock of noisy, squabbling lorikeets gathered, drawn there by the local philanthropists who fed them a breakfast of sunflower seeds. Their brilliance of colour was dazzling, scarlet and gold and electric blue. And handsome, sulphur-crested cockatoos were also in evidence, although according to the hotel manager they were unwelcome, destructive vermin, apt to take apart your fascia and window-surrounds if in the mood. To Tom, who had no fear for his woodwork, they were splotches of immaculate white, with bright, intelligent eyes and comical habits.

He knew there was something wrong the moment he laid eyes on Clare; something amiss in her smile and in her body language and in the tightness of her greeting. She lifted her face for his kiss, but as though it took some effort to do so, and showing none of the shy warmth he had come to expect. Clearly, Thea had been giving her a bad time.

'Trouble, darling?'

They were surrounded by the usual crowd of tanned Sydneysiders, clad in the briefest of shorts or bright summer cottons. Clare kept her eyes lowered. She was wearing a simple skirt and shirt. She looked wonderful and she looked awful, really vulnerable, as though she might have been crying.

'Perhaps it's nothing.'

Tom picked up his bag. 'Thea been giving you hell?'

'Yes and no. I'd rather not talk about it right now.'

He looked at the top of her bowed head. This must be serious. Mentally he cursed the witch. What the hell had she been saying that could cause such a change in his beloved?

'Then let's go – and you can tell me all about it. When am I expected to appear for inspection?'

'I don't know. Perhaps never.'

'*What*?'

'Tom, please. I can't tell you right here.'

It was a hideous drive to the hotel on Captain Cook Avenue. Usually they would be swapping anecdotes, and he would be telling her about Elliot and about the quality of the Cascades' snow, and she would be filling him in on the minutiae of school life that had not made its way into a letter. They might even be kissing, if the driver appeared sufficiently uninterested. Clare hated anything too demonstrative in public.

'How does it feel to have graduated?' he asked, in attempt to break the uncomfortable silence. He put his hand over hers as it lay between them on the seat of the taxi. She drew it away.

'We don't graduate. We just leave school, although the nuns lay on their idea of a bean-feast. Cream cakes, and sandwiches made with white bread. That's thought to be special, in convent parlance. I'll hear about my exam results in January.'

'And then?' As if he didn't know; but there was a hollow, anxious feeling in the pit of his stomach, as though this unexpected reticence was not exclusively the result of Thea's mischief but was something in which he, too, was inextricably bound.

They reached the hotel. The manager greeted them like personal friends, but even this did nothing to lighten the atmosphere. Tom felt more and more as Damocles must have felt with that great, lethal sword suspended above him by a single hair.

'Would you like to come up to my room, or shall we go out to the park?'

Even those words acknowledged his sense of foreboding. In other, happier visits they'd be racing to the room, falling out of their clothes as quickly as decency permitted, making for the bed in a laughing, joyous ferment of pleasure and excitement at being together again after their enforced separation.

'Perhaps the park would be better.'

He knew that he was doomed.

There was a bench shaded from the brilliant sunshine, and away from the couple of families with young kids who were cooking something delicious. The park authorities very considerately provided solid, permanent barbecues for public use. The smell drifted toward them, as Tom and Clare made their way to the isolated seat. A pair of black-headed, sacred ibis strutted around, hoping that a morsel or two might come their way. Even the happy familiarity of it all could not shift the lump of lead in Tom's stomach.

Seated, he turned again to Clare. She hadn't met his eyes once in the last hour. 'Tell me, darling. What's up?'

She was gazing intently at a neighbouring shrub. It had a mass of pink flowers, Tom noticed irrelevantly, and a host of tiny butterflies hovered over it like a golden halo.

'I don't know where to start.'

He wanted so badly to hold her hand, but dared not risk a second rebuff. 'Start at the beginning.'

Clare let out a long, slow breath. 'We had a terrible row, Thea and I.'

A tiny spark of hope rekindled in Tom. Maybe this was nothing to do with him, after all.

'It happens in the best ordered families. Will and I fought all the time.'

'But this was different. Thea never loses her temper. Never. Not with me, not with anyone. But she did this time. She actually screamed at me.'

'What led up to it?'

'I'd been foul to her. I knew I was being horrid, but I couldn't help it. It was like a concentration of everything, leaving school, missing you, missing my school friends. I seemed to have nobody to talk to, to share things with, except for when you phoned. And Thea forgets that I've grown up. She expects me to say, "Fantastic!" when she suggests a ride on a merry-go-round. I'm too old for cosy trips to the Botanic Gardens.'

Tom flexed his shoulders, feeling with relief that he was in the clear. This was nothing more than a natural spat between mother and daughter. To be expected. In fact, the wonder of it was that they had not rubbed up against each other years ago.

'Give her time. She'll come to terms with having a grown-up daughter.'

'No. You don't understand. That was just the background, so that you'd realise why I was behaving badly.'

'Okay. Carry on.' He risked taking her hand in his. She withdrew it and began to twist her fingers together in an action that refuted her claim to adulthood more succinctly than any words.

'Then she told me. Told me about you.'

229

'About me?'

She risked a glance at him. 'Tom, why did you never mention that you were a drug addict?'

'Me?'

'Yes, you. I know it's true, because I asked Douglas afterwards, after Thea had told me everything, and he says that the police in San Francisco have you on their files, although you've never actually been arrested.'

San Francisco. Things fell into place with the awful finality of a condemned man hearing the hammering of nails, as the scaffold with his name etched on it is being erected.

'You want me to tell you about San Francisco?'

'Yes. You said you'd always tell me the truth.'

'And I meant it.'

'Omission is as much a sin as commission.'

Tom took his time formulating what he had to say. 'I wasn't being deliberately deceitful. That, I promise. But I guess there are certain things in everyone's past that are too painful, or too shameful, to rake up. I don't look back at that time of my life with pride. If you'd asked, I'd have told you. But I'm not an addict. I never did mainline, and I never tried the really hard stuff. I came off drugs four years ago. Nearly five. And I'll never again use them. That's a promise, Clare.'

He interpreted the slight shrug of her shoulders as, "that's irrelevant," or, perhaps, "who cares?"

'Tell me about what happened.'

'Sure. If it will help.' He turned to look at her. She still kept her eyes averted, so he could see only her profile. He drew a deep breath to steady himself, while he formulated the right words. 'I explained to you that I resented my people. I always felt like an alien in their midst. That's why I didn't want to go to school where I grew up. Instead I went to Berkeley, in San Francisco. Half way through my second year, I guess I felt the way you're feeling right now. Suddenly I could see no sense in what I was doing. There was no purpose to it. I'd spent my life studying, toeing the party line, being the kid everyone wanted me to be. It's not unusual to kick

230

over the traces at a time like that. I just rebelled.'

'So what happened then?'

'I dropped out of school.'

'And . . .?'

He shrugged. 'I suppose you could say I got in with the wrong set. That's easy enough to do in 'Frisco. There are quite a few of yesterday's hippies who cling to the Beat philosophy. I didn't have to look too far.'

'Thea said you were a stud, up for hire. I asked Douglas and he didn't disagree. Is that true as well, Tom?'

He was silent for a minute, appalled at how all this dirty linen must appear to someone who was eighteen, and had lived her life in a cloistered community of women. He could remember feeling a lifetime older than her, that first night they'd met to talk. At present he felt like her grandfather.

'In a way.'

'But why?'

He shrugged. 'Drugs are expensive, especially when you don't have a regular supply of cash. I couldn't write home and say, "Dad, I need an income to feed my habit." I didn't want to resort to stealing, because becoming a thief was the pits. The first step on a dangerous ladder. So it seemed to me that I should offer something by way of a service.' He stopped to recall the rationale behind his nineteen-year-old thinking. It seemed appallingly lame, when viewed objectively. Then he continued, 'Clare, drugs screw up your mind. Sometimes it's hard to think clearly. At the time, I reasoned that what I was doing was more honest than becoming a petty crook.'

'Being a prostitute? That's what you were, wasn't it? A male prostitute.'

He winced at the contempt in her voice. 'I guess. And I guess I deserve your scorn.'

'But that's not the end of the story, is it.'

'Well . . . no.' What else did she want?

'Go on. Tell me the rest. Tell me the really dirty part.'

'I think that was the really dirty part.'

Her voice gained in strength. 'Oh no. That was just the begin-ning. What about the woman who was your protector?'

'My protector?'

'When you became a kept man.'

'Became a kept man?' But then light dawned. 'You mean, when I met Perdita?'

'Yes. That's what I mean. When you met Perdita Svenson.'

How come Clare knew her name? Of course. Douglas Hamilton.

'Well, Perdita was an older woman. In her forties, anyway. The rest of us were kids. She sort of held court, in that area where we all congregated . . .'

'The druggy, drop-out area?'

'I guess. It certainly wasn't too salubrious. Anyway, the kids gathered at her place because she kept us supplied. And she liked me. That's about all. I sort of moved in, for a period of about a year. In a way, I suppose I was a kept man. I didn't think about it at the time, because I was useful to her. I kept the place together and I did things for her, and I kicked out the undesirables when they became abusive.'

'What sort of things did you do for her?' There was a harsh edge to her voice.

'All sorts. Ran drugs for her, occasionally. Fetched and carried and delivered.'

'Shagged her? Fucked her?'

He winced. 'Yes. We sometimes had sex.'

'That's the most disgusting thing I've ever heard.'

He was temporarily nonplussed. 'Clare, I've always been honest with you about that. I never pretended to be the patron saint of chastity.'

'You don't know anything, do you! I thought you were wonder-ful. I thought you were good and kind, and that you respected me . . .'

'I do.'

' . . . and all the time you were actually scum. You were more stinking than a blowfly, than a maggot on a sheep's bum. I hate you, Tom Goulding, and I don't ever want to see you again. Not ever in my life.'

Tom felt as though he were drowning, and there was no helpful scrap of floating driftwood onto which he could clutch.

'But . . .'

'There's nothing you can say.' She paused, angrily wiping at the tears that were starting to flow in earnest. 'You were shagging my mother, you prick. You were shagging my mother, and all the time I thought you were absolutely marvellous.'

'*Your mother?*'

'You heard me. My mother. Perdita Svenson, nee Potts.' She stood uncertainly, clutching at the tissue which was doing a bad job of stemming her tears. 'And I never want to see you again. Not ever. Not ever.'

She stumbled away, aiming uncertainly for the park gates. Tom wanted to hurry after her, but his feet appeared to be rooted to the ground. His chest was constricted and his throat felt as though it was caught in his grandmother's mangle. He was still in shock from her parting words.

A small boy from one of the picnicking families had been drawn toward their row. He stood, bare footed, open mouthed, staring at Tom. He had a charred sausage in one hand.

'She's cross,' he contributed helpfully. 'You made her cry. You're a bad man.'

Tom stared back at the child. Clare was, indeed, cross, even if he had not intended to make her cry. And his past had come back to haunt him. The kid was right. He was a bad man.

'Oh, go get lost!' he snapped.

The small boy's face crumpled at the ferocity of Tom's tone and he ran back on stubby legs to the comfort of his mother's arms. Tom, totally bereft, could only envy him. He was on his own in a foreign country, with nobody's arms into which he could fling himself. His feet of clay had been exposed, he had lost his love.

In truth, in the last few minutes his life had lost its meaning.

another sheet of...

22

Tom spent a miserable night in his hotel room, longing for the phone to ring, terrified to partake of as much as a comforting slug of whisky in case it did. It would be the kiss of death, he knew, to approach Clare with his breath reeking of spirits. The television offered very little in the way of entertainment, even if he had been receptive to it. As it was, a diet of forced Christmas pap was the last thing in the world he could stomach. A requiem would have been more to his taste than festive celebrations. All he could hope was that a degree of good sense might return the next day, after the eruption of anger and emotion had worked itself out. It seemed a forlorn prospect.

He awoke on Christmas morning with a head like a coconut being crushed in a vice, feeling about seventy and aware with an awful hollowness that his very raison d'être had fallen apart. He wondered whether it was sensible for him to try to contact Clare and talk to her. She lived just along the road, less than half a mile. He'd brought Thea a side of Seattle's best smoked salmon, and teardrop earrings for Clare to match the pendant he'd given her in April. Maybe he could at least deliver his gifts and thus test the ground.

He waited until a decent time after breakfast, then wandered along the road, hesitant about what he was doing, but unable to come up with any other plan of action. Perhaps a night's sleep had given Clare a new slant on things, possibly she was able to see his transgression for what it was; a hideous quirk of fate. There was absolutely no way he could have known, in those days, that seven years later he would be in love with Perdita's daughter, with the infant she had abandoned years earlier.

He'd done some pretty hard thinking in the long hours of the night, before sleep at last took pity on him. Perhaps he should have seen a likeness, but even knowing of the relationship, it was quite difficult to do so. Apart from a similarity of build and an approximation of height, Clare and the Perdita he knew were very different. And how the hell was he to connect the two by any other method? Perdita had never hinted at the slightest knowledge of Australia, any more than he was aware she had given birth to a child. Neither subject had arisen during his time with her.

Memories of that interval surfaced again, making him cringe. There was no doubting that knowledge of his dropout period, and the sleaze and illicit nature of their way of life, would be his cross to bear forever. In that at least, Clare's scorn was well deserved.

Then there was another consideration. Thea knew all this and had imparted it to Clare down to the fact, unknown to him, that, despite never having been arrested, he was still of interest to the police. And it had all been verified by Douglas Hamilton, although heaven only knew how he was in a position to do so. Obviously he was a guy with many irons in the fire. He was also the guy Tom had considered his ally, albeit only after some deliberation. He'd wondered, at the time of Clare's accident, whether Douglas was setting him up. Yesterday's scene would seem to verify those earlier reservations, which showed that you should never put your trust in fellow man.

Tom walked slowly along the pavement, passing houses very similar to those in which lived Thea and Clare and their neighbour. Pretty houses, with their double balconies and ornate wrought ironwork. They were painted in pastel shades which, in the bright sunshine, gave them the appearance of period doll houses. And behind each front door, Tom reckoned, there was a family at this minute opening stockings and presents, and kids squealing with excitement, and dogs not so different from Elliot rolling in the discarded papers, just as Elliot contorted himself each Christmas like an overgrown puppy, instead of an elderly fellow who ought to know better. Thinking of Elliot brought a lump to his throat, because in the old dog he had one friend who was unconditional in his love, and didn't assume that you came to him smelling of Daz, and without a past.

He rang the doorbell three times and waited a decent interval before he gave up. He wondered about leaving his gifts on the doorstep, but thought better of it. Only a narrow garden separated the front door from the sidewalk. Packages left in full view might prove far too much of a temptation for some light-fingered passer-by. He returned to the hotel to face a lonely Christmas meal.

'Mr Goulding?' the manager greeted him.

'Hi.'

'You have a message . . .' Tom's heart leaped, only to sink again as the young man completed the sentence, '. . . from a Mr Hamilton. He stopped by, shortly after you'd gone out. He asked you to ring. Here's his number.'

Tom took the slip of paper gingerly. What the hell could Douglas want of him? To gloat? He dialled the number equally cautiously, like a soldier determined to guard his back from sudden attack.

'Ah, Tom. You gave me permission to call you that.' Douglas reminded him of this fact every time they met, as though in permitting the use of a first name you were conferring an honour on someone.

'Yessir . . . er . . . happy Christmas.'

'Thank you. I'm assuming that your Christmas celebrations are far from happy.'

Tom cleared his throat, still not too sure where all this was going. 'You could say that, sir.'

'Then how about we eat together? I'm on my own and I'd value your company. And I'm afraid I have an apology to make. I should like to salve my conscience, to the best of my feeble ability.'

Mystified, Tom agreed the time. The hotel, he knew, laid on a festive dinner.

They met in the foyer at the allotted hour and shook hands.

'Shall we eat right away? I must admit I have a hole inside me larger than the hold of the Titanic. That's the problem with living on your own. You become lazy about your eating habits. It was better when my wife was with me, because I prepared the meals for us

236

both. Now, I'm inclined to forget about food until hunger gets the better of me.'

Douglas continued to converse doggedly as they ploughed their way through what appeared to be a gargantuan meal. Tom was forced to wonder where so small a guy tucked away so much food. Turkey and mini-sausages, bacon rolls and bread sauce, three sorts of potatoes, peas and carrots all disappeared as though Douglas was laying in stores for the Seven Years of Famine. It was left to Tom to agree and to nod and to say, 'yessir,' and 'no sir,' at the appropriate times.

And after the turkey had disappeared, Douglas tucked into a heavy, fruit concoction smelling richly of brandy, which he explained was traditional, British Christmas fare. It was not until coffee and mints appeared that he introduced the topic far closer to Tom's heart.

'I want to apologise.' Tom raised an inquiring eyebrow but remained silent. 'I'm afraid I very much miscalculated things, and because of my . . . error in judgement . . . I let a very large cat out of the bag.'

'San Francisco?' Tom ventured.

'Precisely.' Douglas wiped his mouth with a napkin, clearly seeking time to select the correct words. 'My work took me there. You may not know, but I deal with ballistics. I was in San Francisco for the Baillie trial.'

Tom nodded. Throughout the better part of November and into December half of America had followed the machinations of that particular trial.

'When we talked last summer, at the time of Clare's accident, you mentioned a Perdita. Perdita Svenson. It occurred to me that this was a very singular name. I've often thought that the time might come when Clare wanted, or needed, to know about her birth parents. Perdita Svenson, I discovered, is well known to the SFPD. It took very little effort on my part to locate her when I was in that fair city.'

Things began to fall into place. 'And, according to Clare, I'm also on their files. That was something of a stunner.'

'Incidental, dear lad. Incidental. They have no interest in you at all. It was no more than an old file, slipped into another, on which you appeared as sharing the same address. You'll be happy to know that I destroyed it myself, with their approval. But I'm afraid the same cannot be said for Clare's natural mother. Alas.'

Tom helped himself to a mint. 'But you can't have known that they were one and the same woman. Perdita Svenson and Perdita . . . Potts?'

'No, indeed. Until I laid eyes on her.'

Tom sat forward. 'You saw her? You visited her?'

Douglas nodded. As before, Tom noticed that, when he became excited, his eyebrows took on a life of their own, behaving like separate, living entities.

'And how is she?'

The eyebrows snapped together over the bridge of Douglas's nose. 'Are you a scholar? Have you read Emil Zola's *Nana*?'

'I'm afraid not, to both your questions.'

'Well, Nana led a life of considerable debauchery. By the time of her death she was so disfigured by all she had put her body through that close friends did not recognise her. Probably syphilis. I thought of Nana, when I saw Perdita. It was difficult for me to equate the prematurely aged, louche person I met with the very beautiful young woman she had been, at the time of Clare's arrival. Very difficult.'

'So you spoke to her.'

The older man nodded. 'Would it bother you if I smoked?'

Tom shook his head. 'If it's okay with the hotel.'

'Och, we have yet to emulate California and ban all smoking. But I shall try to be considerate.' He fumbled for his cigarettes. 'Yes, I spoke to her. Were I the writer of farce, I should have enjoyed that small talk.'

'How come?'

'At first Perdita pretended to have no idea who I was. That is understandable in the circumstances, but I could see in her eyes that it was untrue. She knew very well who I was.'

'Why should she pretend?'

'Perhaps I forgot to tell you, when this matter was raised before, that Perdita and Shaun stole a great deal from Thea during

238

their time in Australia. I presume they had no other form of stipend, so what they could filch from her maintained their habit. And they took most of her more valuable bits and pieces, upon departure.'

Tom drew in a long breath. 'Phew. So Perdita has a record in Australia, as well?'

'No. Thea never filed charges. She always felt she came best out of the bargain. After all, they left her Clare. A more than fair exchange, I would say.'

Tom fell silent, thinking about all he had learned. It did not seem likely to restore his reputation in Clare's eyes, but it did explain a few things.

'Once I had let Perdita know that she was not getting away with her selective amnesia, and also that I was not there to issue her with a warrant, she relaxed enough to fill me in on other details.'

'Such as me?'

Douglas reached over for the ashtray and knocked onto it the long twist of ash that had accumulated. 'Such as you. But other interesting facts, as well. Poor wee Shaun, for example, died of an overdose shortly after they returned to America. Unmourned, I gather. And these days it suits Perdita to see herself as an earth mother, offering the next generation love and understanding. That, however, would not be my description. I see her as a venomous spider, sitting in the centre of her web and luring young and vulnerable children into a life of drugs and debauchery.'

'In her vocabulary, love equals coke and horse and amphetamines and whatever else is in fashion,' Tom confirmed. 'I can tell you, she makes damn sure that they're hooked, those kids. She doles out poppers like candy. That way she can support her habit and keep her disciples under her thumb. She's an evil woman.'

Douglas nodded. 'About that we are in full agreement. It's simply a mystery to me that she has been able to continue her lifestyle without interference from the local police force.'

'Oh, she's always far too smart for the cops to catch her. I can vouch for that. She uses kids, like me, to run for her. And younger.

Under the age of twelve they can't be prosecuted as adults. So she gathers a little troupe of runaways about her, desperate for a bit of affection, and pretends that she's offering them cosy, maternal comfort.'

'Aye. A modern day Fagin. So sad.' Douglas stubbed out the butt of his cigarette. 'And now I come to the part where I owe you a profound apology. I had assumed that Thea, like me, would be interested to know all that I had learnt. After all, I told myself, eighteen years is a long time. She is secure in Clare's affection. So I shared with her my knowledge, having insisted upon her promise not to impart all I was about to tell her to Clare. Or not until some time a long way in the future.' Clearly in need of some form of crutch, he reached into his pocket for another cigarette. His hand shook as he groped for the small tobacco cylinder and lit it. 'Painful as it is to relate, Thea was unable to keep her promise. She lost her temper, she confessed, when Clare exhibited some very normal, if trying, adolescent behaviour.'

Tom felt that something was needed of him. He cleared his throat. 'Thank you for explaining.'

'I feel that, although I have not fired the gun, I certainly loaded the bullets. What bothers me is that, because of my ill-considered action, your relationship may well have been dealt a mortal blow. One from which it will be impossible to recover.'

Tom's emotions had run the gamut from cautious curiosity, through dejection and back to deepest despair. It was like taking part in an autopsy, each organ being removed for inspection. But nothing could restore the corpse to life again. Knowing how it had all gone wrong would not return Clare to him, or reinstate him in her affections. The glass had been shattered, the water spilled. If she could not accept him, warts and all, there was probably very little that he could salvage. But it would be cowardly not to make another effort.

'Mr Hamilton . . . Douglas . . .sir, could you arrange for me to see her again? Yesterday she was so hurt that she couldn't hear me. The ultimate sin, in her eyes, is that I had sex with her mother. But there was no way I could have known this, when we met. Perhaps she'll have come around to that conclusion, by now.'

'It's possible that she might listen to me.' Douglas looked at him with his fierce, eagle eyes. 'I'm afraid Thea Galway and I are not on speaking terms. I was very angry when she admitted she had betrayed my trust. Very angry indeed. But I can certainly weigh in to persuade Clare to offer you a hearing.' He stood up and extended his hand. 'The best I can do is apologise for my part in this tragedy again, and to wish you luck, Tom. I believe you may well be in need of it.'

23

Once, as a ten-year old kid, Tom had seriously transgressed. Will was quite often in trouble, generally because of his propensity to talk big, but Tom's activities, things like fishing in the creek down back or creating tree houses, rarely led him into too much misfortune. On this one occasion, however, his mother had baked some pint-sized apple pies for a charity fund-raiser at the church they attended irregularly. Thelma's apple pies were legendary in their neck of the subdivision.

As he came in from school, the smell of warm pastry drew Tom as surely as the music of the Pied Piper drew the children of Hamelin. The kitchen was deserted. He counted the pies. Thirteen; an odd number to chance upon. He tried to think himself into his mother's way of reasoning. He bet she'd meant to make twelve. She'd said, 'Yes, of course Mrs Smith,' . . . or 'Mrs Brown,' . . . or whoever . . . 'sure I'll bake you some of my pies. A dozen, perhaps?'

Mrs Smith or Mrs Brown could not be expecting thirteen. It stood to reason. Thirteen was an unlucky number. It was a very small step to see that in helping himself to the thirteenth he was actually doing his mother a favour. She would be humiliated in public, if the other women thought she couldn't count to an easy dozen.

The pie slipped down like water unerringly finding its way, leaving in Tom's nose and on his tongue a delectably sticky, sweet aftertaste. Problem was, it did no more than whet his appetite. If Thelma didn't notice the difference between thirteen and a dozen, he argued, she'd probably have a problem sorting out twelve from eleven. The second pie followed the first. And then of course, it behove him to round off the number.

Three pies, even if they were only pint-sized, made him feel thoroughly queasy. He was forced to retire to the bedroom he shared with Will, which was where his father found him some time later. Dale's face looked like a thundercloud. Tom knew he'd blown it.

Even so, even knowing he was thoroughly in the wrong, Tom could still be resentful. When Dale confronted him with knowledge of his crime, desiring confirmation, Tom aroused himself from his wretched state sufficiently to gum his mouth tightly together and refuse to incriminate himself. Dale then launched into a homily about the virtues of honesty, prior to removing his belt.

It was the only time in his life that Tom was licked, and it hurt. Not the physical hurt, which he knew he deserved, but the perceived hypocrisy of a parent who lectured you about the necessity to tell the truth, when Tom had not lied, and at the same time allowed his household to live in a state of continual pretence. He felt that he was being punished for the wrong reason. That rankled.

The only other ramification of this sorry saga was that many years passed before Tom could again smell apple pie, without being overwhelmed by nausea. Will grabbed every opportunity to tease him endlessly.

The memory of this episode came to mind now. Once more he was being castigated, but for all the wrong reasons.

He could feel ashamed of his Beat period, and considerable regret. He did. They were wasted years. Given time, he would certainly have confessed this to Clare. He'd have tried to explain to her the difference in his thinking during that period, between thievery and offering services to women in exchange for board and bed. The rationale was warped, but drugs did that to your mind. He deeply regretted his brief love affair with those poisonous substances. He'd have told her about Perdita as well, and how he had lived as her lieutenant for thirteen or so months.

But, as he'd said to Douglas, to blame him for accidentally bedding her mother seemed totally unjust.

Douglas managed to mediate to the extent that, two days later, Clare agreed reluctantly to see Tom. For no more than to say good-bye. Douglas, calling to inform Tom of this, added his regret and apologised yet again.

'I've spoken with her, but she's still deeply shocked and hurt. I heard a lot of talk about betrayal of her trust.' Tom could hear the genuine contrition in the older man's voice. 'I'm sorry, Tom. I suppose it's asking too much of anyone in her situation to step back and consider this rationally. She just kept repeating, "but my *mother*, Douglas. He was *having sex with my mother*."'

Tom had not known that his heart could sink any lower. It felt lead-lined as it was. Not to mention the bitter taste that invaded his mouth.

He cut short Douglas' attempt to apologise yet again. 'At least she'll see me. You did your best, sir. Thank you for that.'

He was beginning to hate that park. Its pretty leafiness grated on him because such enthusiastic verdancy was in direct contrast with the arid desperation he felt. Clare arrived, walking hesitantly as though she would rather be anywhere but there. She refused to meet his eyes.

'Hi, Clare.'

'Hello.'

She was wearing sunglasses, which acted as a barrier behind which she could hide. Awkwardly they sat as they had on Christmas Eve, side by side on the same bench, looking at the same bushes, the same trees. The tiny golden butterflies still created a fluttering aura around the pink-flowered shrub. The only ingredients missing were the two families happily enjoying their barbecue.

'Clare . . .' Tom began.

She cut him short. 'Before you try to say anything, Tom, I want you to know that nothing will change the way I feel. Don't bother to excuse what happened. Don't try to explain. None of that matters.'

'Then what does matter?'

'I'll tell you. I feel as though I was in love with another person. A person who isn't you. I thought I knew so much about you and all

244

of it was perfect. Now it's as though I never knew you at all. I've been in love with a spectre who doesn't even exist.'

'But I never lied to you. I'd have told you about what happened in 'Frisco, given time. It just never occurred to me to spill the beans, per se.'

'And what would you have said about my mother? How would you have broken that small item of news?'

Frustration made him sound angry. It was back to that single issue again. 'I didn't know she was your mother.'

'And that excuses you?'

Hearing the implacability in her voice, he tried desperately to find something to justify his perceived sin. 'Isn't there anything in your past that makes you cringe, in retrospect?'

'Nothing that I'd be ashamed to share with you.'

'Not even skinny dipping in front of a total stranger?'

She did glance quickly at him and he felt a tiny surge of hope, only for it to be dashed again. 'How can you possibly compare that with what you did?'

He shrugged. 'I was simply using it as an example.'

But somehow he knew that this was going nowhere, there were no more weapons left in his arsenal. Clare was not prepared to hear him or to offer him any possible hope. He dug his hands deeply into his pockets, feeling as though his world had fallen apart.

'That's it then, isn't it.'

'Is it?' he asked miserably. 'What did the sisters teach about forgiveness? Can't you forgive what happened, even if you don't forget? Then we could pick up the pieces and start again.'

She waited, while he held his breath. 'No, Tom. We can't ever pick up the pieces. You know it. I know it. It's over.'

Misery clouded his vision. The trees and the sunshine were still there, but he saw them all through a grey mist. The heat had gone out of his day and out of his life. He made to stand.

'Then I guess we should say good-bye.'

For the first time Clare looked directly at him. 'Tom . . .?'

'What?'

'Can I ask you something?'

245

He shrugged, leaning back against the bench again. 'I guess.'

'Tom, you promised that you'd always be honest with me.'

'And I have been, even if you don't believe me.'

'Will you tell me something, now? Absolutely truthfully?'

Where was this leading? 'If I can.'

She hesitated, looking first across the smooth green of the grass, then back to him. 'What is she like, my mother?'

Perhaps he should have anticipated just this question. It was only natural that she should be curious. Just as it was the last question in the world he wanted to answer.

'Why don't you ask Douglas Hamilton? He spoke to her, only last month. I've not set eyes on her in years.' And prayed that he would never do so again.

'I did. I did ask him. He told me that my father's been dead for years, from a drug overdose. But when I asked him to tell me about Perdita . . . my real mother . . . he said to ask you.' She turned her head away, gazing down at her hands. 'Actually, I didn't want to come this afternoon. I thought it would hurt too much, our seeing each other like this. But I really do want to know about her.'

'Thea's your real mother, Clare. Not Perdita.'

'You know what I mean.'

Yes, he knew what she meant. He thought about the Perdita he had known. A self-centred, scheming person, who manipulated you and everyone else to her own advantage. She had been heavily dependent on heroin and crack for years, and their effect was predictably harsh. Even in the 80's her looks were fading, as the substances she mainlined aged her prematurely. Her skin had a quality of unhealthy greyness to it; her hair, even then, had lost its fairness and looked limp and lustreless. And she could be cruel, denying some unhappy kid the wherewithal to satisfy his craving, until he'd performed whatever task she had in mind for him. Her deliberate cruelty had been the catalyst that drove Tom away in the end, accidentally helping him back into mainstream society. For that, he supposed, he could be grateful to her.

He thought about Douglas' reference to Zola's *Nana*. Douglas had said that he'd not recognised Perdita as the beautiful young

246

woman of eighteen years ago. He'd used words like debauched, so clearly crack had continued to take its toll. Perdita Potts was not privileged to own a portrait in the attic which could carry the burden of her addiction. It was all written, plain to see upon her face and in her wasted body. Tom had read in her eyes, on occasion, her self-knowledge and her desperation.

'What do you want me to tell you?'

'What does she look like?'

The truth is the truth is the truth. That was the tenet of Tom's faith, and because of it he had promised Clare that he would never lie to her. Great. Then he should say, 'she's a hopeless addict, clinging to life while a ticking bomb counts down? If she can't get her fix on time she gets the shakes. And she's gaunt, prematurely ageing; her skin no longer fits and her eyes reflect her hopelessness?'

The truth is the truth is the truth. He took his time, selecting his words with utmost care. He could do this one thing for his goddess, this one thing for his love.

'She's very beautiful,' he began slowly. 'Perhaps, had I known to look for a connection, I could have seen that you must be her child. Her hair is still fair, and long and lovely. Her eyes are her best feature. She looks far too young to have a grown-up kid.'

'Really? And what about her personality? What is she like?'

Tom leant forward, resting his arms on his knees, letting his eyes scan the far scenery. The truth is the truth is the truth. But not always essential.

'She's a warm, generous person. Even though you mightn't admire her lifestyle or condone her drug habit, you'd be proud about the way she does her best. She's a person for whom nurturing comes easily. Now that I know she has a daughter, I think, perhaps, she tries to compensate for having lost you by mothering other kids. They see her as a sort of parent. She was very kind to me.'

'Do you think she regrets having given me up? Thea always said she deliberately gave me to her for my sake. It was an act of great generosity.'

'Of course she regrets giving you away. Which parent wouldn't?

247

And I'm sure Thea was right. She had only your best interests in mind.' He was sufficiently brave to put one hand over Clare's and she allowed it to remain there as she sat, very still, taking in the message of his words.

'Thank you for telling me. I think, one day, I'd like to meet her.'

Tom spoke very gently. 'Don't Clare. Don't for both your sakes. Raking over old coals can be very damaging. Look forward, instead. Go to the uni, get yourself another boyfriend, some guy who doesn't have a past. Marry, and have kids of your own and be happy.'

Clare began crying quietly. She removed the sunglasses and he could see the tears spilling down her cheeks. Some people looked hideous when they wept. Clare managed to look lovely. Tom's heart turned over, just observing those tears.

'Don't cry, darling. If you do I'll start as well. And there's nothing more pathetic than a grown man weeping.'

Clare sniffed. 'I'm sorry. But if you think about it, this is the end of a period. A very important period. You're my first love, and I'm saying good-bye to you.'

Tom wanted desperately to scream, there's no need to say good-bye. We could start again, but he remained silent. He, too, could recognise the inevitability of all this.

He stood and drew Clare to her feet, then took her in his arms. She turned her tear-stained face to his.

'Good-bye, my darling. Enjoy the rest of your life.' He kissed her gently and she didn't resist.

'Good-bye, Tom.'

Then she turned and walked away from him, taking with her his hopes and his love and his heart.

He managed to get a seat on a flight to the States the next day. It meant going via Los Angeles and picking up a shuttle flight, but it was better than mooching unhappily about Sydney. He hoped that he never again was forced by circumstance to visit Australia. The memories which the city held were far too painful.

24

*It is painful to remember those next few weeks. Saying that I regret-
ted my hasty action is too easy, and gives absolutely no understanding of my unhappiness, or my deep contrition. It was terribly hard
to apologise to Clare, but I did so. I selected my words with great
care, pointing out to her how, despite my remorse, I had been moti-
vated only by my love for her.*

*Clare was remarkably philosophical, which I must say
surprised me. I had expected her to be very angry indeed.*

*'Perhaps it was all for the best,' she replied, when I had done
my best to explain myself. 'It would have been awful to discover
after we were married that he wasn't the person I'd thought he was.
Better to learn that now, and not have to divorce him after only a
month or two.'*

*'Marriage is for life,' I was forced to remind her at once. 'The
church does not condone divorce.'*

*Clare looked at me with sad eyes. 'Grow up, Thea, won't you.
We're not living in the twentieth century. Even the Kennedy family
gets divorced.'*

*'That marriage was annulled,' I replied stiffly, because I have
also my doubts about the easy way certain people manage to
change their marriage partners these days.*

*'Oh yeah? Call it what you want to.' And I hadn't even the heart
to scold her for saying, 'yeah,' which is such a sloppy, unattractive
word.*

*But, despite her thoughtful response initially, there was no
doubting her unhappiness. She could scarcely stir herself to go
through the little details of daily living; it was as though a light had*

been quenched inside her. And Christmas had been a disaster. I had invited Douglas, but after what happened he said very brusquely that he could not bear to sit at my table. Although I knew that he had right on his side, I was still extremely hurt. I had taken a great deal of trouble preparing our menu and cooking such items as a traditional Christmas pudding, which is expensive as well as time-consuming. Personally, I find such heavy fare at odds with our Antipodean Christmas, coming as it does in the middle of summer, but I had hoped to please Douglas. So there was that heavy, suet and fruit pudding, and neither Clare nor I had the heart to touch it. I had baked a ham. Clare picked at her portion, pushing it about her plate. I knew that she was still deeply shocked by the revelation that Tom Goulding was not her knight in shining armour, but I thought she might have tried to please me a little, by eating her ham. When she didn't I realised that this was part of my punishment, as well.

I was also deeply shocked when she announced, two days after Christmas, that she planned to meet with Tom again. If there was one thing that gave me a modicum of comfort, it was the knowledge that That Man would no longer intrude into our lives.

You may be questioning my hopes regarding Clare at this moment, and wondering whether I really did assume she might lead a solitary life, similar to my own. I can say, and I hope that this will be believed, that in the months which followed that terrible day in February, I had come to rethink my ambitions for her. Maybe I should have heeded Douglas' advice and not entrusted her to the sisters of St. Ursula's. But that was in the past. I had come to the conclusion that Clare must go on to Sydney University, continue her education and then, perhaps, meet some decent Australian boy who would win her heart. But not too soon. I even thought back to young William Brandon, and contemplated her meeting up with him again. Stranger things have been known to happen. But William, of course, was not a Catholic so I mentally rejected that option.

What I really wanted for her was that she should enjoy a period of growing up, not be precipitated into early adulthood and come to regret her lost youth at a later date. Was that too hard to ask?

So I was able to think, for a period of about three days, that perhaps we were again on course. I had, with some effort on my part, modified my stance. Once Douglas' anger had been given time to cool I might explain to him that I now shared his opinion. Being able to confess that one is in the wrong has always appeared to me to be a sign of maturity. I hoped Douglas would see my change of heart in that light.

And then Douglas actually made contact with Clare behind my back. He engineered things so that she went to meet That Man again. I considered this unforgivable. And when she returned it was obvious that, like hapless players in an awful game of Snakes and Ladders, we were back to square one. My poor darling. I had thought she looked bad before. Now she looked truly terrible. And she shut herself in her room and she wept and wept. Nothing would console her. Nothing at all.

Instead of trying to find ameliorating things to say to Douglas, I could only look fiercely at him over the dividing privet hedge, and feel that in this one thing he was as much in the wrong as I had been earlier.

It was clear to me that this involved Perdita. I discovered, at the mention of her name, that ever since Clare had been mine I had harboured a deep, deep dread, that at some future time the mother might return to claim the daughter. I had sublimated my terror, but I had lived with such a fear forever. As they say, old sins cast long shadows. We were well and truly in that shadow.

After several miserable days, equally unhappy for me as for Clare, because every parent hopes to have the ability to comfort, Clare confided in me a little of what had transpired.

'Tom says that she's a very lovely person, still. And kind. He says that she looks after the young people of the area, perhaps because she regrets having given me up.'

This was so very different from all that I had heard from Douglas that it was on the tip of my tongue to leap in and tell the unvarnished truth. I even opened my mouth to refute such claims. But then I stopped, in mid-breath as it were. These easily uttered platitudes were so incorrect that Clare could not have misunderstood. Tom

251

Goulding must deliberately have described Perdita in this light. And in flash of insight I could understand, and approve of his action. He, like me, was shielding my darling from the sordid truth.

'I suggested that one day I might go to meet her,' Clare continued. 'But he didn't think that would be a good idea. His opinion was that to do so might open old wounds. It must be very hard to give up your baby. For her sake, I don't want to rake over old coals.'

'I think that's a very wise decision,' I said and, amazingly, found myself actually approving of Tom Goulding in this one small, but important, matter.

The HSC results confirmed that Clare had come within the top 2% of the nation. I was pleased for her, but not surprised. By the time of university enrolment in early February, our lives had settled down a little.

I'm not sure which of us was the more unhappy; Clare because of the end of her first love affair, I because of the sense of loss I felt at having been alienated from Douglas. I had not appreciated, until this time, just how important he had become to me. We probably saw each other no more than twice a week, but to be deprived of those pleasant little encounters was like losing the mustard on the ham, the clotted cream atop the fruit scone. Nothing tasted or felt quite the same. When he had some news about my financial affairs – because he still managed my portfolio, for which I was profoundly thankful – he would leave this communication in my letterbox. Something brief might be written upon it, such as 'Please sign here,' or 'I've taken steps to sell these. Sign at the bottom if you approve.' Scarcely a conversation.

To give a new impetus in my life, I joined the Sisters of the Virgin Mary, a group of women based at St. Kevin's who worked among the prostitutes frequenting King's Cross. I can't say that I enjoyed this undertaking but it did fill my days, and I looked upon it as a period of contrition. We provided two houses for those girls who wished to "come off the game" as they called it. We tried to educate them in the skills of home science, in which they appeared sadly *lacking. I suppose it was interesting work, but I should record that it did nothing to ease the ache in my heart.*

Starting at the university did fill the void in Clare's life. For the first time she was surrounded by young people, without the chaperonage of Thea or of the nuns of St Ursula's. Young men as well as young women; people who wore the sort of clothes Thea detested, and did their hair in strange, funky ways, and spoke in a language that was completely alien. And, more to the point, it was really the first time that she found herself among her intellectual equals. Nobody at the university thought it was sad to be clever. This was a huge eye-opener.

And there was more to it. She took her time dipping one hesitant toe into the social life pool of her fellow students, but by the second term she was going to parties where pot was openly circulated, and crack was available if you cared to dig a little deeper. Clare did not. Her natural caution came to her aid, as well as her revulsion that Tom had been a druggie in the past; plus, perhaps, the fear that she might emulate her natural parents. These two facts had a powerful effect on her. She looked at her classmates and wondered why they found it necessary to smoke and to snort. They appeared to have everything as it was. They were the nation's brightest hopes, they mostly came from solid, middle class homes with supportive families and strong values. She concluded that they indulged in drugs as a rebellion against those very values.

The university buildings appealed to her. They were Colonial Gothic, with more than their share of stone carving around the impressive quad. Dominating the immaculate rectangle of grass was a vast jacaranda. Local lore had it that if you'd not started revising for your exams before this tree bloomed in spring, you were destined to fail.

She chanced upon William Brandon close to the end of her first year at the university. She actually spotted his back amid a crowd of guys in the Manning Bar. This particular venue was the more dimly lit and atmospheric of the university's bars, and the preferred watering hole of the philosophy and arts students. William topped the other young men by an inch or two and had filled out, but was still instantly recognisable. She waited until the group broke up. Even two terms at uni had not given her the courage to interrupt a crowd of noisy, companionable blokes.

'William?'

He turned. 'Clare!'

She returned his wide smile. 'How are you?'

'I'm fine.' He looked down at his watch. 'Have you got time for a pint?'

'I'd like a half, please.' She'd found that she could enjoy alcohol in small quantities. It helped her to relax and counter-balanced her natural shyness.

They took their drinks out onto the balcony. It was more than a year since the last postcard with the familiar handwriting had arrived at St. Ursula's. Clare thought how strange it was to have known someone so well through letters for four long years, and yet to know him scarcely at all. He had been a nice looking small boy, a handsome fifteen year old. Now, at nineteen, he was definitely a man.

'What are you doing?' she asked.

'Law. And you?'

'Japanese, with Asian studies.' She thought she read respect in his eyes and knew that she didn't deserve it. There was this perception that Japanese was an especially difficult language, but she had sailed through the first year and faced her end of year exams with no misgivings at all.

'You know, I quite missed getting your letters. I looked forward to them.'

'Not as much as I looked forward to yours. They really did change how the other girls perceived me. No letters, and you were assumed to be a sexless wonder; letters, and you were looked upon with envy.' She paused to sip her beer. 'How's Frankie?'

'She's fine. We're married.'

'Married? When?'

William grimaced. 'About ten months ago. I'm surprised you

didn't see the piccies in the paper.'

Thea would definitely frown upon "piccies," but Thea no longer held sway.

'Sorry. I don't spend my life scanning the society pages. I must have missed your piccy.'

She wanted to ask why William had launched himself so precipitously into marriage. Frankie could be no older that she was, nineteen at most.

William must have read her mind. 'It wasn't exactly what we'd intended. But I got Frankie up the spout and Dad read us the riot act. The timing was a bit unfortunate, to say the least. He'd just launched a blistering attack on the government for sanctioning unmarried mothers per se, and for being so generous with taxpayers' money. In those circumstances it seemed wiser to sprint to the altar, before things began to show. Clare was a very premature baby.'

'Clare?'

He turned to her, grinning, but colour flushed his neck and face. For a minute he looked deliciously confused.

'Yeah. We called her Clare.' He raised one eyebrow slightly. 'As I told Frankie, Clare was my first love, when I was eight.'

'But I'll bet you didn't add that you gave up writing to her about fifteen months ago.'

'What would be the point of telling her that?' He stood. 'I've gotta go. It was great seeing you again, Clare.'

Clare rose as well and gathered together her books. 'And you.'

Side by side they returned to the quad, then parted company in the cedar-vaulted entrance hall, beneath the clock tower. As he turned to go, William thought to ask, 'and what about you, Clare? Any boyfriend?'

She had dated one or two of her fellow students, but nothing had come of these dates. The boys seemed hopelessly immature to her, interested in no more than latest Aussie Rules results. 'Not really. Not any more.'

He shrugged. 'Tough. But the right guy will come along. You're too special for just anyone.'

Clare, walking to her next lecture, thought that the right guy had already come along, and then departed. The problem was, his past history cast very long shadows.

After that first meeting, she and William seemed to bump into each other quite often. It wasn't deliberate – or not deliberate on her part – but once they returned to the university the following year a pattern began to emerge. It was like picking up the threads of a long-time friendship. Quite frequently they ate lunch together in the Garden Courtyard coffee shop. They studied together in the Fisher Library. It was hard to study at home, because the infant Clare was a lively baby and demanded her parents' attention. Gradually, Clare was privileged to learn more about the Brandon set-up. Evidently William's father was still paying for him to attend uni, and William and Frankie had an allowance on which to live. Frankie, she learnt by degrees, was an awful housekeeper, unable to budget from one week to another, even though William was responsible for all the major bills like electricity and property taxes. Clare admired pictures of Frankie and Clare, and William and Clare, and William and Frankie. Not to mention Chloe and Zoe who were Himalayans, and William's wedding gift to his bride. They had dictatorial blue eyes, flat sulky faces and too much fur. Clare could almost hear Thea sneeze at the sight of the feline pair.

Evidently, according to William, Frankie's inability to work out the cost of a week's groceries for the three of them was exacerbated by his mother-in-law. He had very little to say in praise of her. William had a very endearing way of rubbing the back of his neck when he was embarrassed or perplexed. Clare couldn't quite ascertain whether embarrassment was behind his confession that he found Mrs Buchan a trial, or perplexity because he'd assumed that after their marriage Frankie would not need quite so much support from her mother.

And, an added irritation, Mrs Buchan was besotted by the baby; her first, her very first grandchild, and absolutely the cutest thing ever to breathe air. She showered upon the child every possible toy, and they all had to be found shelf-room in the very small apartment which Frankie and William could afford on his father's allowance. In William's telling of it, even a minor trip from bedroom to bathroom became hazardous, an obstacle course to be circumnavigated around a host of infant amusements.

In a way it was like a continuation of his letters, except that now Clare sat across the table from him, and munched on her meat pie as she heard the latest instalment in the saga, and William was a living, breathing, very attractive man on the other side of that table. And, incidentally, somebody else's husband.

25

The following Christmas Tom returned to his childhood home. This wasn't entirely philanthropic, although Clare's words had, indeed, stuck with him. But, bereft as he saw himself to be in his black mood, one Christmas was like another and doomed from the start. Because he was reluctant to leave Elliot, he drove the two thousand odd miles, taking three days and seeing the period as an opportunity to recharge his batteries. There was more to it than that, though. Any flight artificially gobbles up the distance separating places. Early discoverers knew they had encountered somewhere new and very different, because it had taken them weeks and months to reach their destination. Flights of an hour or two don't allow you the luxury of that buffer. The need to bring Elliot along was a useful excuse to establish a zone of neutrality.

Tom had not been back in ten years, and he had no idea what to expect. Total familiarity or a sense of other-worldliness? In the event, he experienced about fifty-fifty of each.

To begin with, the place seemed much smaller than memory dictated, and even more parochial. Counterbalancing that, Thelma and Dale appeared to have aged not at all, and were so warm in their welcome that Tom, guiltily feeling more like the Prodigal Son with each minute, felt like a jerk for having harboured as much as a passing resentment against them in the past. This, of course, lasted as long as their original greeting and the opening of a couple of beers to mark the occasion. Then Tom was invited to come outside, inspect the new Christmas lights.

'You see?' Dale said, as they stood in front of the familiar house, bottles in hand. 'Those old candy canes were looking kinda shabby so I trashed 'em, last year.'

The earlier decorations had been replaced by a series of plastic elves, clearly intended to represent Santa's workers. They lined the short driveway, grinning, cartoon-grotesque faces staring sightlessly at the passing world. Tom thought they were hideous, just as he could sense Dale's pride. In fact, it would have been impossible not to do so. Dale's satisfaction was as tangible as sugar frosting on top of the apple cake. Hell, could his father not remember how he'd railed against such overt displays in the past? Evidently not.

'They're great, Dad. Different.'

Dale clapped a hand on his shoulder. Tom held himself in check and did not shrug it off. 'You think so, huh? Betch'a don't have anything as cute in Seattle, huh?'

'Nope. Can't say we have.'

Dale took a reflective drink from his bottle. 'Poor old Will. Mad as hell when I found 'em. Ran along to Wolfsen's, hoping to get himself a set. Too bad. I'd gotten myself the last they had in stock. You should'a seen his face.'

Tom, also drinking his beer, managed to move away so that his father was obliged to remove his hand. 'How is Will?'

'Great. Great. Been married five years, now. Pity you missed the wedding but your mom'll show you the albums.' He grimaced in sympathy at the prospect of all those happy moments, captured in glossy six-by-fours, to be endured. 'That'll take an hour or two. Three boys. Great kids. That Will Junior's a riot. You'll meet 'em all on Christmas Day.'

Tom reflected that Elliot, who knew very little about children and children's ways, might be happier if confined to the car during this period of invasion. The old guy brought the conversation to a close now. He mooched across to the nearest elf, raised his leg, and directed a stream of piddle down the plastic face.

'Hey!' Dale exclaimed. 'Call him off, won't'cha?'

Was it feasible for a dog to electrocute himself by peeing on an ornament?

'Elliot. Enough.' Although Tom privately thought that his buddy-in-arms had shown very good taste.

259

Christmas was to be endured. Tom endured it, remembering as he did so Clare's remonstrance that he was too harsh on his parents. He did his best, to make amends for those ten years of separation, to thank them for the effort he appreciated they had made on his behalf as he grew up. He tried to empathise with them. He failed in that, but he was man enough to accept his parents and his brother, in a way that was at least half-way to maturity.

You could respect people, he concluded, without liking them or seeking to emulate them. Two days after Christmas, he could bundle Elliot into the car and kiss Thelma's lily-of-the-valley-scented cheek, and allow Dale to clap him once more on the shoulder – and escape back to Seattle and his own world.

He'd watched with interest Will's eldest son, Will Junior, and known that, like his father, the kid was mean as a female skunk in season. He wondered whether the next in line, Tanner, would grow up with the same resentment of his older brother that Tom had felt for his father?

Elliot started the New Year badly, by having a series of tiny strokes. The vet suggested that Tom have him put humanely to sleep, but Tom could not bring himself to terminate the dog's life. Having been assured that the old boy was in no pain, he carried him tenderly home and applied himself to rehabilitation. Elliot was so pathetically grateful, thumping his tail against the floor whenever Tom offered him some small tidbit, or paused to stroke his head. Old, tottery legs had a disconcerting way of finding gaps between the planks, so Tom gathered him up in his arms for transportation along the deck and past the half-dozen houseboats, to the patch of grass where he could follow nature's dictates. On the occasions when he was taken unawares and soiled his box, his abject apology tore at Tom's heart.

He could no longer climb the circular staircase which led to the bedroom, so Tom elected to sleep downstairs on the put-you-up sofa-bed. He had difficulty getting his head down to his feed bowl; Tom created a collar of cardboard on an upturned dishpan and placed Elliot's food bowl safely within that, and in reach of his buddy's grizzly-white muzzle.

Bob and Joey, separately and together, suggested that maybe Elliot had exceeded his shelf life. The rational part of Tom might agree, the sentimental part refused to accept it. Elliot was his rock, his stability. To Elliot he had confided his hopes and his anxieties; with the dog he had shared all the aching pain that followed Clare's termination of their relationship. Even when his sight failed and the effort of raising his head proved almost too much, Tom could not sign his death warrant.

It was left to Elliot himself to do that, and he did it in the time-honoured way, by wandering off.

Goodness only knew where he found the strength. On most days it was all he could do to stagger from his bed to the feeding bowl and back again. But on this particular night he managed to locate the not quite latched door, and take himself off along the deck and over the green sward, and across the road. Tom, searching frantically for him no more than minutes after the escape, could track his paw prints on the damp sidewalk.

Then there was that terrible sequence of sound which every animal owner must dread, the squeal of brakes, the dull thud of metal against flesh and bone . . . the silence. Knowing with an awful surety what would await him, Tom made for the upper level of the street. His heart twisted painfully in his chest.

Elliot had been thrown into the gutter by the force of the impact. A white-faced young woman was bending over his inert body. Tom knew, without even feeling the still-warm body, that Elliot was dead. It remained for him to reassure the shocked driver of the car that it was not her fault, and to gather up his buddy's body and to carry him gently back to the houseboat. Then he wrapped him in his own blanket and laid it in the trunk of his car, for burial the next day.

Joey and Bob were in Oregon, visiting with friends. The house-boat was so empty that to Tom it was like a church, midweek. He thought he could hear his own breathing in the stillness, the awful vacuum.

Desperate, he called Sandi.

'Hi. It's me, Tom.'

They hadn't been in touch for weeks. Months, even. He could hear her surprise and carefully controlled voice. 'Tom! How are you?'

'Miserable. Elliot's dead, and I feel like a jerk. I should have taken him to the vet and I couldn't bring myself to do so. So he walked into a car. Now there are two of us feeling awful; me, and the poor kid driving the car.'

There was a pause of about ten seconds. 'Wait for me. I'll be right over.'

She moved in the next day.

The academic year kicked off in February for Clare with one major difference. She moved out of home and into student digs. She'd expected at least a show of reluctance from Thea, but the stuffing appeared to have gone out of her mother, who confined her objections to a promise that Clare would come home regularly. That was an easy assurance to make; the flat into which she was moving had no washing machine. One reason why Thea went along with the change in address was that Clare would be sharing with Jane Sullivan, of whom Thea thoroughly approved.

Jane had always been the closest of Clare's St Ursula's friends, but she had taken time off after school to visit Europe with her parents. Now she was back, an academic year behind Clare, doing English and engaged to Simon.

Their flat, wedged between the university and Annandale, was like most student quarters, not a thing of beauty, although not a total health hazard either. They shared with Anna, who as third in was assigned the smallest of the three bedrooms. Anna, at present, was an item with Jim, and they saw very little of her.

Clare had assumed, and been assured by both Douglas and Tom, that once at uni and among her intellectual equals, there would be no shortage of boys seeking her out. This had proved to be true, and as she had always hoped they did respect her, but somehow nothing ever came of these embryonic relationships. Like so many things for which we long, the reality did not entirely come up to scratch. The fault was Clare's and she was only too aware of it. Somehow

262

the boys were too eager, or too blasé, or too young, or too cynical. They wanted to hot things up too swiftly, they sought to impose their views on her, or to mould her opinions to suit theirs. In the end, after a spate of minor disappointments, she settled for the celibate life and friendship with William.

The girls saw quite a bit of Lyndal at this time because she, too, was living in Annandale. Things had not gone for Lyndal as one might have imagined. She had left school to begin nursing, which held exactly the right, feminine image to appeal to her father. She lasted about six weeks, by which time she was suffering appalling bouts of nausea each morning. Subsequent investigation revealed the manifest fact that she was at least three months pregnant.

This startled everyone, Lyndal not the least. After all, the old adage has it that only the good girls get caught. Nobody would have ranked Lyndal among their number, unless you translated the words to mean that she was good at *it*. She married Shane before it showed; scarcely the huge marquee-on-the-lawn ceremony about which she'd fantasised and boasted back in St Ursula days, but at least she was two years older than her sister, Diane.

Married life was a huge disappointment. Used as she was to her father's wealth, which had always been casually distributed upon request, to be deprived of an easy income was a disaster. Sex aside, Shane and Lyndal scarcely knew each other, were parents before they had time to grow up, and before their relationship had a chance to mature. Lyndal sought out her old gang members as confidants because she was thoroughly unhappy.

They met regularly, she and Clare and Jane and, as in the past, Lyndal took on the role of narrator and instructor, the other two her audience. This time around, it did not make for happy listening. And little Philip was scarcely three months old before Shane released his frustrations by becoming abusive.

On the occasion when Lyndal elucidated, one morning, the trio was seated at a not-too-salubrious coffee place. The coffee could have been better too, but at least it was cheap.

'He spat at me. It landed on my cheek, a great glob. Then it trickled down my chin.'

'Why?' Jane asked. The element of surprise was missing from this revelation, because verbal abuse had been an integral part of the partnership for some time. They'd endured lengthy descriptions of what he had said to her and she, in turn, had reciprocated. As they sipped their none-too-nice coffee and listened, the baby slept in his buggy. Now, he showed signs of stirring. Lyndal put her foot on one wheel and rocked vigorously.

'Philip was crying. He'd been a bugger all day, screaming and screaming. I was really shagged out. You don't know how exhausting a baby is. And Shane wanted sex. I said "no," and he started to bitch, so we began rowing. We're always rowing.'

'Spitting is disgusting,' Clare commented. She could hear shades of William and Frankie in this precipitous marriage, although William was not into "she said to me" revelations, and she couldn't imagine him resorting to Shane's approach. 'And degrading.'

'But that's not all.' Lyndal wiped away an errand tear. 'When I kept on insisting I was too tired for sex he raised his hand, like this . . .' and she demonstrated, '. . . and I thought he was going to hit me.'

The pair responded as one.

'Did he?'

'You can't tolerate that. Nobody deserves to be hit.'

Lyndal sniffed. 'He didn't. I could see him sort of draw back, as though he realised what he'd nearly done.'

But the combination of insufficient money and too little maturity continued to take its toll. Less than a fortnight later, Shane landed an open-handed slap across Lyndal's cheek.

Jane and Clare were on opposite sides, when it came to advice. Clare thought that Lyndal should up-sticks and leave forthwith, at least allowing a period of separation to cool things. Jane was of the opinion that a marriage was a marriage, and you stuck with it. Jane had always displayed more inclination to martyrdom than others within the gang. But she reluctantly changed her mind when a closed-fist punch succeeded the open handed slap. Lyndal looked truly terrible with her eye half-closed and a great, blue-black bruise

264

staining the socket.

And, unbelievably, although Philip was only five-and-a-half months old, she was pregnant again.

'What if he starts to abuse Philip as well?' Clare asked. She'd only seen Shane from afar, and knew him exclusively from Lyndal's narratives and the observed results of his frustration.

'He adores the baby. He'd never hurt a hair on his head,' Lyndal assured her, wiping away yet another tear.

On this particular occasion Philip was lying on the floor of the girls' flat, practising the motions of crawling. He was an attractive infant, with his mother's dark colouring, but even an attractive infant seemed to Clare no substitute for losing one's youth. Premature maternity held all the appeal of a ball and chain. It was such a surprise to see Lyndal, the outwardly confident leader of their childhood, reduced to abject subjugation. Like the world turned upside-down, the planets realigning. Somehow, they'd changed roles. Clare, who'd been so quiet and self-effacing at school, was now the more mature by a nautical mile; cocky, bubbling Lyndal, who had been the despair of the nuns, was going to pieces in a relationship and cowed by her immature, equally unhappy husband.

She moved home when Shane made quite a good fist of strangling her. Kylie was born four months later.

Jane and Clare agreed it was a relief to see her head back to Nyngan. Hearing the saga unfold in painful detail had been draining and frustrating, the more so that they had been unable to do anything positive.

'But Shane's to be pitied, too,' Clare remarked soberly. 'He must have felt trapped. Eighteen, and the father of one and a half kids. What he needs is time to get on with things, and to grow up.'

'What he wants,' Jane rebutted, 'is to meet up with his mates every evening and drink himself legless.'

The last two years have been terrible. I seem to have lost the two most precious things in my life; my friendship with Douglas in total, and my darling daughter in part. Losing Clare to the university and her new

265

friends was to be expected, you might say a rite of passage, so I could come to terms with it quite philosophically, but to be deprived of Douglas' friendship hurt on a daily basis, like a series of pinpricks.

At first I turned to my belief to fill the void, but for the very first time I found that it did not bring fulfilment. Maybe it was Douglas' own attitude to religion which had sown a tiny seed of doubt. I don't mean to suggest that anything would remove my faith from me entirely, but somehow it did not seem, at this moment, an answer to everything.

I tried to find worthwhile tasks to give my life meaning. Working with the lamentable women of King's Cross did help to an extent although, to be honest, I did little in the way of "hands on" encounters. Although my fellow workers broke it to me very gently, I gather that my attitude, my opinions, my very stance are seen as daunting by these unfortunates. As they must, in the course of their work, encounter men considerably more physically formidable than I, not to mention threatening, this did seem somewhat paltry in my view. I am scarcely a large person, whichever way you look at me. However, I suppose it must be said that I do represent a certain set of values, and being confronted with a person of moral certainty might well be read as intimidating.

So the work I did was more in the manner of housekeeping and preparing homes for the girls willing to "come off the game." And after a while it held no appeal.

I'm not particularly interested in hobbies; not things like stamp collecting or decoupage. I do take a pride in my garden and find quiet satisfaction in seeing it at its best, but those small terraces are scarcely a full time occupation.

I read, I kept up with what was being exhibited at the Art Gallery; but all of these things are considerably more pleasurable when done with another, and while Clare was growing up I had become used to companionship. In truth, I did not enjoy my lonely state.

I know, from what I have read, that people embarking upon one of the Twelve Point programs must start by taking that first, vital step. They must admit that they have a problem which is beyond their ability to solve. Then, and only then, can they progress.

Perhaps you could see this moment as my nadir, when I appreciated just how much I was hurting myself, by holding so implacably to my convictions.

But, even having reached that low point, I found it incredibly hard to take the next, most obvious progression. If I can quote the *Twelve Step* program again, this is when that person must stand up and admit to the failing within himself or herself. I thought and thought about it and I knew that, although I consider myself to have my fair share of the Gallipoli Spirit, I would find it very difficult indeed to walk around to Douglas Hamilton's door and unburden myself with an abject apology. So I wrote a letter. In it I acknowledged that the fault was entirely mine. I knew it, had known it from the moment my mouth betrayed me. I also acknowledged that I had deliberately misinterpreted Douglas' arranging for Clare to meet with That Man, as an excuse to counter my own guilt. I know I was wrong in that, as well.

Then I said how deeply I regretted the coolness which had separated us for the last twenty-seven and a half months, and asked whether he would care to share tea with me on some future occasion.

I record all those words so easily. They slide from the bottom of my ballpoint pen. That does not do justice to the effort they took me to write. Then I folded the sheet and slipped it into an envelope, and placed it in the correct letterbox. I knew Douglas to be at home, because I'd seen him enter his house earlier that day, with a suitcase in hand.

The next few hours were torture. I filled them by clearing up a small patch of weeds on the bottom terrace, lifting every tiny piece of popper-weed, every trace of groundsel, investigating every length of couch grass root. Couch grass can be a real menace in a garden. I took two hours and forty-three minutes to pick my way over a patch of soil that I could have cleared in half an hour. And just as I was straightening my back . . . the front door bell rang.

I peeled off my gardening gloves and untied my calico apron which has pockets on the front for small, hand utensils, feeling like a sinner who seeks absolution but is not entirely certain it is available to her; as an offender must feel when summoned before the magistrate's bench. Then I walked slowly up the two terraces, taking my time to compose myself, because I confess I was terrified. What if Douglas was there to tell me that he spurned my apology? That the most contrite words could never undo my terrible deed? And then again, it might be someone delivering a parcel, or wanting me to buy some shoddy goods . . . and not Douglas at all.

I opened the door almost in slow motion, and when I saw his face I experienced a rush of terrible qualms because he looked so fierce, and his impressive eyebrows were drawn across his face in such a stern line. But in his hand he carried something wrapped around with the sort of paper fancied by florists, and he thrust this something forward, rather in the way that William Brandon pushed his valentine into Clare's hand all those years ago. And the paper fell back to reveal several fine, white roses.

'Knowing your puritan views about tobacco, it's no good suggesting that you smoke a peace pipe with me, Thea,' he said, quite gruffly, 'so I've brought you these as an offering of truce, and in exchange for your letter.'

And he did something that no man except my father had ever done before. He leaned over and kissed me on the cheek.

That was an evening of firsts, for me. Douglas took me out to dinner, to the Sydney Tower, and high above every other building we circled slowly and ate delicious food and watched the great spread of the city, west as far as the Blue Mountains, and out towards North Head, and over the suburbs. I had never dined there before, I had never been invited out by a man. I was sixty-two and I cannot recall ever having been so happy.

And here I should record something else. Douglas apologised to me. He said that it had been a matter of regret, which had given him many sleepless nights.

'I was careless, Thea,' he began. 'I'd not thought it through. It had not occurred to me that you might feel insecure, where Clare was concerned. I knew that her feelings for you were deep rooted. I had assumed this was obvious to you, too. Otherwise, I should never have shared with you my rediscovery of that unfortunate woman who happened to give birth to her. Had I kept this news to myself, none of what subsequently transpired would have come to pass.'

'Perhaps it was for the good,' I ventured. 'Clare has enjoyed her time at university. She has grown up, as I'd hoped.'

'But I'm not sure that young Tom would share your views,' Douglas replied. 'Between us, you and I, we did him a great injustice.'

I held my peace. After Clare related the manner in which he'd spun for her a false picture of Perdita, I decided that perhaps I'd misjudged Tom Goulding, but that did not mean I would have welcomed him any more, back then. Time is a great healer; my hatred had died a natural death, but there would need to be further clear blue water between me and that sequence of unhappy events, before I could bring myself fully to accept him.

And anyway, he was in the past. A part of Clare's history certainly, but of no interest to us now.

Life in Seattle settled down to a pattern. Sandi put her stamp on the houseboat by introducing small, feminine changes. She came home from work each evening bubbling with happiness, and cooked healthful, fat-free meals for them both. Just occasionally she would yield and allow Spencer steaks to be slapped onto the barbecue. She was cautious about extending the hand of friendship to Bob and Joey; although clearly she knew how important his friends were to Tom, and so did not reject them out have hand. By Tom's reasoning, she was determined to hasten slowly, for fear that he might take fright.

To his knowledge she did not, however, give up the lease on her own apartment.

Tom could read her contentment in the way she hummed as she prepared the salad, in all her body language in fact, and it made him feel bad that he couldn't share her exhilaration. Worse, it made him nervous. Not that he was unhappy, but their becoming a permanent unit had never, really, occurred to him. But he did acknowledge that the error was his, in calling her at the time of Elliot's death, and he also accepted that, having made his bed, he should learn to lie on it. He really did try hard to contribute something to the relationship. When Sandi began to drop hints, however, that she should think about giving up work, things began to fall into place and his nervousness showed signs of developing into full-scale panic.

'It makes sense,' Sandi said, from where she was curled up on the sofa-bed. 'I'm going to be thirty-two next birthday. I don't want to wait too long.'

'Too long for what?' Tom asked knowing, but too craven to voice his knowledge out loud.

'Maternity. My biological clock is ticking over, Tom.' She looked up at him brightly, as though issuing a challenge. 'We've been together now for nine months and known each other for goodness only knows how many years. It's the logical step.'

'It is?'

Having broached the subject, Sandi clearly decided that she might as well grasp the tiger by its tail. 'And I think we ought to talk about Clare.'

'Clare? How does she come into this?'

Sandi drew a throw rug over her legs. The evenings were becoming chill as fall approached. 'You know quite well how she comes into this.'

'I do?'

'Sure. And I think we ought to discuss it, before I . . . before we . . .'

'What is there to discuss?'

There were many opportunities to see why Sandi had always been so successful at her job. She'd never let a potential client quietly melt away. She'd pursue him, and woo him, and he'd be signing along the dotted line before he was aware of it. She was tunnel-visioned in her determination, once her mind was made up. It was a quality in her of which he found admirable and terrifying at the same time.

'There's a lot to discuss, Tom. For starters, I think you're still in love with her. Or with the ghost of her. Can you deny that?'

The truth is the truth is the truth.

'I guess I am, in a way. Although I know it's unrealistic.'

'And unfair to me. I want you to tackle your feelings, Tom. Really analyse why you still hanker after her.'

Tom rubbed his nose miserably. He hated this analysis stuff at the best of times. When he found himself unwillingly on the psychiatrist's couch it was six times worse.

'I guess because she was an ideal.'

'That's exactly it! You're in love with an ideal. Probably always were. Have you thought that, probably, that's why Clare put a period to your relationship?'

'No it's not,' he felt compelled to protest. 'It was because I'd... I'd known her birth mother.'

'Which was probably the last straw,' Sandi agreed, as though reasoning with a small child or a retard, 'but I'll bet she knew she couldn't live up to your ideals. You put her on a pedestal, and you wouldn't even allow her to scratch, because scratching sullied the image of how you thought she should behave.'

Tom tried to put up a fight but it sounded pretty feeble, even to his own ears. 'I don't think that's true.'

'Believe me, it's true. And even though that affair is dead and buried, I have to live with the knowledge that I'll never, in your eyes, measure up to the perfect Clare.'

'I don't compare you with Clare.'

'Oh no?'

He winced slightly. The truth is the truth . . . 'Well, not intentionally.'

'Tom, it's like a barrier, always separating us. Everything I do, I know you're comparing with how Clare might have done it. Even when we're having sex, I can almost hear you fantasising that I've got long, fair hair and a face like Botticelli's *Venus*.'

'I don't,' he protested again, feeling more and more dishonest as he did so. 'And you're a very attractive woman, in your own right.'

But Sandi had put her finger on the problem, perhaps without appreciating how deep it went. In his inner moments he had never really accepted that their relationship, his and Clare's, was dead and buried. In those special moments he'd imagine her appearing on the jetty, looking as she'd looked when they'd parted nearly three years ago, ready to apologise, ready to accept his avowal of humility, prepared to pick up the pieces. This perception was so vivid that he could close his eyes and see her, down to the last detail, he could smell her in his nostrils and feel the smoothness of her skin with its fine, blond hairs. And Sandi was right, in that Clare's was the image which appeared behind his lids in that moment prior to sleep, while his hand rested on the angle-sharp hip of another woman. Another woman who had just announced she wanted to bear his children.

Sandi pushed the throw rug aside and stood up.

'I want you to think about it, Tom. If you consider we have a future, then you'll have to bury her memory and come to terms

272

with today, and the demands of the present.' She crossed to the kitchen area and put the filled kettle onto the ring. 'We'll talk about it again, in a few days. Light the fire, will you? Please?'

Clare heard about the accident on the news, that evening. An appalling, freak event, in which an out-of control truck whose brakes had failed careered down the hill, slicing in half the car which happened to be crossing the intersection at that moment. The driver was killed instantly. The infant in the back was not harmed by as much as a hair. The deceased woman was the young daughter-in-law of one of the state's premier politicians, Bill Brandon.

The news was so unexpected, so shocking, that it was like a blow in the solar plexus. Temporarily, it robbed Clare of her breath. Poor Frankie, dead at twenty-one. Poor little Clare, who had lost her mother. Poor, poor William; twenty-two and a widower. It wasn't important that she knew their marriage had been shaky, at best. That would not mitigate the sense of loss, she thought, it would simply add an extra burden of guilt to William's mourning.

The funeral was held the following Friday, at the Anglican cathedral. Clare sat a long way back, because she had never even met Frankie and was certainly not family. She could recognise William's mother, who seemed scarcely to have aged since her youngest child was a small boy at prep school, and William's father, Bill Brandon, was easy to identify, too. His son was a younger replica of him. William, himself, slowly following the coffin and its crowning corsage of white arum lilies along the central aisle of the cathedral, looked ghastly, drained of colour, clearly still in shock. Clare's heart ached for him, and for Frankie's parents who appeared equally bereft. There was no sign of the baby, so Clare assumed that she must be being cared for elsewhere.

Clare waited another week before she called.

'William? It's Clare. I'm so very sorry. How are you getting on?'

'I can't tell you. But it's grim.'

Clare paused. 'Would you like to come over? My flat-mates are away, so I'm on my own tonight and I could cook us something. Or we could buy take-away.'

William didn't even wait. 'I'd love to see you. I feel as though the bottom's fallen out of my world. But you don't have to cook. There's a Lebanese place I know. I'll pick us up something.'

He arrived an hour later, clutching a paper sack containing assorted aromatic dishes. The spicy smell preceded his appearance. He still looked dire, as though he'd not slept in a fortnight. His skin was waxy, totally unlike his usual representation of healthy Australian manhood, his chin was covered in stubble, his hair appeared not to have made the acquaintance of a comb in some time. Clare, seeing him, felt like crying herself, for his obvious hurt.

'William . . . ' All the pain she felt for him was in her voice.

Then she welcomed him into her arms and, some time later, into her bed.

She had no intention of anything, apart from offering comfort. She didn't see them as a couple, she could not envisage a future for them. Because of his father's public profile, and because William was still officially in mourning, they never went out together. Only Jane and Anna knew that William even visited, let alone spent the night, but they'd frequently seen Clare share lunch with him at uni, so this logical progression did not present a problem. His haunting the flat was totally reasonable, in the light of an old friendship, and his obvious need for support during this terrible period.

It was William, not Clare, who wanted more. His two-year-old daughter was at present living with his in-laws. William wanted to include the child, and asked Clare to come with him when he picked up his daughter to share the weekend. Clare resisted, only too aware of how Frankie's parents might interpret this.

'William, be reasonable,' she protested. 'Look at it from their point of view. The Buchans are still hurting from the loss of their daughter. They're bound to misunderstand, if I appear on their front doorstep with you. They might even think to wonder why you called your baby after me, and leap to all the wrong conclusions. You'll be adding unnecessarily to their agony.'

So, instead, William collected little Clare and they picnicked together, along with Jane and her fiancé, Simon. It was Clare's introduction to her namesake and she thought the little girl enchanting, and at the same time a bit scary.

'I know so little about babies,' she confessed, aware of her ineptitude and needing to explain. 'I'd be terrified to pick her up, in case I hurt her.'

William tossed the child, squealing with delight, into the air and caught her. Clearly this was a favoured game.

'Babies are tough,' he replied. 'Or Brandon babies are, anyway.'

But, even so, Clare was more comfortable preparing soldiers of toast for Clare's tea, or reading a story to her if pressed; and was happy to let William demonstrate his paternal skills by changing her nappy. It wasn't really playing at happy families, she reasoned, because it was so one-sided. William might like to leapfrog over some of the formalities imposed by society, Clare did not share his enthusiasm.

Because, despite liking William as she did . . . loving him, even . . . prolonged exposure to him revealed the less mature side of his personality which she'd always assumed to be there but had never, actually, witnessed.

He was, for starters, entirely subject to his father's bidding. William was an only son, trailing in the wake of three sisters. Perhaps he was all the more precious for that reason. Bill Brandon had mapped out his son's career for him from the first, which was one reason why Frankie's ill-timed pregnancy and their hasty marriage were seen as so inopportune. William was to gain his law degree, he was to enter the family law firm, he would proceed thence, in the fullness of time, into a full-blown career in politics. He would pick up his father's mantle, as it were.

Fine.

'But what if you don't want to?' Clare argued. They were in the small garden at the back of the apartment which William had shared with Frankie. Clare found it uncomfortable, that apartment. It was entirely Frankie's, it bore her seal, as powerful in its way as was the Great Seal of England, endorsing the rights of the sovereign. William was watching little Clare's progress towards the sandbox.

'But I do want to.'

'Have you ever thought about anything else? Thought about saying, "to heck with all this. I'm going to chuck it in and sail around the world?"'

'Why would I want to sail around the world?'

Clare lay on her back on the lawn which needed a mow, and let William do the child-watching bit.

Why, indeed. But Tom had done that, in a way. He'd tossed his books into the bin and cocked a snoot at his parents and at the expectations of everyone, and just dropped out for a couple of years. Which was how, of course, he came to meet up with someone called Perdita Potts. Svenson. When he'd confessed to his Beat period Clare had been appalled. Comparing what he had done with William's almost unthinking agreement to toe the party line, Tom's gesture seemed less outrageous. Quite reasonable in its way, and certainly brave. It was a pity about the drugs, of course, but there was any number of students quietly going about their studies at the uni, and experimenting with a host of illegal substances on occasion. The bogie-man of drugs seemed less shocking, with maturity. Some kids had no need to experiment, others felt it a part of the growing-up process, just as the girls at St Ursula's had felt it essential to taste sex, if you wanted to be considered a woman. Another step towards adulthood.

Which brought a natural progression of thought to another matter. William was hopeless, where sex was concerned. It was hard not to compare him with Tom, who had always insisted upon their making love, which took time, and who'd rejected sex, which was all over in three minutes. William was definitely a three-minutes-sprint-roll-over-and-go-to-sleep sort of lover, and he disliked it when Clare suggested there was another way. Thought it a slur on his manhood, muttered that Frankie had been less choosy.

Of course, there were certain things about him which would always be endearing. He was kind and well mannered and intelligent in most things and very, very familiar. One day, he would make some other woman a terrific husband.

Some other woman? Clare sat up abruptly. That was the conclusion she had reached, almost without direction. William Brandon was a terrific bloke, and one day he would make another person very happy; but that person wasn't Clare Galway.

The Quest

27

Clare flew out of Kingsford Smith Airport on a steaming hot day at the end of January. The jumbo jet climbed steeply and then banked, so she could see below the great spread of the harbour with its hundred small inlets and bays, and to the south the huge expanse of water that was Botany Bay. Then the plane corrected itself and headed out across the Tasman Sea and towards America.

She had left uni back in November, having graduated with honours. She had said goodbye to William before that.

William had sulked. Probably, Clare concluded, thinking about it now as the plane climbed towards its cruising altitude, her rejection of him was a first. Apart from the tragedy of Frankie's death, William's life had always been sun-kissed. He'd been born with that proverbial silver spoon in his mouth, and more than his fair share of brains, brawn and looks. It made for a very appealing combination. William had never, she thought, been forced to struggle for everything. He was ill-prepared to fight for Clare. She could recall in minute detail his look of amazement as she explained to him, as gently as she could, that perhaps it would be better if he moved his things, his toothbrush and sports gear, out of her digs. There really could be no shared future. She was happy – no, eager – to remain his friend, but that was as far as it went. When sulking, William's face took on a petulance at total variance with his normally sunny openness. He'd flung his clothes into a bag, emulating the unrealistic way that people packed in movies, then slammed the door behind him in a singular display of peevishness. Frankie had been dead just eight months.

His single status had not lasted long, though. Within a month Anna, her flatmate, had come to Clare hesitantly asking whether she would mind if she, Anna, went out with William? Clare smiled secretly and gave them her unstinting blessing. No need to explain to Anna that William was useless in bed. She'd find that out for herself, in the fullness of time. And Anna was sensible, nice, and socially acceptable to the Brandon parents. Given time and the inclination, she would make an excellent politician's wife. Perhaps she could do better than Clare, and teach William how to be a real lover. Perhaps William would, by then, be receptive to her tuition.

The plane had ascended through a blanket of light cloud. Looking down into it, you could imagine that the cloud was a tangible substance, like soapsuds floating on a watery surface. Clare had flown only once before, and that no further than Proserpine and the Whitsunday Passage, in a tiny, propeller-driven plane. Everything about this flight was fascinatingly new territory.

Was she out of her mind, to undertake this venture? Was she asking too much, seeking too deeply? She'd discussed its implications at length with Douglas, fully aware that, now relations between the two households were harmonious, to have Douglas as an ally was akin to receiving Thea's blessing.

No, that was going too far. Thea had needed a great deal of convincing and so doing had, indeed, taken the combined persuasive skills of both Clare and Douglas. She was prepared to accept that her position as Clare's mother was incontestable. Sacrosanct. She was less easily convinced that to stir up old ashes might not prove disastrous to Clare. She didn't itemise her fears, but Clare knew precisely to what she was referring.

'I'm over Tom, I promise,' she had explained and reiterated. 'I might not even bother to visit Seattle. Probably won't, actually.'

'Then why go at all?' Thea had argued. 'You have no need to seek out Perdita. And there's a chance that she disappeared ages ago. More than a chance. A probability, in my opinion.'

The tone of her voice suggested that this was a contention devoutly to be hoped.

'Look upon it as part of growing up,' Clare had reasoned. 'Like cutting my hair.'

'There was no need to that, either. Your hair was wonderful.'

Clare, abandoning her contemplation of the floor of cloud, ran her fingers through her short crop. It might indeed have been wonderful, but that long plait had also been heavy, and a pain when it came to washing and drying. Her present cut was considerably easier for travelling.

What was she seeking, in flying to San Francisco? That Perdita might open wide her arms and weep, because her long-lost daughter had been restored to her? Douglas had spoken with considerable caution against any raised hopes. He'd informed her that her birth father had died some time ago. He'd explained to her about the drugs in Perdita's past. He'd gone on to remind her, very gently, that people could change, and that abuse of poisonous substances accelerated that change. But Tom had painted an altogether different picture of Perdita, and over the past three years Clare had clung to that preferred version. A nurturing person, Tom had said, still beautiful, still perhaps regretting the loss of her child.

Clare had decided to hedge her bets. There was that part of her which stuck to the child's creation, the story of ultimate sacrifice and perfect denial. That rendition encompassed the 'princess' mother of folk legends and nothing but noble sentiments. The other part of her, however, heard the implications behind Douglas' carefully weighed words. He, after all, had spoken to Perdita more recently, and his description was more lucid for what it left out than for what it included. Although he was her ally in agreeing to this trip, Clare could read in his reticence a warning, that she might well be disappointed. He'd gone so far as to suggest that she brace herself for this possibility. On a practical note he'd also introduced her, via e-mail, to friends of his in Sausalito, with whom she could stay.

Sandi moved out of the houseboat on the last day of January. Tom arrived home from work that evening to discover her absence and the presence of a note on the table, held down by a paperweight which contained swirling snow around the Eiffel Tower. It was a particularly tasteless small item that he'd bought for her in Paris, by way of a joke. He'd also bought her some French scent which had cost a fortune and at close quarters made him sneeze.

Darling Tom, I've tried, and I'm adult enough to know that I've failed. I just can't imagine spending the rest of my life playing second fiddle to a phantom, a might-have-been. You've heard that saying, about not crying over spilled milk? Darling Tom, as far as I can see you'll be weeping into that puddle of spilled milk for the rest of your life, until you're a wrinkly old man with only your memories to keep you warm in bed. And the irony of it is, I can't imagine there's a woman alive who'll ever live up to your perception of the idealised Clare. Least of all Clare, herself. Can't you see? You've created in your mind a fucking paragon. And I don't plan to apologise for my choice of words.

But perhaps without me about you'll be able to stop — and to think. *Think about what you* really want *in a woman. A saint? An impossible ideal? Or a living, breathing person, with warts and imperfections?*

I'll be at my old address, and I'd appreciate it if you'd forward my mail. Don't bother to call. I can't see any reason to prolong the agony — for either of us.
Sandi.

P.S. I've left you a present. It's in the bathroom. I hope it's more complementary to your lifestyle than I've managed to be.

Still clutching the sheet of paper, Tom sat heavily on the nearest chair and waited for the anticipated cloud of regret to overwhelm him. It did not transpire. Instead, gazing at Sandi's letter with unfocused eyes, he was stunned by the immense onrush of relief that he felt. She had gone. She would not be coming back. He could unburden himself of the knowledge that he constantly failed her, could not return her devotion by so much as a part. The unbalanced nature of the scales had been an endless cause for guilt on his part. But now he was alone, mercifully alone, and it was not entirely bad.

He stood, finding his legs were not altogether steady and poured himself a scotch. Since the time when, on the morning following Clare's accident, Douglas Hamilton had produced his hip flask and offered Tom that exquisite fillip, he'd discovered in himself a liking for the occasional single malt. Right now he found it equally heartening as that baptismal dram.

Sandi had moved back to her old address. So he'd been right, she had retained the lease all along. Wasn't that also a case of hedging your bets, he mused? Might he have accepted more wholeheartedly the concept of babies and happy twosomes, had she committed herself a hundred per cent to him? But by maintaining that bolt-hole, surely she was being similarly cautious. He read the letter again, wondering whether, this time around, he'd experience the inevitable pain. But, again, he could feel nothing but overwhelming relief. Sandi was a fantastic woman. She was smart and beautiful and sexy. She'd make another guy incredibly happy. That other guy was not Tom Goulding and it was as well for both their sakes she recognised this, and acted on it. He could only be grateful to her, for her strength in making the decision for both of them.

The P.S. mentioned a present, in the bathroom. Hell, the bathroom? What sort of gift did that imply? A plastic duck to accompany him into the shower?

It didn't take long to discover, because at that minute there was a bang, followed in quick order by a scuffle, a whimper and a shrill bark . . . all emanating from the general direction of the lavatory. Tom opened the door, cautiously.

The most ludicrous animal hurled itself toward his chest. A brown animal, with flying ears and lolling tongue and feet like floor mops, and a shaggy coat like an unkempt hearthrug. Tom staggered back, propelled by the force of the assault. He toppled heavily, onto his butt. The animal rewarded him by slobbering copiously all over his face, now conveniently positioned. Tom shoved it away. The beast, all high-charged energy and coiled muscles, and clearly overjoyed at being released from its enforced

281

incarceration, continued in determined style to express its appreciation. Tom strong-armed it aside again, added a vocal growl of disgust, and scrambled to his feet. The animal hurtled skyward and managed to plant a sloshy kiss on his ear.

'Quit it! NOW.' Tom shouted.

The dog, because clearly it was of that general persuasion, sank to the floor, but looked as though another assay was only seconds away. When not in his face, Tom could regard it more objectively. It was clearly male and about half grown, perhaps. And he could see what had prompted Sandi to choose this particular specimen, before all others. There was a definite look of Elliot in the silly, half-smiling face and Heinz-57 mixture. Except that Elliot had been wise and dignified, and this animal was clearly brainless, and had no more connection to dignity than marshmallows resembled jalapeno chillies.

'STAY.'

Amazingly, the dog stayed, although its entire body still trembled with pent-up enthusiasm. Tom glanced inside the bathroom. His eyes swept over the capsized water bowl with DOG now printed upside down, and the huge pool of piddle into which the mat appeared to have fallen, and the heap of shit in the corner.

Just retribution, he thought, for his lack of remorse. Sandi must have known. It seemed appropriate.

He wrote to her that evening, expressing regret that things hadn't worked out, contrition for his part in their not doing so, and hope for her future with some other lucky guy. He also thanked her for his present.

I think I'll call him Mortlake, he ended, *because Elliot was named after Elliot Bay, and it's the continuation of a theme. And it shortens well to Mort, which is also appropriate, because if he doesn't learn a few manners mighty quick he will be dead. That I can promise. Look after yourself, Love, Tom.*

San Francisco was lovely. All that Clare might have hoped. Douglas' elderly friends were kindness themselves, insisting upon escorting her to all the tourist places, to Ghiradelli Square and along Fisherman's Wharf and on the cable cars. They went across to Alcatraz by ferry, and climbed the steep incline up which hundreds of unhappy men had plodded in the past, towards the grim buildings at the top. Clare hated the place. She could almost feel the despair of the inmates and was happy to re-emerge into the wintry sunshine.

John Gordon had been with the SFPD for years and had been instrumental in calling upon Douglas' forensic expertise. His wife had retired from the School Board and wanted to know all there was to know about Australian education. Clare found it quite hard to equate St. Ursula's with mainstream schools, so found herself hedging a bit. She was on safer territory when discussing the academic claims of the University of Sydney.

And, strangely, once in San Francisco she found that any desire to meet with her birth mother had dissolved. Just wasn't there. She had to remind herself several times of the purpose of her trip. One part of it, at least. Because, despite her repeated avowals to Thea, always in the background was the possibility that she might travel north to Seattle, and seek out Tom.

Three years. Three years since they had met in the small park for the last time, and she had forbidden him to contact her, ever again. And what had happened in that time? Well, she'd grown up, for a start. She'd come to appreciate Tom, with hindsight, for his more important qualities, and to dwell on them, rather than casti-gate him for his transgressions. She could even say that she'd put whatever had happened between Tom and her mother into perspec-tive. It didn't necessarily add up to wholesale forgiveness, but it did go some way towards understanding.

She couldn't say that she'd definitely be heading for Seattle . . . but then again, she'd not ruled it out.

It took fifteen days for her to reach the point when she could ask, casually, for instructions to reach Haight-Ashbury. Clare and the hospitable Gordons were enjoying breakfast; pancakes and the curiously sweet bacon which Americans seemed to prefer and which, in the pan, dwindled before your eyes to crisp ribbons.

There was a wall of sea fog which shrouded the bay across from Sausalito, blanking out the island of Alcatraz and making every-thing feel damp. Evidently this was not so unusual. The mists could roll in from the Golden Gate in minutes, and disappear as quickly. Douglas had given her the street and number where he had tracked Perdita to earth. He'd also warned her that her birth mother was not in the habit of staying long at any single habitation. When she recited this address it was clear from their response that the Gordons were not impressed. Clare had simply talked about 'friends' loosely and in a detached fashion. She'd made no claims to kinship.

'But like all that area, hon,' Judy Gordon explained reassur-ingly, 'coming up in the world. Cute houses, but rundown. Close to the park too, but that's not necessarily an asset.'

'Seedy,' interjected John. 'Dropouts and dealers.'

'But your friends might have made a good choice, in the long run,' Judy continued. 'Our new commissioner's determined to clean up the district. Maybe they'll have made a killing, in a year or so.'

Clare had become an honorary grandchild, to augment their existing brood. When she'd protested that she was outstaying her welcome, they were quick to refute this and point out the pleasure that her being there afforded them. On this cool morning in late January the pair gave her instructions and sent her on her way with a host of warnings and offers to accompany her, which she speedily rejected. With chaperones there could be no "out" clause, should her nerve fail. She picked up the bus by the Sausalito waterfront, sat as it trundled across the Golden Gate Bridge, seeing nothing but a blanket of pearly-white fog. She'd done the journey often enough, though, to imagine the great, rust-red structure and the glimpse of the Pacific beyond the headland.

Haight-Ashbury should have been lovely. Might well become so again, any time soon. The architecture was quaint, the position, tucked between the great Golden Gate Park, and much smaller and intimate Buena Vista Park, should have been ideal. Like the curate's egg – in parts it was.

The houses were as Judy had described them. In a way they

reminded Clare of Sydney architecture, in being narrow, terraced or closely abutting, and intrinsically charming. You could see only too clearly where people were making a push to improve their properties. And it was easy enough to find the house where Perdita Svenson might or might not still lay her head. That was the advantage of the American system of numbering their houses on a grid system.

Clare found that her steps slowed as she approached the address. Even if she'd not known where to look, she might have noticed that, particular house anyway; but for all the wrong reasons. For its awfulness. The house looked incredibly sad. On either side trim properties had conifers in tubs abutting the entrances and fresh paint-work. Their neighbour, by way of contrast, had not been blessed in living memory by so much as a token lick of paint. The door to the garage, opening onto street-level, hung abjectly from broken hinges. Sills and porch were apologetic in their peeling exteriors, shabbiness seemed to have entered the soul of the place.

On the opposite side of the road a low wall with piled rubble behind indicated that here a similar structure had already given up the struggle and been granted merciful release. Clare seated herself on the available surface and wondered for the umpteenth time why she was here. The closer she came to meeting her mother, the more confused she felt, and the more inclined to abort the whole thing. She sat on the wall for an hour, while she struggled with the entire spectrum of her motivation. Did she really expect that she would be received with open, welcoming arms? Better council was to brace herself for the disappointment of her mother's non-appearance – or for her reluctance to acknowledge kinship.

During the hour she watched an assortment of kids come and go through the dilapidated porchway; kids who could have represented the United Nations in their race and ethnic backgrounds. The only thing they had in common was their extreme youth, and the fact that their clothes all looked as though intended for someone much larger. Was that the current, juvenile fashion? Or necessity? Clare tried to guess their possible ages, but apart from assessing that none could be older than fifteen, and most were nearer twelve, it could be no more than conjecture. One or two looked in her direction but without curiosity, more passed within arm's reach without a glance her way. They might have numbered a dozen in total. It looked quite a small place to shelter such a crew.

Two minor events broke into that hour, during which Perdita Svenson did not put in an appearance. At one time a stout woman appeared from an abutting property and castigated a couple of youths with an abrasive stream of what Clare took to be Spanish. The boys responded with several extremely vulgar gestures which left nothing to the imagination, while telling the good woman where she could put herself. Some time later, in order to stretch fast-numbing muscles, Clare walked along the road to the edge of the park and bought herself a coffee from the booth there. She seated herself once more on the wall, warming her fingers around the cardboard beaker, and thought again of what Tom had told her. Perdita, he had said, saw herself as a mother to street children such as these, perhaps trying to compensate for that early loss of her infant daughter. It certainly made sense. Probably all her money, or whatever she had available, went into food and clothes for her "family." It stood to reason that she'd see this as far more important than paint and structural repairs.

Time crawled by with the listlessness of a lizard on a frosty morning. It wasn't exactly cold; but the inactivity, and the unyielding hardness of the stone wall, made for discomfort. Clare was about to give up her vigil, reminding herself that at least she'd tried, so need never reproach herself in the future, when she noticed a figure coming up the rise.

They had parted, mother and daughter, when Clare was not a month old. There was no reason in the world why she should connect to this figure . . . except that somehow she did. Perhaps even the walk was recognisable, in the way that one can glance in a shop window and register a certain familiarity, before awareness dawns that what you have glimpsed is your own reflection.

Strangely familiar, yes – but reason told her differently. This could not be Perdita, because this woman was a far cry from Tom's description. Beautiful, he'd said. Beautiful? Perhaps once. But not now, certainly not now. The skin of this woman's face sagged over the cheek-bones as though it had lost any elasticity it once possessed. And it was grey. Her hair was similarly lack-lustre. It might once have been fair, but you'd need a good imagination to appreciate that now. Perdita, Clare had worked out, was probably forty-four or five. Still quite young. This sorry person could have been touching sixty; not far from Thea's age. Although, the thought made itself manifest, Thea was still trim and always immaculately groomed.

The woman came abreast of Clare's perching place. Two of the boys, who had been lounging about and clearly awaiting her arrival, approached her apprehensively. They were restless, edgy. Clare could not hear the exchange that ensued, but she could read the body language easily enough. It did not translate into warm maternity. Apparently one of the boys, a child of perhaps eleven or twelve, had transgressed. Perdita, if Perdita it be, swore at him. The boy remonstrated, his voice high, pleading and whiny. The woman raised her voice and railed at him.

' . . . and don't come back until you have!' she concluded shrilly.

'Aw . . . Perdita . . . '

The woman had a plastic bag of groceries in one hand. She swung the bag back, then drew it sharply forward so that its arc brought it in contact with the child's temple. He grunted and fell clumsily to the ground. Clare could hear the crunch as something heavy, perhaps glass, met bone.

'Aw . . . gee . . . Perdita . . .' the companion child remonstrated. He was larger, and possibly of Mexican parentage. Perdita rounded on him fiercely.

'I don't run a charity here.' Her voice was sharp. 'If you can't earn your keep you can fuckin' well find some other place.'

The smaller boy had scrambled to his feet. He looked dazed and a trickle of blood ran from his temple, down through his fingers.

'I'll get it,' he whimpered. 'I will, honest. Just gimme . . .'

He stopped abruptly, mid-sentence, as Perdita drew the bag

back a second time. Then, sobbing, he backed out of range and set off down the hill. His buddy waited long enough to scream at Perdita, 'You torturer! You mother-fuckin' bitch . . .' before following him.

It was only then that Perdita appeared to notice that she had an audience. She looked directly across at Clare who still sat, stunned, on the low wall. Even had she wanted to, Clare could not have made one move in her direction. So this was her birth-parent? The warm, loving person carefully described by Tom?

It was as though the world had ceased to turn. They were separated by the width of the road, and yet afterwards Clare could have sworn that her mother looked deep into her eyes – deep into her soul – and recognised her daughter. And . . . and this was the terrible thing, the part to which she returned again and again . . . Perdita's look was of pure, unadulterated hatred.

Clare left San Francisco the next day.

28

February of that year brought a spell of unexpectedly mild weather, encouraging spring bulbs into precipitously enthusiastic growth. Joey, in Martha Stewart mode, bought and planted primroses in tubs for their and Tom's decks. On Sunday afternoon Tom took the enthusiastic Mort for a leg-stretch around the edge of the lake. There was a well-constructed walkway, which took you over a series of small islands, and wintering-over waterfowl congregated alongside. Tom knew no more about waterfowl than to identify Canada geese and buffleheads, but the walk appealed to both pooch and master. Tom approved because it was attractive, Mort because of the entertainment the geese provided. He'd quickly discovered that he could create a pleasing diversion by executing a series of joyous bounces among any birds sufficiently stupid not to seek instant entry to the water. Then he would stand, triumphant, at the lakeshore, tongue lolling, head to one side. Compared to Elliot's sober wisdom he was still a hopeless, brain-deprived idiot. Tom couldn't imagine how so stupid a dog had managed to worm his way into his affections.

Once home, Mort lay contentedly out on the deck like a guy who knows he's done his duty for the day, and can now relax with a clear conscience. Tom flipped the cap off a bottle of beer and joined him, stretching out on an inadequately dusted-down deck chair. The Cascades were thickly snowed, the sky beyond them, despite the gentle sunshine, a clear ice-blue. Tom had tried to follow Sandi's parting words and only look forward. She'd used the "crying over spilled milk" maxim, concluding with the somewhat tart observation that it looked likely he'd still be weeping into that puddle of milk as an old man.

But today, just this once, he planned to allow himself the minor indulge of a few might-have-beens. Not morbidly, but leniently, as befitted the day. There was no need to flagellate himself.

This time four years ago he had found himself lost in the Blue Mountains, and he had climbed a cliff-face, and become embroiled in an episode of magic. It had been an enchanted period and an enchanting one. He need only close his eyes and he could see Clare in front of him, he could smell the sweetness of her skin and feel the texture of her hair. He could hear the cracks of thunder as they made love that first time, on the ledge of rock. He could hear, too, her scream as she fell.

It was an easy step to recall all the hopes he had harboured for them. He'd imagined her here, sitting on this deck, looking across the lake toward the mountains, and appreciating their beauty as he appreciated it. He'd seen himself introducing her to the area, knowing that she would be receptive to all that Seattle had to offer. He'd indulged in fantasies of them together in his bed.

He grimaced. Sandi was right; he should bury the images of Clare and start over. Easily said, less easily executed.

Footsteps along the boardwalk intruded upon his shadow world of memories. A woman's walk, so it was probably Joey come to remind him he was sharing dinner with them tonight. Bless the woman, she fussed over him like a mother hen with one precious chick. Even more, since Sandi's departure. He'd always suspected that she and Bob had been prepared to tolerate Sandi for his sake alone.

'Tom?'

He opened his eyes with a jolt. His fantasy world and reality were becoming uncomfortably intertwined.

The voice came again, a shade louder a lot more anxious. 'Tom? Are you about?'

Mort disappeared around the side of the houseboat and fired off a warning salvo of staccato barks.

Tom hauled himself out of the chair, rubbing his neck. 'Clare?'

She was standing on the jetty, looking uncertain. She had a small duffel bag which she'd deposited on the decking, and she was wearing jeans and some sort of top, and her anxious look melted away as she saw him . . . and she smiled slightly . . . and she was there . . . and she was . . . she was . . . Clare.

Mort decided, upon reflection, that this person presented no threat to his beloved master. He moved without pause from challenge mode to that of frenzied welcome. Tom pulled him down, before his enthusiasm precipitated them all into the water.

'Quit it, you hopeless animal.' Still in shock, he turned back to Clare. 'Where did you spring from?'

'I didn't spring. I've taken ages to get here. I think I took the wrong bus. I've walked from the university.'

He put out a hesitant hand, as though fearing that the person before him was a phantom, a figment of his imagination, and his fingers would encounter nothing. But her smile was real enough and gaining in confidence, and the hand he grasped belonged to no spectre.

'Come and sit down. Can I get you anything? A drink?'

She followed him aboard and he hastily unfolded a second, still cobwebby chair. 'Sit here . . .' He indicated where he'd been dreaming minutes earlier. 'Mort, go to your basket.'

'Are you sure you don't mind? I mean, I don't want to intrude upon your new life.'

'My new life? Oh, right. No, you're not intruding upon my new life. It's great to see you.'

Mort didn't understand orders which implied exclusion. He made a valiant attempt to award Clare his moistest kiss. Tom hauled him down again, apologising as he did so.

'This isn't Elliot?'

'Hell, no. This witless imbecile is Mort. Mortlake, actually. But his name is extremely appropriate, because if he doesn't learn some manners mighty soon he will be dead.'

Clare seated herself. 'What happened to Elliot?'

'He died. Old age.'

She lowered her eyes and Tom's heart flipped in return. He'd not had time to compose his responses, or to practice. It was like putting back the clock three years.

291

'Oh. I'm sorry.'

'Can I get you a drink?' Tom repeated, as a hundred reactions and emotions and sensations vied for supremacy. He could hear himself sounding like an idiot.

'A beer would be nice.'

When he went indoors she followed him, and looked about the tidy interior of the houseboat appreciatively. 'This is lovely, Tom. Just as you described it.'

'Thanks.'

Mort had decided that he'd done enough welcoming. He returned to the slumber which Clare's arrival had interrupted. They took their drinks back onto the deck. The silence had all the ease of the eye of a storm; the atmosphere was as charged as a drum-roll preceding an execution.

When they did speak, it was together.

'Tom . . .'

'Why . . .?'

They laughed self-consciously. It was ghastly. The old comfort and camaraderie of the past had been forgotten, or refused to surface. They might have been two strangers, had it not been for the huge legacy of unfinished business and confused hurt which separated them as tangibly as a pile of soiled linen.

'No, you start. Your turn. Tell me what you've been doing.'

Clare appeared to find her beer fascinating. Her eyes followed a drop of condensation as it trickled down the outside of the glass. 'Well, I went to university, as we'd always planned. I graduated last year.'

'Congratulations. I don't need to ask whether you graduated with honours. Who could think anything less of St. Ursula's star pupil?'

'Well, yes. I suppose not.'

'And you've cut your hair.' A sin, if ever there was one. Her gorgeous cascade of flax, replaced by a short bob.

She put up a hand self-consciously. 'Oh that. Yes, I cut it off to celebrate my twenty-first birthday. A mark of growing up, I suppose.'

Then grow it again and stay young, Tom wanted to blurt out, but managed to hold his tongue.

'And how's your mother? And Douglas?' Actually, he'd heard from Douglas as usual, just before Christmas. A very standard card, featuring a picture of Ayers Rock, with a perfunctory note.

'They're all right. Chugging along, I suppose you'd say. They made up their quarrel.'

'That's great.' Once again the silence threatened to enfold them. Tom made a supreme effort.

'And . . .? Any boyfriend?'

That drop of condensation must hold all the allure of the radium in Marie Curie's crucible. Clare could not drag her eyes away.

'Not really. Certainly not now.'

'But . . .?'

She met his eyes briefly, before returning to admire the foamy surface of the glass. 'I met up with William again. William Brandon, who used to write to me. Do you remember him?'

'Sure.' Tom might have added that there was scarcely a word she'd said which he didn't remember, but somehow this was not at all as he'd dreamed of their meeting again. In those images Clare had flung herself into his arms, avowing contrition for having judged him so harshly, and promising never again to depart. They'd never, in his imagination, struggled to find common ground.

'Well, William got married, straight out of school. He and Frankie had a baby, called Clare. Then, a year ago, Frankie died in a car crash. It was so sad.'

'I'm sorry.'

'Yes. Well, after that I thought we might get together. But William has a lot of growing up to do. He was still doing it when I left.'

'So, how long ago did you leave Sydney?'

'About a month ago.'

Tom stood. The sun had disappeared as the winter evening threatened to close in, Suddenly, you realised that it was still February.

'Let's go inside. I'll light the fire.'

Clare stood uncertainly. 'Are you sure you don't mind? I can easily . . .'

He led the way, Mort taking this as his cue to squeeze between them and enter the living room first. 'Where are you staying tonight? Are you booked into a hotel?'

'No. But I can easily find somewhere, if you . . . if your wife . . .'

He hunkered down before the free-standing stove, scratched the match along the coarse surface of the box and let the flame toy with the kindling paper. 'Clare, I'm not married.'

'Not . . . not to Sandi?'

'Nope. Not to anyone. And you're welcome to stay here. I don't have a second bedroom, but that sofa you're on is a bed.'

Did those words really emanate from his mouth? Was he actually telling Clare, his angel, his goddess, that she had exclusive rights to the fold-away bed? Was he totally cracked?

'Thanks. If you're sure.'

This was all so painful that it was with relief he greeted Joey's hail.

'Ahoy there, land-lubber!' Joey's round, cheerful face appeared in the doorway. She pushed Mort down as he did his best to lick her to death.

'Joey, come in. Do you have room at the dinner table for a guest? This is Clare. Clare Galway.'

Joey's look was so openly curious that Tom all but blushed, for her and for him. 'I don't believe it. The fabled Clare?'

It was evident that this overt avowal of prior knowledge was doing nothing to set Clare at ease. Tom sprang to her rescue.

'In person. And hot from Australia.'

'Sure we can squeeze another one at the table. And grate a bit more cheese. You're welcome, Clare.'

It made it easier, there being four of them, while Tom adjusted to the unexpectedness of it all. He hadn't realised until he saw her, until after that original frisson of joy had melted away and been replaced by nothing at all, that the legacy of his hurt would make itself so manifest. Although Joey and Bob kept a flow of conversation sparking in their usual manner, and the banter was as quick-witted as ever, Tom began to wonder with mounting resentment why Clare had seen fit to invade his cubby hole, his haven, and to uncover old wounds.

This thought was followed immediately by amazement that, at the moment when his dreams were being fulfilled, they should not provide the happy ending on which he'd set his heart. And glancing at Clare, he knew with certainty that she was having a similar problem. What had she imagined, arriving unexpectedly this afternoon? The end of the fairytale? That he would open wide his arms, say, 'Come, my darling . . . all is forgiven,' and the credits would roll? In which case, no wonder she appeared so on edge.

They didn't stay long after dinner. Joey's and, by implication, Bob's, idea of a cosy evening was to play some sort of childhood game like Chutes and Ladders, but with their own version of crazy rules. And at any time you were entitled to create your own rules to suit your particular strategy. A game could take hours to complete. When in the mood, these evenings could be riotous, but Tom was not in the mood tonight.

Back home Clare seated herself again on the sofa, Tom fed the fire and said, 'I'll put on coffee.'

After these simple tasks were executed he slouched in his own chair and wondered where they might go from here. Could he talk the evening away in trivial nothings which kept them well and truly separated from Sydney and the Blue Mountains, see Clare safely to bed, and wave her farewell in the morning? Or should he take the bull by the horns and ask her straight out her purpose for being here?

Clare precipitated either course of action. 'You must be wondering why I've come. I owe you an apology, Tom.'

'An apology?'

'Yes. Do you mind if I explain?'

The coffee-maker completed its task with a series of splutters. 'Let me get your coffee first.' Then, both supplied, he stretched out in a deliberate attempt to appear at ease and said, 'Fire away.'

'I have to go back quite a long way. Do you mind?'

He shrugged. 'Nope. We've all the time in the world.'

Clare wrapped her hands around her mug, as though seeking confidence from its warmth. 'Well, you need to remember how it was, at the convent. You know all about Lyndal, and how she came back each term with new things to tell us, about boys and boyfriends. In a way it was like Ten Little Indians. As we grew older, one by one the other girls lost their virginity, and returned to school with stories to tell and photographs of the current boyfriend. Everyone except me. I knew that there wasn't a hope in Hades of my meeting anyone, or not until I got to uni, and in a way that would be too late.' She paused and created time by sipping her coffee. 'Then you came along.'

Tom grimaced. 'I sure did.'

'No, I'm not suggesting that it was as calculated as that. I might not have found a boyfriend yet, but I'd thought long and hard about it. I knew what I wanted, when he did appear. Not going as far as what he'd look like exactly, but how he'd respect me, and not just be after sex, which in Lyndal's bible was the only weapon we girls had at our disposal. But I knew that he'd appreciate other aspects of me, not just the physical. Tom, do you remember how you appeared out of the bush, that afternoon when you climbed the escarpment?'

'Could I forget?'

'I suppose not. Well, somehow I knew at that minute that you were the person. Just like that. And when we talked about it later, you said that you'd felt something similar.'

'*Some Enchanted Evening*. Eyes meeting across a crowded room. Yup, I remember.'

'And after that it was all so wonderful. I suppose you could say that, once we'd met and talked, I became more and more certain that you were the man I'd been dreaming about and praying to find. Does that make sense?'

'I guess.'

'And part of that certainty was that you were everything I'd imagined. You looked so right, and I made no allowance for the possibility that you might have faults. Perfectly ordinary, human characteristics, but not catered for in my reckoning. I suppose I was in love with an ideal.'

'And then you made the sad discovery that I was a normal guy, with my share of human frailties.'

Clare stared into the dark liquid in her mug. 'Oh, it was far worse than that. I might have come to terms with your Beat period and a bit of pot smoking, given time. But I suppose, like all adopted kids, I'd created a huge myth about my natural parents. Thea had always been vague about them to protect me from the truth, but she'd let me assume that they longed to keep me, and circumstances made it impossible. When she lost her temper and spilled the beans, two myths went up in smoke simultaneously. Your supposed flawlessness, and my parents' heroic self-sacrifice. And it sent me into a tailspin.'

Tom drained his cup. 'Understandable, I suppose. It must have been tough.'

She looked up, glancing briefly his way. 'But not half as tough as I was on you. That's why I came, to say how sorry I am. The look of hurt in your eyes has stuck with me all these years.'

He tried to accept this avowal of contrition with as much graciousness as he could muster.

'Thanks. Apology accepted.' He paused. 'How come you changed your mind?'

Clare held out her mug. 'Could I have a refill, please?'

Tom rose and replenished both mugs. He handed her the sugar.

'William.'

'What?'

'I rethought things because of William. We'd been friends, platonic friends, for some time before Frankie was killed. You know, doing student things. We shared lunches and studied together. He told me all about how he'd come to marry Frankie. Evidently, even when they became an item years and years ago, he'd never imagined them actually becoming Darby and Joan together. Frankie was his school-boy idea of a great date. Pretty in a cutesy-pie way, big breasts, happy to roll in the hay, but an absolute dimwit. A total galah, was how William described her. Galahs are supposed to be the morons of the parrot world. Frankie and William had absolutely nothing in common apart from the sex, but once the baby was on the way there

297

was no turning back. William's father did the shot-gun wielding stuff, but Frankie's parents were equally determined to get them together.'

'And how does this equate with you and me?'

'Wait, I'm getting to that. After the accident, his in-laws took the baby and William half-moved into my digs. I really liked him and I honestly thought I was over you, but all the time I found myself comparing him with you, and it was like comparing a boy with a real man. You're only seven years older, but that seven years made a huge difference. And when I reasoned it through, the difference is that you had lived more, you had experienced that time in San Francisco and come off the drugs, which must have taken enormous strength of character. And you'd created a career for yourself, without any help from your parents. William has never made a major decision in his life – his father does that, smoothing the path before him the way people smooth the ice before the stone, when curling. It was the difference between maturity and a really nice, but totally puerile kid. Do you understand?'

For the first time since her appearance Tom saw light at the end of the tunnel.

'So there's something in being a passé, over-the-hill sort of guy, with a less-than-squeaky-clean history?'

'Has to be. But there's more, Tom. There's something I must thank you for.' Once again her mug appeared to hold some hidden fascination. 'I was in San Francisco a week ago.'

Tom sat very still, his face like a poker player's. 'Nice city.'

'A lovely city. And I visited your old haunts.'

He anticipated what was to come. 'Uh huh.'

'And I saw the beautiful person who gave birth to me.'

'You did, huh.'

Clare kept her face averted, but the way she brushed her hand across her eyes spoke volumes. Tom leaned across and handed her a clean tissue. He kept his voice gentle. 'There's no need to cry. I understand.'

Clare scrubbed at the tears as they started to flow in earnest. 'And, of course, I could see at once that she really is the wonderful, caring person you told me about, just as she's this great beauty. Because Tom Goulding never lies.'

Tom shrugged slightly. He leaned forward. 'I guess I discovered that you were right. There are moments when the truth loses its importance. The lies were worth it to me, to spare you any unhappiness. And Perdita has absolutely nothing to do with you, Clare. Nothing at all.'

Clare took his hand and cradled it against her cheek. 'I just wanted to thank you, Tom. I know how hard that must have been for you.'

For some reason he was unable to move a muscle.

'I guess I'd better explain something as well, as this is confession time. Sandi saw it before I did, and she was pretty blunt about it. You weren't alone, back then, in falling in love with the ideal rather than the reality. I put you on a pedestal from the moment I clapped eyes on you. I said at the time I thought it was magic. And I guess I didn't want the magic to end, I didn't want you to be anything less than total perfection. That's why I hated the sordid bits like that hideous Rock, when they intruded upon my dream. So in a way we were both playing out each other's fantasies.'

Clare smiled mistily at him through unshed tears. 'I always said you were a hopeless romantic, Tom. You winced every time I used even a mildly indelicate word.'

He shared her smile. 'Hell, yes. I wanted you to become a Stepford wife, or at least a Stepford fiancée. My goddess didn't even know indelicate words.'

'Poor Tom, didn't I always say it? You're an emotional baby. No street smarts at all.' She leaned over and gently swivelled his watch around, so that the dial was on the inside of his wrist. 'How on earth have you managed to survive so long without me?'

And for the very first time their eyes met, truly met . . . and that was enough.

Epilogue

I can look back now and appreciate that I made mistakes. Don't we all? Clearly, my worst mistake was to tell Clare about Tom's past. This was a betrayal of trust, twice over. His past life was his affair, and for him to confess in his own time, in his own way. Telling myself that it all turned out for the best is no excuse, even if it did work out that way. I've grown, matured. I can accept my mistakes and live with them, even if at times I find it hard to forgive myself.

And they're so happy, Clare and Tom and the baby. My grandson; Jacob, after Tom's grandfather.

However, the reason I've written this tale is because I wanted to set the record straight, and to explain to you exactly how things came to pass. . . and to thank you. Without you, my dear, I should be facing a bleak future; one in which my bitterness, my burden of guilt would, given time, have become a canker. I might have lost my daughter, my delight. I may well never have known my adorable Jacob. That's the debt I owe you, and it's a debt I can never repay in full.

I remain, your loving wife,

Dorothea Hamilton.